WHEN DESTINY SEEKS
TO DESTROY YOU

SHATTERED

-BOOK TWO OF THE GLITCHED SERIES-

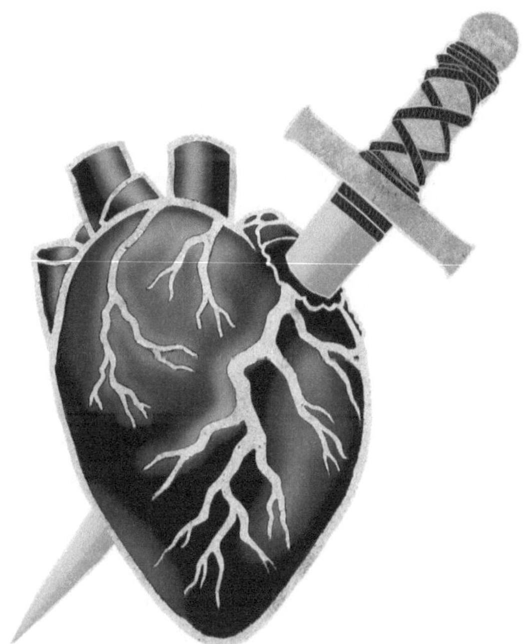

EISLEY ROSE

This book is dedicated to everyone who, at any point in their lives, has ever felt or been told they aren't good enough.

I want you to know that it is complete and utter bullshit and that every inch of you, both inside and out, is absolute perfection.

Don't let others' insecurities stop you from living your truth.

- Shattered Inspirational Playlist -

Prologue:
    "Afterlife" by Holding Absence

Chapter 1:
    "Wrath" by Clejan & Ohd Beats

Chapter 3:
    "Popular Monster" by Falling In Reverse

Chapter 4:
    "Nightmares in Paradise" by Palaye Royale

Chapter 6:
    "There's Fear in Letting Go" by I Prevail

Chapter 7:
    "Blank Space" by I Prevail

Chapter 9:
    "Alone" by I Prevail

Chapter 11:
    "I See Red" by Everybody Loves an Outlaw

Chapter 12:
    "Deep End" by I Prevail

Chapter 15:
    "Everytime" by Ana Done (Violin Cover)

Chapter 29:
   "Easy to Love" by Bryce Savage

Chapter 30:
   "Sound of Madness" by Shinedown

Chapter 31:
   "Youngblood" (feat. Lauren Babic) by Bilmuri
   "Lovely" by Billie Eilish & Khalid

Chapter 34:
   "Adrenaline" by You Me At Six

Chapter 36:
   "Moral of the Story" by Ashe

Chapter 37:
   "Breath" by Breaking Benjamin

Chapter 38:
   "All the Things She Said" by the Weight of Atlas

Chapter 39:
   "Mine" by Kelly Clarkson
   "What If You" by Joshua Radin
   "Not Strong Enough" by Apocalyptica feat. Brent Smith

Chapter 40:
   "Little Girl Gone" by CHINCHILLA
   "Bang" by AJR

AN ANCIENT PROPHECY

"Fear not the one soul split in two, for they are destined to save this realm. Both bathed in blood and consumed by fire, absolution must be at the helm.

"One of the two souls forgotten, the other believed to be dead. Their lives painfully intertwined yet distanced by fated bloodshed."

—The Oracle at Delphi (371 BCE)

PROLOGUE

A disheveled, broken shell of Alessa stood before the motel's bathroom mirror after she had allowed herself to be overcome with grief for three days and nights. Her hair had dried days ago in a haphazard, chaotic mess in which her dark strands had frozen, sticking out every which way, and her reddened cheeks shone brightly against her pale complexion.

As Alessa stared at her pale pink lips and the dark circles beneath her red, puffy eyes, she gasped as Damon's smile flashed in the reflection before her.

Suddenly, she was back in Eric's château amongst the dancing flames. Reliving the terrible memory, she reached out for Damon, lying on the ground as Camden carried her over his shoulder out of the bedroom.

Snapping back to reality, Alessa fell forward. She gripped the edge of the motel bathroom's white countertop and caught her breath.

The sound of running water from the shower slowly returned, and the room began filling with steam from the hot water.

Turning on the faucet, Alessa reached beneath the running water and splashed her face. The cold liquid saturated her hair, and her breathing slowed as she focused on her wet dog appearance in the reflection.

Glancing to the side of the sink, Alessa eyed the small blade Camden had left on the bathroom counter. With the water still running from the tap, she squeezed her eyes shut tight.

Unable to rid herself of the distressing image of Damon's body, Alessa's fingers wrapped tightly around the knife's handle, and with a shaky breath, she lifted the blade to her neck.

With trembling lips, Alessa held out a handful of hair and cut through, chopping her long, wet locks, even with her jawline.

Tears fell from her bloodshot eyes as dark, wavy strands drifted lazily down to the floor.

After the final slice of the blade, Alessa wiped away the remaining tears from her face using the back of her hand.

"No more tears are to be shed until Kai is safe," Alessa demanded of her reflection in the mirror.

Continuing like this won't help Damon. He's beyond my help now. But my sister isn't, and I need to focus on finding her. I can still save her. I will save her.

Closing her eyes, she inhaled steadily, focusing on closing off her heart. Opening them, Alessa glared at the expressionless woman staring back at her.

Exhaling slowly, she set the knife on the counter, undressed, and stepped into the tub. After pulling the curtain closed, her skin turned a light shade of red from the heat of the running water.

Damon's ring caught the light from the overhead bulb, and

as she stared at her finger, Alessa scrubbed the painful memories from her skin.

After turning off the shower, she stepped out of the tub and dried off with a towel hanging on the back of the door. She grabbed clean clothes from a plastic bag on the floor between the toilet and sink.

As she emerged from the bathroom, Camden was taken by surprise.

He peered up at Alessa with an apple in hand. "You're up. And you're clean," he said hesitantly before swallowing his mouthful of fruit. "How are you feeling?"

Alessa tilted her head to the side and flashed a pensive smile. "Alive."

"I see you gave yourself a haircut. Looks nice." Camden gave a reassuring nod before taking another bite out of his apple.

"I needed a change, and I realized being laid up in bed feeling sorry for myself wouldn't help us find Kai."

He pointed at Alessa with the hand that held the apple. "Just so you're aware, over the past few days, the government has cracked down on the state's borders, so we won't be able to leave Illinois for at least a few weeks."

Alessa pulled Damon's laptop from his backpack, sitting on the chair before a small table. "That's fine. While we wait, we can research and form a plan, including a list of people to interrogate."

Camden threw his apple core into a small trashcan beside one of the beds before unbuttoning his shirt. "Right. Well, you can get started while I jump in the shower."

"Hey, Cam," Alessa called out as he walked toward the bathroom.

With his hand on the door handle, Camden turned his head toward her.

Alessa stared into his hazel eyes. "Thank you for taking care of me. You didn't have to, but you did, and that means more to me than you'll ever know."

Camden stared back at her, his expression serious. "You didn't leave me; I won't leave you."

Licking her lips, she glanced at the floor, breaking eye contact. "Go take a shower, already. You stink." She grinned.

"I stink? You should've smelled yourself just a few hours ago! You were ripe," Camden laughed, throwing his shirt at Alessa.

She caught the light blue button-up before tossing it onto Camden's bed.

Hang on, Kai. We're coming for you.

CHAPTER ONE

The heart rate monitor beeped consistently and loudly.

Beep ... Beep ... Beep ... Beep.

Cain marched across the floor of the makeshift hospital room that had been created in his uncle's new home. Brushing his medium brown hair out of his eyes, Cain pointed at the unconscious man. "He's been like this since the procedure. It's been over two weeks. How can the doctors not know when he will wake up?"

Cain rubbed his hands together nervously. "Kai, we never should have trusted those so-called doctors—"

She placed her hands on his shoulders reassuringly. "You and I both know there was no other way around this. Your Uncle Eric would have never known a moment's peace. My people would have hunted him down until the day he died had he continued to live in that body."

Beep ... Beep ... Beep ... Beep.

Bending down, Cain rested his forehead against Kai's and exhaled loudly. "You're right. Of course, you're right, but now there's this glaring chance I could lose him."

She took his face in her hands. "That's not going to happen. His neurosurgeons are world-renowned and are the best money could pay for."

Cain gripped Kai's fingers, roughly removing her hands before he continued pacing back and forth. "I understand that, but he's been off the sedation meds for over 24 hours and nothing." He gestured toward the unconscious man lying on the hospital bed.

"You must give him time to heal. You were both warned that this had never been done before. His brain has been through more than we will ever know."

Cain approached the bedside and groaned aloud. He gripped the raised railing, and his eyes furrowed as he stared at the handsome middle-aged man. "It's going to be quite a change going from Eric's old body to—"

"Lucas," Kai interjected. "His name is now Lucas."

"Right. Lucas Greenfield of Greenfield Farms." Cain smirked as if he were entertaining an inside joke. "Gotta wonder if the actual Lucas knew what he agreed to when he sold his business to us all those years ago. I can't imagine he read the small print about him giving my uncle his life if it were ever required."

Lucas's heart rate increased gradually.

Beep ... Beep ... Beep ... Beep.

"We got quite lucky his dad recently passed and that he has no other familial ties," said Kai.

"Luck had nothing to do with it, my pet. Uncle Eric—I mean, Lucas—had this as his backup plan. Our men and The Elite's Bodyguards had been hired as staff on his sugarcane plantation for years, just in case we had to enact the next stage in our plan. The extermination of his few remaining employees should go relatively unnoticed."

Cain touched the back of Lucas's hand, and his eyelids suddenly fluttered.

Cain gasped excitedly. "Uncle Eric?" Clearing his throat, he looked around the room to ensure no one heard him. "I mean, Lucas, sir?"

Kai leaned over the raised railing. "Sir, can you hear us?"

The once unconscious man's eyes flew open, and he stared at Kai. Smacking his dry lips together, he lifted his hand to rub the slumber from his eyes. "Did it work?" Lucas asked. Hearing his changed voice crack, Lucas tilted his head in surprise, and in his scratchy voice, he demanded, "Get me a mirror."

Darting to the side of the room, Cain snatched a handheld mirror off the dresser and handed it to his uncle.

Turning the reflective surface toward him, Lucas sucked in the disinfectant-scented air. "It worked. They did it," he said in awe, tracing his well-defined cheekbones beneath his fingertips.

Kai walked backward toward the exit door. "I'll let the medical staff know you're awake."

As soon as the young woman disappeared, Lucas side-eyed his nephew. "I see you still have your pet," Lucas snapped disapprovingly.

"Kai's been punished for what happened with her serum. I didn't tell her that her serum failed and her sister survived; all she knows is that the Spartans stopped the final stages of our cleansing, and that is why she was punished." Cain smiled at the memory of him lashing her backside. "Kai handled the whipping quite well; it must be her Spartan upbringing."

Lucas tilted his head and examined his strong jawline in the reflection. "Mm-hmm. But why keep her around at all? Don't tell me you've fallen for the girl."

Cain's eyes darkened as he glared at his uncle. "She's more like an enticing, obedient plaything that has been extremely useful, so her life isn't inconsequential to me." He tilted his head to the side in contemplative thought. "Yet."

Lucas scoffed. "You had me worried there for a moment. I thought maybe you had developed feelings for the girl."

Cain waved his hand in the air and sat beside his uncle. "Enough about Kai. How are you feeling? Do you remember everything about your old life? Your other body?"

"For having my consciousness uploaded into another, I have to say, I'm feeling pretty damn good." Lucas grinned at his handsome reflection. "My original body, Eric, wasn't blessed with this good-looking face, and now my new self, Lucas, has his entire life to live without the Spartans hunting him down." He pulled his pale green gown to the side, exposing a circular scar on his neck. "Good. They placed it just where I asked them to. I don't want to forget why I'm doing this."

Cain nodded. "So what now?"

Lucas set down the mirror and placed his hand upon his nephew's. "We introduce our genetically modified sugarcane to the world. One way or another, we will have control."

CHAPTER TWO

Two weeks later...

Alessa stood alone at the end of Chicago's Navy Pier, watching Lake Michigan's choppy waters.

Since the night the American people were informed of Eric Lansing's smallpox release, no one had dared leave their home in fear of contracting the deadly virus, emergency personnel included. Unable to make it to the hospital, people were dying in their homes, and the smell of decaying bodies wafted across the city. Those who were fortunate enough to survive stayed isolated in their homes, waiting for a cure.

Tilting her head back, Alessa closed her eyes against the bright sun. With summer nearing, the temperature was warming, and the southwesterly wind blew the tails of her thigh-high burgundy fitted tailcoat jacket wildly about.

The United States government had been searching for Eric Lansing since the night of his château's fire but to no avail. No one could be held responsible for the company and its actions, as everyone who had worked at or been affiliated with Erebos Industries disappeared overnight.

Scientists were scrambling to find a legitimate cure for the fast-spreading virus as thousands more died around the globe every day. The President of the United States was still being kept in a secret location for fear of her safety, but the American people were being informed via news anchors that she would be receiving the approved vaccine soon, which was the first positive news the world had received in months.

Squawking seagulls flew above Alessa as she exhaled deeply, absentmindedly rotating Damon's ring around her finger. Turning away from the lake, she walked back toward the Navy Pier's entrance with only the boisterous birds to accompany her.

Three weeks later...

Alessa was back in Pennsylvania, standing on the rooftop next to Pat's apartment building. Holding binoculars up to her eyes, she prepared to watch the interaction between Pat and the lawyer she had hired to help care for her friend.

The lawyer looked around the empty street before pressing the button for Pat's apartment. He held up the collar of his coat and spoke into the microphone hidden in a button. "Check, check, one, two, can you hear me?" he asked, glancing up at the rooftop where she was stationed.

Alessa gave the man a thumbs-up after hearing him speak with her in-ear monitor.

Pat hollered into the crackly speaker. "Who is it? What do you want?"

"Uh, hi. My name is Brody Grammer. I'm a lawyer who specializes in death benefits. Can you please let me up so I can discuss a few things with you?"

"I don't plan on dying any time soon so you can bugger off," Pat grumbled.

The lawyer chuckled and readjusted his bag's strap on his shoulder. "Oh, no. It's not about your death; it's about you receiving death benefits due to someone else's passing."

Questioning the unknown man's motives, Pat hesitated. "Nope. Never heard of ya. Go away."

The lawyer pressed the button beneath Pat's apartment number, buzzing his apartment once again. Only once the sound of the speakers turned on did he speak. "It'll only take a moment. It has to do with Jane."

"Uh ... Jane, you say? Okay, then. Come on up. Better have your mask on."

Alessa watched the lawyer's shoulders drop with a sigh through the building's windows on each landing as he climbed the stairs to Pat's apartment. Finally, he reached Pat's door and knocked.

Alessa watched the men's interaction through Pat's living room windows.

Pat stilled momentarily before positioning his mask over his mouth and nose. "Just give me a second." After opening the front door, he ushered the man in. "Come on in, quickly." He closed the door behind him. "What is this about you say?"

"Ah, yes. I am a benefits lawyer, and you have been left in Jane's will," the lawyer said matter-of-factly.

Pat's face fell from behind his mask, and his body stilled. "Jane's ... dead?"

The lawyer grabbed a handful of documents from his bag. "She took it upon herself to contact your bank to pay off your apartment's entire loan, and then she left you with a sizeable inheritance."

Pat stared off into the distance and sat down on the couch. "Jane's dead?" he repeated.

"Yes, she is. I assumed you already knew. I am very sorry for your loss."

"So, she's not coming back," Pat said to no one in particular.

The lawyer licked his lips nervously as his eyes darted back and forth. "No, sir. She won't be back."

Pat sat silent for a moment, his eyes tearing up, and he sniffled. "Okay." He cleared his throat once again. "What is it, you said, now? Thanks to Jane, I own my apartment outright?"

"Yes, sir. And not only that, but you should consider getting an escort to the bank to deposit this check."

Pat held out his hand and took the small check. "Escort? Why do I need an escort? How much is it for?"

"Oh, I'm sorry." Remembering the man was blind, the lawyer chuckled nervously. Obviously, you can't read it. It's for 1.2 million."

Pat's jaw dropped open. "You said what now?"

"A little over one million dollars."

Pat's grip on the check tightened as his breathing became ragged.

The lawyer peered around the room at the disarray and realized Pat had no one to help him. "Actually, my morning is free. Would you like me to escort you?"

"Um." Pat swallowed. "Would you?"

"Of course." The lawyer nodded. "Would you like to go to your bank right now?"

Snapping back to reality, Pat stood up. "Yeah, I guess I would. Let me grab my coat." He walked over to where his coat was haphazardly thrown on the side table. Glancing out the window, he could see the outlines of the sun's bright rays and felt them warm on his face.

"Thank you," he whispered into the illuminated darkness to an invisible Jane.

Sighing loudly, Alessa dropped the binoculars and headed for the rooftop's ladder. "I hope you have a good life, Pat."

With a knot in her stomach, Alessa trudged up the grassy hill to the spot she had chosen for the two gravestones to be placed.

Sitting side by side, the upright headstones were tragically beautiful, reflecting the sunlight, each colored stone reflecting her friends' distinct personalities.

The left one glowed ruby-red, and the right one was the deepest of blacks. The red headstone had Reagan's name on the front, and the black headstone had Mackenzie's. Both had their individual dates of birth and identical dates of death laser-etched into the front of the stone.

Standing before her two best friends' headstones, Alessa swallowed the hot vomit that inched its way up the back of her throat. Not only were they dead because of her, but the ground beneath her feet was regrettably empty since their bodies had perished in the fire.

With trembling lips, she held back the urge to scream. "I'm so sorry," she apologized. "I'm so sorry for everything. I miss you both. So much."

She inhaled shakily. "I promise on my life, if Eric is still alive, I will track him down and make him pay."

CHAPTER THREE

In her dream, Alessa aggressively questioned the Bodyguard tied to the chair. The person's face changed every time she beat the side of their skull with her brass knuckles.

Bright red blood splattered the four walls, and Alessa screamed in frustration as she collapsed to the floor. Rocking back and forth on her heels, she held her head as the gravely injured Bodyguard cackled from the chair to which they were bound.

"You'll never find her."

She looked up at the Bodyguard, whose head was dangling at an impossible angle while they flashed a demented grin. "She's already dead; you just don't know it yet."

Invisible hands yanked Alessa's head back, and a sharp object pierced the base of her skull.

Gasping aloud, Alessa's eyelids sprung open, and her crimson irises caught the flickering light illuminating the corner of the motel room. "Shit!"

She grabbed a nearby towel and ran for the lamp she had inadvertently set on fire while sleeping. Whipping the fabric at the flames, she huffed with her red irises still aglow. "Come on. Fucking go out." Eying the ice bucket filled with water on the table, Alessa dunked the singed towel and tossed it into the flames. As the small fire was extinguished, leaving the motel room air thick with smoke, she breathed a sigh of relief, and her irises returned to their sky-blue hue as her adrenaline lessened.

Fanning the smoke away from her face, Alessa opened the small motel window, encouraging the brown fog to escape.

In an exhausted haze, Alessa shuffled back to her bed. She plopped onto her stomach and leaned over the edge of the bed, grabbing the book *History of Sparta* from the bedside table.

Propping herself up on her elbows, Alessa saw the tattoo on the inside of her right upper arm that she had gotten in Damon's honor: "*Molon Labe*" was spelled out in Greek; its meaning, "Come and Take Them."

King Leonidas of Sparta had spoken the infamous words during the Battle of Thermopylae in response to Xerxes's demands that the Spartans surrender their weapons.

The image of Damon smoldering before her, holding her in his arms as they danced at Eric Lansing's château, came to mind as she stared into the distance.

Falling in through the motel room's front door, Camden exhaled. "Whew!" Recognizing the smell of smoke, he followed his nose and looked toward the corner of the room. He saw the charred corner and wrapped the bright green and pink feather boa around his neck to usher the smoke out the window.

"What the hell, Alessa?" he groaned. "This again? Soon, motels will get smart and start talking to one another, and then they'll find the pattern of burning rooms. They will stop accepting cash-only payments if we keep leaving rooms like this."

Alessa rolled her eyes. "It's not like I can help it," she grumbled, returning her attention to the book.

After fanning a sufficient amount of smoke out of the room, he belched loudly and stumbled across the room. "You have another one of those firestarter dreams?" he slurred while falling into a chair.

Alessa looked up from the book and pointed her finger at Camden. "Ding ding ding. Uh, Cam, are you drunk?" She squinted her eyes, trying to focus, and leaned her head toward him. "And is that glitter you've got all over you?"

Camden grinned sloppily while pointing his finger back at Alessa. "Ding. Ding. Ding. You got it." He stretched back in the chair and groaned loudly as his joints cracked and popped.

Alessa squinted, peering over at the small clock on the side table. "What time is it?"

He shrugged with an exaggerated blink. "Uh, like three or something?"

Alessa scoffed after reading the time. "Uh, no. Try 4:30. What were you doing out that late? I highly doubt it had anything to do with—"

"No, Alessa," he sighed and shook his head. "It had nothing to do with finding Kai." He struggled to take off his first shoe. "Look, we've been at this four months. For four months straight, I have thought of nothing but finding your sister."

"Hey, now. We've also been trying to locate Eric Lansing."

He threw his shoe under the table with an audible sigh. "Even in Rogue Command, we were allowed a night off occasionally, just to let loose." Camden tossed his second shoe and wobbled, falling over to the side while he stumbled across the room.

Rushing over to help Camden, she steadied him. As he leaned in close to Alessa, the scent of whiskey smacked her in the face. "Wow, Cam." She could also smell the nauseatingly sweet women's perfume wafting off his skin and coughed. "You kind of smell like a strip club."

He blinked slowly and chuckled. "Guess that makes sense since that's where I was. And, oh, were the ladies accommodating tonight!"

Alessa ducked out of his arm and backed away as Camden unbuttoned his shirt. As his shirt fell open, he touched a bite mark that was visible on the side of his neck. "Some much more than others," he laughed to himself.

Alessa fanned the strong scent of alcohol away as she stepped back. "Jeez. I mean, I can't say you haven't earned some free time ... to do as you wish." She rolled her eyes with a slight smile as she walked back to her bed.

Stripping out of his shiny dark green button-up, Camden tossed his shirt onto the bedside table before he stumbled toward the nearest bed. Camden groaned, falling face down onto the covers.

Alessa raised an eyebrow and cast a sideways smile. "But you surprised me by spending your free time at a strip club."

Camden flipped onto his back and crossed his ankles as he closed his eyes. "Hey, now. We can't all be Saint Alessa."

She chucked a pillow at his smug face. "Oh."

Camden caught the pillow with an outstretched hand just before it struck his face. "Mmm. Thanks," he said, tucking the pillow behind his head.

After eyeing Camden's muscular torso, Alessa's eyes dropped to the floor. "Well, seeing as I'm up for the day, I'm going to grab a cup of coffee. You want me to bring anything back?"

"Yes, surprise me, and make sure you get something to eat," Camden mumbled as he drifted off to sleep.

Alessa got dressed in blue jeans and a black corset top before shrugging into a black leather jacket. She turned around and air-saluted her friend's unconscious form before she headed for the 24-hour diner just down the street.

Even though it was August, nighttime in Wisconsin could be chilly, and tonight was no exception. As she pushed open the door, a ding announced Alessa's entrance. She stumbled into the intimate diner and was immediately greeted by a smiling waitress with a soft voice and an intense Northern accent. "Go ahead and sit anywhere, hun. I'll be right with you."

She sat on a stool at the bar and read the small menu posted on individual signs in front of every other seat. The local news was playing on the television set above her.

Two news anchors sat behind a desk.

"With the distribution of the legitimate vaccine, the mutant smallpox virus has been contained in just under four months. There hasn't been a new case in over one month, and the global vaccination initiative has been deemed successful."

"As was previously reported, Eric Lansing is technically still missing; however, it is believed by many he perished in the fire at his château four months ago. However, if you do by chance have any information regarding him or his company, Erebos Industries, the United States government is asking you to call 1-888..."

"What can I get you?" the waitress interrupted the anchors.

Alessa tore her eyes away from the small television hanging above the counter. "Oh, uh ... can I get a hot mocha? And a chocolate chip muffin, please."

The waitress flashed half a smile. "I can make you a hot chocolate."

Alessa dipped her head. "Sounds good to me. I'll take it."

The waitress tucked her notepad away without jotting down her order. "That it?"

"Yep."

The waitress nodded toward the television as she walked behind the counter. "Can you believe everything that son of a bitch has put us through?" She poured a cup of steaming water into a mug and poured the chocolate powder before mixing it with a silver spoon.

Alessa pressed her lips together as she played with Damon's ring. "No, I cannot."

The cocoa nearly sloshed out of the mug as the waitress set it down in front of Alessa. "Well, I can tell you if I were ever to see him in person, I'd have no problem putting a bullet through that man." She pressed a finger into the space between her eyebrows. "Right between the eyes. It'd be no different to me than hunting a buck."

Alessa wrapped her hands around the warm ceramic mug and chuckled, staring into space. "Or kicking him off a high cliff and watching his face contort in anguish as he panics, knowing he's about to die. But it won't be a quick death—no. Every mistake he's ever made in his entire life will have time to flash before his eyes as he falls toward the earth until finally, *thump*."

The waitress's head tilted to the side as her eyes grew wide.

Alessa cleared her throat and blinked, erasing the vivid image of Eric's dead body from her mind. "Or yeah, what you said." She laughed light-heartedly to break the awkward silence.

"Damn. I thought I was dark." The waitress raised her

eyebrows and side-eyed Alessa before turning around. "I'm just going to go grab your muffin."

"Oh, could I have two more muffins? So three total?" Alessa shouted at the waitress as the kitchen doors swung shut.

The anchor on the left spoke again. "One positive piece of news for the nation is that Greenfield Farms promotes a new genetically modified sugar substitute. The company claims its product has no terrible aftertaste or adverse health reactions.

"Greenfield Farms boasts the artificial sugar isn't engineered in a lab but is grown in the same manner as sugarcane. It is a genetically modified plant that is superior in how it is processed. This changes the chemical makeup, thus tricking the body into thinking it along the same lines as drinking water."

The second news anchor sported an exaggerated grin and laughed. "What a concept."

The waitress dropped off a small paper bag. "Your muffins."

"Thanks." Alessa forced a smile before she returned her attention to the news story.

"If there's a product that tricks my body into thinking sugar is as healthy as water, sign me up," the first anchor proclaimed. "The sugar substitute has been in development for close to ten years."

A picture of the Greenfield Farms logo popped up on the screen, followed by a video of a handsome, sandy-complexion, middle-aged man with wavy medium blonde hair and dark grey eyes.

The man reached out and firmly grasped hands with someone from the crowd.

"Lucas Greenfield is the CEO of the biotechnology company Greenfield Farms," the reporter continued.

Alessa held the mug up to her lips and sipped the steaming chocolate. Glancing back up at the television, she recognized the woman's profile on the screen and nearly choked on the hot liquid.

Standing directly behind Lucas was her sister, Kai. Sure, her naturally straight-haired blonde hair had been dyed a toffee-brown and curled, but otherwise, the young woman looked exactly like Kai.

That has to be Kai. It just has to be.

Forcing down the hot chocolate still in her mouth, Alessa threw cash on the counter before snatching up the bag of muffins and sprinting out the door.

CHAPTER FOUR

Alessa burst into the room, slamming the motel door into the wall. "Cam!"

Springing upright in bed, Camden held his fists in front of his face, prepared to fight. "What? What's wrong?"

As adrenaline coursed through her veins, she fell forward and grabbed his thick biceps. "I saw her!"

Confused, he blinked slowly. "Who'd you see?"

"I saw my sister. I saw Kai."

Camden rolled his eyes and placed his hands behind his head, falling back into bed. "Not this again."

She jumped up and ran back to the motel door, slamming it closed excitedly. "I know what I saw."

Yawning, he rubbed the heels of his palms into his closed eyelids. "Alessa, you did not—"

Snatching up the chair, she plopped down and hurriedly whipped out Damon's laptop, placing it on the table before her. "Kai's hair was curly and dyed brown, but it was most definitely her." She nervously bit her lower lip before muttering under her breath. "It had to be her..."

"Mm-hmm." Camden sat up and groaned. "What time is it?"

Alessa was fervently typing on the laptop's keyboard. "You were asleep for maybe an hour."

His jaw dropped as he stared up at her. "You couldn't have waited to tell me you saw your sister's doppelgänger until I got more than an hour of sleep? Even if it was her, there's nothing we can do right now. I'm going back to bed," he grumbled.

Alessa's eyes locked on the computer's screen. "That's fine. I've got research to do."

Over the next several hours, Camden snored behind Alessa as she dug into the company, Greenfield Farms, and its CEO, Lucas Greenfield. She watched any footage she could get her hands on, searching for her sister in every frame, and found legal documents for which they had applied, including permits and licenses.

By the time Camden awoke, Alessa had found dozens of videos where the same woman she believed to be Kai could be seen.

Camden stretched his arms while extending his legs off the edge of the bed. "I'm going to need some painkillers, food, and hydration." He reached for the full glass of water on the bedside table. "Find anything worth looking into?"

Alessa rotated toward Camden, and the computer screen's glow reflected off the side of her face. She grinned wildly. "Did I ever."

He sat, arched his back, and cracked his spine with a sigh. "Okay, then." Camden stood and headed toward the bathroom. "First, I'm going to take a restroom break. Then you can show me everything."

While waiting for Camden to return, Alessa saved all the documents she had found to the computer's drive.

He rubbed the back of his neck as he made his way to the half-full pot of coffee. "Wow. That was a night." Picking the pot up by the handle, he noticed the coffee was hot and fresh. "Have you been awake this whole time?"

Alessa's eyes never left the computer screen as she clicked the mouse, positioning the files one after another. "Uh-huh."

He grabbed a container of creamer from their small refrigerator. "Hey, where'd you put the meds?"

She pointed at the table between their beds, her attention never leaving the computer screen. "In the drawer beside you." Alessa impatiently watched Camden reach down and pull the pill bottle out of the drawer. "Could you possibly move any slower? I need you to get over here to show you all of this. We have a lot to cover."

Camden's eyebrow arched as he swallowed the painkillers. "So, you're serious. You think you may have actually found your sister?"

She snatched the laptop off the table and plopped down on the edge of Camden's bed. "Sit down already, and I'll show you everything."

He exhaled loudly, sitting beside Alessa with his coffee in hand. "Okay, okay. I'm ready."

She pointed at a picture of an attractive middle-aged man with medium-length blond hair and storm-grey eyes. "This is Lucas Greenfield, CEO and founder of Greenfield Farms."

Camden held his drink up to his lips, blowing the steam. "Yeah, I've seen his pretty face before. What does he have to do with anything?"

"I think he knows where Eric is, or at least he's in his inner circle. I haven't found exactly how he's connected to him, but in my gut, I have this terrible feeling that he is."

Alessa paused as Camden took a drink of his hot coffee. "Please continue," he urged.

"So, this Lucas Greenfield guy grew up in a small town. His dad was a farmer who convinced him to grow a new plant type that could be used as a genetically modified sugar substitute. Together, they spent the last ten years investing in the development of the product, and it's finally getting cleared in the United States."

Alessa opened the next tab, displaying a video of the product being consumed by a smiling family, all wearing pastel colors while dancing in a field of orange and white wildflowers. A feminine voice said, "Ambrosia, the genetically modified sugar that won't add inches to your hips. This delectable food is made organically in the ground, not in some scientists-run lab. It's the first of its kind. Ambrosia doesn't mimic sugar within the body's cells but instead tricks the taste receptors into believing it tastes sweet. Ambrosia, the future of health."

"Wow." Camden took the final swig of coffee in his mug. "Yeah, I'm gonna need a lot more of this to get through the day if you keep making me watch that cheesy shit." He stood up and poured himself another cup of coffee as Alessa continued.

"And this footage is from Lucas's most recent public speech. If you look right here"—she paused the video—"you catch a glimpse of Kai."

Sitting back on the bed, Camden leaned into the computer screen and squinted at the grainy picture. "I guess?" He pressed the enter key to continue the video, and his eyes widened. "I think you may be onto something."

Alessa turned her head to look at him. "What did you see?"

He set the mug down on the bedside table and pointed at the computer screen while standing up. "Those men on either side of Lucas are Rogue Command Bodyguards." Heading to the bathroom, he unbuttoned his pants.

Alessa hollered, "How can you tell?" She dipped her head down before the computer screen. "They just look like—"

"Any other Bodyguards? Yeah, I know," Camden shouted from behind the closed door. "You just have to trust me; I trained with them since we were toddlers. It's like how you recognize your sister. Well, those are like my brothers. However, just because this guy has Rogue Command Bodyguards doesn't mean he is associated with Eric Lansing. Companies use our services all the time."

Alessa bit her lower lip in frustration and slammed the laptop shut. "Right. Well, there's a press conference two days from now. I think we can make it if we leave soon."

"I'm just brushing my teeth," Camden replied. "Go ahead and pack up."

Alessa shoved her clothes into plastic bags before carefully placing Damon's laptop into his backpack.

Exiting the bathroom, Camden met Alessa's eyes while rolling up the sleeves of his burnt orange button-up. "All right, let's go get your sister."

CHAPTER FIVE

After a two-day drive, Camden and Alessa arrived in Kansas. They followed signs posted along the back roads advertising the location of Greenfield Farm's marketing event.

Camden groaned. "Damn, this makeshift parking lot is full."

Alessa played with the fake hair on her long, bright blonde wig. "Do you think I could use my microchip to record today?"

Camden shook his head and turned the steering wheel. "I don't think you activating is a good idea, especially out in the open with civilians."

Alessa scoffed and rolled her eyes before applying pink lipstick. "It's not like there's a trigger here. If I record it, I can replay it in my mind whenever I want."

"You have yet to prove you can control your microchip's glitch. As far as I've seen, you do the most damage when you're unconscious; however, I don't want to try and tempt fate. You're just too volatile right now. Your microchip must be tamed, not explored in front of innocent bystanders. We're not completely sure of—"

"How dangerous I am?" Alessa interrupted.

Camden tilted his head in contemplation. "That's one way to put it."

A parking attendant used their wands to direct the heavy traffic into the makeshift parking lot, guiding Camden into an empty parking space.

"I hate it when you call it that. A glitch," Alessa grumbled, unbuckling her seatbelt. "It's like I'm faulty or something."

"I mean"—Camden shrugged with a sideways grin—"if the shoe fits."

She adjusted a large-brimmed sun hat atop her wig. "Whatever. How do I look?"

Checking her out from head to toe, he smiled devilishly. "I mean, you could definitely pull off the blonde look."

She playfully slapped his muscular shoulder. "Yeah, okay."

Cam handed her white sunglasses. "Put these on. You'll use these to record the event instead of your microchip. To start recording, you push, right"—he stretched his arm across Alessa and lightly touched the button built into the side of her frames —"here."

Alessa's heart rate unexpectedly sped up as his fingers lingered beside her face, and she swallowed hard. Her cheeks blushed pink, and she pulled away. "Uh, thanks."

Camden grabbed for his door handle. "You ready?"

Flattening the dress over her abdomen, she peered nervously out the passenger side window. "What if my sister is here? What do I do? I've been searching for her for so long." She anxiously spun Damon's ring around her finger. "I haven't even considered what would happen if I found her."

Camden let go of the door handle and turned toward Alessa. "I can't tell you that. This is probably one of those situations in which you won't know how you'll react until the time comes."

He ran his hand through his hair, sighing loudly. "But unless we get out of this car, we'll never know how you'll react because there's not a chance in hell you'll find her in here."

After giving her hand a reassuring pat, Camden opened his car door. With a deep, steadying inhale, Alessa stepped out of the car onto the pavement.

After walking around the car, he took Alessa's hand within his own as they scanned the large crowd. "This is quite the turnout."

Lucky for them, the day was sunny enough, so Alessa didn't draw any attention to herself since she was simply another woman wearing a large-brimmed sunhat and sunglasses.

Camden pulled Alessa close, entwining their arms as they made their way up a grassy hill toward a large pavilion. "I guess we'll just follow the crowd."

An elegant Indian woman wearing a burgundy silk wrap shirt and black slacks entered the makeshift stage from the right side and set up a cordless microphone on a stand.

Alessa pointed. "Looks like they're about to begin."

The woman standing before the crowd tapped on the microphone, causing a high-pitched sound to reverberate off the nearby trees. "Attention, attention. One, two, three. Can everybody hear me?"

The crowd hooped and hollered in response.

She flashed her white teeth in a wide grin. "That's great. Good morning, everyone! We will start today's festivities by introducing our company, the product meant to better your lives, and what we stand for.

"First, let me tell you a little about myself and my role in all of this. My name is Veda, and my position at Greenfield Farms is personal assistant to Lucas Greenfield. Mr. Greenfield and his father spent years on their family farm growing organic vegetables and fruits until one day, his father had the brilliant idea of cross-breeding plants to find the perfect combination for a healthy sugar substitute.

"Ambrosia is the result of their successful endeavor. Ambrosia is the first genetically modified sugar substitute of its kind. It was not developed in a lab and is a plant-based product."

Lucas Greenfield stepped onto the pavilion from the side stairs and adjusted his tailored fitted suit as he strolled beside Veda.

Glancing to the side, Veda's cheeks blushed a light red as she introduced the CEO. "And here he is, the man of the hour, CEO of Greenfield Farms, Lucas Greenfield."

The crowd erupted into a chorus of cheering and clapping as Lucas took center stage in front of the microphone.

Camden and Alessa's eyebrows scrunched in confusion as they looked around the fanatic crowd.

Camden bowed his head toward Alessa. "What the hell is going on? This is giving me real cult-like vibes."

Agreeing with Camden, she nodded. "History shows when people are given an option to better their lives, they jump on the bandwagon. No matter how ridiculous the claim."

Stepping up to the microphone, Lucas Greenfield held his hands up to silence the crowd, but they only cheered louder. Pressing one hand to his chest, his smile grew.

"Yep, this isn't creepy at all," Camden sarcastically remarked.

Alessa glared at the handsome middle-aged man and pressed the record button on the side of her sunglasses.

Lucas stretched his neck up and to the left before beginning his speech, sending spine-tingling chills from Alessa's head down to her toes.

What the fuck was that? Why did that seem eerily familiar?

"Thank you for the warm welcome, and we are so grateful for your presence here today. My father, God rest his soul, passed away a few months ago, so he isn't able to see the results of his hard work." He chuckled. "Excuse me; all of *our* hard work."

"Way to be modest," Camden remarked snarkily from the corner of his mouth.

Lucas continued. "Unlike every other genetically modified sugar substitute currently on the market, Ambrosia has no life-altering effects. No weight gain, headaches, low blood pressure, inflammation, depression, kidney damage, cancer; the list goes on and on. Ambrosia has been proven not to have one single side effect. How are we so sure? Here are the volunteers who have been consuming our product for three years now, and they can all tell you without a doubt they have not experienced a single side effect."

Lucas pointed to a large group of men, women, and children who marched up the stairs, using both sides of the stage. They stopped behind him, and he beamed confidently from center stage.

"These brave souls accepted the challenge by drinking and eating only food prepared by our company chefs for the past three years. They have been part of a highly monitored control group in which everything they ate, from ice cream to pasta, was made with Ambrosia instead of sugar or a different sugar substitute.

"Sixty participants started with type 2 diabetes. Every person with this diagnosis has been cured through diet alone.

"Every day, the participants journaled how they felt emotionally, mentally, and physically. By the end of the first six months, all reported a change in their mental health for the better; their energy was sky-high, and they were pleased the product did not have an aftertaste." Lucas Greenfield laughed as if his statement were hilarious.

The crowd laughed loudly before applauding the participants beaming on the stage.

Alessa squeezed Camden's arm, and he bent down. "Is it just me, or are their smiles kind of—"

"Creepy?" he finished for her. "Yeah. It's like there's a light on, but nobody's home."

Lucas Greenfield continued once the sound from the crowd cheering and hands clapping died down. "Now, I know my claiming these facts can only go so far. This is why we have set up several free testing stations throughout the U.S. and overseas. We stand by our promise; you will taste nothing but sheer bliss once our product has hit your tongue. Guaranteed." Lucas Greenfield winked. "See you in Kansas City, Missouri, at Union Station in two days."

Camden joined the awkward clapping as they turned away from the stage. "I guess we know where we're headed."

CHAPTER SIX

While Camden drove them to Kansas City, Alessa reviewed the footage she had recorded.

As they sat in the Union Station's busy parking lot, Camden shoved the last bite of a cheeseburger into his mouth. "Find anything suspicious in the footage?"

Frustrated, Alessa silently shook her head back and forth.

"Okay, so what about in any of the files you saved? I saw you reviewing that footage on our way here as well. Any dirt on Lucas Greenfield?"

Frustrated, Alessa sighed. "Not a damn thing." She slammed down the top of the laptop before balling her hands into fists.

"Hey, now. Alice didn't do anything to you." Camden grabbed the computer from Alessa's lap and placed it gently in the back seat.

"Alice?" Alessa laughed incredulously.

Camden rubbed his hands along the steering wheel. "She's like our third wheel, so I named her."

Alessa shook her head, looking out the window at the growing crowd. "You are a strange man."

"So if this man is squeaky clean and truly is who he says he is, are you sure we should be following this guy? I mean, you didn't see Kai at the press conference."

Her head whipped back around. "Yes, we absolutely should be following Greenfield. You saw those people's grins frozen in place like they weren't even human."

"That was weird," Camden agreed.

"And there's the fact he's hired not only Bodyguards but Rogue Command Bodyguards, specifically. He has to be hiding something. Besides, there is something eerily familiar about him. I can't place my finger on it, but my intuition tells me he's somehow linked to Eric."

Camden pointed down the road. "Can your intuition take me to one of the bars we passed on the way here? I'm thirsty."

Alessa's eyebrows raised while she tucked her brunette hair strands beneath the long blonde wig. "You do realize the event we're about to attend provides an abundance of drinks. Surely one of them has to be alcoholic."

He grabbed ahold of the car's handle and scoffed. "No way am I about to drink the Kool-Aid at a massive gathering held by a man with a cult-like following. In the history of humankind, when has that ever ended well?"

Before opening his door, Camden fixed his crooked, dark brown, shaggy wig.

Exhaling loudly, Alessa and Camden stood side by side behind their car, watching the crowd flow toward the stage set up in front of Union Station's front doors.

Seven long tables were set up on either side of a podium, with Greenfield Farms' workers standing behind each one.

Everyone was sporting a T-shirt with the Greenfield Farms logo on the front.

On each grouping of small paper cups, a label described the liquid in which Ambrosia was used instead of sugar or a sugar substitute. The first was labeled iced tea, then dark soda, light soda, and finally, yellow and pink lemonade.

Some of the foods presented were chocolate brownies, a piece of cherry pie, half a bagel, a slice of bread, and jelly.

Of the fourteen tables set up, each had a line of one hundred people deep and was quickly growing.

After joining a line, Camden noticed Alessa nervously twisting Damon's ring around her finger. "Tell me more about your sister."

"Huh?" Alessa glanced over at Camden.

"Kai. I'd like to hear about her."

Her forehead scrunched. "What exactly would you like to know?"

"Anything, really." They took a step as the line moved forward.

Camden licked his lips. "Well, we've been on this adventure for nearly half a year, and I have yet to hear about the woman beyond her physical description. What are her likes? Her dislikes? What makes her tick?"

"Oh, um." Alessa cleared her throat. "Okay, her likes? Unlike me, she preferred the sun over the moon. I mean, she *does* prefer the sun," she corrected herself.

"That's a start."

They simultaneously took another step.

"And you know how I told you, Damon and me falling in love wasn't a thing I ever counted on? Kai wants, no, she craves to be loved. I've always been afraid of her falling for the wrong guy because of her subconscious need to be loved.

"What happened to us at our cabin made me abhor love and personal attachments, but it made Kai cling to the concept. I have always felt responsible for what happened to us; how we needed to be brought into the Spartan society because of my killing my parent's murderers and being fucked up from it."

Camden gently grabbed Alessa's elbow and turned her toward him. "You can't possibly blame yourself for what happened to your family."

She bit down hard on her lower lip, trying to keep her emotions buried deep.

He placed his thumb on her chin and tilted her head, forcing Alessa to look into Camden's green and golden eyes. "Thanks to you, your sister is alive. She *is alive*, Alessa."

She closed her eyes and took a steadying breath.

Stepping forward, Camden kept Alessa distracted from her dark thoughts. "What kind of person is she?"

Alessa chuckled, glancing off to the side. "She's bold, and clever, and funny. Her heart is so big. She's brave, strong, intelligent. Oh, is she intelligent! She is on her way to becoming one of the top scientists in research and development at the Colorado compound."

Stretching her neck, Alessa peered through the sea of people for Kai's familiar face.

"What's your first memory of her?"

"You mean besides my parents being murdered? Um..." Alessa squeezed her eyes shut as the cabin flashed before her. Blinking them open, she saw Lucas Greenfield standing on the stage behind the podium. "I think it was when my elder brought us back to his home. We were standing just outside the room where he and his wife discussed whether or not to keep us."

"Well, that's fucked up," Camden scoffed.

Alessa shrugged nonchalantly. "Tis' the way of Spartans."

Stepping up to the rectangle table, they each grabbed a tiny cup of yellow lemonade before pretending to take a drink. While bringing the cup to her lips for a second time, she glared at Lucas Greenfield as he remained behind the podium with a cheesy smile plastered on his face.

As Alessa turned to walk away from the tables, Lucas was approached by a handsome man with dirty blond hair and a young brunette wearing a dark grey pencil skirt with a midnight blue silk button-up.

The young woman's striking brown hazel eyes looked past the young man as she took him by the crook of his elbow and pulled him toward her. After whispering something in his ear, he perked up and turned his head to the side before excusing himself.

Recognizing the woman, Alessa gasped. "Kai?"

Alessa dropped her cup and its contents onto the ground as she pointed at the young man and brunette hurrying off the stage.

Alessa tried to yell over the crowd. "Kai!"

Camden smiled nervously at onlookers as he grabbed Alessa by the arm. "Shh. Keep your voice down," he encouraged.

Alessa pushed Camden backward. "How can you tell me to pipe down? That's her; I saw my sister!"

"Be smart, don't do this here," he warned.

"How can I let her go?" Alessa shrieked.

She nearly dragged him all the way back to the front of the lines before Camden inconspicuously jabbed his fingers into Alessa's jugular, rendering her unconscious.

He caught Alessa as she fainted and swept her up into his arms. "I'm so sorry; my wife has a medical condition," he apologized to the nearby concerned witnesses. "This happens all the time; she'll be fine. Her medication is in the car." Camden pushed past the people. "Excuse me."

Laying her down beside the car, Camden grabbed his med kit and cracked a smelling salt capsule. Holding it before Alessa, he bit his lip in frustration. "Come on. Wake up."

Jerking upright, Alessa dry heaved and pressed her fingertips deep into her temples. "What in Hades?"

He picked her up underneath her arms and stood her upright. "Come on, let's get you in the car." Camden opened the passenger side car door and helped Alessa in.

He walked to the other side of the car while Alessa took her hat and wig off in silence.

Camden pulled off his wig and shook his head before starting the car. "You gave me no choice. You were losing your shit after seeing your sister."

Alessa began trembling from head to toe as the adrenaline kicked in. "Cam, shit. I'm so sorry. But—she's alive! I saw her with my own eyes. I was starting to think I had hallucinated, but that was definitely Kai."

After tossing the hat and blonde wig into the backseat, Alessa plucked the sunglasses from her face and peered down at the shades. She had recorded everything.

"Her hair is much darker, and I've never seen her with curls that tight, but it's her. I knew it. I fucking knew she wouldn't leave me." Alessa's voice cracked as she grinned wide.

Camden half-smiled. "I'm happy for you," he said, his voice strained.

Catching onto Camden's hesitation, Alessa turned to him. "What? What's the matter?"

He tilted his head from side to side. "Did you not see how friendly she was with that guy who also worked for Lucas

Greenfield? For you thinking Lucas has something to do with Eric Lansing, don't you think it's not a great look for your sister to be working with him?"

Alessa stared at him, silent.

"And why'd she go and change her appearance? Something about this isn't adding up."

Alessa huffed before pressing her back into the seat. "In the entirety of Spartan history, not a single citizen has gone undetected. Her microchip is no longer registering on their radar, just like mine, but if something happened to her after I went on my mission and she was forced to leave Sparta, she'd have to look completely different. Once it was on the Consilium's radar that she was still alive, they wouldn't ask questions until her dead body was brought to them."

Camden threw the car into reverse. "Wait a minute. If that's the case, are you saying they might kill you once they realize you're still alive?"

Alessa pursed her lips and stared out the front window before responding. "They could very well, yes."

Camden's eyebrows raised in surprise. "Okay, then, how about we not find out and stay as far away from Spartans as possible?"

Alessa exhaled and rubbed her hands nervously up and down her thighs. "I haven't exactly been home to tell them I'm not hanging with Hades in the underworld, so to the best of their knowledge, I'm dead. But I'm thinking right about now might be the time to tell them."

Camden shook his head. "First, tell me why your sister would be tempted to leave Sparta to assist a company interested in genetically modifying food?"

She raised her hands in defeat. "I—I can't answer that.

Honestly, I have no idea, but what I do know is we need to get her out of there."

"And how exactly do you suggest we do that?"

"By going home." Alessa sighed. "I need to talk to my elder. He's the only one I trust besides you, of course. And I guess it's time we figure out what is going on with my microchip."

Camden turned the steering wheel. "I've already told you. It's glitched and—"

"Technopathy, right," Alessa interrupted. "But how do I control it? Can you teach me?"

Camden tilted his head to the side in contemplation.

"No? I didn't think so. Maybe my elder or even the Council will know how to help me. All I know is we can't keep doing this on our own."

Concerned, he ran his fingers through his hair. "You know they'll never accept me because of who I was. How will I hide the fact I'm Rogue Command? It'll be an achievement if they don't kill me on the spot for being a Bodyguard."

"How will they know? Your eyes don't turn golden unless you're connected to one of those remotes, am I right?"

"Well, not exactly. I am forced to activate when connected to a remote, but my eyes also activate like yours when I tap into knowledge, memories, or skills. Hold on, are you telling me after all these months of interrogating and fighting Bodyguards that you've never noticed my eyes activating gold?"

She looked up at the roof, thinking back to them interrogating the Bodyguards. "No, I don't think I have. However, I am rather busy when we are conducting business, so you'll have to forgive me for not looking deep into your eyes. But, are you saying as long as you hide your ability to activate, we could pass you off for being Special Operations or something?"

Camden turned onto the highway. "If we went down that route, I'd have to be one hell of a good liar. I'm sure they will quiz me down to the size of the shit I squeezed out that morning."

Alessa scrunched up her nose in disgust. "Ew, Cam, really?"

"I'm just saying if you want me to say I'm something as specialized as that, I'll need to have one hell of a back story."

"That's fine; we've got about fifteen hours' worth of time."

"So, are you telling me you want me to head for Colorado?" He peered up at the street signs they were quickly approaching.

Looking out the front window, she nodded her head. "Yes, Colorado. And Cam, don't worry about Spartans coming after you. After they see what I'm capable of, they're not going to fuck with you."

He side-eyed Alessa as she slid her sunglasses back over her eyes.

He exhaled loudly while taking the exit. "Or they'll want you exterminated."

With an exasperated sigh, she pressed play on the side of her sunglasses and watched the recorded footage play on her right lens. "It's you and me against the world, Cam. Gods help anyone who comes between us."

CHAPTER SEVEN

Blinking slowly, Cain stared down at Kai, asleep in his arms.

The golden morning glow filtered through the fingerprint-covered window, illuminating her blonde eyelashes. Even though Kai's hair was dyed brown, her eyelashes remained a natural ashy blonde.

Propping himself up on his elbow, he looked at the tan skin on Kai's exposed neck. Her artery lay just below the surface, which Cain could easily slash. She'd bleed out easily within five minutes if the cut were deep enough. Or he could prolong her suffering for days.

Cain hardened, imagining hot, dark red blood coating her tan skin.

His fingers twitched in anticipation as he reached for her throat. As Cain traced an artery down the side of the young woman's neck, he recalled the first time he met her during the cave tour. "Kai, my pet," he whispered.

It was toward the end of spring, but the winter chill still clung to the wet sides of the cave where the tour group entered.

Since Cain's time in the cult as a young child, his urges had been dark and deadly. Growing up, his Uncle Eric had encouraged him to find an outlet for these feelings of malice that threatened to consume him.

For years now, every few months, he had chosen a new victim. A camping excursion, a group hike, or a cave exploration were all wonderful ways to meet people who were ripe for the picking.

Cain would befriend a person of interest and research every aspect of their lives on social media. If they seemed distant from their family and friends or had no internet presence, Cain would get them to open up about their lives so he could further assess whether they were good candidates.

After his victims were deemed worthy, Cain would lure them somewhere secluded and torture them, mutilating them beyond recognition until they begged for him to release them from this world.

Cain's inner demon would be satiated for a short while until his overwhelming urge to kill would consume him, and he would return to the hunt.

Today, after months of peace, Cain's inner demons were speaking to him again, and he was itching to find another worthy target, this time at a cave tour.

Walking into the dark entrance behind the group leader, Cain stopped to look up at the large stalactites hanging from the ceiling when someone collided with him.

Stumbling forward, a young blonde put her hands out to catch herself, but Cain had reached out and grabbed her by the arms.

She gasped as he held her in mid-air.

Surprised by his protective reaction, Cain cleared his throat. "Um," he said, helping her stand upright.

Once she regained her footing, the young woman brushed her light hair from her eyes and stammered apologetically. "I am so—so sorry. I just lost my balance and—" Kai caught her breath, looking up into the man's striking grey-green eyes.

Grinning, he flashed his pearly white teeth. "It's not a problem. I'm sure you're not the first to trip while walking on a cave's uneven ground."

Blushing, she glanced away. "Uh, yeah, you're probably right."

Still holding onto her, Cain asked, "What's your name?"

"Oh, um, Kai," she said breathlessly.

"Mmm. Kai," he purred. "I like it."

"I'm glad?" she laughed nervously, backing away from him. "We should probably pay attention and get back to the group before we lose them." She pointed behind him at the others who had walked away, leaving them with only the light from the entrance and the flashlights on their heads.

"Oh, yeah, you're right." Cain turned around and extended his arm. "Ladies first."

Squinting into the darkness, Kai marched ahead, trying her best not to trip again.

Walking close behind, Cain could smell the woman's scent, and he hardened. Growling under his breath, he was frustrated by the weak, human response. Cain had never become aroused without violence being involved, and it made him feel as though he were losing control.

As the guide instructed the group on how to climb the interior wall, Kai peeked back at Cain and smiled shyly.

Shifting his hips to the right, he attempted to hide his

growing bulge. What the fuck is wrong with me? Get it together.

The instructor climbed the rock wall and called down for the next volunteer.

Kai excitedly raised her hand high up in the air. "I'll go."

Cain walked up behind Kai protectively. "I'll spot you."

While securing the rope around her torso, Kai prompted, "You never told me your name."

He reached around and pulled the rope tight, making Kai groan. "Cain."

"Like Cain from the bible? Isn't he the one who killed his brother and had the ability to possess humans?"

He grinned devilishly. "That's the one." He pointed up at the awaiting instructor. "You should get going."

"Right." Kai spun around and exhaled loudly. Reaching up, she grabbed onto the rough, vertical rock. Her legs worked together in an elegant dance as she climbed the wall.

"Beautiful," Cain muttered under his breath as he watched her from down below.

"Mmm," Kai groaned, stretching her limbs in the early morning light.

Cain watched her body wriggle against the white bedsheets. "Morning, my pet."

Kai's eyes remained closed as her lips parted into a slight smile. "Morning."

He kissed her gently on the lips. "Caffeine?"

She nodded her head excitedly. "Yes, please."

"Ready for today's press conference?" Pushing himself upright out of bed, Cain walked over to the hotel room's phone and called down to the front desk. "Two mocha lattes for room 214."

She sat upright with her back against the headboard. "We start the day with station ten interviewing Er—"

Cain's head whipped back around, and he glared at Kai, waiting for her to correct his uncle's new name.

She backtracked quickly. "I—I mean, Lucas, at 9 am, and then it's a day full of back-to-back interviews."

Cain sat down on the edge of the bed, facing her. "Kai, you need to be more careful. You can never, ever say his real name in public."

She nodded fervently. "I know. It was a stupid mistake; I'm sorry."

Cain placed his fingertips beneath her chin, lifting her face to his. "Think of it like he's in witness protection. Because of what those damn Spartans did to him, he had to change his entire identity."

"It's still hard for me to believe Spartans started that fire and tried to kill him just because he was trying to make the human species stronger. I mean, the misfortunate side effect of it killing those that reacted to the medication wasn't a part of the plan, but every medical advancement has curveballs." She turned around and sat on the edge of the bed, stripping out of her nightgown.

Cain squinted as he held back the truth: his uncle had meant to kill those who had deadly genetic anomalies, and they had every intention of ending the lives of millions more, but Kai's sister, Alessa, had stopped them.

He stared at the faded whip marks across Kai's back. "It's hard for me to believe you haven't been in contact with anyone from home since you left."

Kai's back stiffened as Cain ran his fingertips up and down

the shiny, scarred lines. "I have told you so many times that I can never go home. They can't know I'm alive, or they'll kill me for abandonment." She glanced over her shoulder. "I'm yours. Forever."

Cain growled, his cock tingling in excitement as his pet confessed her allegiance to him. "You promise?"

Pulling himself against her back, he knelt on the bed and playfully bit Kai's shoulder.

She moaned before turning around to face Cain, and their lips melted into one another as Kai pressed her breasts against his chest.

They fell back into bed, their limbs entangled, and by pleasuring Kai, Cain satiated his blood lust, delaying his urge to kill a while longer.

CHAPTER EIGHT

After driving well into the night, Camden pulled into the parking lot of a small motel.

He turned off the engine before brushing the hair out of Alessa's face as she slept. "Alessa."

"Mmm?" she mumbled.

"We're stopping for a few hours. We both need to get some sleep. Stay here while I get us a room."

As Camden headed for the front lobby, Alessa stepped out of the car, yawning while she stretched her stiff joints.

Even though the sun had set over seven hours ago, the night sky had an eerie dark pink and orange tint.

Arriving back at the car, Camden pointed at room nine. "That one's ours, and sorry, but there were only rooms with one bed available."

Before Alessa could open her mouth, Camden assured her, "I will be fine sleeping on the couch."

They grabbed their necessities and shuffled sleepily toward their room as Alessa rubbed the goosebumps covering her arms. "Cam, don't be absurd. We've bled and sweat together; I think we can handle sleeping beside one another in the same bed."

He put the key in the lock and turned it. "Okay, but remember, I'm just a man."

Alessa chuckled and glanced up at Camden. "What is that supposed to mean?"

He tilted his head down, gazing into her pale blue eyes. "I can't help it if I wake up, well"—he cleared his throat—"excited."

Alessa's lower jaw dropped, and she pressed her tongue to the side of her mouth. "Oh, gotcha. Uh, I promise I won't take it personally." She looked away before her red cheeks could give away her level of embarrassment.

Camden and Alessa threw their bags off to the side of the room on their way to the bed. Exhausted, they collapsed onto the covers and fell asleep within moments.

Alessa woke up eight hours later and was slow to move. Blinking, she realized she had snuggled into Camden's bare chest, and his arm was wrapped protectively around her.

Not knowing how to handle their close proximity, Alessa's eyes darted back and forth between Camden's face and his hand resting comfortably on her shoulder.

While biting her lower lip, Alessa reached her right arm up and out from her friend, but as his hand dropped onto the bed, he shifted, causing Alessa to startle.

She rolled off the bed with a hmph and landed on the thinly carpeted floor.

Peering up over the edge of the bed, Alessa felt as though she would die of embarrassment.

"Smooth. Real smooth," she criticized herself as she crawled to the bathroom on her hands and knees.

Hearing the *click* of a closing door, Camden stretched his

arms over his head before pulling his neck to the side. With a loud *crack*, he groaned. "Oh, man."

Throwing his legs over the side of the mattress, Camden sat up and glanced around the room. "If I were coffee, where would I be hiding?"

Eyeing the tiny coffee machine sitting atop a nearby table, Camden walked unsteadily toward it while rubbing the sleep from his eyes.

Alessa exited the bathroom as the liquid streamed into the paper cup. "Oh good, you're up." She eyed Camden on her way to the far corner. "I'm running to the car to get us a change of clothes."

Unable to form words without caffeine, Camden grunted in understanding and turned back to watch his coffee drip into the paper cup. He closed his eyes, and the next thing he knew, Alessa was tossing a plastic bag onto the bed.

"Your clothing, good sir."

"Mmm. Thanks," he grumbled, tearing the tops off three coffee creamer packets.

She walked into the bathroom with a handful of new clothing and closed the door as Camden sat on the bed, nursing the hot liquid.

Exiting the bathroom, Alessa sat in the squeaky red chair near the motel's door and grabbed her black hiking boots as Camden sipped the last of his coffee. "You ready for this?"

She hesitated before lacing the first boot. "I don't have a choice. I realize now I need to go back to get help bringing my sister home."

Camden snatched his clean button-up short-sleeved shirt and cargo pants from the plastic bag on the bed.

Alessa pressed her hand to her heart in feigned surprise.

"Why, Cam, I do believe that's the least dressed up I have ever seen you."

He rolled his eyes and dressed as Alessa finished lacing her other boot.

"All right. Let's do this," Camden said, securing the belt around his waist. Swooping down, he grabbed his hiking boots before marching out the door with his black shoes in hand.

Chasing after him, Alessa bolted for the driver's side door. "I'll drive."

Camden tossed the keys to her, and she caught them easily in her outstretched hand. "I guess that makes sense, seeing as I have no idea where your invisible house is," Camden agreed.

They slammed their doors closed simultaneously before reaching for their seatbelts.

"Where are we heading?" Camden asked.

Alessa started the car. "It's not just a house, Cam. It's an entire hidden city."

"Uh-huh." Camden's forehead furrowed in confusion. "And how exactly do they accomplish that? Hiding an entire city?"

She placed a hand on the steering wheel while throwing the car in reverse. "Well, an invisible forcefield surrounds it, which deters unwelcome visitors. It makes people feel sick the closer they get to it, like, to the point where they become violently ill. Ever hear the phrase altitude sickness or high-altitude cerebral edema? The symptoms mimic those."

"Interesting. And your city is smack dab in the middle of the Colorado mountains?" he laughed incredulously.

"Yes, exactly. Spartans founded it, and we reside in total secrecy thanks to our advanced technology. You can think of our forcefield as a sort of mirror. Our city's perimeter reflects the surrounding woods' image, giving the illusion that the woods continue as if there is nothing beyond the perimeter but more forest."

Camden opened a bag of chips and popped one in his mouth. "How do the Spartans ensure millions of visitors don't come across this segment of the mountains and start to clue in on what is happening?"

Alessa cranked the steering wheel left. "It's actually an offshoot from an incredibly difficult hiking trail section. Have you heard of the Continental Divide Trail?"

Camden squinted in disbelief. "Surprising as it may be, I have actually."

"Well, if you find the sweet spot, you can find our city. If you were a microchipped Spartan, you would have a built-in GPS to find the city."

Camden stopped chewing and glared at Alessa. "How violently ill are we talking?"

"It can cause a killer headache, nausea, dizziness, disorientation, an overwhelming feeling of foreboding..."

Camden's face flushed, and his jaw dropped. "You expect me to follow you into Spartan territory with all these fun symptoms on board? I don't have one of your Spartan microchips installed, and yours isn't in tip-top working order. Who's to say yours is even going to work?"

She huffed. "Mine is not—"

Holding up a finger, Camden continued. "How do you expect us to get through this forcefield when we want to do nothing but turn the other way?"

Rolling her eyes, Alessa turned onto a back road. "I will be fine. I highly doubt my microchip is completely demolished; it's probably just fractured. You, on the other hand, are going to have to push through it. And you will feel as though you are suffering from one hell of a hangover when it's all said and done."

Holding his tongue, Camden growled.

"Don't worry," Alessa patted his leg. "Soon after we cross the border, I'm getting you a temporary microchip. It fastens itself just behind your ear. I can get one from Sera in the medical ward."

Camden shoved another chip in his mouth and shook his head disapprovingly. "Who's Sera? How do you know I'll push through the symptoms til' we arrive at the medical ward?"

"Oh, you'll survive." She chuckled reassuringly before returning her attention to the road. "From what I remember, the symptoms greatly lessen once you make it past the outlying forcefield." Alessa turned the dial, increasing the radio's volume before mumbling, "I hope," under her breath.

CHAPTER NINE

Nearly two hours into the drive, Alessa pulled over to the side of the windy road halfway up the mountain. After parking the car, she jumped out and leaned into the back seat, grabbing Damon's backpack by its strap.

Camden startled awake and shook his head back and forth. Glancing out the passenger side window at the wooded, elevated landscape, he asked, "We're here?"

"We're here." Alessa got out of the car.

"Really?" Camden reached back into his seat, grabbing his large pack containing the rest of their supplies and clothes. "This is it?"

Alessa nodded. "I'm not sure what you expected, but yes, this is it." Walking toward a tiny building, she pointed at the metal door. "I advise you to use the bathroom before we head out."

Camden arched an eyebrow. "That's a bathroom?"

Walking toward the brick bathroom, she laughed. "I mean, it does have a toilet."

After relieving herself, she stood on the gravel before the woods, squeezing the straps on Damon's heavy backpack.

Adjusting his pack, Camden strolled up beside Alessa. "Okay, magical compass, which way do we go?"

Closing her eyes, Alessa focused on the faint, familiar, high-pitched squeal resonating in the back of her mind. It was New Sparta's forcefield calling out to her like a beacon.

She opened her eyes and nodded her head. "This way."

Searching for the sun's location, Camden looked up only to find the thick leaves on the branches extending from one tree to another. "What direction is this?"

"Doesn't matter. It's the direction to New Sparta."

Camden followed behind Alessa onto the unmarked path before them. "So, what wildlife should we expect to encounter while on this magnificent journey?"

Following her intuition, Alessa marched forward, swatting low-hanging branches as they hung before their faces. "Oh, um. I guess the typical ones, like owls, deer, some wild sheep..."

Behind Alessa, Camden climbed up the rocky terrain. "Well, that doesn't sound so bad."

She huffed, stepping up onto the side of a boulder. "I mean, there's always the off chance we encounter some moose, bears, or mountain lions."

Camden stood still. "Did you just nonchalantly mention the possibility of my having to fight a bear or two while a mountain lion watches from the sideline?"

Alessa laughed, securing her backpack's straps. "For the most part, they'll leave us alone. I have a foghorn and bear spray if they decide to attack. Typically, wildlife wants to live and let live. Besides, it's not the bears we need to worry about."

Camden's eyes widened. "What's worse than a bear?"

Alessa looked at him over her shoulder. "Man. Man is much worse. Just focus on taking deep breaths and relax."

"Good luck telling a Russian to relax," he scoffed.

On the first day, they ventured high into the mountainside, walking in and out of the treeline. The first time Camden followed Alessa out of the shade of the woods, he sighed aloud. "Wow."

Snow-capped mountain peaks reached toward the heavens with dark green trees scattered along their mountainsides. Sunlight filtered through the thin, fluffy clouds wrapped around the furthest peak on the rocky terrain, and birds of prey flew high above, searching for their next meal.

They exhausted themselves hiking into the evening until Camden and Alessa could hardly distinguish what was directly in front of their faces, even with their headlamps turned on.

"We'll stop here for the night," she conceded, setting down the backpack in a pile of crunchy leaves. Pulling out a couple of high-intensity flashlights, Alessa strategically placed them in their one sleeping bag.

She then yanked out a warm, thin jacket from Damon's backpack while Camden dug in his elongated bag for the self-heating blanket.

"I didn't realize how deep into the trail we'd be going. I'm much better at time management with a map in hand." Camden shook out the blanket, activating its heating core. He glanced around nervously. "Aren't we a bit exposed here?"

Alessa spread out the double-wide sleeping bag and chortled. "I'm sorry I forgot to grab a paper map from New Sparta's gift shop on how to get there. We're no more exposed than anyone who has decided to take this trail."

"How is it we haven't seen a single other person out here?"

"Hadn't thought about it, but it might be due to the time of year. There might be some festivals in cities around here that take priority."

Camden sat down and scooted into the bag. "How do you know which direction to keep going? I feel so lost right now."

Alessa shivered, and Camden held the bag open for her. "Thanks." She snuggled into his chest, and he wrapped his warm arms around her. "I get this feeling. It's like being connected to New Sparta by an invisible string." Content, she moaned, happy Camden was sharing his body heat. "Oh, yeah."

"I understand why people take on the dangers to see nature's beauty. Those views today were incredible." He swallowed before speaking down into the top of Alessa's head. "We have enough supplies to make it to New Sparta, right?"

Alessa hesitated before choosing not to include their lack of food in her response. "We'll be cutting it close on water, but if we need more, we can always go out of the way to refill at the river."

A cold chill shot through Camden, and he shivered. "I think I'd prefer the shortest path. I'm not one for sleeping outside. I enjoy the finer comforts in life or a bed at the bare minimum."

Staring up at the bright stars sparkling high above them in the night sky, Alessa mumbled as she fell asleep, reminiscing about Damon and his love of nature. "I get it. Nature isn't for everyone."

Alessa stood frozen in place before the tall, burning building. She watched the flames rise from the drug manufacturing plant as it consumed its metal supports.

The employees ran about frantically, screaming for help at the top of their lungs.

As she looked down at her bloodied hands, Alessa was sitting on the floor of Eric Lansing's bedroom. The flames were licking up the walls when she heard Damon's gurgling breathing.

Suddenly, Damon was lying in her arms, blood seeping out from between his parted lips.

"Damon! No, no, not again," Alessa whimpered.

"Don't give up on me. Don't let me go," he begged as the breath escaped his lungs.

Her forehead scrunched in anguish. "I would never give up."

Damon reached up and cupped her cheek with one hand. "I'm still here, babe."

Distraught, Alessa shook her head. "I—I don't understand."

Damon's face transformed into Hades', and he spoke the most bone-chilling words. "He yet lives, and you still owe me a life. If you cannot deliver on your promise, I shall take a life of my choosing."

With a loud gasp, Alessa startled awake in Camden's embrace.

"Are you okay?" Camden pushed her hair out of her face. "You started trembling, really bad, and then you were damn near convulsing."

"I, um. Yeah, I..." Alessa sat upright and looked around at her surroundings, trying to embrace reality.

The orange and pink sunrise shone through the trees as she tried to catch her breath.

Pushing Camden away, Alessa reached for her water bottle on the side of Damon's backpack. "I'm just dehydrated."

Camden shook his head in disbelief, stood up, and began wrapping the sleeping bag into its small pack. "I know you've been having nightmares about the past; you can't hide it. Are they always this bad, though?"

Alessa chugged down the remnants of her first water bottle and shook her head back and forth. "This dream was different. It wasn't a memory; it was something altogether new."

Camden squinted in confusion, waiting for Alessa to continue, but the tension remained as she changed the conversation. "We better eat a granola bar and head out so we can try to make it by mid-morning tomorrow."

The second day was spent in near silence as they tripped, jogged, and took occasional water and food breaks, all while getting bit by various annoying insects.

Losing what little hydration she had left through sweat, Alessa felt the chill in the evening air. Knowing they should preserve their strength, she hollered out to Camden. "Hey, we should stop."

He looked around at the identical, tall trees surrounding them. "Here?"

Alessa sighed and dropped Damon's backpack. "Yeah. My bones are tired, and this spot looks good."

Camden stopped hiking and rubbed the stubble upon his chin. "Are we nearly there? I'm feeling a little off."

"Headache? Fatigue? Nausea?"

He nodded in agreement. "All of the above."

"Those are the first signs of altitude sickness, but they're also the first signs we're on the right path and headed in the right direction." Closing her eyes, she concentrated on the louder, high-pitched squeal. "Yeah, we're really close. I just need the night to rest. Besides, we can't see enough in the darkness with just these two headlights and the few flashlights we have."

After taking a small drink from their water bottle, she handed it over to Camden before preparing the sleeping bag.

Camden exhaled loudly after chugging the remainder of the water. "I'm going to need more of this."

Alessa gave an apologetic smile while shrugging into her warmer jacket. "That's the last of our water. And we're out of food as well."

He tossed the empty bottle near his bag and picked out the wood to make a fire. "Well, shit. I'm not so great at hunting. I mean, I guess I could try." Camden stared into the dark wilderness while holding the two sticks.

Alessa had already found two rocks and moss, and as he stacked the logs, she struck the two rocks together, lighting the moss aflame, and threw it into the wood pile.

She grabbed the self-heating blanket as Camden bent down and gently blew on the flames, encouraging their growth.

After finding a larger log, Alessa sat down with the blanket wrapped around her and gestured for Camden to sit beside her.

Sitting against the fallen log, he wrapped himself into the blanket, snuggling into Alessa's side. Looking down at the top of Alessa's dark head of hair, Camden asked, "What will it be like? Your home?

She grinned and exhaled. "My memories are probably a bit unbelievable, but I can tell you it is beautiful. Statues of gods and goddesses line the main street, and ornate buildings stand tall on either side of the street, each with a specific purpose. We have festivals yearly to celebrate those who have come and gone, the gods and goddesses, and our hopes and dreams. Oh, and our elders can control the climate within the boundaries of our city. That's probably my favorite thing."

Intrigued, Camden tilted his head. "Really? How does that work?"

"I've never been interested in learning about the science of it all, so I'm not sure how to explain it. All I know is they use our technology to control the weather. I'm more interested in the medical field."

Camden's breathing quickly turned into light snoring, and she relaxed into him. "Night, Cam," she sighed before joining him.

Alessa was running in the woods when she heard a loud voice call from the darkness.

"Alessa!" Damon bellowed from the trees.

She whipped around and gasped. "Damon? Damon!"

"Alessa!" he yelled, but from farther away.

She frantically ran through the trees, pushing the branches away from her face. "Where are you? I can't see you!"

"You're so close. Come find me," his voice called out.

Dropping to her knees, Alessa cried out in anguish. "Where are you? Please tell me!"

Damon crouched down beside her and whispered into her ear. "I'm right here."

Alessa's eyes sprung open as the hot breath of death licked up the side of her neck. Gasping for air, she realized she was alone and panicked. Searching her surroundings, she bellowed, "Cam?"

"Over here," he yelled reassuringly, standing over a cliff, looking out at the horizon. "Come look at this," Camden urged.

Wrapping the warming blanket around her shoulders, Alessa shuffled to his side. Stopping before him, Alessa rubbed her fingertips against her tingling lips.

Camden flashed a sideways grin. "Lips feel like they're asleep or itchy?"

Her eyes narrowed, and one side of her lips lifted curiously. "How'd you know?"

"In Russian lore, that means you'll be kissed soon."

Alessa laughed out loud. "Yeah, okay. It's more likely you'll kiss someone sooner than I will." The leaves beneath her feet crunched as she moved closer. "Now, what is it you wanted to show me?"

"I want you to pause a moment and take a breath. Smell the wildflowers, touch the tall grass; I know you've been through a lot, but look at this view. Isn't it incredible?" He pointed over the cliff.

Above them, wispy white clouds decorated the light blue sky. Directly below the rocky cliffside, half a mile before a dense cloak of trees stretched a meadow of colorful flowers.

Alessa's eyes lit up with the familiarity of the meadow and treeline, and her entire body vibrated with the intensity of New Sparta's beacon.

"Home," she exhaled. After throwing Damon's backpack over her shoulder, Alessa sprinted down the side of the mountain toward the meadow. "Grab our gear!"

"Wait up!" Camden yelled, throwing the blankets into his pack.

After finally catching up to Alessa at the cliff's edge, he stood next to her, panting. "What do we do now?"

She rotated toward him, grinning up at him wickedly.

"What's so funny?"

She pulled her backpack tight and secured its buckle across her chest. "Tighten your straps." Then, Alessa stepped back off the cliff.

"Alessa!" Camden screamed as he lunged for her. Looking down, he saw Alessa clinging to the edge of the cliffside, grinning up at him. "This is the easy way down. Come on."

The color drained from his face. "You're joking."

She extended her foot to another foothold and worked her way further down the rocks. "I'm not. Now, get moving."

Grumbling and uttering an incoherent slew of curse words, Camden tightened the heavy pack on his back before dropping down, just as Alessa had done. Clinging to the side of the rocks, he slowly followed her down to the meadow.

As Camden jumped down from the final section of the cliff, he joined Alessa, who had been waiting for him.

"Just a little while longer," she promised. Sporting a giant grin, she jogged out into the meadow.

Sighing loudly, Camden begrudgingly followed her into the wild grass, which was growing tall amongst the purple, pink, and white flowers.

The brisk wind pushed the white, puffy clouds across the pale blue sky as they ran steadily toward the thick treeline.

With the onslaught of terrible symptoms, Camden stopped and blinked his eyes wide, bending over with his hands on his knees, breathing heavily. "I think ... I'm starting ... to hallucinate."

Alessa wiped away the sweat on her forehead with the back of her arm. "You feelin' it bad, huh?"

The hum vibrating the air around them was impossible to ignore. They were getting much closer.

"You're gonna have to suck it up; we need to keep moving

forward." Alessa licked her lips in determination and pressed on.

Shaking the worsening fatigue and nausea away, Camden stood upright and trudged behind Alessa. Within minutes, he felt significantly worse. "This ... sucks ... ass." He coughed the phantom water from his lungs. "Feels like I have the flu or something."

She turned around and jogged back to him. Grabbing his bicep, she pulled him onward. "You have to keep going. You're only going to feel worse before it gets better, and if you stop now, I guarantee you won't continue."

Camden swallowed the vomit forcing its way up the back of his throat and stared forward in determination. "Run," he exhaled breathily.

"What?"

"Run. It's the only way I'm pushing through this."

Letting go of Camden, Alessa sprinted forward, and with newfound excitement, she darted between bushes, jumped over logs, and kicked off tall standing trees.

Camden clenched his teeth and blinked wide, chasing after her, fighting the disorientation. "I'm not sure ... I'll survive ... getting through," he admitted, his face ashen.

"You will! You have to!" she yelled over her shoulder. "Remember, the symptoms will lessen significantly once we cross the border. They won't go away entirely until you get the temporary implant, but you will feel human again."

Approaching a high cliff, Alessa stopped running and waited for Camden to join her. She pulled on his arm as he stepped beside her, and they continued toward the edge of a high cliff.

He wiped away the sweat that had gathered along his eyebrows. "Uh, Alessa?"

They stilled, standing before the edge, looking down at the rushing river beneath their feet.

Alessa stared at the shimmering wall separating the outside world from New Sparta. Wrapping her arms around Camden's chest, she grasped her hands behind his back and walked slowly backward toward the cliff's edge. "Do you trust me?"

Nervously licking his lips, he nodded. "Of course I do, but—"

Holding her hands tight, she kicked back off the rocks. "Then close your eyes!" she yelled as they fell backward.

Believing he was being pushed over the edge of a tall cliff, Camden screeched as he fell through the invisible wall. "What the hell—"

Their bodies shimmered as they crossed the border, rolling one over the other.

Breaking free from her grasp, Camden got up on all fours and vomited violently into the grass field. As his loud retching replaced the peaceful sounds of nature, Alessa stared back at the shimmering wall from which they had just fallen through. Looking at the outside world, she smiled excitedly. "That never gets old."

Camden vomited once more, and Alessa turned toward him. "Sorry," she apologized, moving closer. "You'll feel better in a few minutes."

As the waves of nausea decreased, Camden rolled onto his back with a groan and looked up at the sky. "Go ahead and kill me now." His heart felt as though it were going to pound straight out of his chest.

Suppressing laughter, Alessa shook her head. "Just focus on your breathing. In through your nose, out through your mouth."

He saluted her weakly. "Will do."

Glancing to the left at a thick patch of woods, Alessa exhaled, "Home," as Camden propped himself up on his elbow.

"Why is it so hot? I swear it was just thirty degrees cooler before we went through the border," he complained.

"Remember how I told you our elders control the climate?" She shrugged out of her jacket, exposing her raspberry-colored tank top. "Ah," she sighed. "That's better."

"Help me get out of my layers, would ya?" he grumbled. "The last thing I need is to get overheated while feeling like absolute shit to begin with."

Alessa tugged Camden's arms from his jacket, exposing his fitted grey T-shirt. He flashed a sideways smile. "Thanks."

"You look like you're feeling a little better." Alessa folded up their thin jackets and shoved them into Damon's backpack. "Got some color back in your face."

Camden rubbed the back of his neck. "I no longer feel like death, so that's a positive. It feels like I've got an intense hangover."

"We'd better get moving; we don't want to get found by the patrol. Do you need help standing up?" Alessa reached her hand out toward him.

Camden swatted away her outstretched hand and struggled to get up independently. "You, stop it. I'm good. Who are the guards?"

"Spartans assigned to patrol the perimeter in case, well"—she shrugged—"anything like we just did occurs. It never has, but I guess 'had' would be the correct term since we technically just did it."

"You'd think they would've set up alarms or something. You know, just in case."

Slinging Damon's backpack over her shoulder, Alessa held

her hand out for Camden. "I'll let them know your thoughts on the matter. You gonna be okay carrying your pack?"

He swung the large bag over his shoulder and took a deep, steadying breath. "Show me the way, oh fearless leader."

Turning toward the treeline across the grassy meadow, Alessa nervously licked her lips. "This way."

CHAPTER TEN

Nearly an hour into their walk through the wooded portion of the Spartan city, they came across a quick-moving stream.

Collapsing to his knees, Camden threw his pack off to the side before dipping his hands into the flowing water. He hungrily gulped the cool liquid from within his cupped palms.

Shrugging out of Damon's backpack, Alessa knelt beside him. After using the back of her arm to wipe the dripping water from her chin, Alessa looked up at the sun's position. "The sun will be setting in less than a few hours."

"So what's the pl—" Camden was interrupted by the snapping of a twig.

Springing to her feet, Alessa stood with her fists raised protectively in front of Camden.

Five men emerged from the tall trees with weapons raised, pointed directly at them.

"Your names and rank?" the leading Spartan demanded.

Alessa's heart filled with hope as she stared at the man in disbelief. "Quade?"

Taking a step forward, the Spartan yelled. "Answer me!"

She put her hands up in surrender. "Quade, it's me. Alessa, Custos."

He tilted his head in consideration. "You can't be. Alessa's dead."

She moved slowly toward her childhood friend with her hands in the air. "Do I look like I'm dead?"

Quade's eyes drifted from Alessa's head to her toes, and as his offensive stance softened, she teared up.

With a nod, she ran toward her best friend. As she collapsed into his arms, Quade dropped his weapon.

Wrapping his strong arms around Alessa, he held her tight and buried his face into her warm neck.

As his grip lessened, she backed up and looked into her friend's beautiful, deep brown eyes. "I've missed you terribly," her voice broke.

Realizing his men were still on high alert, Quade held out his hands. "Lower your weapons. She's one of us. It's Alessa."

"Alessa?" one of the other men questioned.

"Chambers, it's good to see you," her voice cracked as she struggled to control her emotions.

Quade grabbed hold of her arms and stepped back. "How is this possible? It's been what—"

"Nearly five months," Alessa finished for him.

"Who's he?" Quade directed at Camden.

She grinned nervously. "That's Camden. He saved my life."

"After she saved mine." Camden scooped up the pack and marched behind Alessa.

Quade eyed the tall blond man while snatching his weapon up from the ground. "He's not Spartan. How'd he get past—"

Alessa smiled guiltily, holding her hands out in front of her chest. "I helped him."

"More like forced," Camden interjected.

Alessa shot Camden a menacing glare. "Okay, I forced him through the forcefield. Speaking of, we should probably get to the medical ward to get him a temporary chip so the symptoms don't kill him."

Camden's eyes widened. "I'm sorry. Did you just say they could kill me?"

She shrugged, shaking her head back and forth. "I won't let that happen." Alessa looked back at Quade. "Can you escort us to the medical ward? I want to get home before the sun sets; we've had a rough couple of days trying to get here."

"Of course we can. Sera needs to check him out anyway. Let's go, guys," he directed toward the patrol. "Want me to carry the pack for you?"

Grabbing Damon's backpack, Alessa swung it over her shoulder. "I'm good, but thanks."

Quade matched her stride but directed his comment at Camden, who followed close behind. "Welcome to New Sparta. Alessa has always been an interesting friend and keeps on surprising us. How did you two meet? And how exactly did you gain her confidence so that she would tell you everything?"

"We have a lot to catch up on," Alessa interjected. "All you need to know right now is that I trust Cam with my life. I would never have brought him into our home otherwise."

"I trust you, Alessa. Which means I also put my trust in whoever you do." Quade touched her forearm. "I have so many questions. How did your friend survive getting past the forcefield? Where have you been? How are you alive but not connected to the database? How—"

Alessa cut him off. "We have so much to catch up on, but"—she eyed the other Spartan men—"we should do it in private."

Camden cleared his throat. "To answer some of your questions, we met at a drug manufacturing plant in Texas a few months back; I gained her confidence by being there for her when she needed someone, and I got past the forcefield because I am one tough mother fucker. Even though while I was crossing, I thought I was going to die."

"Well, that's reassuring." Quade cracked a grin. "That our forcefield made you physically ill but didn't completely deter you. Maybe we need to amp it up a bit."

"No." Camden laughed. "I think for the average human, the amount of juice it gives is more than adequate to keep them away."

Quade looked questioningly at Camden before Alessa jumped in. "Cam is significantly stronger than a human in the general population. That, too, will need to be discussed in private."

"Got it. Well, once we get to the medical ward, my wife Seraphine will get you hooked up, and you'll feel much better." Quade's facial features lifted in excitement. "I can't believe I forgot to ask: where's Kai? If you're alive, surely she is as well."

Alessa glanced around nervously.

Quade understood and directed his patrol to walk ahead of them. Once they were far enough away, Alessa responded quietly. "Yes, she's alive. I'm not sure how or why, but I have an idea of how we can find her, which is why I returned. I need to talk to my elder and the Council of Elders, but it can't be public knowledge yet."

Quade nodded. "You do realize after her mysterious disappearance, if she were to be found alive, she would be declared—"

"A traitor? Yes, I am well aware. This is why it is between you, me, and Cam. I will tell Sera later, but for now—"

"No one can know."

"Precisely."

As Quade, Camden, and Alessa emerged from the treeline, they descended onto a path lined with pebbles. The townspeople of New Sparta went about their day as if nothing of significance had happened, utterly oblivious to the fact that one of their own was back from the dead.

Becoming savvy to the fact their guards were parading people through town, the citizens of New Sparta turned to see who it was. Astonishment crossed their faces, and mumbling began as soon as Alessa was recognized.

Camden clucked his tongue. "Oh, boy. Here we go."

Alessa grimaced. "Yeah, I am not digging the attention we're getting."

Camden lifted his chin, nodding toward a shaven-haired Spartan with a birthmark surrounding their eye. "Hey, is that Spartan over there a man or a woman?"

Alessa shrugged. "Does it matter?"

"I mean, well, no. I guess not. I just always had this idea in my mind of Spartan women being feminine, wearing scantily clad flowing dresses while Spartan men were rugged and muscular."

She shook her head in disbelief. "That's thanks to Hollywood and their sexualization of women. I'd like to think we're more forward-thinking than those in the general population. As long as those who can carry children eventually fulfill their obligation of continuing the Spartan bloodline, it doesn't matter what gender they identify as.

"If you truly think about it, gender is in itself a human construct defining how a boy or girl should act, and since in our culture women are encouraged to be strong and fight, that doesn't exactly fit with the outside world's definition of 'feminine.'"

"About that, why do Spartans encourage their women to fight now? From the brief history lesson given to me by the internet, didn't they not allow women to engage in battle back in the day?"

Alessa scoffed and disregarded his notion with a flick of her wrist. "That was back when they had the luxury of choosing who could fight."

Camden pursed his lips together and nodded. "I see. So, as soon as your population dwindled, women climbed the social ladder."

"That's one way to put it. Another way would be they didn't have enough bodies to allow us not to fight. Now, the entire population is trained for battle regardless of gender."

Quade interrupted their discussion. "I'm sorry, but I just can't stop thinking about your situation. You being alive doesn't make any sense, Alessa. How are you off-grid? Are you still able to activate?"

Taken back by his question, Alessa stilled while she contemplated how to respond.

Hearing live music in the distance, she became distracted. "I think we figured out it was an injection I was given while being tortured," she mumbled while slowly moving forward as if in a trance.

"Shit. I'm not exactly sure what I was expecting, but hearing you were tortured..." He swallowed. "I mean, you look okay. Are you okay?"

Alessa's eyebrows furrowed in concentration as she listened to the familiar voice. "I am now. For the most part."

Leaving Quade and Camden behind, Alessa snaked

around the bodies standing before her, blocking her view. As she stepped out from behind a particularly tall Spartan, her breathing faltered.

Standing before her was Damon.

CHAPTER ELEVEN

Alessa's jaw dropped as she stared in disbelief. "Damon?" she mumbled.

Unable to tear her gaze from his tanned face, she moved as if in a trance, weaving stealthily through the bodies separating them.

Noticing the sudden change in Alessa, Camden stepped to the side to see who she was moving toward. His eyes widened in surprise. "Damon?"

"How do you know Damon?" Quade demanded.

"Something's very wrong. He shouldn't be here." Camden dropped his pack to the ground.

As if being pulled by an invisible string, Alessa moved forward.

Damon's lips moved to the song lyrics, and her eyes wandered down to his olive-toned fingers, watching them pluck the strings of his guitar.

With every step, Alessa's heart beat for Damon once more, lifting the dark veil that had settled within her soul.

His lips curled into a relaxed smile, and tears welled in Alessa's eyes as she pushed through the crowd.

Glancing off to the side where Damon's dreamy gaze was directed, Camden froze. "Who is that?" As realization dawned upon Camden, he panicked. "Oh, wait. No, no, no. That's impossible. That can't be." He looked toward Alessa before breaking into a run. "Oh, shit!"

Leaning to the side with his guitar balanced precariously on his thigh, Damon pressed his lips against a woman's red-painted mouth.

Devastated, Alessa's heart shattered as she watched Damon kiss another woman.

"Don't!" Camden yelled, rushing toward Alessa.

As Damon pulled away, Alessa's broken heart filled with rage, and as she recognized the lightly tanned woman in the short, tight dress, her eyes flashed blood red.

With a spark of rage igniting their microchips, the Spartans in front of Alessa screamed before dropping to the ground with their heads cradled in their hands.

Overcome with hate, Alessa sprinted forward, and with a warrior's cry, she lunged for Brielle with outstretched arms.

Damon jumped back in surprise as Brielle was grabbed by the back of her hair and tackled to the ground.

After landing flat on her back, shock was written all over the woman's face as Alessa sprang on top of her.

Jumping over the crouched bodies, Camden screamed at Alessa to stop. "Alessa! No!"

Not understanding what was happening, Damon lunged for Alessa. "What the f—" he began but was cut off by blood pouring from his nose. With his skull feeling as though it were splitting in half, he grabbed the sides of his head and hit the ground.

Terrified for her life, Brielle screamed at the top of her lungs as Alessa punched, scratched, and slammed the back of her head and torso hard against the ground.

The Spartans, all kneeling with their heads in their hands, cried out in agony as Alessa's microchip glitched, unintentionally attacking anyone within a one-hundred-foot vicinity.

Having lost all control, Alessa pounded on Brielle as Camden ran to break up the women.

"Stop!" Camden yelled, sprinting toward the fighting women. "You're killing your people!"

Wrapping her hands around Brielle's neck, Alessa screamed, her eyes flaring with hatred. "She needs to die," she said between clenched teeth.

Flying at Alessa, Camden ripped her away from Brielle, and after rolling over one another, he landed on top. Blood flowed from Camden's nose as he struggled to restrain Alessa. "Please don't make me do this," he begged while holding her down in the grass.

Struggling beneath him, Alessa's only response was a feral growl.

Camden bowed his head, and his forehead wrinkled as he let go of her shoulder and pressed his fingertips deep into the side of her neck. "Forgive me," he said as Alessa gasped loudly before falling unconscious.

Simultaneously, the Spartan's intense pains within their heads vanished, and they helped one another to their feet. Searching the crowd for answers, they whispered amongst one another while looking toward Alessa.

Hearing Brielle inhale loudly and cough, Damon rushed to her side. He gingerly pressed his hand against the side of her face as she coughed up blood. "Bri, oh gods. Don't worry, we'll get you to the medical ward."

As audience members ran up to help the injured woman, Damon's jaw flexed as he eyed the unfamiliar blond man from behind.

Adrenaline coursing through his veins, Damon stood with his fist raised, ready to seek blood. "What the fuck was that ab—" he demanded as he ran for the man kneeling above Brielle's attacker.

Gripping the blond's shoulder, Damon pulled him back to see who had attacked Brielle. All of the air inside of Damon's lungs was sucked out of his chest, and he collapsed to the ground.

Damon's heart clenched, and his face scrunched up in distress. "Alessa?"

CHAPTER TWELVE

Immediately following the attack on Brielle, Camden and Alessa were surrounded by Spartan guards with raised weapons aimed directly at them.

The citizens of Sparta, who had been enjoying the show, fearfully backed away as the guards took charge of the situation.

Quade jumped between his guards and Camden and Alessa to diffuse the situation. He eyed Camden. "You'd better come with me."

"Understood." Camden draped Alessa's unconscious body over his shoulder before being escorted by no less than twenty armed Spartan guards to the medical ward.

Her limp hands slapped against Camden's torso as her arms dangled behind his muscular back.

As they approached the building, medical staff ushered in those still suffering from headaches as a woman wearing deep red scrubs with gold detail rushed out the front doors.

Her eyes grew wide as they locked onto the parade of Spartan guards.

"What's going on? I couldn't make out what had happened on the intercom through all the garbled noise," she asked Quade.

"Sera, you're not going to believe it—" Quade began but was interrupted by Brielle's wailing.

Seraphine's jaw dropped as she watched the woman be carried into the building with Damon trailing close behind. "What in the name of—"

Quade grabbed his wife's hand. "Sera, Alessa's alive."

Seraphine's eyebrows furrowed, and she fervently shook her head back and forth. "Don't toy with me; that's not funny. That's impossible, and you know it."

"I thought so, too." He nodded at Camden as he walked past them, and their eyes met as he carried an unconscious Alessa over his shoulder.

Seraphine blinked slowly before inhaling deeply. "You're sure it's Alessa?"

Taking both of his wife's hands within his own, Quade nodded. "I am quite sure. We spoke before—"

Seraphine looked around at her fellow Spartans kneeling on the ground, everyone with their heads between their hands. "Before what? What happened to all of our people?"

Brielle's cries echoed down the hallway, demanding Seraphine's attention. "I've got to address Brielle's wounds. Who did this to her?"

Quade looked to the ground and sighed. "Alessa. She attacked her."

Seraphine narrowed her eyes in disbelief as they hurried down the hallway. "Why would she do that? Does she even know Brielle?"

Quade shrugged his shoulders and raised his hands. "I have

no idea if they know one another, but she attacked Brielle after seeing them ... kiss."

Seraphine's face fell. "Oh, gods."

"The only reason Brielle is still breathing is because Camden stopped Alessa from killing her."

Seraphine held her hands up under the decontamination field. "Who's Camden?"

"He's the guy you just saw holding her. She brought him across the barrier."

Seraphine laughed incredulously. "So many things you are saying do not make sense. How could she do that? Oh," she interrupted her train of thought, "I guess that means you need to grab a temporary device for him. I don't have time to question him right now, but I trust you know how to quick-install a device while I work on Brielle?"

After the glass case released her arms, she entered the chaotic room where Brielle was being examined. Her eyes met with Damon's as the doors closed behind her. "Damon, I need you to leave. Now," she instructed as her assistants gloved and gowned her. "The entire facility. I don't need you sticking your nose where it doesn't belong."

"But I—" he began.

Seraphine ignored him, continuing, "And you are not to set foot inside Alessa's room until we have a clear idea of what's going on. I need to make sure it even is Alessa."

Exiting the room, Damon ran his fingers through his hair and muttered, "Like hell," under his breath.

"I mean it!" she yelled over Brielle's screams. "Stay away from Alessa!"

Camden and Alessa were taken to the secluded part of the medical ward, where one of the armed guards followed him into a room at the end of a hallway while the rest stood outside the double glass doors.

Only once the thick, clear doors sealed behind him did the guard address Camden. "You need to set her down."

Doing as he was told, Camden gently laid Alessa down on the hospital bed. A tear lay stagnant in the corner of one eye, and he brushed a few brunette strands of hair from her face.

"Come with us," the guard stepped back, and the doors opened.

Camden's eyes narrowed in distrust. "You're sure about that? You want to leave her alone?"

"She won't be alone. Guards will be posted outside her room at all times. It is imperative we debrief you for only once you are cleared will your temporary device be inserted. You will expire if we don't take care of that soon."

"Oh, well, if that's the case, I'll be right back, doll." Camden raised the bedrails on either side of Alessa before bending forward. "Don't you dare wake up while I'm gone." He pressed his warm lips against her forehead before walking out the door in front of his armed escort.

Approaching the secluded wing of the medical ward, Damon glared at the blond man walking in front of the heavily armed Spartan guards.

Half of the Spartan guards remained in front of the bulletproof glass doors, standing erect.

Damon marched toward the guards with closed fists and

demanded, "Move, NOW!" As they split down the middle, he ran straight into Quade's extended hand.

Quade's hand pressed hard into Damon's sternum. "Stop. You cannot be here."

Damon smacked Quade's hand away from his chest and stepped forward defiantly. "Are you kidding me right now? Alessa's in there! You can't keep me away—"

"I am well aware of that fact. But given the circumstances—"

"Fuck the circumstances!" Damon growled. The veins in his neck bulged as he held back his rage for the sake of his friend. "You *will* move out of my way or get hurt. Either way, I am getting in that room."

Quade side-eyed the guards to his left and right before sighing deeply. "If Sera finds out I let you in—"

Damon looked past Quade. "Imagine if Sera was on the other side of those doors and I were standing in your way. What wouldn't you do to get to her?"

Quade rolled his eyes before stepping out of the way. "Gods help us," he mumbled. "Don't do anything stupid; I have to go check the guy out," Quade hollered before walking away.

Bending forward, Damon looked into the ocular scanner beside the doorframe. After the device scanned his eye to verify his identification and clearance status, the doors opened, and with an exasperated sigh, Damon stepped into the dimly lit room.

The doors sealed themselves behind Damon as he moved hesitantly toward Alessa. Unable to take his eyes off her face, he stepped beside the hospital bed and lowered the railing.

Staring at Alessa's unconscious form, Damon couldn't help but imagine her body dissipating before him as if she were merely a mirage. Reaching out, he grasped the ends of her shoulder-length dark hair, and his breathing hitched as he played with the soft, delicate strands.

She was truly there with him in the land of the living.

Alessa's eyes darted back and forth behind closed lids as she relived Brielle dosing Damon with the deadly pill.

Alessa and Damon were once again grasping onto the catwalk as it crashed into the flames. Then suddenly she was holding Damon in Eric's bedroom, as blood seeped from the corners of his mouth.

As the hot flames quickly spread throughout her dreams, Alessa jumped awake with a gasp.

Damon jumped back, and her blurry vision cleared as Alessa blinked away the sleep.

"Where the fuck—" she stopped mid-sentence as Damon's face came into focus.

Tears welled in her eyes, and the color drained from her face. "No, no, no. You can't be here." As her stomach flipped, she scrunched her legs up in bed and squeezed her eyes shut.

While watching Alessa's reaction, Damon rushed toward her and grabbed the back of her neck, pressing his lips against hers.

Pulling away, he breathlessly pressed his forehead against Alessa's. "I'm here. I'm real, sydämen liekki."

Opening her eyes, Alessa stared into Damon's ocean blue irises, and her heart fluttered. "Damon?"

With tears in his eyes, he nodded frantically up and down. "Yeah, baby. It's me."

She eagerly pulled Damon into her, and their lips

frantically moved against one another as their pulses quickened.

"Wait, wait." She broke away from his desperate kiss. "This can't be real. You died. I watched you die."

He chuckled in disbelief. Grabbing her hand, he pressed it against his chest. "Can you feel my heart beating? Baby, I haven't seen you since you left to investigate Erebos Industries. It is I who thought you were dead since you disconnected from the database—"

Alessa pulled her hand out of his grasp and shook her head back and forth in confusion. "You don't remember finding me?"

Ignoring her question, Damon grasped Alessa's hand. "You're still wearing my ring."

She looked down at his ring. "Of course I am."

"After your microchip disconnected, I went looking for you. Even though everyone told me I was crazy, especially my father."

Alessa's eyebrows furrowed in confusion as she listened.

"When I didn't find you—"

"But you did find me," she interjected.

Ignoring her, Damon continued. "What took you so long to come back home? And who is the guy you brought with you? I heard he isn't even a Spartan. But how could that be? You would never have brought him here if that were the case, would you?"

Pushing Damon back, Alessa remembered the reason she fell unconscious. The intense burning began behind her eyes, and Alessa closed them while inhaling deeply.

"Brielle," she huffed and stood before Damon. "Did I hallucinate, or did I see you kissing *Brielle*?"

Alessa glared up at Damon as he hovered above her five-foot-six-inch frame.

He stared down at her, his eyes wide. "How do you know—"

"I know *she* isn't a Spartan," Alessa spat. "And guess what, you *did* find me, and together, we found Camden in Texas at the drug manufacturing plant that we all burned to the ground."

Tilting his head, Damon's eyes narrowed in distrust.

"And I took so long to come home because I was focused on finding my sister. From what you had told me, she wasn't in the best of graces here in New Sparta, so I figured coming home could be worse for her."

He stepped toward Alessa with outstretched hands. "How could you possibly have known—? You're saying I told you?"

Alessa's jaw dropped. "What in the Hades is going on? How do you not remember—? Wait, did you get an injection at the base of your skull? Come here, let me see."

Alessa grabbed his shoulders and forced him down before her. He grumbled as she searched his hairline for the identical scar she had from the memory loss injection.

"What are you doing?" he demanded. Grabbing Alessa's hand, Damon rotated to face her while still on his knees.

Tears welled in Alessa's eyes as she struggled to understand what was happening. "How did you survive the fire? When Camden carried me out, screaming your name—" Alessa's eyes flickered red as she recalled the heartbreaking moment.

Damon jumped back. "What just happened with your eyes?" He shook his head. "How do you know about the fire?"

"You were lying on the floor. Your chest wasn't moving. You were dead, Damon. Oh, gods. I never would've left you if I knew—" she cried, agony gripping her heart.

Damon took her by the shoulders and shook her. "Alessa, how do you know about the fire?"

Tears fell down Alessa's reddened cheeks as she felt the intensity build within her. "Because I was there! We were there ... together."

Damon's back straightened, and his eyes went blank momentarily before continuing. "No, sydämen liekki. I was there with"—he swallowed—"Brielle."

Alessa froze. "What? No, that's not—"

"We went to the party determined to take down Erebos Industries. Things took a turn for the worst, and if Brielle hadn't been there to save me—"

"The fuck you say?" Alessa began hyperventilating. "Brielle, SAVE YOU?" she screamed, feeling herself lose control once again.

"The day I accepted that you were never coming back was the hardest day of my life, but Brielle helped me through my darkest days and got me through the pain."

"You mean the pain SHE caused?" Alessa demanded through clenched teeth.

Damon sighed loudly. "What are you saying?"

"Brielle is the reason you nearly died in the fire at Eric's château. She's the one who forced the pill down your—"

"Alessa, enough!" Damon backed away. "Brielle and I ... we're ... together."

Alessa's hands balled into fists as the rage within her heart lit the room's electronics on fire. As every device exploded, the lights above sparked before shattering.

A painful stabbing sensation appeared in the base of Damon's skull as he frantically looked around the room.

"She took you from me, and now you're in love with her?" Alessa's chest heaved up and down before she closed her burning eyes. "Why the fuck did you come in the room and kiss me like I was your long-lost love, only to rip my heart out and stomp on it? Get out. Just get out," she growled.

The fire alarm sounded, echoing off the walls of the enclosed room.

"Alessa, I—" Damon stepped toward her.

Opening her blood-red eyes, she glared up at Damon. "Leave. Now."

Seeing her red irises, he froze. "Why is your activation red? What happened to you?"

Alessa gripped her bedsheets, swallowed, and squeezed her eyes shut. "After everything, how could you?" Alessa wailed. Grabbing her chest, she collapsed to her knees as the flames throughout the room intensified.

"Shit," Damon cursed in Greek as he bolted toward the exit.

As Damon ran out through the clear double doors, Camden bolted in. "What did you do?" Camden yelled at Damon as their shoulders slammed against one another.

Camden grabbed the extinguisher off the wall and sprayed foam all over the electronics, after which he threw the emptied container into the unoccupied chair and crouched before Alessa.

The doors closed before Damon, and he stood before the speakers, listening to their conversation.

Camden held Alessa's face between his hands, redirecting her focus. "Hey, Alessa, breathe. I need you to take slow, deep breaths. That's right. In and out. I'm here for you." Camden demonstrated how to take slow, calculated breaths, and her irises returned to their bright blue color as her microchip unglitched.

Alessa's entire body shook uncontrollably as she fell into

Camden's arms. "It's so unfair. I just got him back only to lose him," she cried into his chest.

CHAPTER THIRTEEN

On the third day of Camden and Alessa's quarantine, Seraphine stared into the brightly colored holographic image displayed before them in mid-air. "This is remarkable."

The phlebotomist handed Alessa a cotton ball, and she pressed it against the bleeding vein in her arm. "In my opinion, the most remarkable thing is how I still have blood after the amount the medical staff has drawn, but what are you referring to?"

Alessa was exhausted from the around-the-clock surveillance and the never-ending battery of tests and blood work.

"I think I figured out what happened to your microchip; I'm just not sure how it happened." Seraphine held her thumb and pointer finger to the hologram display of Alessa's brain. Separating her fingers, she zoomed in on the three-dimensional image of the cellular construct of Alessa's brainstem.

Pointing at a golden discoloration within the bundle of threads, Seraphine explained, "You see this right here?"

Camden and Alessa squinted and leaned in simultaneously. "I guess?" Alessa said.

Camden shrugged. "Sure."

"What is it?" Alessa asked, stepping closer to the large screen. "Why is my brain—"

"Glowing?" Camden finished for her.

Seraphine rubbed her hands together in excitement. "As you know, we've been unsuccessful in consciously reconnecting you to our database for the last week, leaving only one possibility since you're clearly still alive."

Alessa groaned. "Stop talking in riddles and get on with it, Sera."

"Your DNA is incompatible since, at a cellular level, your microchip has become a part of you. Essentially, your DNA no longer reads as being human."

Alessa scoffed. "Then what does it read as?"

"I couldn't say. It doesn't recognize it as any known species. It's like your brain had to reconstruct itself, imbedding the microchip to survive."

Alessa laughed incredulously. "Yeah, okay. This actually makes sense based on how my life has been going."

Camden nodded at the screen. "I mean, it does make sense if you think about it."

"What does? My not being human anymore?" Alessa retorted.

He side-eyed Alessa. "You said you remember being injected with some type of serum that felt as though every synapse in your brain was being set on fire. What if it changed you at a cellular level?"

"The fuck, Cam. Are you suggesting my sist—" Realizing she was about to give away her sister's part in all of this, Alessa cut herself off.

"Your what?" Seraphine asked.

Alessa bit her lower lip and placed her hands on her hips. "I—I'm not sure, but I am sick of being so focused on myself. Now that you've determined I'm not the enemy, can we please discuss Damon and the demon spawn he was kissing when I first arrived?"

Seraphine cocked her head to the side. "Her name is Brielle."

"Oh, I am well aware of her name," spat Alessa as she threw her cotton ball in the trash can.

"How can that be? Did you meet her before the other day?"

Alessa pleaded with Camden. "How can I explain any of it without sounding like I've lost my mind?"

He shook his head with a sympathetic glance. "You can't. If I were Seraphine, and you told me what you're about to tell her..."

Alessa spun Damon's ring around her finger. "But I can't just not say anything."

"I am *right* here," Seraphine interjected. "I can hear you both. Just tell me already."

Alessa sighed in exasperation. "Okay. Maybe if I say it quickly, it won't sound as crazy."

"Before I remembered anything, including who I was, Damon found me and saved me from being attacked by Eric Lansing's Bodyguards. While my memories slowly returned, he helped me seek revenge against the three men who tortured me. During our time together, he introduced me to Brielle, thinking she'd help us, but instead, she sold us out, and in her anger, she dosed Damon with the red pill."

Seraphine's jaw dropped as she sat down slowly, and her eyebrows raised.

"Damon and I found Camden at Erebos Industries' drug manufacturing plant in Texas. After we set it on fire—"

Seraphine's jaw dropped as she looked back and forth between Camden and Alessa. "Wait, that was you?"

"Yeah. And then, when we arrived at Eric Lansing's château, my memory returned and—" Alessa shook her head as the violent images flashed before her eyes. She pictured Damon's lifeless body lying on the floor, blood dripping from the sides of his mouth.

Camden cleared his throat. "And I drug her out of the fire while she thrashed about, desperate to get back to Damon."

Alessa anxiously rubbed her hands together while she paced back and forth. "I'm not sure how Brielle got to Damon. I don't remember seeing her anywhere at the party, and we were there hours before the fire began."

Seraphine stared at Alessa, her expression serious. "How did the fire start? The fire department never determined a cause. Did you set it?"

Alessa stopped walking and turned toward Seraphine. "I didn't mean to. Honestly, Damon had just taken his last breath, or at least I thought he had, and suddenly, I had the overwhelming feelings of dread and rage consume my entire body, heart, and soul. Before I knew it, the Bodyguards dropped like flies, and every electronic in the room burst into flames."

Camden rubbed his hands together as he sat in the rolling chair. "Over the past few months, we've determined she's somehow developed technopathy, the ability to control electronics, since the first time her microchip glitched."

Seraphine's eyes narrowed. "Glitched?"

Alessa shot her friend a sideways grin. "'Glitched' is the

term Cam gave my microchip malfunctioning. He thinks it sounds cooler than 'fucked up.'"

Seraphine sat forward in her seat. "If the gods truly have blessed you with this incredible gift, have you been honing your skills?"

Alessa's eyebrows lifted, and she chuckled. "Uh, no. Setting shit on fire without meaning to, thanks to emotional outbursts and messed up dreams, is more my forte. Besides, I've been a little busy with—"

She glanced up at Camden, who was shaking his head back and forth.

Catching on to his meaning, Alessa stopped mid-sentence and let the remaining thoughts about her sister dissipate.

"Busy doing what?" Seraphine rolled up to her computer screen.

Alessa shrugged while scrunching up her face. "Oh, um, you know. We've been trying to locate Eric Lansing. I don't believe he died."

Seraphine typed busily on her keyboard, the keys clacking as she entered information into a document pulled up on the screen. "Interesting. Why's that?"

Alessa pursed her lips. "Call it a gut feeling."

"Mm-hmm. So far, the story you've told is pretty far out there. I'm not saying I don't believe you, but I've never seen Brielle threaten Damon. And as far as I can tell, their feelings appear authentic and genuine."

Alessa squeezed her eyes shut and swallowed the bile that crept up the back of her throat.

Seraphine turned around and faced Alessa. "I hate to see you in pain, and it's not that I don't believe you, it's just that—"

"It's hard to believe without seeing for yourself," Camden interrupted.

"Kind of, yeah," Seraphine agreed. "Let me just get this straight. You claim Damon's memory has been tampered with, Brielle killed him, and your microchip has glitched, giving you the ability to control electronics. Is that the gist of it?"

Alessa nodded yes while biting her lower lip.

"I still have a few questions that haven't been addressed yet. Like, why was Camden at the plant in Texas, and could your sister still be alive? If you are disconnected from the conscious part of our database, what's to say Kai isn't as well?"

Alessa's eyes widened, and she turned around to hide that she wasn't telling the entire truth. Alessa walked across the room, away from Seraphine. "Cam was being held as a prisoner and being tortured when Damon and I found him restrained and nearly dead. I used what little medical training I could remember to save him."

Seraphine's eyes narrowed as she looked at Camden from top to bottom. "For being tortured, you appear incredibly well put back together."

Alessa turned back around to face Camden. "She's going to figure it out. We should go ahead and tell her."

Camden's neck muscles tensed. "You're sure she won't outright try to kill me?"

"What? Why would I do that?" Seraphine side-eyed Camden as her muscles tensed. "Alessa, why would I want to kill him?"

Alessa held up her hands defensively. "Okay, Sera, you can't utter a word to anyone. And I mean no one. I'll tell Quade when we bust outta here because you are the only two I trust in the whole world, but no one else will understand because they don't have my back like you two do. You are my family."

Seraphine balled her hands into fists and bolted up out of her chair. "Say it already."

"He was a Bodyguard, Rogue Command, to be specific."

Seraphine's fist rose protectively in front of her face, and her eyebrows rose and she backed toward the exit. "What the fuck did you just say?"

Alessa lunged for her friend's hand. "He isn't anymore, Sera!"

Seraphine shook her head back and forth. "Alessa, you know once you're in, there's no getting out."

Alessa grabbed her friend's hands and held onto them desperately. "I would never intentionally put anyone in harm's way. Do you trust me?"

The doctor stilled and stared at them, her body language indicating she still wanted to take flight.

"Sera, you *know* me. Would I ever put your son in danger?"

After a brief hesitation, Seraphine exhaled. "No." She shook her head, looking back and forth between Camden and Alessa. "You would never hurt Soren."

Alessa grasped Seraphine's hands within her own. "I need you to trust me. His fellow Bodyguards were torturing Cam. He had somehow gone against his engineering once he realized the depths of their depravity, and they were trying to kill him."

Seraphine nervously licked her lips before peering over at Camden. "Is this true?"

Camden nodded stiffly. "It is. Alessa saved me, and I saved her."

"But once you saved her from the fire, wasn't your debt repaid?" Seraphine asked.

Camden's cheeks reddened. "Indeed, it had been." He glanced at Alessa. "But I just couldn't leave her after all she had been through."

Alessa cleared her throat. "We became close friends, and we trust each other entirely."

"Okay, then." Seraphine's shoulders dropped as her muscles relaxed. "If you trust him, I guess I do, too. And I won't say a word. But if the Council of Elders finds out—"

"They won't. However, I will need you to lie and say you did the scan of his brain and found no evidence of him having a microchip."

Seraphine's jaw dropped. "How can you ask this of me? If the Consilium finds out—"

"If they were to find out somehow, I would say I messed with the equipment, I swear it. Once I convince the Council to look into Greenfield Farms, they will be too distracted to care about Cam," Alessa pleaded.

Seraphine glared at her friend. "You are playing a dangerous game. And what about Kai? Is she still alive?"

"I—I don't have an answer for you. I am hoping to know more soon. But I need you to clear me so I can talk to my elder. We've already wasted three days, and he's the main reason I came home."

"Alright, Alessa. You have my official approval." Seraphine pointed at Camden. "And you behave yourself. I'm putting my life on the line, so don't screw me over."

Camden saluted the physician. "Ma'am."

"You must keep your technopathy in check until your elder can work with you." Seraphine stood in front of the glass doors. "And Alessa, I highly advise you avoid Damon and Brielle for now."

Alessa's eyes flared blood red as the doors opened, granting her freedom. "I promise no such thing," she grumbled under her breath.

CHAPTER FOURTEEN

"Camden, I need you to take this seriously," Seraphine explained as they walked through the glass doors. "You are not to leave Alessa's side until the Council of Elders gives you the okay. This is for our citizens' safety and yours. Plenty of our people don't trust you yet, which means it could be dangerous for you to be caught alone."

Camden tilted his head. "Rightfully so. They don't know me."

"Exactly. So you are not to leave Alessa's side for the time being."

He chuckled. *I'd love to see them try.*

Seraphine stepped directly in front of Camden. "You need to take this seriously. I have been instructed to pull the juice on your microchip if you disobey orders. There will be no warning, no second chance. Do you understand?"

His smile disappeared as he looked at Seraphine and addressed her with utmost respect. "I understand and will not bring shame to your name in any way. You vouched for me; I shall do as you ask."

Seraphine nodded and stepped back with a sigh. "Thank you. And Alessa, you go straight to your elder. No side quests. Swear to me."

Alessa rolled her eyes as she exhaled loudly.

Seraphine painfully grabbed her friend's upper arm. "Swear it."

Alessa glared at her friend's fingers wrapped around her arm. "I swear it. I will head home this very instant; no detours."

Seraphine released her arm. "Okay, then you two are free to go. I will see you later."

Alessa lunged at her friend, pulling Sera into her arms. "Thank you. Truly."

After a quick squeeze, Seraphine pulled back. "Yeah, well, don't make me regret it."

Seraphine walked away down the long hallway, leaving Alessa and Camden to see their way out.

Emerging from the large building, Camden raised his hands to the heavens. "The sun! Oh my gods, it feels so good, the warmth against my skin."

Looking at her friend, Alessa chuckled and shook her head, walking further down the pebbled path. "You are so dramatic."

"Hey! You can't be walking off without me. You heard Seraphine, I'm your shadow from here on out."

"Well, come on, shadow, we've got time to make up. I honestly didn't expect them to keep me for so long."

Camden looked down at the ground and grinned. "I'm just surprised they didn't kill you on the spot."

"I'm sorry, what?" Alessa laughed, shocked that her friend had that thought cross his mind.

"Yeah, I pretty much had it pegged 50/50 or maybe even 25/75 that your people were going to take us out so I'm pretty happy to still be around."

Alessa stopped walking and stared at Camden incredulously. "Hold on, you thought there was a pretty good chance of us being killed on the spot, yet you still willingly came with me?"

"Of course. First, I don't have anything better going on these days, but I enjoy keeping you company. If you go, I go, right?"

Alessa scoffed before continuing down the path toward her small cabin. "Okay, Jack."

Alessa's elder was standing just off the walkway, spinning a long spear used by warriors.

Seeing Alessa's father figure spinning a weapon in his hands, Camden promptly turned around. "Nope, no way am I meeting your father for the first time with him whipping a dory around."

She laughed and grabbed Camden's arm, turning him back around. "Oh, don't be a baby. Once he knows your intentions are honorable, he won't hurt you. But we might want to explain that rather quickly."

"Elder!" she screamed while running down the grassy hill toward her childhood home.

Her elder held his hand up into the sun, which was setting directly behind the running woman. Recognizing Alessa, her elder dropped his weapon and extended his arms.

As Alessa fell into his chest, he wrapped his arms around her in a tight embrace. Her elder placed his hands on either side of Alessa's face, looking deep into her blue eyes. "Alessa! I was informed you were here, but I refused to believe it until I saw it myself. How are you here? How are you alive?"

"Oh," she cried. "I intend to bore you with every detail since my departure."

Camden slowly walked through the grass toward Alessa and her elder.

"Who is this?" her elder asked.

"This is Camden. He's saved me more than once, and I him. Also, he's kind of my prisoner right now. The Council won't let him leave my side until he's earned their trust. Not sure how that will happen, but it's not really up to me, is it?"

Her elder extended his hand toward Camden. "Well, if this is true, I thank you. I can't believe Alessa allowed anyone to save her. Spartan women are quite headstrong."

Grasping her elder's hand, Camden grunted as his hand was crushed beneath the older man's grip. "It was my pleasure."

Letting go, Alessa and her elder walked toward the cabin. "Let us go home and catch up. I want to know everything."

An hour later, Camden and Alessa sat beside one another on the couch across from her elder. Strategically placed candles illuminated the room, creating an intense ambiance.

"And that's everything, from when I left to start my mission until now," Alessa said.

Her elder sat unmoving in his chair, staring into space. His jaw dropped before speaking. "You're sure about all of this?"

With tear-filled eyes, she nodded her head.

"Okay. So, about Kai. You cannot tell anyone about her still being alive. The Council will not hesitate to send an assassin to take her out. As far as they're aware, she's a traitor. I will work on changing their minds. If I am unable to do so, you are aware of what that means for the two of you if you can extract her?"

Alessa nodded in silent agreement. She and her sister

would have to leave New Sparta and live on the run for the rest of their lives.

"As far as Brielle goes, I never liked her, and starting tomorrow, I will entrust a few to keep an eye on her. But Damon seems captivated by her, so you should be careful. He is very protective of Brielle."

Fuming, Alessa bit her lower lip painfully and blinked away the burning sensation from behind her eyes.

With the whistling of the tea kettle, Alessa's elder stood up. "And you'll need to borrow a gown from someone if you don't already have one. I kept all your clothes, but you know we Spartans like to celebrate. New Sparta's anniversary is next week."

Alessa glanced over at Camden, shaking her head in disbelief. "How could I forget? It's always right after my birthday."

"I had completely forgotten your birthday was coming up," Camden apologized.

She dismissed his statement with a wave of her hand. "It's just another year. I'm honestly surprised I'm still alive."

Her elder returned with a tray lined with mugs and their tea steeping in a clear glass tea infuser. "Which is a huge accomplishment with what you've been through. For some reason, your life was destined to be fraught with difficulty."

Camden watched the dark amber tea seep into the clear water. "I've noticed this as well, with what Alessa has told me of her past."

Her elder's eyebrows raised in surprise. "So, he knows *everything*? How unlike Alessa to share her life with someone she has known for so short a time. It took you, what, three years to trust Quade?" her elder pointed out.

Alessa pursed her lips together and cleared her throat. "More like four."

"So, what's different with Camden?" he asked point-blank while pouring the tea from the glass pitcher into each mug.

Interested in hearing her reasoning, Camden took his steaming mug and rested his foot on his knee while lying back against the couch cushions. "Yes, Alessa. Why me?"

Taking her hot mug, Alessa squirmed uncomfortably on the couch as her cheeks blushed light pink. "It's hard to explain. Have you ever felt an instant connection to—no, no, it's not like that. Um, you see..." she stumbled on her words.

Running her hand through her hair, Alessa started again. "The only way I can describe it is that my soul recognized his. I know that sounds crazy—"

Camden sat straight up. "No, it doesn't at all. That's actually how I would explain it as well: why I trusted you from the beginning and why I didn't leave even after my debt was paid."

Alessa's elder eyed the both of them while blowing on his hot mug of tea. "Interesting."

Alessa and Camden broke eye contact, and she exhaled loudly as he cleared his throat.

Her elder tapped a finger against his ceramic mug. "One thing I am unclear about: you said you died."

She sipped her hot tea, feeling the burn on the back of her throat. "Mmm, yes. Several times."

"Okay, then, how did you escape the Ferryman?"

"Ah, well, uh, I didn't."

Her elder's eyes narrowed. "Explain yourself, child."

Alessa groaned, shifting on the couch. "Alright. So, when I died, I went to the underworld and spoke with Hades, who—"

Camden's jaw dropped. "You did what?"

"—exchanged my one soul for four others. And it couldn't be just any souls. It had to be the four we agreed upon."

Alessa's elder sat forward. "Why couldn't it be any soul? Didn't you give him plenty with all the Erebos Industries employees you killed?"

"If I recall our conversation correctly, Hades explained that souls have different values assigned to them, and each is worth more depending on their body count. This also includes lives that were taken indirectly, thanks to them. So, Eric's value is quite high."

Her elder took a drink from his mug. "I guess that makes sense in an odd sort of way."

"And on the way here, Hades spoke to me in my dreams—"

"Say what now?" Camden interrupted.

"—and he said, 'He yet lives, and you still owe me a life.' Our deal was made for Craig, Henry, Miguel, and'—"

"Eric," Camden bolted up out of his chair. "Alessa, you should have told me," he chastised, pacing the room.

She placed her mug down on the table. "I'm so sorry. I wasn't sure if it was an elaborate dream or if I was hallucinating, but now, I'm sure it was real. I feel it in both my heart and soul."

Alessa's elder shook his head back and forth. "Hades is not known for being one of the more understanding gods."

"You don't think I know that? I was sure I'd be able to kill Eric Lansing. I honestly thought I had until his body never turned up, and then Hades began showing up in my dreams with his threats."

Camden stilled and turned to face Alessa. "Threats? What threats?"

"Just one. If I don't deliver Eric's soul to the underworld soon, Hades will take what is dearest to me."

Alessa's elder pressed his lips together and stared ahead in stunned silence.

"I hate it when gods speak in riddles," Camden grumbled before downing the rest of his tea.

Alessa's elder stood up and set his mug on the wooden table between them. "I must retire for the evening. It'll require extra energy to convince the Council of our need to investigate Lucas Greenfield and his company, Greenfield Farms. It sounds like we need to get to him sooner rather than later."

Alessa watched her elder walk away down the hallway.

"He's right. We all need to get some sleep," Camden insisted.

Taking Camden's hand, Alessa wobbled back and forth before shaking her head. "Oh."

Grabbing her shoulders, Camden held her firmly in place. "Are you okay?"

"Uh, yeah. I—I'm suddenly absolutely exhausted." Alessa yawned, and her eyelids fell.

He scooped her up into his arms in one fell swoop. "You're coming down from your adrenaline high. You've been on high alert since you returned. Alright, tell me which way to walk, and I'll get you to bed."

"Down the hall, and my room's the first door on the right. You can stay in Kai's old bedroom across the hallway," she said with her eyes closed.

Holding her against his chest, Camden walked down the hall as instructed. After opening her bedroom door, he set Alessa on the soft bed. Rolling her back and forth, Camden pulled the covers over her shoulders, tucking her in.

"Good night, my fiery one," Camden whispered in his native Russian tongue before walking out the door and closing it behind him.

CHAPTER FIFTEEN

Fire licked up the walls of Eric's château, and as guests ran frantically screaming, their clothes caught aflame.

Alessa watched in horror as skin melted from their bodies, exposing charred bone and muscle.

She whipped her head to the side, and suddenly, Eric's bedroom was before her. Damon's body lay in the middle of the room, amongst the fallen Bodyguards. His eyes were wide open as his lips moved silently.

"Damon!" Alessa screamed, unable to escape the rising flames. "Damon, I'm here!"

Awaking from the nightmare, tears streamed down Alessa's face as she screamed, "No!"

Running into her room, Camden sat down next to her and held out his arms. "I'm here, Alessa. I'm here."

Falling into his embrace, Alessa covered her eyes and cried. Her body shook violently as she gasped for breath.

Camden folded his arms around her. "You've dealt with a lot this past week. Go ahead. Let it out."

After a few minutes, Alessa took a few slow, calming breaths before telling Camden about her dream. "I was back in the fire. Damon was alive this time. I saw he was alive but couldn't get to him."

Camden allowed Alessa to speak her peace as he silently sat with her. Eventually, her body stopped shaking, and her mind fogged with sleepiness. "Cam?"

He laid her back down. "Yes?"

Alessa's eyes closed tight as her words slurred. "Will you please stay with me?"

Camden glanced nervously around the room. "This isn't exactly a motel with two beds, and I'd rather not piss off your elder. I'm pretty sure he could easily take me out."

She held onto his hand. "Please?"

Camden sighed and lay down beside Alessa.

Feeling the warmth of his body, Alessa scooted back into Camden, and he wrapped his arms around her protectively.

"I've got you. Go back to sleep," he whispered in her ear.

The next time Alessa awoke, the sun shone brightly through the bedroom window. With a loud groan, she sat up in her childhood bed.

Beside her was the imprint of Camden's body, and as she laid her hand down on the still-warm sheet, she smiled.

Where would I be without Cam?

After shuffling down the hall, she entered the kitchen, her hair looking like a hot mess.

Looking up, Camden nearly spit his coffee out. "Good

morning, sunshine. Your hair tells an interesting story; you hardly sleepin' or sleepin' hard?"

Alessa grabbed a ceramic mug and poured herself a cup of hot coffee. "Both."

"Your elder left early this morning to meet with the Council. He gave me explicit instructions for us to meet Quade at noon in Training Room 3. Said we'd have it all to ourselves for the rest of the day."

Alessa glanced over at the clock on the wall. "Shit, why'd you let me sleep so late? It's already ten o'clock. That doesn't give us much time to shower, get to the mess hall, eat, and meet Quade. We gotta go!" she yelled as she hurried down the hallway, hot drink in hand.

After she showered and caffeinated, Alessa ran from the house with her hair still wet, laughing and pushing Camden playfully as they headed for the mess hall.

As Alessa nearly fell over, she caught herself on a smaller tree trunk growing just outside the path. Looking up, she saw Damon standing in a grassy field before a class of his young adult students.

He stopped talking and stared straight into her soul.

The overwhelming pull to run to him and fall into his arms instantly brought tears to her eyes.

As Damon's bright blue eyes stared back at Alessa, he moved toward her until Brielle placed a hand on his arm and touched the pendant hanging around her neck. Whipping around, Damon's back straightened, and he walked back to the front of the class, continuing with his lecture without a second glance back at Alessa.

Watching Brielle stand beside Damon with her hand possessively on his arm, Alessa struggled to breathe as they glared at one another from across the meadow. "You're dead," she mouthed at Brielle with a wicked grin on her face.

As the color drained from Brielle's face, Camden grabbed Alessa by the shoulders and pulled her away. "I'm going to enjoy every second, watching your life drain from your body," Alessa promised under her breath.

"Don't give her the satisfaction. We'll figure out a way to break him from her spell."

"A spell..." Alessa cocked her head, repeating the words inside her mind. "Interesting thought. It is almost like she has some hold over him."

"How much longer 'til we get there? I'm starving," Camden complained as they jogged side by side down the path.

Turning around the next corner, she raised her hand, pointing at the first of the tall buildings. "We're here."

Buildings varying in height and width lined both sides of the paved street. They were made of tan, white, and light grey rocks, some built with large white columns extending from the roof down to the front steps.

"Oh wow," Camden said, admiring the gorgeous main street. He slowly spun in a circle. "This is incredible."

"I didn't get to show you around when we first arrived. I was knocked unconscious on our way here by some asshole." Alessa grinned.

Camden flashed a cocky, sideways grin. "I hear he was a devilishly handsome asshole."

She laughed before giving him a brief tour. "The original Sparta was known for its beautiful architecture. When our people escaped, they couldn't exactly bring the statues and structures along with them, so our engineers designed New Sparta from scratch."

"Wow. Everything is just so—"

"Large?"

"And elaborate." Camden pointed at the library. "Does that building in particular need that many columns?"

"Well, it is our library, which is historically known for its beautiful architecture."

Camden stopped walking, and his face scrunched up in contemplation. "How exactly would that be known? Wasn't Sparta destroyed?"

Alessa rolled her eyes with an exasperated sigh. "We had original settlers who knew what it looked like, which is why the updated library in New Sparta is damn near identical to the original, just on a smaller scale."

"Interesting." Camden continued walking by her side. "Who are the statues meant to be?"

She blocked the sunlight with her hand and looked far into the distance, down the main road to the three small figures. "You can see those? From back here?"

He leaned down and tapped the side of his temple. "Enhanced sight."

She shook her head back and forth and whispered. "Oh, right. Sorry, I forgot about your chip. But wait, you don't need it to activate to tap into its usefulness?"

He laughed under his breath while looking into her blue eyes. "The statues' importance?"

"Oh, right." She cleared her throat, returning her gaze to the marble statues. "The two male figures standing are the gods Artemis and Apollo, and the goddess sitting on the fountain's edge is Athena."

Alessa pointed at the elongated building they were passing. "And this building here is one of our training centers. We have multiple gyms along the backside, connected by a covered walkway. There are three communal housing units. One is where the women live, one is where the men live, and one is where the children live with those appointed to train them."

Camden tilted his head in confusion. "So, the kids don't stay with their parents?"

She shook her head back and forth. "Nope. At age five, they are moved into a separate area to help them desensitize and adapt to being warriors."

He bit the inside of his cheek before asking, "Would you be okay with that?"

Alessa nervously cleared her throat but did not respond.

He pressed. "Sending your children away? Five is pretty young, even if it is just a few streets away."

"Mmm, yeah. That's something I plan on never finding out."

Stopping in the middle of the path, Camden turned toward Alessa, his eyebrows furrowed together. "Why is th—"

"And this is the main mess hall, right here. Where we make and serve all the fresh food," she directed Camden toward the double doors before opening one and ushering him in.

"Thank the gods. I am starving!" he bellowed, rushing forward.

After lunch, Camden jogged behind Alessa while trying to catch up with her. "Hold up!" he yelled before releasing a loud belch.

"Really, Cam?" Alessa asked, feeling quite full from the meal as well.

"I should not have had that second serving. Whew." He rubbed his hand over his shiny navy blue button-up shirt.

"Maybe not. But you also could've worn a little looser of a shirt. We're here to practice, not look good."

Camden winked. "You think I look good?"

"Oh, dear gods." Alessa laughed and opened the door.

Stepping through, Camden gasped. "*This* is what Spartans call a training room? It's more like training paradise."

The large room was filled with gymnastics equipment: uneven bars, two balance beams, several sets of rings dangling from the ceiling, trampolines, and a rock wall reaching onto the ceiling and extending across the far wall. It was positioned just before an elaborate obstacle course that took up half of the large building.

To the side of the room, Quade stood before long lanes that looked like a bowling alley.

"Hey!" Alessa hollered as she ran up to her friend and hugged him.

"It's been a minute." Quade let Alessa go and nodded toward Camden. "Camden."

"Quade," he replied.

"So what's the plan for today?" she asked, directing his attention toward the electronics at each lane's end.

Each electronic was encased in thick plastic with a tube dangling above it, extending down from the ceiling.

"The Council of Elders needs to be reassured that you are not a danger to New Sparta and its citizens. Your elder spoke with them already; their main concern was your inability to control your technopathy.

"They want reassurance that what happened with your accidental attack on the Spartans won't happen again."

Alessa spun Damon's ring around her finger while rocking back and forth. "That's understandable, but how can I prove to them I won't lose control again? I honestly don't know if I can promise that."

Quade pointed at the far end of the first lane. "You see the small radio down there?"

Listening to Quade, Camden crossed his arms and leaned against a nearby pillar.

She looked to where Quade was pointing. "I do."

"Today, you will be honing your technopathy in a safe environment, with people who care about you so you won't be tempted to freak out. Each piece of equipment is enclosed in a fireproof tube connected to its own fire extinguisher."

"How very efficient," Camden complimented.

Quade looked back over his shoulder at Camden. "It was her elder's idea. I simply found the engineers to help implement it."

"This is actually really neat. But how long will I be expected to practice? I've only accidentally set things on fire; it's never been intentional."

"Yet," Quade replied. "And you're not to leave this building until eight o'clock by order of the Council of Elders."

Alessa's eyebrows rose. "Eight hours? I'm supposed to train for eight hours straight? I mean, if I were working physically, that would not be a problem, but this is a very different scenario."

Quade tilted his head to the side. "That's just today. Starting tomorrow, it's twelve hours each day. Eight to eight with a half hour for lunch."

Both Alessa and Camden's jaws dropped as Quade stepped forward.

"I don't think you understand. If you can't prove to the Council you're in control of your abilities, they will consider you a threat. And you will be eliminated."

Camden's muscles stiffened, and his back straightened as

he stood protectively behind Alessa. "I'd like to see them try," he growled.

"We don't have much time to prepare, which is why we're working so hard over the next week. We're going to make sure by the time the celebration is held, they are convinced you won't incinerate the microchips inside everyone's heads."

Alessa closed her eyes and inhaled deeply. "Okay."

Camden gently grabbed Alessa's elbow. "Do *not* push yourself. I know you. You will push through the pain, and then you'll pay for it later."

She placed her hand on top of Camden's in reassurance. "I don't have a choice."

Camden sighed loudly, running his fingers through his hair before flashing a sideways grin. "Okay, then. I'll be right over here. You go kick that radio's ass."

She stood beside Quade, ready to focus.

A half-hour in, Alessa's elder arrived to talk her through the rest of the training. By the end of the first day, Alessa could focus her abilities on just about half of the electronics. She was learning to set things on fire with intention and master things that were less explosive, such as turning electronics on and off with just her mind.

When the eight o'clock hour arrived, Alessa collapsed in Camden's arms.

He carried her out of the building and back to her elder's cabin while speaking words of reassurance. "I've got you, my fiery one."

CHAPTER SIXTEEN

For the next week, Alessa awoke every morning fighting exhaustion, only to spend the next twelve hours working hard on controlling her glitched microchip's abilities. Nearing the end of the seventh day, Alessa had grown weary.

Glancing at her elder, she threw her hands up in frustration. "Isn't this good enough? Since being home, I haven't trained physically, and my head can't take much more."

Her elder eyed Camden before instructing him to move to the end of the final lane, directly in front of a portable DVD player. "You, stand there."

She watched Camden stop at the end of the lane and stand with his hands clasped together in front of him. "What are you doing?"

"You think your training is done? That you are good enough?" Her elder held his hand out toward her friend.

She squinted suspiciously at Camden.

Her elder cleared his throat before continuing. "The Council is bound to push your limits. You must be prepared."

Camden tilted his head slightly downward and eyed Alessa. "I trust you."

"Wait, wait. Are you expecting me to trigger the electronic *behind* him? I can't do that." Alessa shook her head adamantly back and forth, backing away from the line. "No. Not a chance. I'll seriously hurt him."

Alessa's elder grabbed her by the arm as she walked past, pulling her to an abrupt halt. "You don't have a choice. They will do everything they can to justify your destruction. And if you die..." he tilted his head toward Camden.

Her gaze darted toward her friend, and with a deep sigh, her eyes rolled into the back of her head. "So will he. Ugh, fine."

She trudged back to the starting line and rubbed her hands together.

"You can do this. I believe in you," Camden encouraged with a forced smile.

Glancing off to the side, Alessa side-eyed Quade, who just entered the room. "Great. More of an audience to watch me kill my friend." Her attention returned to Camden. "Okay, you got this. You got this..." she mumbled under her breath.

With a deep inhale, she closed her eyes and focused all her pent-up rage on the DVD player. Envisioning the atoms within the small black electronic bouncing erratically off one another, increasing in speed, Alessa's irises burned blood red.

Opening her eyes, she imagined herself looking through the muscular Bodyguard standing before her, but she could only focus on his body shaking violently.

Gritting his teeth, Camden fought against the feeling of being burned alive.

"Focus, Alessa. Don't give up," Alessa's elder called out to her.

Alessa's eyes darted back and forth between the look of agony on her friend's face and the trembling, smoking electronic directly behind him. "I—I—" she stuttered.

The vein on her elder's neck bulged as he screamed. "Do it!"

"I can't!" she screamed, falling to her knees. "I can't do it," she cried as her eyes unglitched back to light blue.

Camden's body relaxed as the sensation of being lit aflame ceased.

Shaking the tingling sensation from his skin, Camden ran over to Alessa. "It's okay; I'm okay." The scent of burning electronics permeated every inch of the training room as Camden bent in front of the Spartan.

"I'm sorry, I'm so sorry I couldn't—" she began.

Glancing up at her elder, Camden scooped Alessa up in his arms. "We're done for the day."

Her elder's eyes darkened. "We need to—"

"I said we're done," Camden growled before heading for the exit door with Alessa in his arms.

Staying silent on the side of the room, Quade watched Alessa and Camden barge through the doors. Glancing at Alessa's elder, he asked if she would be ready for the test with a simple look.

Alessa's elder silently shrugged before he turned on his heel and walked away.

As Camden trudged down the path with Alessa nestled against his chest, Damon was walking up the path with Brielle and a small group of Spartans.

Seeing Alessa's arms wrapped around another man's neck caused Damon to snap, and he yelled at them. "Alessa?"

He ran up to the man holding Alessa. "What's the matter?"

He glared at the blond man and stepped forward menacingly. "What did you do to her?"

Alessa was barely able to lift her head, and when she realized it was Damon checking on her well-being, she was sent further into despair. This was the first time she had seen him since the medical ward, and she was too tired to form a coherent sentence.

Alessa could feel his hot breath upon her skin, and she knew if she had the energy, she would have tried to reach out and touch him.

Camden tried pushing past Damon, but the Spartan stood his ground.

The Bodyguard's jaw dropped as his tongue hit the side of his mouth. "Move out of my way, Spartan," he spat, trying to restrain himself.

"Not until I know why she's—"

"Damon!" Brielle huffed, out of breath after catching up to him. "Damon, leave them be. Can't you see you're upsetting the poor girl?"

Camden's eyes narrowed as he glared at Brielle.

Her left cheek was still quite bruised, her lower lip had a decent crack down the middle that had scabbed over, and a white bandage stabilized the bridge of her nose.

As Alessa lifted her head with what little strength she had left, her eyes flickered red.

"She's going to hurt me again!" Brielle screamed and jumped behind Damon.

"No, I'm not," Alessa croaked. "I promised on Camden's and my life I wouldn't try to kill you. Again." She laid her head down on Camden's chest and closed her eyes.

Damon's heart ached to be the one holding Alessa, but the

second Brielle touched the pendant on her necklace, his vision went hazy, and he backed away without resisting.

"Come on, sugar bear," Brielle urged Damon further up the path. "Oh, yeah. See you tomorrow!" Brielle grinned wickedly back at Alessa before pulling Damon away.

"That is one strange woman." Camden turned Alessa away, and they continued toward her cabin. "Let's get you home."

CHAPTER SEVENTEEN

After lying in bed for hours, Alessa was unable to fall asleep after her long day of training. Throwing her covers off, she sat upright in bed. "I've got to get out of here."

She slipped on her combat boots and cracked open her bedroom door. The high-pitched creaking noise from the old wood was deafening, and she squeezed her eyes shut, hoping no one had heard.

Listening to Camden's continued snoring, Alessa exhaled and tip-toed toward the front door.

After snatching up the red and black plaid blanket tucked into the bin by the couch, Alessa snuck out of the cabin and inhaled the cold night air.

Her lungs burned as she ran alone in the dark, and Alessa's heart felt light for the first time in a long time. Damon was alive, even if he wasn't her boyfriend anymore, but Camden didn't leave her when she needed a friend, and she was home. Hopefully, she would have her sister back soon as well.

Unintentionally, Alessa ended up at the edge of the cliff where she and Damon used to sit and talk all night long.

Inhaling deeply, Alessa howled loudly into the darkness before smiling big.

Laying back on the warm blanket, she looked up at the dancing stars. They took turns twinkling their vivid reds, striking blues, bright whites, and pale yellows.

A rogue tear fell down Alessa's cheek as she found the constellation Lyra. With the closing of her eyes, Alessa exhaled a shaky breath of hot air, blowing the water vapor into the night.

Just as she was about to give in to the breaking of her heart once more, a familiar voice spoke from the darkness.

"Couldn't sleep?"

Sitting upright, she gasped. "Damon, what are you doing out here?"

He strolled toward her. "I couldn't sleep either."

Turning her back to him, she wiped the tears from her face. "But what are you doing *here*?"

He gestured to the empty spot on the blanket beside Alessa. "Mind if I join you?"

Unable to speak, she pressed her lips together and shook her head back and forth, forcing herself to look straight ahead at the moon's reflection on a snow-capped peak.

"Honestly, I'm not sure how I ended up here. Maybe subconsciously, I knew this seemed to be the only chance to talk to you, what with you being a celebrity around here."

She sighed loudly, looking out into the darkness, and bit her lower lip. "I'm no celebrity. Everyone is afraid of me." She paused and subconsciously played with Damon's ring still on her finger while fighting back tears. "What did you want to talk about? You don't believe anything I tell you."

Damon shook his head back and forth. "That's not true. I'll admit what you've claimed is shocking, but I want to hear everything that happened to you over the last year. What you've been up to? What took you so long to come back?"

Alessa nervously licked her lips and looked down at his ring, knowing full well she couldn't hide anything from Damon. She laughed nervously. "Ugh, I hate crying. It makes me look weak."

"What's wrong?" he asked, leaning into her.

Alessa's breathing hitched. Unable to look at him, she played with her fingernails as she spoke. "After I awoke with no memory, I tried living my life as best I could. I tried moving on. But I had these terrible nightmares that plagued me night after night. Turns out they were memories from when I was tort—"

Alessa swallowed and shook her head while clearing her throat. "Anyway, Bodyguards attacked me at a nightclub and —" she exhaled loudly and looked down at Damon's ring once more. "No, I can't. It doesn't matter; you won't believe me."

Damon started to reach forward but thought twice about it and pulled back. "Just tell me your truth."

"Okay ... you promise not to interrupt me?"

He nodded while pretending to zip his lips with an invisible zipper.

She took a steadying breath before turning to face him. "My memories were violently erased when Eric Lansing's men caught me, but about a month after I went missing, you found me. After saving me from Bodyguards at a nightclub, we were involved in a car chase. Then we drove to Brielle's apartment, where she dosed you, and I pushed you through an open window onto a moving train."

Damon remained silent as his eyebrows rose.

"Yeah. Throughout this time, you somehow convinced me to seek revenge against those who stole my memory. We started in D.C. with Craig before arriving in Florida, where we took out Henry. He led us to Miguel in Texas, where you and I went to the false cure's manufacturing plant. We found Camden, the man I brought home with me, and we all headed for Chicago.

"As you got sicker, we finally got to Eric Lansing's château, where I remembered everything, including who you were to me. But our reunion was short-lived as you died on the floor of Eric's bedroom," Alessa's voice cracked as she struggled to keep it together.

Damon rubbed his hands together and looked down at the blanket between his feet.

"When you" —she swallowed hard—"died ... I freaked out, and my microchip glitched, somehow allowing me to control electronics. This is how the deadly fire started at Eric's château."

Damon stared at Alessa, his face emotionless. "Uh-huh. Well, uh... that is one hell of a story."

Alessa threw her hands up in frustration and groaned. "I know it sounds insane, but I'm telling the truth."

He held his hands up in a peaceful gesture. "I believe you believe it's the truth."

Alessa shook her head back and forth as hot tears welled up in her eyes. "If that's not the most twisted way of saying you don't believe me." She stood up, her blood boiling.

Damon jumped out in front of her, stopping her from walking away. "Sydämen liekki..."

Alessa's jaw dropped, and her breathing hitched as she nearly collapsed. "What did you just call me?"

Damon stepped back. "I'm sorry. Old habits die hard, I guess."

"No—don't." She stepped toward him, placing her hand on his chest. "Don't apologize for saying something I've been desperate to hear."

"Alessa," he said with a tone of warning. "I'm with Brielle."

Her eyebrows scrunched up, and her hand folded in on itself. "So, you love her then?"

Damon glanced off to the side. "I didn't say that. Look, when I thought you were gone, Brielle had my back. She helped pick up the pieces, and I owe her—"

Growing irritated, Alessa huffed. "I think it's time you leave. I'm not sure what you were hoping to get from this; I just wanted some time alone before there's the genuine possibility I'm put to death. Now, I have an important day tomorrow, and I don't have time to entertain your bullshit." She bent over, snatching up the blanket.

"I know I shouldn't, but I still care about you," Damon confessed.

As Alessa stood up, she turned around and faced Damon with her blanket cradled in her arms.

He took a few steps forward, minimizing the space between them, and tucked a stray dark hair behind her ear. "I know I'm with Brielle and shouldn't feel this way, but I can't stop caring about you."

She stared up into his intense eyes. "Why shouldn't you care about me? We've been through hell and back. Me, quite literally."

Damon's ocean blue eyes bore through her. "Just answer me this..."

"Yes?" she asked, breathily.

"What is your relationship with the man you brought with you, your bodyguard?"

Her face scrunched up in shock that he used that exact term. "You have got to be fucking kidding me. That's the real reason you came out here searching for me: to find out if the guy I brought through the barrier is my lover?" She backed away.

Moving forward toward Alessa, Damon stuttered. "I— I know I don't have any right to—"

"No!" Alessa fumed. "You don't. But for your information, no, we are not romantically involved. You are the only one I have ever wanted. When I saw you alive, I felt like I could finally breathe again. But after seeing you with *her*," she swallowed back the tears. "And your knowing that I am here. I am right here standing before you, and you're choosing to stay with her. It's breaking me all over again."

Damon exhaled. "I hate knowing how much I've hurt you and how I continue to hurt you. " His shoulders drooped. "But I'm with Brielle."

"You still love me; I know you still love me. And I'm going to prove to you that Brielle is the bitch I know her to be."

Damon cocked his head. "That isn't necessary, I know who—"

"No." Alessa's eyes glowed red, illuminated in the dark of night. "You don't know what she's capable of. For some reason, you can't remember."

He put his hands up defensively and slowly backed away. "I mean, I could say the same thing about you. What happened to you? To make you like this." He lifted his hand in a gesture, pointing out her change in eye color.

Taking slow, deep breaths in and out, she lowered her heart rate and unglitched. Opening her blue eyes, she looked away from him, out into the darkness. "I lost my life, my memories, my sister, and the only man I have ever loved. I ... lost ... everything. At least, I thought I did."

"Alessa—" he pleaded.

She held up her free hand and stopped him from moving

toward her. "You need to leave. There are only so many times my heart can break before it shatters completely and hearing how much you love another is more than I can handle the night before I'm expected to defend my right to continue living. I'll see you tomorrow. At my trial."

"It's not a—"

She glared at Damon. "Don't lie. We both know if I don't pass the tests, I'm as good as dead."

Damon turned to leave. "I have no doubt you will pass."

Alessa scoffed as she wiped away a fallen tear. "You've never before flinched away from me. You have no idea who I am anymore," Alessa whispered into the darkness.

Damon stilled. "I still want you in my life. I want to try to be friends." Not knowing what else to say, he licked his lips nervously and headed back up the hill.

Closing her eyes, tears seeped through her eyelashes, falling down both cheeks.

Friends. The word stung like a thousand cuts. *He wants to be friends.*

Feeling half of her soul walk away, Alessa resisted the urge to run after Damon with every fiber of her being. As she stood alone, feeling as though her heart were being torn from her chest, hot tears fell, leaving their salty taste pooled on her upper lip.

CHAPTER EIGHTEEN

Unable to sleep, Alessa awoke after only a few fitful hours. She sat on the cliff's edge and watched the sun kiss the horizon.

The sky changed from a dark blue hue to striped pink and orange as she sipped her hot coffee.

This is the day I could join my parents in the underworld.

Alessa gripped her mug and watched the creamer swirl amidst the rich, dark brown coffee. *No, no, no, I cannot fail. They won't hesitate to execute Camden if I can't complete the test. Fuck!*

Setting the mug down in the long grass, Alessa exhaled loudly and stood up. "Let's get this over with."

The long, blood-red skirt of her warrior's dress flowed behind Alessa as she marched toward their city's arena. Built high on a cliff, the impressive building overlooked the entire Spartan city, memorializing the time when their civilization was the most powerful of them all.

Camden stood off to the side of the main path, and as Alessa passed him, he joined her, sticking protectively close as they walked together.

Breaking the tense silence, Camden's jaw dropped in awe as they approached the tall arch. "Wow."

The beige, oval-shaped outdoor arena had an opening on one side, through which they could see a small airplane parked in tall grass. Packed-down sand coated the floors, and the built-in seats made of off-white stones encircled the center of the arena.

Alessa pointed up toward the sky. "The gods are welcome to watch any festivities, or trials, from the heavens."

The entire Council of Elders and their heirs, including Damon, sat in elevated seats, awaiting her arrival.

She stumbled forward a few steps as the importance of every single council member being there for her trial hit like a ton of bricks. "Fuck," she mumbled under her breath while eyeing the man sitting straight-backed next to Damon. "Damon's dad is here."

Camden glanced up at the man who looked like an older version of Damon. "Why's he so important?"

Alessa shook her head and bit her lip, looking down at the ground as she walked toward the spectators. "He's the head of the Consilium. His being here confirms if I fail, we die."

Camden looked up at the serious look on the older man's face and swallowed hard. "Oh."

Alessa stretched her neck nervously. "He'd be the one to signal our execution."

"Well, then, it's simple. Don't fail." Camden grinned nervously.

Off to the side were sixteen long lanes, and at the end of each lane stood a single electronic of various sizes and shapes, waiting to be set aflame.

Sixteen? Shit. That's a lot to handle back to back.

Peering over the cliff into the meadow below, Alessa

noticed a smaller airplane and thought it odd, but she couldn't fathom how it could be related to her trial.

Sensing her nerves, Camden grabbed her hand and pressed her fingers to his lips. "My fiery one, you've got this," he reassured her.

After releasing her hand, Camden sat in the front row beside Alessa's elder, who was seated rigid and tight-lipped.

With a deep breath, Alessa held her head high as she approached the elders and heirs.

Locking eyes with Damon in the crowd, her heart faltered, knowing if she failed the task at hand, she could very well be put to death on the spot.

"Welcome, Alessa," boomed a loud voice through the microphone.

Tearing her gaze from Damon, Alessa nervously flattened the stomach of her scarlet and gold dress.

"You have been asked today to demonstrate your new *skills*." He spat the last word as if it were toxic. "If you can prove to us you are in control of your power and swear not to use it against other Spartans, you will be permitted to live. As will your partner."

Fuming on the inside, Alessa bowed her head to the council members sitting before her. "I thank you for considering my life worth saving," she said through clenched teeth while staring at the ground.

"We also request you not make any more attempts on Brielle's life. As long as she is in Spartan territory, she is our guest and will be treated as such."

When the woman's name was mentioned, Alessa's eyes flashed red. She took a deep, steadying breath and blinked her eyes back to their deep blue hue before standing up.

"You have my word," she said without breaking eye contact with Damon's father.

One of the council elders stood in front of the first lane, holding out his hand to direct Alessa.

Armed guards stood at the ready, surrounding the entirety of the inner arena.

With the weight of knowing if she failed just one of their requests, both her and Camden's life would be ended, Alessa joined the elder at the start of the lane and inhaled a shaky breath.

Closing her eyes, Alessa used her rage toward Brielle to her benefit and triggered her microchip. Glitching, she opened her blood-red irises and stared at the boombox at the end of the first lane.

Instantly, it set on fire.

Moving to the second lane, she remained glitched as she cocked her head and set the computer on fire.

The third was a cell phone, the fourth a walkie-talkie, and so on down the lanes.

Beads of anxious sweat gathered across her forehead, and her limbs began shaking from exhaustion.

Fighting the urge to vomit and pass out, Alessa approached the sixteenth lane, where the tiniest of microprocessors was set out, lying on a small table.

To Alessa's surprise, Damon stepped in front of the table.

She turned toward the council. "What is this?"

Seeing her red eyes, everyone in the stands reflexively leaned back. "We need to ensure you can control your abilities around our citizens, and Damon has graciously volunteered."

Rolling her eyes in annoyance at Damon's unbending belief in her, Alessa's hands balled into fists, and she met his ocean blue eyes.

He flinched, and her heart dropped as she glimpsed a moment of fear in his eyes. *He doesn't even recognize me.*

Closing her eyes, Alessa cleared her mind and buried her heartache deep as she focused all her energy on the microprocessor directly behind Damon.

Opening her eyes, she stared at the electronic, not breaking contact for even the briefest of seconds, for fear of killing him.

Damon's jaw muscles tensed as he gritted his teeth in pain, refusing to move as it would mean certain death for Alessa. *Come on. Come on. You can do this. You have to. It's not like you've never felt pain before. Suck it up!*

The veins on the back of Damon's hands bulged from his balled fists, his fingernails dug into his palms, and sweat dripped down from his hairline. Just as he felt he could no longer take it, Alessa's eyes flashed brighter red, and the microprocessor behind him burst into flames.

Damon released an audible breath of air as she blinked her eyes back to blue and returned her attention to the seated council members.

A chorus of hand clapping echoed as she struggled to remain standing upright.

"And now, the airplane."

Alessa looked down at the two-seater plane and then back at the elders. "What about it?" she huffed.

"You are to make the entire engine explode or implode; I'm not sure how your abilities work."

Alessa's face dropped. "I-I've never done that to something that large be—"

Damon's father's jaw muscles clenched. "Do it or you declare failure."

Pushing through the physical pain and mental exhaustion, Alessa clenched her teeth together and stared down at the white, reflective plane. Pinpointing the buzzing sound, she focused all her hate and frustration on the one section of the aircraft projecting the noise.

She balled her hands into fists, and her feet were planted firmly to the ground, struggling to hold up her trembling body. Focusing all her remaining energy on the engine, hot tears fell down her cheeks, and blood trickled from her nose until, finally, the engine exploded, and a puff of smoke rose from the flames.

Alessa's elder clapped his hands together and screamed at the top of his lungs, "Well done!"

Just as Alessa was about to collapse, Camden swooped in and put his arm around her midsection while taking her right hand within his own.

Damon's father addressed Alessa with a sour look as Camden helped her stand upright. "Congratulations. You not only remain a Spartan but are celebrated as the only Spartan in our history to have survived having their microchip disconnected. We will be keeping a close eye on you—" he smiled as if he knew a secret she did not—"as we expect great things from you, Alessa."

Realizing the sinister meaning behind his words, she stiffened in Camden's arms.

They're going to try to weaponize me.

"You may have the rest of your day to do as you wish. Tomorrow is New Sparta's celebration. We expect to see you there."

Alessa curtly nodded with tight lips, and after side-eyeing Damon, she grumbled at Camden. "Get me out of here."

Helping her away from the council, Camden whispered into her ear. "Where do you want to go?"

She tore her gaze from Damon's gaze. "Anywhere but here."

He led her into the nearest wooded section of the hill before scooping her up into his arms.

Too weak to fight the act of kindness, Alessa melted into his thick arms and pressed against his muscular chest.

Camden approached a small lake and set her down on the rocky terrain before removing his clothes.

"What are you doing?" Alessa sleepily laughed as he tossed his shirt onto a nearby bush.

He unbuttoned his pants and took off toward the shoreline. "We are going swimming. You need a break."

Smiling gratefully, Alessa untied the rope around her waist and slowly peeled her dress over her head. Chasing after Camden, she stomped the soft fabric into the small pebbles.

Without hesitation, he dove into the lake. Breaking the surface, Camden flipped his shaggy, dirty blond hair up and back. "Whew! That's got a bite to it."

As her legs hit the chilly water, Alessa squealed. "Oh, shit!" Swimming toward him, Alessa took a deep breath and relaxed into the strokes until she grasped his outstretched hands.

"Lay back," he instructed.

Her body automatically stiffened in response. "What, why?"

Camden's strong hands pulled her into him, and his lips were mere inches in front of hers. "Trust me."

Alessa's breathing hitched, and as she consciously tried to relax her muscles, Camden lifted her to the water's surface. Slowly, Camden rotated her as she lay on her back.

Alessa closed her eyes as she floated on the water, and her worries melted away with the Bodyguard's warm fingertips barely touching her skin and the cool liquid embracing the curves of her body.

Camden's face relaxed into a warm smile. "By the way, happy birthday."

Her head whipped toward him with a look of astonishment. "You remembered?"

He continued slowly spinning her. "Of course I did. Just wanted to make sure you weren't aiming to reduce the writing on your tombstone less by making your death date and birth date one in the same."

"Cam, you are ridiculous," Alessa laughed.

"I may be ridiculous, but I'm also incredibly funny. And good looking, I might add," he grinned.

Alessa extended her arms further out in the water. "What am I going to do with you?"

"Oh, I could think of a few things," Camden winked.

Laughing hysterically, Alessa splashed her friend and squealed as Camden splashed her back.

***

After Alessa completed her trial, Damon followed her and the man into the woods.

She did not look good after all the tests. I hope she's okay.

He approached the lake stealthily, hiding behind several tall bushes near the shoreline.

Why do I feel like such a creep? It's not like I'm spying on her; I'm simply ensuring she's all right by watching her from afar. So, I'm spying on her. Dammit.

Damon shook his head after losing the argument with himself.

Watching the blond man hold Alessa up made Damon's blood boil. "Fuck," he growled before turning away.

"Damon!" Brielle squealed from behind him.

He jumped and moved quickly away from the bushes. "Hey ... You."

She squinted, looking past him at the shrubbery. "What are you doing back here?"

"Oh ... uh ... nothing." He draped his arm across her shoulders and pulled her close, kissing the top of her head. "How about you?"

She grabbed ahold of his arm, dangling down. "I was just looking for you. How did everything go? Did you take care of her?"

Damon tilted his head to look down at Brielle. "She passed like I knew she would. What do you mean by—"

With her free hand, she pressed the pendant hanging from her neck, triggering his ability to activate, and his irises turned silver in color as he stopped speaking mid-sentence. "You had mentioned showing me the history of Sparta and describing the intricacies of how the transportation device works, maybe even how the forcefield works."

Damon stared straight ahead, his eyes transfixed. "I did?"

Brielle squeezed his hand. "Mm-hmm. You did. Why don't we head for the intelligence center so you can pull up the info for me to see?"

"That sounds nice," Damon drawled as if in a daze, continuing down the path with Brielle.

CHAPTER NINETEEN

The following day, Camden and Alessa were on their way to the mess hall when a young child charged at them.

Watching the small figure bounce up and down, Alessa held her hand up to block the sun. Finally recognizing the little boy's voice, Alessa's heart leaped into her throat.

She ran toward the boy with outstretched arms. "Soren? Soren!"

Scooping him up into her arms, Alessa fell to her knees in the middle of the path and held his face between her hands. "Oh, my gods. You are so big now! What are they feeding you?" Alessa laughed, tears welling up in her eyes.

Quade was panting after catching up to his son. "There was no point in keeping him away any longer."

"He's been begging non-stop to see you since he got word of your return," Seraphine yelled out further down the path.

Alessa squinted up at her friends from down on her knees. "Thank you."

"Auntie Alessa, I've missed you," Soren confessed while burying his face into her neck.

Alessa sniffled. "I miss you too. Would you like to join my friend and me? We're heading to the mess hall right now."

Soren giggled. "Of course! I'm always hungry." He placed his hand within Alessa's and pulled her toward the city's center.

Seraphine and Quade fell into pace behind them.

Soren peeked over his shoulder at Camden as he walked on the other side of Alessa. "Who is your friend?"

"My name is Camden, but Alessa calls me Cam. Nice to meet you, young man," Camden purred in his slight Russian accent.

Soren's eyes narrowed suspiciously. "How did you meet?"

"Ah, well, I needed help, and your aunt helped me."

Alessa blushed and tried to hide an embarrassed smile. "And when I needed help, Cam was there to help me. And now, we kinda come as a package deal."

"Uncle Damon has to be very excited to have you home, Auntie."

Taken back, Alessa stopped walking.

Seraphine took her son by the hand. "Oh, Soren, that's enough for now. I'm sure you're overwhelming your auntie with all your questions."

Soren squealed joyfully as Quade picked his son up and threw him on his shoulders.

"Let's run ahead and get to the food first," Quade said excitedly before jogging ahead.

Seraphine shook her head at her husband and son before she risked a glance at Alessa. "I'm sorry about—"

Alessa held up her hand to stop her. "No, it's fine. He doesn't know any better."

Seraphine pointed ahead at her family. "I'm going to catch up to them."

Pressing her lips together, Alessa nodded silently and watched Seraphine run toward her husband and son.

"You know it's not going to get any easier. You're going to see Damon damn near every day."

Alessa rolled her eyes and started forward with a huff. "I know that."

"Then what's your plan? Behind your eyes, I can tell you've been formulating one."

She glanced up and off to the side, picking up the pace.

"Alessa?" he demanded.

She whipped around. "I know he still loves me! I can see it in his face when she's not around."

Camden stepped forward. "When is she not around? It's like she's got an invisible cord wrapped around him and is always near his side. When have you been around him without her?"

Ignoring his question, Alessa turned around and continued toward the mess hall. "It's almost as if he's longing to talk to me but can't for some reason."

Camden sighed loudly. "Maybe you're looking too far—"

"You've had to have seen it as well," she interjected. "He's got this look in his eyes, but then she pulls him back, and his entire demeanor changes."

Camden rubbed the back of his neck and chuckled. "Perhaps she's leaking mind-controlling serum into the palms of her hands."

Alessa tilted her head in contemplation. "That's not a bad idea."

"I was joking, and yes, it is a ridiculous idea."

"No, but seriously, something is going on. He would *never* choose her."

Camden touched Alessa's forearm. "Well, he did and is continuing to do so."

As Camden's words sunk deep into her heart, a sharp stabbing pain shot through her chest, and she closed her eyes.

"I didn't mean—"

"Yes, yes, you did." Alessa swallowed, and they continued the rest of the way in silence.

As the double doors opened, the large, crowded room silenced. Camden and Alessa walked the food line, and the whispers began one table at a time.

"Ignore them," Camden said in Alessa's ear as they approached the counter.

Glancing across the room, Alessa saw Damon sitting with a few of his close warriors. His arm was lazily draped over Brielle's shoulders, their fingers intertwined as she sat relaxed, back against him, while talking to the women in the group.

Feeling as though she were struck hard in the gut, Alessa re-lived a moment in time when she and Damon had sat that very same way, her hands laced with his.

Slowly backing away, unable to take her eyes off the love of her life, she shook her head back and forth. "I can't do this," she confessed before running for the nearest exit.

Bolting from the mess hall, Alessa sprinted out of the city and into the meadows surrounding them. Her lungs burned as she collapsed to her knees and screamed. A circle of light exuded from her as her voice turned raspy, and as the bright halo returned to Alessa, the earth surrounding her was scorched a good thirty feet in all directions.

She stared ahead, numb, while listening to the birds tweeting back and forth in the tall trees nearby.

"Well, that's a new trick." Camden plopped down beside

her on the burnt ground. "Don't let the elders see you doing that, or we're both dead."

Camden inhaled deeply before beginning. "Look, I understand you're hurting right now, but the elders expect you to attend the celebration tonight, and Damon and Brielle will be there. Together."

Alessa closed her eyes, and a single tear ran down her cheek.

Wrapping his arm around her, Camden squeezed Alessa from the side. "Fuck them. No one will even pay them any attention; they'll be so jealous of you."

She wiped away the tear with the back of her hand. "And why is that?"

"Now I'm insulted," he huffed. "Because I'll be going as your date, of course."

Alessa rolled her eyes and smiled.

Camden's eyebrow raised as the left side of his lips lifted in a sideways grin. "I happen to look damn good in a suit."

Alessa ran her fingers across the charred grass. "I remember."

"I was going to tell you after we ate lunch, but this seems as good a time as any," Camden began.

"What?"

"I spoke with your elder this morning, and he said the Council agreed to look into Lucas Greenfield."

Alessa beamed as she whipped her upper body to face him. "Really? Why didn't you say something sooner?"

He shrugged his muscular shoulders. "I figured you'd need a pick me up at some point today. Looks like I was right."

Alessa bumped his shoulder with her own and chuckled. "You know me so well."

"I do, don't I?" He placed his hands on her shoulders and

squeezed. "I don't know about you, but I'm starving, so here's the deal. I will grab us food while you head down to the small lake we found the other day and pick a good picnic spot."

"That sounds perfect," Alessa agreed. Standing up, she rubbed the ash from her fingertips onto her black skirt.

"Good thing your burnt grass blends in with your dress."

"It wouldn't matter. I don't plan on seeing anyone else today."

Camden walked back toward the mess hall, calling out over his shoulder. "You mean except for the entire city later tonight."

She sighed before yelling back at him. "Just go get our food, smartass!"

CHAPTER TWENTY

Alessa sat on the toilet, lacing her white heels up her calves. "You know, it's probably time I make my home in the women's barracks. I was staying with Damon before I left, and I can only imagine my elder would like his privacy back."

Camden dressed in Kai's bedroom, across the hall from the bathroom. "I wonder how the Spartan women would feel with me living there since the Council named you my babysitter."

Alessa uncapped her magenta lipstick and laughed at her reflection in the mirror. "Oh shit, I forgot. I guess I'll talk it over with my elder; see if they've gotten any closer to giving you leniency."

"You can talk to him in the morning. Tonight, we have fun. You about ready?"

She smacked her freshly painted lips together. "Yep, you?"

Camden stepped out of the bedroom and closed the door behind him. "I think I'm good to go."

After one final check in the mirror, Alessa sighed. "You can do this," she said to her reflection before entering the hall.

Camden stood before Alessa at six-feet-three inches, a good

half a foot taller than her. He wore a creamy white corset vest with golden reverse boning channels atop a white long-sleeved button-up shirt. Noticing his black pants were tight in all the right places, Alessa blushed and unintentionally bit her lower lip.

Her heels clicked across the wooden floor as she approached him. "Camden! You look, just, wow." She pressed her fingertips into the stiff, dark golden boning channels on his corset. "The artistry is incredible. Where did you get this?"

Camden's eyes bore into hers as she looked up at him, her fingers splayed across his chest. "You're one to talk. Have you seen yourself? You were right to keep that dress. And those heels." He whistled. "You, my fiery one, look good enough to eat."

Alessa forced herself to breathe and cleared her throat, intentionally breaking the moment's intensity. "You mean this old thing?" She picked up the skirt's fabric and spun it around. "Do you think he'll remember it?"

Camden placed his fingertips below her chin and gently tilted her head back. "I truly don't think he will, but your beauty will not be wasted on him."

With a shrug of her shoulders, Alessa blinked away tears. "It's worth a shot."

"You're not wrong." Camden leaned in and kissed the tip of her nose. "It can't hurt to try. Now, let's get to the party and have a few drinks. The Russian in me is greatly in need of a release."

Alessa guided him out the front door. "Um ... so ... about our parties ... they can get rather indulgent."

A UTV pulled up in front of the cabin. "Would you like a ride?" the driver asked.

Alessa pulled up her skirt and sighed. "Perfect timing, yes, please."

Camden turned his head toward Alessa as they sat down beside one another. "What exactly do you mean by indulgent?"

"Well, to be perfectly honest, we Spartans love our wine almost as much as we love to ... well ... have sex."

Camden's interest piqued, and his eyebrows rose.

"So you may see or even partake in some things tonight," she chuckled and raised her hands before her chest. "I'm not here to judge; I'm simply warning you."

Camden straightened his already perfectly placed golden tie. "Well, thank you for the warning."

The entire city was illuminated by lights strung up above from one side of the road to the other. At the city's entrance, the marble statues of the gods and the goddess were decorated with floral bouquets, and elaborate decorations were strategically placed throughout the city's center.

Spartans were scantily clad in thin, gorgeous, flowing gowns, more traditional warrior uniforms, and handsome suits.

Off to the side, in a small alcove, a group of Spartans were drinking, laughing, moaning, kissing, and fucking. Hard.

A woman was bent back against the stone; their dress was pushed to the side with someone else's head pressed between her spread legs. Her mouth opened, and she moaned loudly. Looking over the man kneeling before her, the woman's eyes met Camden's, and she licked her lips.

His eyebrows raised, and his cheeks blushed. "You were not kidding."

Exiting the vehicle, Camden cleared his throat before tilting his head toward the expansive dance floor in front of a DJ booth. "After the first few drinks, you, me, dance floor. I'll be right back."

He removed his hand from Alessa's lower back and hurried toward the bar.

Standing alone, Alessa wrapped her arms around herself, suddenly feeling the crowd's eyes on her.

Scanning the party for familiar faces, Alessa saw Quade and Seraphine laughing with a few others on the other side of the room, and as her eyes drifted away, she caught Brielle and Damon engaged in a serious conversation off to the side of the DJ's booth.

Whipping around, Alessa slammed into Camden's chest. "Oh! Oh, I'm sorry," she apologized, brushing her hair out of her eyes. "Did any of it spill on you?"

"Don't worry about it, I'm good." He glanced behind Alessa, where she had been looking when distracted. "Oh, I see. It's the D-bag."

"Cam!" She smacked his shoulder. "Stop it," she chastised before taking a drink from his grasp.

"I mean, his name is Damon, and douchebag starts with a D. It's a play on words; I thought you'd be impressed." Camden smiled lazily. "I got us each a double. Figured we'd need it, and now I know we do." He held up his glass to Alessa. "To our health!" he exclaimed in Russian before tilting his head back.

"Bottoms up." Alessa downed the alcohol.

Her face scrunched up in disgust, and he laughed. "Whew. It burns so good," Camden said.

Alessa coughed before handing Camden her empty glass. "If you say so."

Balancing the glasses, he rotated. "I'll be right back. To get through this night, we'll need more liquid courage."

As he headed back to the bar area, a member from the Council of Elders approached the microphone and tapped it, sending a high-pitched squeal resonating throughout the city.

"Good evening, everyone, and thank you for celebrating the founding of New Sparta!"

The crowd erupted into chaos as they hooted and hollered, their cheers echoing off neighboring mountains.

After the boisterous celebration, the speaker raised his hand. "Alright, alright. Silence! We will start the festivities by honoring our Spartan history. A group of our young men in training will perform the pyrrhikhê for us."

Out of the corner of her eye, Alessa noticed Hades leaning against a pillar, sporting a cruel smile with a colorful drink in hand.

Camden snuck up behind Alessa and leaned into her ear. "The fuck is that?"

She gasped, jumping in surprise. "Ah! Don't do that."

Her attention returned to the pillar, but the image of Hades was gone.

As an uneasy chill descended her spine, she took the drink from Camden's extended hand and leaned back into his chest, turning her head to speak. "It's a war dance performed by our people to honor those lost in battle. We Spartans dance every year on the day we celebrate the establishment of New Sparta."

The men on the dance floor held their shields out in front of their naked torsos while rotating their spears in the air. After several minutes of grunting, turning in random patterns, and pretending to fight one another, the music ceased, and the dancing stopped abruptly.

Camden blinked dramatically and lifted his glass to his lips. Throwing back his head, he chugged the alcohol. "Well, I'd be fine if I never have to see that again."

Alessa rolled her eyes and smiled before she finished her drink.

"And now"—he set their empty glasses on a gold-painted

naked waitress's platter—"we dance." Camden jerked his head back toward the painted woman before Alessa laughed and grabbed him by the arm, pulling him toward the dance floor.

As they stood in front of one another, they grinned excitedly.

For the first time in a long time, Alessa had forgotten to be sad and was genuinely having fun.

The music began, and Camden and Alessa stepped backward and forward before extending their right arms at the elbow. Holding it up in front of themselves, they encircled one another.

Dropping their right arm, they raised their left and repeated the action, rotating in the opposite direction.

Camden sauntered toward Alessa and placed his hands on her hips before turning her around. Stepping further into her, he wrapped his arms around her collarbone and pressed her back into him.

"I don't know any of your dances, and since I'm leading, I recommend you just go with it," he whispered in her ear.

Intrigued, Alessa placed her hand on his.

Camden grasped Alessa's hand and rotated out and away before he pulled her back into his chest. Resting his forehead against hers, he looked intensely at Alessa with downward-cast eyes.

They swayed back and forth before Camden pressed into her chest, pushing her back, and stepped forward three steps. He raised her hand above her head and spun Alessa in a fast circle.

Catching her by the elbow, Camden extended Alessa's arm to the side before guiding her to the left. After a quick trot across the illuminated glass dance floor, he lifted her arm, spinning Alessa in a circle.

Camden stopped her, and they were face to face before he spun her back the other way.

Her lips separated into a broad smile, and her heart felt light.

Flying around the dance floor beneath the stars, Camden and Alessa never took their eyes off one another as the tension built between their bodies.

Her heart nearly leapt out of her chest as the music intensified, and her grin widened.

As the music ended, Camden gripped the back of her neck and dipped Alessa.

She stared up into his gorgeous hazel eyes and saw a primal need she recognized from Damon in the past but had never seen in Camden before.

With the song's ending, Camden stood her upright and pressed her against the front of his vest. Their chests rose in unison as they looked into one another's eyes.

Sensing someone's gaze, Camden's eyes darted behind Alessa. He saw Quade standing amongst the crowd, signaling for Camden to meet with him with a nod to the side.

Camden sighed. "Looks like I'm being summoned."

Alessa turned around and saw her friend staring intently at them. "All right. Go see what he wants."

He grasped her chin between his thumb and first finger. "Do not get into trouble while I am gone."

Rolling her eyes, she grinned mischievously. "I don't seek out trouble; it always seems to find me."

"Either way..." He released Alessa from his hold before lifting her hand to his mouth. His dark gaze lifted to Alessa's eyes as he pressed his lips against her fingers.

Alessa's breathing hitched with the intensity of his gaze,

and she stared at his playful grin before he turned his back and walked away.

Taken aback by the strange feelings stirring deep inside, Alessa whipped around to leave the dance floor when she crashed into someone's chest.

"Oh! I'm—" Alessa faded, looking up into Damon's blue eyes.

He laughed nervously. "Where are you off to in such a hurry?"

"Um, nowhere, really. Just away." As she tried to get by Damon, he grabbed her elbow.

"Dance with me," Damon demanded.

Alessa narrowed her eyes as she looked up at him. "What about Brielle? Where is she?"

"Let me worry about her. Alessa, please. Just one dance." His thumb rubbed back and forth on the back of her arm.

Alessa's heart felt as though it were caught in a vice. Incapable of speaking, she nodded slowly.

He led Alessa onto the dance floor, and they put their hands in front of one another, as the specific dance requested.

They stepped toward one another before stepping back away. While spinning Alessa in place, Damon saw the tattoo on her right inner arm, identical to his, and his breathing stopped for a moment before he regained his wits.

Alessa's back stiffened, and she froze as Damon touched her stomach. She closed her eyes, feeling the heat from his trailing fingertips as they danced across the front of her beaded torso.

He cleared his throat. "Beautiful dress," he complimented.

Alessa chuckled at the thought of him having seen the dress before in Chicago. "Oh? You didn't used to think so."

Damon stepped before Alessa and held his hand above her,

awaiting her to place her hand in his. His eyebrows furrowed. "What's that supposed to mean?"

She sighed before raising her hand to his. "Never mind."

Damon spun Alessa several times while his free hand guided her by the waist. "So, what's his story?" He pulled Alessa into his chest and wrapped his arm around her, placing his hand upon her lower back.

"Who?" Alessa asked as they stepped to the side, one foot over the other.

He leaned her slowly to the side. "The blondie."

"His name is Cam, and I don't understand why you keep asking me about him. But, if you must know, we're just friends. Why do you keep asking? It's not like you believe a word I say," Alessa spat angrily.

Damon lifted Alessa, rotating her in a circle.

As Alessa glared at Damon, he grew visibly frustrated. "It's not that I don't—I've always believed you. You've never given me a reason not to."

They placed their hands in one another and stepped one foot over the other in the opposite direction before Damon spun Alessa around.

As she crashed into Damon's chest, Alessa's heart fluttered, and her insides burned. "Why is this time any different?"

As they looked into one another's eyes, they spun around the dance floor, their bodies moving due to muscle memory.

The song neared its end and Alessa touched Damon's cheek. His eyes closed and he tilted his head to the side. "I don't understand it," he said, opening his eyes and looking questioningly into hers. "The moment I see you, my insides ball in a knot, and I feel—I feel..." Damon trailed off.

"What do you feel?" Her throat tightened as she held back the fleeting feeling of hope.

He shook his head in dismissal. "But, then, with Brielle—it's like this uncontrollable need to be with her. It's almost—"

"Unnatural?"

As the music ended, Damon placed his hand on Alessa's and removed her hand from his face.

Stepping toward him, she begged. "Come back to me, Damon. Please come back."

Feeling the familiarity of those words, he blinked in confusion before pressing his fingertips into the sides of his temples. Looking behind Alessa, he saw Brielle staring daggers at them. "Bri..."

Alessa watched in dismay as Damon rushed off the dance floor toward the other woman.

Looking frantically around the dance floor, she caught the eye of every Spartan in attendance, including Camden, before running toward the empty glass gazebo at the far end of the field.

Hot, angry tears spilled down her face as she flew past the partying Spartans, and she ran up the few stairs before falling into the gazebo's railing.

"Fuck!" she screamed, cursing at the night sky.

As she cried up at the stars, the sky flickered dark purple before returning to its onyx-black color. Alessa wiped the tears from her eyes and tried to focus on the sky. "What was that?"

The alcohol kicked in just in time to interfere with her stepping over the railing, and she landed hard in the grass.

"Oh..." She wiped the tears. "That was weird."

After brushing off her skirt, Alessa stood up and walked unsteadily toward the full moon. "Good timing," she congratulated the alcoholic stupor as she plopped down in the grassy field and passed out cold.

CHAPTER TWENTY-ONE

Alessa awoke with a groan as the bright morning sun shone through her closed eyelids. "Ugh, my head."

Throwing back the covers, Alessa discovered she had been undressed down to her bra and panties. "Wait, how did I get home? And in my bed?"

Grabbing her thin housecoat from the hook on the wall, Alessa opened her bedroom door and stepped into the hallway. With eyes half-closed, she palmed her way along the wall to the kitchen, where Camden sat at the small table drinking a cup of coffee.

"Good morning, Sunshine," he grinned, lifting the mug to his lips. His eyes scanned her head to toe as her housecoat sloppily hung open.

"Mmm," she painfully groaned in response.

He handed Alessa an orange-colored liquid inside of a clear glass. "Your elder made you this tonic; says it'll help you. Drink up."

Her face scrunched up in disgust as she smelled its contents. "What is it?"

"I'm not exactly sure, but I recommend not focusing too much on the tiny chunks floating around."

Alessa dry heaved.

Camden chuckled. "Just chug it."

After exhaling loudly, Alessa shook her head, working up the courage to guzzle it down. "Bottoms up," she said, tilting her head back and drinking its contents.

"Gross," Camden said in Russian.

Her body shivered from head to toe. "You didn't have to drink it," Alessa scoffed.

He sipped his coffee, hiding his entertained grin. "True."

Alessa rinsed the glass in the sink. "How did I make it home last night?"

"Oh, that's a funny story. I was making a new friend with a woman Quade had introduced me to when, to my surprise, I saw this incapacitated individual fall over a gazebo railing. When I went to go check on said person, I found her passed out."

Alessa grimaced, blushing with embarrassment.

"And with the night's festivities only getting more—"

"Oh, I know how they get." Alessa poured herself a cup of coffee.

"I did not feel comfortable leaving until I had her safe in her bed."

"So, we didn't—" She pointed back and forth between her and Camden.

He eyed her, and an eyebrow arched. "Does it feel like we did?"

She shifted her hips back and forth, accidentally allowing her housecoat to fall open a bit more, exposing her underwear and bra. "No, I guess not."

After swallowing the lump in his throat from watching her

wiggle about, Camden cleared his throat. "Trust me, if we had, you'd know it."

Her eyebrows raised, and she slowly nodded, closing her housecoat in slow motion. "Uh-huh, well, thank you for taking care of me, and I'm sorry for not allowing you time to *make friends*." Alessa did air quotes.

"Yeah, well," he walked over to the counter and stood in front of Alessa before bending her backward and placing his mug in the sink directly behind her.

Alessa's thin housecoat opened further as she bent backward, and Camden's chest brushed up against her breasts.

"I only care about one friend," he said, his hot breath caressing Alessa's lips.

Alessa's elder burst in through the front door to the cabin. "Morning!"

Alessa whipped around and dropped her mug in the sink as Camden stepped back with a smirk. "Good morning, sir."

Alessa's elder beamed. "I have excellent news. I've just come from the Council of Elders, and after consulting with the Consilium, they have agreed to investigate Lucas Greenfield."

"What is a Consilium?" asked Camden.

Alessa turned around, holding her housecoat together. "The Consilium is the worldwide group of elders with the final say in everything we do. Damon's father is the leader."

"Interesting. Okay, then. That's great news." Camden pointed at Alessa. "You need to get dressed. We need to get to training."

"Yes," her elder agreed. "I will be helping the two of you step up your training. You need to remember what it's like to get your ass kicked so you know how to recover and keep fighting."

Alessa eagerly nodded. "Thank you. This is one step closer

to getting Kai back. Do you think they will grant me access to surveillance footage at each of their taste tests? I know they have several more scheduled over the next few weeks."

Her elder poured himself a cup of hot coffee. "I don't see why not. But they still can't know about Kai. That will have to be handled delicately."

Alessa stared down at the floor. "Because she's a traitor in their eyes."

"Precisely," her elder agreed.

Alessa looked up at Camden, and their eyes met. "Um, I should go get some clothes on."

Camden cleared his throat and pointed out the front door. "I'll wait for you out front."

Her elder narrowed his eyes as he watched Camden exit the cabin, and then, turning around, he watched Alessa disappear around the corner into her room.

"I'm excited to get back to my medical training with Sera," she hollered from the bedroom.

Alessa's elder stood outside her bedroom with his coffee in hand and his back pressed against the wall. "Uh-huh."

"I mean, don't get me wrong, I like finding my strengths and encouraging my abilities to grow, but I'd like to have a change of pace; break it up a little."

Her elder cleared his throat. "You certainly have your work cut out for you. Training physically, mentally, searching for your sister... So, Camden and you seem to be getting rather close."

"Yeah, well, he's my best friend. Sera has Quade and is busy being a mother, a wife, a doctor, and a mentor, and Quade is a father, a husband, a warrior, and a guard. They're all too busy, and I don't need to involve them. Cam has my back and is helping me find Kai." Alessa emerged from her bedroom and stood in the hallway across from her elder. "He's my strongest ally right now, besides you."

Her elder pulled Alessa into a tight embrace. "You are never alone. I will always be here for you." He pointed at her head before moving his finger to her heart. "Whether it's in here or in here."

CHAPTER TWENTY-TWO

Three weeks passed quickly as Camden and Alessa trained physically and mentally with her elder.

Forced to keep his true identity a secret, Camden fought as any other person in the general population would, keeping his activation under wraps, which was more challenging than he thought it would be.

Alessa had kept her distance from Brielle as per her orders, and on the other side of New Sparta, Damon had started looking into Lucas Greenfield as instructed by the Council of Elders.

Damon focused on the computer screen in front of him as Brielle complained in the background.

"I don't understand. Explain to me again why you won't get the implant?" she whined.

Damon leaned forward, focusing on his research. "I hate this fucking computer. I miss my laptop. I loved that thing."

Brielle strolled up behind him, wrapped her arms around his shoulders, and placed her hands on his pecs. "Damon, I'm talking to you."

He jumped with her touch. "Yes, what? I'm sorry, I'm a little busy," he half-heartedly apologized.

"Why won't you just get the implant?"

"Oh, that again," he groaned, shutting off his monitor. "I've told you, I don't like the idea of being tracked, of opening my mind up for possible hackers."

He stood up, and her hands dropped.

"But your people have run test after test, and it's been proven safe every time. They need someone they trust, like you, to take a leap of faith. Someone has to be the first to get the implant. You'll be able to access so much more information! The World Wide Web will essentially be available to you at all times. You'll be unstoppable." Brielle wrapped her arms around his neck and stood up on her tiptoes.

"Besides, sugar bear, your mind is too strong to be hacked." Her deep red lips separated into a seductive smile before she leaned in and kissed him.

Damon pulled back after pecking her on the lips and removed her hands from around his neck. "I'd love to continue this, but I must meet with Quade." He snatched his black leather jacket off the back of a nearby chair and opened the front door.

Running to the door, she rubbed her fingertips against the locket dangling around her neck before calling out for him. "Damon! One last kiss."

His eyes flashed silver as her fingers pressed into her necklace, and with a deep inhale, he leaned down and kissed her again. He shook his head back and forth, and his eyes turned back to blue. "I've got to go."

She leaned out the doorframe. "Hurry home to me."

Watching him leave, she huffed aloud. "It's getting harder

to control him. I need to convince him to get that implant, and soon."

On his way to meet Quade, Damon slowed down as he passed Alessa's house. He watched Camden leave the cabin, and the instinctual urge to check in on her kicked in.

Damon rubbed his hands together, nervously approaching the front porch, and marched up the few steps to the front door. Turning the handle, he opened the wooden door and cleared his throat as he entered the familiar living room. "Hello?"

Recognizing the sound of a shower, Damon stood frozen in the entryway. As the sound of water ceased, Alessa stepped out into the hallway, wrapped up in a towel, utterly oblivious to his presence.

While walking barefoot into her bedroom, she peeled the towel from around her body, and it pooled on the floor behind her feet.

Damon's breathing hitched as she strolled naked into her bedroom. Wiping imaginary sweat from his brow, he panicked. "Fuck. I shouldn't be here." Against his better judgment, he allowed his instincts to take control, and he followed her to the bedroom, where he stood quietly, watching her dress.

After wiggling into a pair of panties, she pulled the straps of her bra on before she turned to face the hallway.

Damon ducked back behind the doorframe as Alessa grabbed a black tank top from the bed.

As Alessa approached the full-length mirror propped up against the wall, Damon snuck back around the corner. His gaze landed on her stomach, and his eyes nearly bulged out of their sockets as he saw her abdominal scar in the reflection.

Forgetting Alessa didn't know he was there, the door slammed against the wall as Damon rushed into the room. "Dear gods. Alessa, what did they do to you?"

"Shit!" she screamed, whipping around. "What are you—"

He placed his hands firmly on her hips and twisted her around to face him. Falling before her, Damon gasped. "I know you said they tortured you, but—"

Grasping the bottom of her shirt from just below her breasts, Alessa pulled the fabric down, covering the scar. "Damon, stop it, please—"

Ignoring her resistance, Damon pulled up the bottom of her shirt, and his fingertips nearly touched the raised edges of her scar. Jerking back, she tugged her shirt back into place.

Damon's face contorted in pain. "To leave a scar like that—"

Alessa turned away from him, her face blushing red in anger. "Yes, Damon. I am well aware of what someone goes through to have a scar like that," she snapped.

Wiggling into a pair of forest green women's cargo pants, Alessa huffed. "What are you doing here? I highly doubt it was to crash my getting dressed and tell me how terrible a scar I have." She sat on her bed and tugged on a pair of black combat boots while awaiting his answer.

Adrenaline was pumping, and he flexed his hands to make them stop shaking. "Uh, no, I..." He cleared his throat. "I was passing by and saw Camden leave."

She zipped up the side of her boot. "You saw my friend leave and wanted to check in on me? I haven't seen or heard from you in weeks. What made you want to see me now?"

Damon dug his hands into his cargo pants pockets. "Hey, just because we're not together anymore, it does not mean my feelings for you vanish. I still care about you."

Bemused, she chuckled. "You care about me. So much so that you choose to stay with the woman who killed you?"

His eyes rolled back into his head, and his entire body recoiled. "Not this again—"

"Damon, I can't do this right now. What do you want from me?" she asked, stepping toward him. "You don't want me anymore. You've made that abundantly clear, so why are you here, alone with me, in my room?" She took another step toward him. "What do you expect from me?"

He sighed, noticing her still wearing the ring he gave her when they were together. "When I saw him come out of your cabin, knowing your elder isn't home—I mean, you're already breaking the rules by having an outsider here..."

Her face scrunched up as she laughed sarcastically. "So you came into my home unannounced to watch me dress to uphold my honor? Have you lost your mind? Besides, my relationships are none of your business. So what if me and Cam were screwing each other every single night, all night long, fucking until all we can do is pass out beside one another, unable to utter a single word because all our strength was used screaming one another's names in ecstasy?"

Picturing them together, Damon's jaw muscles flexed, and his cheeks burned.

Alessa leaned in toward him, tears threatening to spill over her eyelashes. "That's what I thought," her voice cracked.

Walking around Damon, she headed for the front door.

He ran before her, blocking her path. "I would hate it, okay? I hate the thought of another man touching you, let alone"—he swallowed—"making love to you."

"You're one to talk. How do you think I feel about you and your bitch?"

Damon tilted his head toward Alessa. "Her name is Brielle."

"I said what I said. Now, get out of my way," she growled.

He stood firm in his stance. "I don't think it's appropriate for you to have brought an outsider into our home."

Alessa glared at Damon incredulously. "Are you kidding me right now? What is Brielle, again? Oh yeah, an outsider." She marched up to him and was mere inches from his lips, glaring up into his eyes. "It doesn't matter what you think anymore. I'm. Not. Yours. Anymore. Now, MOVE."

Damon blinked back what felt like the sting of tears as he shrunk back.

Her eyes flashed blood red. "I highly suggest you move on your own accord before I make you."

Stepping to the side, he finally allowed Alessa to pass.

Watching her storm out the front door, Damon shook his head in confusion as he shrunk to the floorboards. "What is happening to me?"

CHAPTER TWENTY-THREE

Lucas Greenfield stood in front of a green screen displaying a picturesque video of a sugar cane field beneath a clear blue sky. "Greenfield Farms: the future of health," he said into the camera as it panned away.

The commercial's director tipped his head toward Lucas. "That was great. Everyone take a fifteen-minute break."

Lucas Greenfield loosened his necktie while marching offset to the private dressing room. His adult nephew, Cain, was close behind.

Once in his room, Lucas plopped down in his chair before groaning in front of the large mirror. "I am too exhausted to keep up this front."

Cain quickly closed the door behind them. "You can go back home after today's recordings. We should have enough footage to pique the public's interest in our product."

The reporter's voice was projected from the television in the background.

"In local news, a violent brawl broke out at a popular bar this evening. Everyone interviewed at the scene says the attack was unprovoked, and only moments earlier, the suspects were laughing and having a good time.

Fifteen individuals were killed, including the suspects, and fourteen were injured. Unfortunately, at the time police arrived, the five suspects continued their rampage and would not stop the attack."

"Cain, son," Lucas said. "Turn that babbling woman off, will you?"

With the press of a button, the news reporter was silenced, and the screen blackened.

Sitting in front of the mirror, Lucas stared at his reflection, rotating his face back and forth. "I am grateful for this younger, stronger man's vitality. I am sure it will be of good use to me."

The dressing room's door opened, and Kai stepped in. "You are doing an incredible job."

She closed the door, and her high heels clicked across the floor as she handed Lucas a thin folder containing the following week's schedule. "Your interview with Good Morning America has been moved from Friday to tomorrow."

"What?" he demanded, his angry eyes piercing Kai's.

Her eyes darted back and forth between Cain and Lucas's. "Their rep called just a little bit ago, but if you need us to move it, we can—"

"No. No, that's fine," he dismissed her with a flick of his wrist.

"Eric, it's no—"

Before she had time to correct her mistake, Lucas's hand smacked the side of her cheek, and she fell to the floor.

Cain didn't move as he stood tall above Kai, disgust written across his face.

Tears sprung to her eyes with the reddening of her cheek. "I—I—I'm sorry." Kai swallowed. "Lucas."

Pulling his pant legs up, Lucas crouched down in front of Kai, placing his hand on the side of her face. "You will never say that name again. I am Lucas, now; Lucas Greenfield."

Kai lay stunned on the floor, her hand covering the stinging mark left on her cheek. "I—I understand. It will never happen again."

Standing upright, Lucas adjusted his metal cufflinks. "Interviewing with Good Morning America tomorrow morning will work. I hoped to get home sooner rather than later, but spreading the word about our product is worth pushing back my few days of relaxation."

After his uncle left the room, Cain held his hand out for Kai and helped her up by her elbow.

Standing up, she swayed back and forth, blinking the dots from her vision.

"You okay?" he asked.

Forcing a smile, Kai nodded jerkily. "Yes, I should've never let that slip. I am so, so sorry."

Cain removed her hand and pressed his lips gently against the discolored spot on Kai's cheek.

"My uncle means well. It's just that a slip-up like that could mean life or death. You must be more careful; consider the big picture and what we will achieve with our product." He placed his thumb and first finger on Kai's chin, holding her firmly. "You know I love you, my pet?"

The stinging of her cheek subsided as the joy in her heart overrode the pain. "I love you, too," she smiled.

He wrapped his arms around her waist and pulled Kai in for a kiss. "You know, we couldn't have made it this far without you."

Kai winced with the pain of Cain's lips on hers, forcing her cheekbone to feel the brunt of it.

He walked toward the exit, pointing at Kai before leaving the room. "You should put some makeup on that; it looks like it's going to bruise."

Kai plastered a slight smile on her face before rotating to face the mirror. She grabbed a makeup brush and a dab of coverup from a tube, and as she glanced up at her reflection, Kai eyed the darkening spot.

Stroking the brush across her skin, she applied a streak of tanned liquid over the bruise.

CHAPTER TWENTY-FOUR

Alessa slammed open the surveillance room's door before she grumbled incoherently and plopped down in a chair beside Camden.

Rotating his chair to face her, he raised an eyebrow. "You okay?"

"Yeah, it's just—I'm fine," she barked. "I'm looking forward to this distraction right now, and later on today, I'm meeting up with Seraphine to continue where we left off with my medical training. So, I have nothing but great things to look forward to. Now, where are we with Greenfield?"

He slowly rotated back toward the three-dimensional image projected in front of them. "Uh, okay then. Lucas is currently in Atlanta."

"Another one of their taste tests?"

He pointed at the crowd and zoomed in on the individuals eating and drinking the products laced with the modified sugar. "They're growing in popularity. If I weren't so afraid of what would happen if I consumed the sugar substitute, I'd be tempted to try it."

Alessa strolled up to the holographic image. "That's just one of the questions I have. What are they playing at? You and I know nothing good can come out of this if Eric is behind the ploy. What is their end game, and what will this do to all these innocent people? How are Eric and Lucas linked? I can't figure it out, and it's eating me alive." She blew out a puff of air in frustration and crossed her arms.

"That's why the elders sent in your people to get footage like this. We need to find the link between Lucas and Eric. One based on facts, not your feelings."

They continued watching the live feed provided by the fellow undercover Spartans, who were hidden in plain sight amongst the crowd.

As the music faded, the crowd clapped and cheered in anticipation.

Camden leaned back in his chair, propping one leg atop the other. While leaning to one side, he set his elbow on the arm of his chair and balled his hand into a fist, pressing it against his lips.

The ever-handsome Lucas Greenfield approached the microphone, sporting a huge grin. Stretching his neck to the left, he exposed a small circular scar before starting his speech.

"Stop!" Alessa screamed, jumping up and pointing her finger at the scene.

Camden held up his two fingers in mid-air, pausing the footage.

Spinning her left hand, Alessa rewound to when Lucas stretched his neck. Timidly walking forward, she approached the man's three-dimensional image.

Standing before him, Alessa reached out, stopping herself just before touching his neck.

"What?"

She glanced off to the side. "But that can't be."

"What is it?" Camden urged.

Alessa looked back up at Lucas and narrowed her eyes. "I'm not sure how he did it, but somehow, this *is* Eric."

Camden uncrossed his leg and sat upright in his chair. "Excuse me? Did you just say what I think you did?"

Alessa looked up at the image in awe. "Lucas Greenfield *is* Eric Lansing. They are one and the same."

"No, no. That's not possible." Camden stared up at Lucas Greenfield. "Is it?"

Alessa cocked her head and looked back at her friend. "You sit there, telling a Spartan with a microchip implanted in her brain that has fucked up so royally it has given her the ability to control technology that someone changing their appearance isn't possible?"

Camden's face scrunched up in defeat. "Touché. So, what, you think he pulled a *Face/Off*?"

Zooming in, she grabbed his image from the screen, separating him from the rest of the footage. "I think it's even more advanced than that. I see no resemblance to Eric Lansing except his mannerisms and the scar he once showed me."

She stared at the handsome middle-aged man, looking him up and down from head to toe. "I can't present this as evidence to the council to convince them this is Eric. I won't be taken seriously."

Camden leaned forward onto his knees. "Not yet, at least."

Relaxing her eyes, Alessa glanced behind the figure of Lucas Greenfield into the background of the picture. "Oh, my gods."

Camden rubbed his freshly shaven chin. "What now?"

Alessa moved hesitantly toward the group of people in the

projection. Using her fingers, she moved the bodies standing before a woman with toffee brown hair.

"Kai," Alessa whispered. Extending her hand forward, her fingertips disappeared into the woman's projected image.

Camden's eyes widened. "Is that—"

She nodded her head as tears welled in her eyes. "Yes. It's Kai."

"What is she doing working for Eric Lansing?" Camden walked up behind Alessa.

She swallowed the ball of emotion creeping up the back of her throat. "I'm not sure, but we can't say anything to the elders about this. We can't tell anyone."

Alessa closed her eyes and focused on destroying the image in her mind before opening her red irises. The audio became a low screeching noise as the image turned into fluorescent zig-zagged lines.

Camden's jaw dropped. "Did you just destroy the file?"

"I had no choice. If anyone realized that was my sister, they'd send in an assassin. In the eyes of my people, she's a traitor. And unless I can prove otherwise, she doesn't stand a chance of a fair trial."

Camden shook his head back and forth and placed his hands on Alessa's upper arms. "This is a dangerous game you're playing. Are you sure about this?"

Unglitching, she stared at the lines stretching across the corrupted file. "I don't have a choice. She's the only family I have left. I have to save her."

Camden wrapped his arms around Alessa and held her against his chest. "If you truly believe Lucas Greenfield is Eric Lansing, we must resume your microchip training."

Alessa pressed back and stepped out of his embrace. "Agreed. We need to be ready for anything."

CHAPTER TWENTY-FIVE

The following day, Alessa's elder was packing a backpack in the living room.

Mid-yawn, she mumbled, "Morning," as she leaned over the counter and poured herself a cup of coffee. "Where are you heading?"

He side-eyed Alessa while stuffing clothes in his bag. "You know better than to ask questions."

"Never hurts to try." She blew the steam away from the mug she was grasping while leaning against the kitchen counter. "How long will you be gone?"

"I'm not sure, a few weeks? A month?"

Staring off into the distance, her thoughts about Kai ran wild.

Her elder pressed his lips together. "Alessa, are you okay?

"Hmm?"

He sighed. "I know you and Damon aren't on the best terms, but I need you to attend his class today. I've already sent Camden on ahead."

"You did what?" Alessa scanned the room. "Why do we need to—"

Alessa's elder held his hand up to silence her. "Stop. You know Damon is your best chance at honing your skills. If you plan on engaging with Bodyguards soon, you must be mentally and physically prepared. Last night, the gods sent me a message in the form of a dream."

She sighed before drinking her hot coffee. "And? What did they tell you?"

He zipped his bag. "You are about to be tested."

Alessa blinked and looked down into her coffee cup. "In what way?"

"In more than one way." He swallowed. "And there's nothing I can do—I am not to interfere, so I am trying my best to do what I am allowed."

"What does that mean? Do you know what is going to happen? Will I bring Kai home?" She stood up straight, her voice dripping with excitement.

Exhaling loudly, her elder slung his backpack over his shoulder and pressed his lips against Alessa's forehead before nodding.

She beamed as he turned around. "Did they tell you when or how?"

Alessa's elder pursed his lips and shook his head while he opened the front door. "Be safe, my eldest daughter of Sparta."

He closed the door behind him, ending Alessa's interrogation.

With newfound energy and excitement, she rushed to get ready and ran out the front door.

Taking a shortcut to the academy where Damon was teaching, Alessa entered the gardens. Turning the corner, she was violently struck in the neck.

Her back made a *thud* as it smacked the ground, and her head immediately followed, ricocheting off the hard surface. Gasping for air, Alessa's throat made high-pitched noises from being closed off from the impact of the person's arm.

Emerging from behind the tall bush, Brielle grinned in satisfaction as she watched Alessa writhe in pain. "Stay away from Damon."

Alessa massaged her sore neck. "Or what?" she squeaked.

Brielle fingered the locket dangling from her neck and leaned down over Alessa menacingly. "More than anyone else, you know what I'm capable of. Don't. Fuck. With. Me," she growled before turning around.

Alessa sat on the ground, catching her breath. She focused on her breathing as well as burying her rage down deep so she didn't end up killing Brielle right then and there.

Game on, bitch.

Walking into the building, Alessa rubbed the sides of her trachea while stretching her neck's sore muscles as she stepped up beside Camden.

He looked at her out of the corner of his eye. "You okay?"

"Mmm." Alessa flashed a false smile while attempting to focus on Damon at the front of the room.

Next to the olive-skinned teacher was a short, pale woman standing with her hands clasped behind her back. She paced back and forth, staring out into the crowd. A strip of freckles danced across her nose, and her bright red hair stood out against her deep brown eyes.

"This is Lexi. She is a new addition to this compound from our Motherland, Greece. We've actually known one another since childhood, and I can say from experience we are honored to have her join us here in the United States."

She ceased moving back and forth, stopping directly next to

Damon. Raising her eyes to his, she asked him in an Irish accent, "What do you say we give 'em a little show?"

Damon scoffed and rubbed his hands together. "Oh, I don't think they'd—"

Camden cupped his hands around his mouth and bellowed across the room. "I think they would."

Meeting Camden's defiant glare and grin, Damon scowled. Turning back to face Lexi, he forced a smile. "Okay, then."

Lexi's eyes lit up as she positioned herself on one side of the line in the middle of the room. "It's been too long, old friend."

Damon shook his head and stood in front of her on the other side, leaning down toward her.

The woman's left eyebrow arched as she grinned mischievously. "It has been too long since you have had your ass handed to you, that is."

Damon's features scrunched up. "The fuck are you talking about?"

"Go!" she yelled with a huge smile plastered across her face.

Grabbing for his neck, Lexi wrapped her right arm around him as she threw her body across the line. Jumping past Damon, she smacked the back of his head playfully with a loud giggle.

Growling at her inability to take anything seriously, Damon lunged for her.

Unfortunately for Damon, Lexi used being small to her advantage. As he danced forward, she side-stepped out of his way.

Anticipating her step to the side, Damon jabbed Lexi in the ribs.

She stepped forward unsteadily and kicked above his head. Wrapping her legs around Damon's neck, Lexi squeezed her thighs around his windpipe before she slammed him down to the ground.

"Oh!" the whole room echoed at the sound of his body hitting the mat.

Damon grunted aloud as his back hit the thick mat. *Motherfucker.*

Using his fist to punch through the tiny gap she had made between him and her, Damon used his brute strength to separate them. Grabbing hold of her thighs, he lifted her over his head, but, yet again, she got the best of him.

After coiling herself around him like a snake, Lexi pulled out a small baton from the side of her thigh. Whipping it out, the rod extended, and she smacked his lower back.

As he fell to his knees, she squeezed his windpipe closed with her thighs.

"Give?" she asked, sporting a wicked grin.

With blood vessels popping in the whites of his eyes, Damon held his fingers up, signaling his acceptance of defeat.

Lexi held her hand out, releasing him from her grasp and helping him to his feet.

The room erupted in hushed whispers and excited smiles. The students didn't know whether to clap or be upset that this new person had just taken down one of their greatest teachers.

"Wow..." Alessa hissed.

"What?" Camden smiled big.

"Damon doesn't lose. Ever. You don't understand how significant this is. Something must be off."

Camden waved a hand in dismissal. "Eh, I'm sure it's nothing. The guy's bound to lose sometime."

Blood seeped in between Lexi's white teeth as she smiled at the crowd. "Getting old already?" she asked.

Damon rubbed his neck while addressing Lexi. "I took it easy on you, being my childhood friend."

Lexi's eyes flared as she flashed a sideways grin while entering the crowd. "Justify it however you'd like. But a loss is still a loss." She winked.

He cleared his throat and attempted to project his voice toward the room full of Spartans. "On that note, I will have you join small groups and practice skills for the next half hour."

Locking eyes with Alessa, Lexi moved through the crowd toward her and Camden, standing at the back of the class, away from the others.

Lexi approached the two as they stretched their limbs. "Mind if I join you?"

Alessa nodded toward the rest of the Spartans. "Wouldn't you feel more comfortable not making friends with the outcasts?"

Lexi shook her head while wiping the sweat from her brow. "No, I wouldn't."

"Haven't you been warned about the woman with the red glowing eyes?"

Lexi's eyes grew wide. "Is that you?" she asked excitedly.

Alessa looked straight at Lexi and thought of Brielle. As the hatred stirred inside her, Alessa's eyes flashed red.

Lexi stepped forward toward Alessa. "That is incredible."

Alessa stopped stretching her arm and cocked her head to the side, intrigued. "You're truly not afraid?"

"Why would I be afraid? You're like any other Spartan but with a much cooler activation color."

Camden snickered. "And except for the fact she could make your head explode."

Lexi's jaw dropped. "Really?" she asked, her voice dripping with excitement.

Entertained by her reaction, Camden's eyes squinted, and he sported a half-grin. "You are a bit messed up in the head, aren't you?"

Lexi chuckled. "Wouldn't be the first time I've been told that." She glanced from Camden to Alessa. "So what's with the red activation? Of all the colors we could change to, I've never seen red."

Alessa sighed, mentally preparing herself for the emotionally draining conversation she was about to have. "I went through some pretty intense trauma, and it caused my microchip to glitch, which gave me the ability to control technology."

"Gods. You're a technopath?"

Camden's eyes narrowed. "Exactly. I'm surprised you know anything about the subject. When we arrived, everyone treated Alessa like an alien."

Lexi looked past Camden at Damon, standing at the front, who was talking to Brielle. "That is the weirdest thing."

Camden followed her gaze. "What is?"

"Never thought I'd see Damon in a serious relationship."

"He's not," Alessa aggressively shot back at her with red cheeks.

"Oh." Lexi eyed Camden, who shook his head no in response to her unspoken question. "My mistake." Changing the subject, Lexi punched the air. "I'd be curious to hear the entire backstory when you have time."

Alessa glanced over at a distracted Damon. "Wanna get out of here and head to the gym? I can show you a few moves I've been working on."

Lexi grinned excitedly. "Oh, hell yes."

Camden scanned the room. "They all seem pretty distracted. Let's go."

They snuck out the nearest door, closing it quietly behind them, and ran laughing toward the gym.

"What's your accent?" Alessa asked upon entering the gym.

Lexi breathed through the stitch in her side. "Celtic."

Camden smiled at her. "I like it."

Blushing, Lexi looked away. "And yours? I hear a hint of, what, Russian?"

"Very good," Camden said in his native tongue. "I'm impressed."

"I did grow up with Russia nearby." Lexi clapped her hands together. "Enough talk. I want to see what Alessa is capable of."

CHAPTER TWENTY-SIX

Sweat dripped from Camden and Alessa as they sparred in front of Lexi.

Grinning wickedly, Alessa's eyes glitched a fiery red as she focused all her energy on the microchip buried deep inside his brain.

Camden's hands sprung to the sides of his head, and as she brought him down to his knees, blood poured from his nose, and he grunted in agony.

Enough. Alessa unglitched, and her eyes returned to their pale blue hue.

Camden exhaled loudly as he caught the towel Lexi had thrown his way.

Lexi's face furrowed as she watched Camden collapse to the floor. "You doing okay, there?"

"I'm sorry, Cam," Alessa apologized, placing her hand on his upper back.

He grabbed her hand. "Don't be." Camden wiped the blood away with the fluffy white towel. "You need to practice on someone, and who better than someone as strong as I am?" he laughed wholeheartedly.

"Wow." Lexi stared in awe. "That was riveting."

Embarrassed by all the attention, Alessa's cheeks reddened as she helped Camden up to his feet. "We need a break."

With his nose still actively bleeding, Camden wiped the blood away with a clean tissue before shoving a bit of another one up his nostril. After washing his hands, he turned around toward the Spartans. "Food?" he asked, hopeful.

Alessa eagerly nodded her head. "Food."

"Yes! Maybe we can beat the lunch rush." Camden sprinted out the doors.

Lexi and Alessa followed Camden out into the glass-covered hallway.

"So, what branch are you?" Alessa asked Lexi.

"Warrior. And my secondary is historian."

"Well, that has to be interesting. In my late teens, I enjoyed reading up on Spartan history, but I haven't had much time these days to sit and read."

Lexi bobbed eagerly. "It is; I really enjoy it. What is yours?"

"Warrior and medical."

Lexi shivered. "Oh. I can handle blood and guts on the battlefield; I just can't put it all back together. I can't visualize how all the parts go together and what they should look like through all the chaos."

Walking into the mess hall, Alessa could feel the air in the room become tense. As her eyes met Damon's gaze, her breathing hitched, and she looked away.

Camden shook his head and scrunched his face up in a sarcastic grin. "It's not like everyone stopping and staring at us is awkward in the least bit. Nope, not at all. Let's grab some food and get out of here." Camden pointed at Alessa. "Don't you fuck this up for me; I'm starving. You leave Brielle alone," he instructed before jogging up to the counter.

Brielle stood up from her seat at the table near Damon and strolled over to Alessa. Cutting off Lexi, she stepped directly behind her enemy. "Poor baby, your neck looks a bit bruised. You feelin' okay?" she asked with a smug grin.

Fuming, Alessa ground her teeth together to keep from glitching right then and there. She pumped her fists while struggling to keep her rage in check.

"I'd watch it if I were you," Brielle whispered menacingly into Alessa's ear.

Alessa's heart rate spiked, and she could feel the burning behind her eyes. "Is that supposed to scare me?" Alessa growled.

Noticing Brielle standing close to Alessa, warning bells sounded in Damon's head, and he hurried over in their direction.

Brielle spied Damon walking over to them, and she smiled sadistically. "It should."

In the blink of an eye, Alessa snatched a food tray from the stack before them and whipped around, smacking Brielle upside the head.

With a thud, Brielle hit the ground, and Alessa tossed the tray onto the floor beside her with a loud bang.

Damon dropped to his knees, lifting a dazed Brielle into his arms. "The fuck? Alessa! The council will—"

"They won't do shit. I promised not to kill her; not once did I say I wouldn't strike the bitch if she deserved it. And boy, did she deserve it."

Damon stared up at Alessa, confused by her act of violence.

Alessa turned toward Camden. "Will you grab me

something to eat? I need to get out of here; the smell of bullshit is making me sick."

Lexi stared at Alessa with a slack jaw before she started laughing hysterically.

"You got it." Camden nodded before jogging down the food line.

Following her out of the mess hall, Lexi chuckled. "I don't know what that was about, but it was *badass*. Remind me never to get on your bad side."

Alessa couldn't help but smile at the woman making light of the situation and was grateful for her light-heartedness.

After grabbing several burritos and sauce packets, Camden sprinted after them as they exited the building.

Catching up to the women further up the path, Camden handed them their food as they continued walking.

Alessa took the burrito and a sauce packet. "Thanks."

"Thank you." Lexi smiled at Camden before unwrapping her burrito. "So, what was all that about?" she asked before taking a bite from her large wrap.

"Oh, um..." Alessa took a bite of her burrito, chewed, and swallowed the hot meat before continuing.

With a full mouth, Camden nudged Alessa. "You might as well just tell her. She's going to find out sooner or later."

Rolling her eyes, Alessa inhaled deeply before choosing her next words. "Damon and I were together. Now, we're not." She took a bite of her burrito as they continued walking. "And we have just reason to believe Brielle has brainwashed Damon or something because he doesn't remember certain events that most definitely occurred. Like him being left in a burning building."

"Interesting." Lexi slowly chewed while lost in thought.

"You say his memory is on the fritz, and he was in a fire. Something about this sounds eerily familiar to me."

Alessa's eyebrow raised as she looked over at the woman. "I highly doubt that. This is a new experience for all of us."

Lexi finished her burrito before addressing Camden. "Will you show me where the historical scrolls and books are kept?"

Camden peered over at Alessa, who shrugged her shoulders. "Sure, let's go," he answered.

Alessa finished the wrap and threw the wrapper away in a nearby trashcan. "You two have fun. I'm going to head to the outside training course. I have some pent-up frustration that needs to be released."

"Meet you at the cabin later?" Camden asked.

Alessa nodded before walking away. "Eventually, yes."

CHAPTER TWENTY-SEVEN

Camden led the way into the large building and held his arm out toward the hundreds of stacks of books. "Behold, the library of New Sparta."

"Mm-hmm," Lexi responded nonchalantly, walking around his extended arm to the nearest computer.

Her blasé attitude took him aback. "I'm sorry, you seem disinterested for someone who seemed to love history and books."

"Oh, no, I am very interested in books. They've been my best friend since I was little. I've always had a harder time connecting with people."

Camden sat down at the next computer. "Then why the lack of enthusiasm in your response?"

"It's a nice library, don't get me wrong, but it's nothing compared to the one in my home base. It is probably about twenty times this size." She opened the search bar on her monitor.

"Oh, well then..." Camden cleared his throat. "So why did you want to come here?"

Shaking her head back and forth as if searching her mind for something specific, Lexi clicked the search icon. "You mentioning them both having been in a fire and him forgetting her ... it struck me as something I had read or heard before. I'm usually rather good at remembering subject matter and its origin, but you're not quoting an exact lesson or phrase, which has my brain scrambling to figure out why it sounds so familiar."

Camden turned on his computer screen. "Do you have a photographic memory?"

"Technically, all Spartans do to some extent, but I was just born with a powerful ability to recall the information," Lexi responded, squinting while looking closely at the screen.

"That'd be cool to have."

She scoffed. "Until everyone thinks you're too weird to befriend. It's quite lonely."

Camden glanced over at Lexi from the corner of his eyes. "I'm sorry. That had to have been difficult."

She shrugged, keeping her eyes on the screen. "I mean, yes and no. If people don't want to be my friend, I don't want to be theirs, so it all works out."

Camden tilted his head in consideration. "Well said."

"Shit. There are only 506,312 articles mentioning fire and 343,279 mentioning memory loss." Her concentration broke, and she faced Camden. "You know what I'm looking for, but what are you researching?"

"I know he's a dick, but Damon has always put Alessa first and laid his life on the line to help her. I know if I was in love with a woman as much as he was with Alessa, no amount of memory loss serum could take away those feelings, but his attitude toward her is almost ... mechanical at times."

Lexi bit her lower lip. "Interesting."

"It's not like I want him to go after Alessa, but from everything she has told me about Brielle, I don't trust that woman with an ounce of my being. And the fact he is fawning over her as if she is a goddess is beyond me."

Lexi turned back to her computer and typed on the keyboard. "Worms."

"What now?"

She pulled up an image of what she was describing. "Worms are specially developed teeny tiny, computerized, living creatures that burrow themselves deep into a person's brain, targeting and erasing certain moments in time, including people."

Camden cringed. "That sounds made up."

"I wish it were. If I ever had any implanted inside me, I'm not sure I would want to continue living. There's no known way of getting rid of them."

Camden stares at Lexi. "How do you know all of this?"

She tapped the side of her head. "I'm interested in all the weird stuff. My brain works differently."

Camden returned his attention to his computer monitor. "I see that. Well, I guess I know what I'm researching."

Alessa stood beside a large lake, focusing on the hay barrel at the field's far end.

An earpiece had been placed atop the large barrel so Alessa could concentrate on it.

She closed her eyes and felt the familiar hum start at her toes, working its way up her body until a burning sensation was behind both eyes. Focusing on the overwhelming emotions of seeing Damon lying amongst the flames in the château, Alessa pictured his face behind the jumping fire before Camden had carried her from the room.

Opening her eyes, Alessa's irises glowed red as she focused intensely on the electronic.

With tears in her eyes, she instructed the earpiece to explode, and it did, igniting both it and the hay barrel.

"What did she say to you?" Damon yelled from halfway down the grassy hill.

Alessa whipped around and saw Damon charging toward her. She quickly wiped away her tears and buried her turmoil down deep.

"You gave her a concussion!" he chastised.

Alessa rolled her eyes. "She's lucky that's all I gave her."

He grabbed Alessa by the arm, pulling her against his chest. "I already told you, she saved my life. I owe her everything. She doesn't activate like us; I have to protect her."

Alessa glared up into Damon's silver eyes. "You owe her nothing. I'm the one who—"

Damon wrapped his fingers around Alessa's throat and stretched her neck upward. "Don't," he growled.

Alessa didn't portray an ounce of intimidation as Damon held her tightly by the throat. Leaning into him, her irises burned bright red. "Let ... me ... go."

Blinking his silver irises back to blue, Damon shook his head as if waking himself from a terrible dream and released her from his grasp. Flexing his hand in disbelief, he stared at his fists while taking a clumsy step back. "I'm not sure what came over me just now, but I need you to know this isn't a game—"

"A game?" she demanded, rubbing her neck. "Do I look like I'm having fun? Because if you think I am, you are sorely mistaken."

Damon rubbed the back of his head. "I know how hard this must be for you. It's hard for me, too. It's like I'm split in two."

Alessa laughed, devoid of humor. "That I don't doubt. *My Damon* would've never laid a hand on me. Not in anger. Not in frustration. Not ever."

His face dropped. "Alessa, I—"

"Don't," Alessa glared. "I'm not the only one who's changed. You need to get away from me."

He pressed his lips together, but his feet didn't move.

As Alessa glared at him, blood poured down from Damon's nose as he felt the base of his skull squeeze.

"Walk ... the fuck ... away," she growled.

Wiping the blood from his upper lip, Damon ran up the hill away from Alessa, not once turning back.

CHAPTER TWENTY-EIGHT

"A violent mob consisting of ten people broke out here in Manchester, New Hampshire, today," reported a news anchor with bleached, short, spikey hair. "There does not seem to be an agenda behind the attack as men, women, and children were among the victims.

"The motive behind the attacks is unknown, but they are believed to have originated in a bar. The ten individuals leading the acts of violence were killed on-site after continuing to charge the police and refusing to be taken into police custody."

The redhead sitting beside the blonde spoke. "Seven people lost their lives in addition to the ten attackers. So far, no weapons were found on the persons."

"I'm sorry. Did you say no weapons were used during the fighting?"

"That's correct, Tom. Also, footage of today's events was sent to us via a bystander, but we will not be playing it on television due to its graphic nature."

Visibly distraught, the redheaded news anchor swallowed.

"Again, no weapons were used, and yet the vicious manner of the attacks took lives. That's all the details we have confirmed with the police, but we will keep you updated as we know more."

They nervously licked their lips while adjusting themselves in their seat. "Well, this is a bit disturbing, to say the least."

"Yes, Rebecca. It is."

CHAPTER TWENTY-NINE

A Spartan guard marched into the restricted area of the weapons building to find Brielle and Damon standing before a large monitor. "What are you two doing in here?"

Brielle whipped around as Damon remained staring at the empty screen. "Oh, uh—"

The guard pointed a finger aggressively at Brielle. "You, especially, should not be in here."

Grabbing Damon's elbow, Brielle turned him to face the guard and pressed the pendant dangling around her neck.

Damon blinked excessively, glancing around the room as if waking from a dream.

Her face scrunched up, feigning innocence. "I'm sorry, we were on our way to see Murphy, but we snuck into a room to makeout on the way there."

The guard's right eyebrow arched. "Then why is the monitor on?"

Damon mouth opened to respond, but he couldn't remember why.

Brielle shrugged. "Not sure. It was on when we got in here. But we really should get going, right, sugar bear?"

Damon looked questioningly at Brielle as she took him by the hand and dragged him out the door. "Uh, yeah."

Shaking his head to clear his mind, they exited the room. While walking down the hallway, he questioned Brielle. "Why are we here? I don't remember how we—"

"You don't remember? Oh, sugar bear, you have been under so much stress lately. We're here to get your upgrade."

"Wait, what? The last time I remember discussing it, I said I needed more time to think about getting the procedure done."

"That was over a month ago, and as of this morning, you were adamant about getting it. Don't you remember?" She pushed Damon ahead of her into the surgeon's suite. "Now, go on ahead, have a seat. They're waiting for us."

Murphy grinned ecstatically as he greeted Damon and Brielle. "Damon! Brielle! I was hoping you hadn't decided to back out. Just go ahead and have a seat. I'll go wash up."

The surgeon exited the room as Brielle directed Damon to the chair.

Damon plopped down in the procedure chair, confused but willing.

"Sugar bear, you need this. I know you more than anyone else in the world. You've been feeling a bit off lately. Am I right?"

Damon's face scrunched with worry. "I thought I was hiding it better. I'm sorry—"

"Shh. Don't worry about it. I get it." Brielle rubbed the pendant hanging around her neck. "If you do this, you'll be the first of the Spartans to truly be able to go above and beyond your already impressive abilities. You'll be able to tap into your full potential, if not more. I mean, the possibilities will be endless." She beamed.

Damon exhaled. "You're right."

"That's good. That's good. I'll be here the whole time, just outside the room." She flashed a forced smile as the technician injected Damon with a sleeping agent and paralytic.

She was escorted from the surgical suite as his eyes fluttered.

Damon's hands were strapped to the chair's arms, and his head was secured to the headrest. His chair was tilted back and raised to the height of the surgeon standing behind him.

"Ready to make history?" the surgeon asked the other three medical professionals in the room.

The entire room sighed as the surgeon flipped Damon's chair so he was facing the floor, and he drilled into Damon's skull to place the additional microchip next to his original one.

The new chip attached itself to the original with feeler-like appendages, intertwining its information. If the doctor had visualized the worms, he would've seen them glow like glow sticks as they connected to the new chip.

Watching the procedure through the glass window, Brielle rubbed frantically at her necklace.

Oh, Damon, if only you knew you just made a deal with the devil.

Seraphine withdrew the thick needle from the fake patient's bicep before placing a circular adhesive bandage over the injection site. "And that's all there is to it."

Alessa pretended to be interested but was distracted after seeing Damon emerge from one of the procedural rooms with

Brielle latched to his arm. While walking away down the hallway, he aggressively rubbed the back of his head.

"Alessa! Earth to Alessa." Seraphine scoffed and threw down the syringe with a metallic *clang*. "I know administering vaccinations isn't the most exciting thing, but if you don't know how to administer the vaccine properly for Mpox—"

"It's not that." Alessa shook her head. "I am interested, I am. It's just—what was Damon doing here? I didn't see him on the schedule for anything."

Seraphine shrugged. "I'm not sure, but I know you should focus on your training, or you'll never again be cleared for surgery. Now, back to your training." Seraphine cast Alessa a stern look.

Cringing, Alessa put her hands up defensively. "Sorry, it won't happen again. Now, what will you be teaching me about? How to administer an enema?"

Seraphine laughed and rolled her eyes. "How about we jump on the simulation lab and run a catastrophic injury?"

Alessa's eyes widened, and she grinned wildly. "Yes! Gods, yes. Let's do this!" Alessa ran to the Sim Lab. Snatching a waterproof coat off the wall, she buttoned it up and bounced up and down in front of the fake patient. "Put me in, coach."

Seraphine smiled as she followed suit, buttoning her waterproof coat before approaching the computer screen. "Okay, you ready for an intense one?"

"Give it to me. I need a good distraction," Alessa encouraged, rubbing her hands together.

Seraphine typed in a disaster code and pressed enter. "Ask, and you shall receive."

Suddenly, the room darkened as if the day had turned into night, and now and then, a flash of light, similar to lightning, would light up the room. Then, a *boom* of thunder would occur. "This is so incredible!"

Seraphine shrugged with an entertained smile. "You asked for it."

A man's scream echoed throughout the room, and the manikin's left leg bent in half. Blood gushed from the open wound where a piece of his femur poked out from his skin.

Floating in mid-air were the man's vital signs. His heart rate was sky-high, and his blood pressure and oxygen level were falling fast.

"Okay, assess. What do we have? Tell me what you need," said Seraphine.

Alessa's eyes darted from the man's head down to his toes as her fingers dove for the spraying blood. Pressing her fingers into his wound, she spoke with a slight shakiness. "Looks like we have an arterial bleed secondary to a femur break."

"What is the primary objective?"

Alessa closed her eyes to concentrate on her remembered training. "To stop the bleeding quick, or he'll bleed to death."

Seraphine nodded her head, staying next to her friend's side. "Good. And how are you going to do this on the battlefield? You have no blood transfusions; there is no surgical ward."

Alessa glanced around, nervous. "Uh ... um..."

"Think, Alessa, think. You don't have much time," Seraphine urged.

"Okay." Alessa swallowed her nerves and licked her dry lips. "I need to reset the femur and apply a tourniquet."

"Good. Now, move. You're running out of time." She pointed to the man's vital signs, which were tanking.

"I need something to brace his leg once we force his bone back into place and a tourniquet to tie around the wound."

Seraphine turned around and pulled out the requested items from the nearby medical kit. "Done. Where do you need me?"

"Over here, like this," she demonstrated. While Seraphine stood on one side of the manikin, Alessa stood on the other. "Ready? Three, two, one, go!" Alessa yelled as she forced the bone back into place with a cracking noise.

"Hold the sticks on either side of their leg so I can wrap it tight."

The beeping noise from the floating heart rate monitor slowed as the manikin's heart began to fail.

"Alessa, we're losing him," warned Seraphine.

Working fast, Alessa wrapped his leg before tying the tourniquet around his leg. As the bright red liquid squirting from the wound site lessened, Alessa felt hopeful she could save her patient. But as she stared helplessly up at the manikin's failing vital signs displayed on the floating monitor, she realized it was because of his excessive blood loss, and his heart was about to stop completely, no matter her heroic efforts.

Alessa looked the man up and down. "Come on, come on, think." Her glowing red eyes finally landed on the manikin's head, where she could see the tiny outline of the Spartan's microchip glowing. "I wonder..." she mumbled, focusing all her anxiety and panic on her ability to glitch.

As her eyes flared red, she focused on increasing the manikin's ability to produce platelets and instructed them to go directly to the wound site. She directed them with hands extended over the man's torso and down onto their thigh. As the bleeding stopped, she returned her attention to the microchip within the person's head and instructed it to release EPO, replenishing the lost red blood cells.

"Wait, what's happening?" Seraphine stood back,

confused. She watched the patient's vital signs return to normal as Alessa moved her hands over the patient. The doctor returned to the computer monitor to confirm what she was witnessing.

The beeping slowed to eighty beats per minute as Alessa's glowing red eyes scanned the patient's body. The patient's heart rate normalized, their blood pressure stabilized, and their oxygen saturation level returned to one hundred percent.

"This can't be," Seraphine said in awe.

Alessa unglitched and looked up at her friend. "What?"

Seraphine told Alessa to join her in front of the monitor. "Come here."

Stepping beside her mentor, Alessa looked where Seraphine was pointing and gasped.

"Your patient was programmed to die. They were meant to bleed out. I purposefully gave you a scenario in which no one could survive, not even a Spartan, but somehow you managed to save them."

Alessa's eyes darted to the repaired manikin. "What does that mean?"

Seraphine's shoulders lifted as her jaw dropped. "I—I'm not sure. I've never seen anything like it."

CHAPTER THIRTY

Starting her day at the gymnasium, Alessa raised her arms into the air before she sprinted forward into a sequence of cartwheels, front handsprings, and backflips. Reaching forward, Alessa grabbed the first of a set of uneven bars.

She spun around the lower bar and propelled herself to the higher of the two.

As the unexpected memory of Damon's fingers tightly wrapped around her neck flashed before her eyes, Alessa nearly missed the bar. Sloppily grabbing hold of it, she felt her shoulder dislocate, and as she fell, she grunted in pain.

Bracing herself, Alessa tensed. When she fell into a strong set of arms rather than striking the ground, Alessa gasped in surprise.

The familiar scent of musk and cinnamon surrounded her. "You shouldn't be doing this without a spotter."

Unable to breathe, Alessa wriggled out of Damon's grasp.

"Wait, come here." He reached for her arm, but Alessa jerked away.

Remaining in place, Damon dropped his hand. "Let me

help you. You need your shoulder popped back into place, and it'll be ten times harder without another person."

Exhaling loudly, Alessa positioned her arm so Damon could help. *I hate that he's right.*

Grasping her arm, Damon pressed his free hand against Alessa's neck to hold her in place. "Ready?"

She clenched her teeth and shook her head.

Pulling the arm, Damon quickly maneuvered the bone back into place, and an audible *pop* was heard as it slid back into its socket.

"Ah!" Alessa screamed before stretching her muscles and rotating her arm to make sure it was back in place. She eyed him from their close proximity. "Thanks. What are you doing here, anyway?" She walked away from him. "Shouldn't you be teaching a class?"

He rubbed his hands nervously on the front of his thighs. "Oh, I, uh, had the day off from teaching."

Camden strolled through the gymnasium's front doors, wearing black slacks and a burnt orange button-up.

Damon's eyes scrunched up in annoyance. "Does he ever dress normally?"

"Is what you're wearing your definition of normal?" Camden scanned Damon's white tank top and dark green cargo pants. "If it is, then no, I never dress like *that.*"

Camden looked at Alessa. "Ready to spar?"

Gripping her injured shoulder, she started to reply, "Actually, no, I—"

"She just dislocated her shoulder, so she shouldn't spar for at least an hour. But I don't have any plans," Damon interrupted, his eyes flashing gun-metal grey.

Sensing the tension between the two men, Alessa shook her

head back and forth. Stepping between them, she put her hands on Camden's chest. "Cam, no. This is a bad idea."

Camden's lips curved up playfully as he looked past Alessa at Damon. "What? It's just a little spar. Challenge accepted." He took Alessa's hands within his own. "It'll be fine. It'll be okay," he reassured Alessa.

Lexi walked in through the gymnasium doors as Camden and Damon stood before one another on the oversized sparring mat. "What's going on?" Lexi asked Alessa. She pointed at the men. "Was this on today's agenda?"

Alessa shook her head back and forth. "I'm not sure, but it can't be good. And no, it was not."

Damon yelled, "Begin!" and Camden stepped to the side before bouncing up and down, grinning wildly as Damon's face remained stern.

Lexi crossed her arms and cringed. "I have a bad feeling about this."

Alessa hissed as Camden dodged one of Damon's hits. "You and me both."

Damon advanced, but Camden stepped back, deflecting hit after hit.

Rotating just out of his reach, Camden punched toward the side of Damon's head, but instead of striking his skull, Damon caught Camden's arm on either side.

Yanking him forward, Damon twisted his upper body and pulled Camden toward his shoulder, flipping him up over his shoulder.

Landing flat on his back, Camden grunted, and his eyes widened with the shadow of Damon's heel raised above him.

Quickly rolling over, Camden dodged Damon's heel as it slammed hard into the mat. Springing onto his feet, Camden faced his opponent and squared his shoulders.

With a *crack*, Damon's nose broke as Camden's fist popped him.

As the force of Camden's punch pushed Damon's head back, he pushed Camden's forearm away. Blocking another hit with his free hand before swinging back at his opponent, Damon forced Camden to move backward.

With a controlled inhale, Camden forced his own activation to stay buried deep down as he was forced to be on the defense. *I could really use my database of stored moves to kick his ass right now.*

Camden deflecting Damon's hits, one after the other, further enraged the Spartan, who had believed he would quickly take down Alessa's friend.

As their arms smacked against each other, the men grunted with the force of the impact. Dancing violently with one another, the two opponents groaned loudly until Camden did a backflip onto one of the elevated platforms.

Landing with his two feet firmly on the ground, Camden stood for two whole seconds before Damon's foot connected with his sternum. After being kicked square in the middle of his chest, Camden flew through the air until his back slammed into the brick wall.

Seeing his chance to end the fight, Damon rushed Camden with his fist held high in the air.

Unable to hold back his activation any longer, Camden's eyes opened, and his irises glowed golden in color.

Alessa's eyes widened as she watched, horrified. "Oh, shit." She covered her mouth. "You need to leave. Now!" she shouted at Lexi, pushing her toward the exit doors.

Lexi held her ground. "What? Why?"

Damon's entire body had left the ground, putting all his

force into his balled-up fist, heading straight for Camden's smug face.

Alessa shoved Lexi toward the exit as she turned around to watch Camden and Damon continue their fight.

Camden calmly held up his hand in front of his face. Wrapping his long fingers around his opponent's knuckles, he easily caught Damon's fist and squeezed his hand, pinning him in a headlock.

"Just trust me. You need to leave, now!" Alessa pushed her friend out the doors.

Slamming them closed behind Lexi, Alessa turned toward the two sparring men. Camden had Damon secured in a headlock, and as Damon's neck muscles bulged, the blood vessels in his eyes began to burst.

"Cam, you need to stop!" Alessa begged, running toward the men.

Grinning with blood between his white teeth and his eerily golden eyes, Camden glanced up at Alessa, his muscles straining. "Not until he announces defeat."

Her eyes darted back and forth between Damon's silver eyes and Camden's golden glowing irises, and her eyes flared red as she sent a spark of pain into Camden's Rogue Command microchip. "I said that's enough," she barked.

Camden released Damon, and the Spartan collapsed to the floor. While gasping for breath, he twisted around to face his opponent. Shock crossed Damon's face as he stared at the Bodyguard's golden irises.

Scrambling to get away from Camden, Damon pointed at him threateningly. "What the fuck? You're one of them!"

Alessa rushed toward Damon. "Damon, listen—"

He backed away, his face scrunched in disbelief. "How could you?"

She put her hands up in front of her chest defensively. "I know who he is. You're just going to have to trust me. Damon, you cannot say a word to anyone."

Damon stepped forward, his chest puffed out in anger. Raising his arms, he pointed at the Bodyguard. "You brought him HERE?" His face dropped as he ran his fingers through his dark chestnut brown hair. "You'll be put to death for this."

Camden growled as he moved protectively behind Alessa. "They can try."

"Stop! Just listen! Yes, he is *what* you think he is, BUT he is not *who* you think he is."

Damon stepped back, away from Alessa. "What does that even mean?"

"Throughout all our years together, have I ever lied to you?" Alessa demanded.

Damon was angrily pacing back and forth. "What?" He stopped pacing, placed his hands on his hips, and looked away from her. "No. Never."

"I'm going to need you to remember that."

He side-eyed Camden before returning his gaze to Alessa.

Alessa licked her lips before continuing. "You are going to take whatever amount of time you need to, to stop freaking out, and then you will meet me by the lake, by your cabin. So I can explain myself."

Breathing heavily, Damon stared at the ground, unsure how to proceed.

"Damon?" Alessa urged.

"Yeah, yeah, okay," he huffed, turning to leave.

"Not a word to anyone," she called out to him.

With a deep inhale, the veins bulged in Damon's forearms, and as he balled his hands into fists, he punched open the exit doors.

Alessa rushed over to Camden and placed her hands on his chest.

He rubbed his hands up and down her arms. "I don't think you should be alone with him," Camden confessed, his voice dripping with worry.

She glanced nervously back at the door Damon had just exited. "I need to convince him you're not a threat."

He licked the blood from his split lower lip and closed his eyes. "I get it. Do you want me to stay close by?"

"No, I don't think he'll try to hurt me." *Again.*

She pressed herself into Camden's chest and wrapped her arms around his muscular back. "Don't worry, I'll talk him down."

Camden's eyebrows rose in concern. "It's not that I don't trust you, but I haven't seen you be able to calm him down once since coming here. If anything, your presence riles him up."

Annoyed with the accuracy of his statement, she rolled her eyes. "You're not wrong, but the old me would've been able to calm him down, so I'm going to have to try. Or else there's a very good chance we're dead by morning."

CHAPTER THIRTY-ONE

Standing before the still lake near Damon's cabin, Alessa closed her eyes.

The memory of her and Damon swimming in the water after the game of Capture the Flag played on the backs of her eyelids.

The cold water hit her sticky skin, and Alessa gasped. After stripping out of her archery gear, she jumped up and tucked her feet under her rear into a cannonball.

Damon yelled as the water struck him in the face and laughed as Alessa came up for air, gasping.

"Shit, that's cold! Ah," she cursed, swimming for the shoreline.

Laughing hysterically, Damon followed close behind. "Oh, come on, it's not that bad."

Alessa stepped onto the shoreline and stood with her arms crossed in front of her chest, looking back toward the city. "What do we do now? I'm so far from my room."

Damon ran his hands through his wet hair, wrung out his shirt, and eyed Alessa.

With his eyes piercing hers, he closed the distance between them, reached behind her neck, and bent down, pressing his warm lips against her cold ones.

Her mouth opened, and her tongue playfully flicked Damon's. He released an unintentional moan before pulling back to utter one simple sentence.

"To answer your question, my place is right over there." He turned his head and pointed out his cabin with a glance.

Blinking away the memory from her tear-filled eyes, Alessa paced back and forth before the still water, nervously picking at her fingernails.

With the rustling of leaves, Damon walked out from the curve along the path. His jaw muscles twitched as he approached Alessa. "I took out my rage on some punching bags. They may or may not be broken open at this point." His face dropped. "So, tell me. What the fuck is going on? What are you doing with a Rogue?"

Licking her lips nervously, she rubbed her hands together. "Okay. Just calm down, please."

"How can I? You go missing and are suspected dead. Then, when you finally show up months later, you have a Rogue Command in tow."

Rushing toward him, she pressed a hand onto his muscular chest. "Damon, keep your voice down," Alessa demanded. "Breathe. I—I need you to breathe."

Glancing down at her hand, Damon took a slow, deep breath before closing his eyes.

She placed her second hand next to her first hand. "Again."

Feeling the pressure of her palms against his chest, Damon took another calming breath.

Opening his eyes, they silently stared at one another as Alessa felt his heart beating beneath her palms.

"Are you ready to listen?" she asked.

Taking her hands within his own, Damon nodded. "Go ahead."

Removing her hands, Alessa turned from him and looked across the water. Sitting down, she scrunched her knees up to her chest. "Come sit beside me. What I'm about to tell you can't be heard by anyone else nor repeated."

Damon hesitantly sat down beside Alessa. "Okay."

She looked at him intently. "Not even Brielle. Do you understand?"

Damon gulped the lump in his throat. "Got it."

Alessa rubbed her hands together and looked down at the grass. "I'm trusting you with my life, Camden's, and Kai's. Please don't betray me."

"Alessa, I swear I won't tell Brielle. But what do you mean by Kai's life?"

Hearing Damon say her and Brielle's names in the same sentence made Alessa cringe, and she glanced away angrily.

"I will tell you everything about Cam, Kai, Eric Lansing, Lucas Greenfield..." She exhaled. "Are you expected anywhere soon?"

Damon shook his head back and forth, his face scrunched in apparent confusion. "Wait, you haven't already told me everything?"

"Heh," she chuckled. "It's good you don't have anywhere to be. This could take a while. All I ask is, please hold all of your questions until the end." *How can I keep emotions from taking over?* "I'll start with Cam..."

Damon remained silent for over an hour as Alessa explained everything from Camden's involvement with Erebos Industries to Kai's disappearance and recent reappearance to Eric Lansing becoming Lucas Greenfield.

After her spiel, Alessa stood breathlessly as her chest heaved up and down. She stopped pacing back and forth and looked directly at Damon. "Well? Tell me what you're thinking."

Damon continued looking at the lake. "Let me get this straight. Camden is a Rogue Command Bodyguard gone rogue who is now working with you to take down Lucas Greenfield and his company, Greenfield Farms, because you two think Eric somehow changed everything about his physical appearance to adopt a new persona. And since Eric's MO is to attempt world domination, this new company has to be in on his new scheme, but we're not sure what that is just yet."

Alessa stared at him expectantly with her eyebrows raised and lips pursed together.

"And you think you saw Kai working with Greenfield Farms when she's supposed to be dead."

Frustrated, Alessa shook her head in defeat and threw her hands in the air. "You don't believe me."

Damon shook his head, still looking across the lake. "It's not that; you've just presented a lot of information, and I need a second to process it."

"Above all, I need you to believe me when I say Camden will not hurt me. Or anyone else here." Her eyes narrowed. "Except you, it seems. He seems to have it out for you. I'm not sure what happened between the two of you when we were in Texas and Chicago to make him dislike you so much."

Damon glanced down at the ground and sighed. "After everything you've been through, I can't exactly blame him." He chuckled. "I'm not saying I like the man, but I am glad you've had someone to keep you safe."

Alessa scoffed. "You don't think I can survive without a man to save me?"

He tilted his head and dropped his hands. "That's not at all what I meant."

"Damon, this entire explanation is tough for me, but if we are going to take down Lucas Greenfield and extract Kai, I'll need you on my side. You are the strongest warrior I know and the only one I trust with my heart and soul. If I can't trust you to have my back, I'm not sure I will survive."

His face scrunched up in distress, and he stood up. "I will always have your back. Keep gathering evidence against Lucas Greenfield and keep Kai in your sights, but do not give any information to the Council regarding her being alive. You are correct. They will eliminate her immediately upon receiving the information. Unless—"

"What? Unless what?" Alessa interrupted.

"Unless she can be useful and give us information regarding Eric—I mean, Lucas."

Alessa's face lit up with hope. "So you're saying there might be a way for Kai to return?"

Damon tilted his head in consideration. "It's a long shot, but with enough evidence presented to the Council of Elders and the Consilium before her extraction, we could greatly increase the odds of her not being executed."

Alessa bit her lower lip to contain her excitement.

He pressed his hands together nervously. "I'll need to speak with my father face to face."

"Your father?" Alessa's eyes narrowed. "I thought he was only here to oversee my trial, and then he was returning to Greece."

"He's still here, but you don't need to worry about it. You need to focus on getting your sister back. Do you truly believe it to be Kai? There's no way you could be mistaken?"

Alessa shook her head with tears in her eyes. "No, Damon. It's her."

"Wow." His eyes teared up, and he rubbed his nose, looking across the lake. "Both thought to be lost, both found. It's almost like it's fate."

"I am not important enough to be a part of anyone's fate."

"I used to think you were mine."

Alessa struggled to stay standing, feeling as though she had been punched in the gut and had her heart ripped from her chest.

Damon froze, shocked the words had spilled from his mouth. "I—I'm sorry. I don't know where that—um," Damon stammered.

Turning away, Alessa looked out at the water and struggled to think about anything else as she fought back tears.

"Uh—" Damon awkwardly rubbed his hands together as he backed away from the lake. "Keep me posted on any additional information you get on Lucas Greenfield, and let me know when the Council gives the go-ahead to take him down. I will be there, fighting by your side."

Alessa closed her eyes and nodded silently as tears poured down her face.

Walking to his cabin, Damon watched Alessa's head jerkily agree with his statement. "I'll see you later."

Alessa straightened her back and exhaled shakily before uttering two simple words. "Goodbye, Damon."

CHAPTER THIRTY-TWO

The news anchor sat behind their desk, ready to speak to the audience.

"Thank you for joining us for the ten o'clock news on the most watched station in the Wilmington area.

"Tonight, we start with the increase in violent behavior that seems to be spreading from town to town. Each case is similar in that no weapons are used, and the mobs are not ceasing their activity until they are taken down by force. The members of the mobs have been as young as sixteen, and for some reason, the attacks begin in establishments that serve alcohol.

"As far as the police can tell, the attacks are entirely random, and the victims aren't being targeted based on one determining factor. The surviving victims are being left horrifically maimed. There have even been talks of acts of cannibalism.

"The police are asking the public to remain alert and observant. If there is any bizarre activity, immediately seek shelter and call the emergency line."

"And now, onto more positive news," the anchor beamed.

"Congratulations is in order as United States presidential candidate Barnes has appeared to have won both the popular vote and the electoral college votes. Mail-in ballots are still being counted, but it seems his promise to 'win the election by a landslide' has been kept."

CHAPTER THIRTY-THREE

Damon was walking past the medical ward when he heard a familiar melody being hummed. He snuck around the corner and hid behind the tall bushes on the garden's edge.

Alessa was sitting on a maroon blanket with a small figure curled up on her.

A child dressed in a light blue medical gown was lying on Alessa's legs, his head in her lap.

While Alessa hummed the familiar melody, her fingertips caressed the boy's hair, comforting the sick child.

Damon listened in secret to the haunting melody his mother had taught him as a child, which he then, in turn, had taught Alessa when they were together. His insides twisted into a confusing mess.

Hearing a squeal from behind, Damon whipped around to see Brielle running toward him.

Damon hurried toward Brielle to keep her from alerting Alessa to his presence. "Bri, when did you get back? How did you know where to find me?"

She flashed her pearly white smile behind beautifully

painted red lips. "Just now, and I always know where my man is."

As she pressed her lips against his, he callously kissed her back.

Pulling away from him, Brielle looked up into his eyes. Sensing his hesitation, she urgently rubbed the pendant around her necklace.

His eyes suddenly glimmered silver, and his smile widened. Wrapping his arms around her waist, he picked her up off the ground and spun her in a circle, facing away from Alessa. "I've missed you," he mumbled into her neck.

Brielle stared off into the distance. *My grip on him is slipping.*

Clearing her throat, she pulled away from Damon and pointed back down the path. "Look who I found."

Blocking the sun from his eyes, Damon held his hands above his eyes, squinting into the bright light. His father appeared from the light, walking down the path toward them. "Shit ..." *What could he possibly want?*

Taken back by his reaction, Brielle glanced at Damon's dad and then back at him. "Is there a problem?"

Damon brushed her off to the side. "You have no idea."

"Damon, my son," his father called out before holding his arms wide for a hug.

Damon awkwardly walked forward into his father's embrace, barely patting his father's back, before his father stepped back.

Holding Damon by his biceps, his father looked him up and down. "Let me see you. It's been too long."

"We just saw each other a few weeks ago at Alessa's trial, and you hardly spoke two words to me. If memory serves me right, you acknowledged my presence by saying my name. That's all."

"Ah, yes, well," the older gentleman faltered. "That's different. That was all business, and we didn't have a chance to speak in private."

"Why break that tradition now? It's been a few years since we've spoken about anything outside duty," Damon retorted.

"Wow. That long already?" his father laughed cordially.

Damon's back stiffened in obvious discomfort. "It's been since I told you what I had planned for my mother's ring, yes."

His father side-eyed Brielle. "It's been a long time since I've last gotten to speak with my son. We have a lot to discuss. We need our privacy. You understand," he said dismissively.

"Oh—oh, yes, I'm sorry, sir." Brielle kissed Damon on the cheek. "I'll see you later."

Damon pursed his lips together and forced a tight-lipped smile while nodding at Brielle.

His father watched Brielle walk away. "She's an interesting choice. Sexy, for sure, but another non-Spartan? I'm starting to think you're choosing women to retaliate against your responsibilities as an heir."

"What are you doing here, father?" Damon demanded.

"Can't a father simply show up just to see his son?"

Damon scoffed before walking down the path toward his cabin in the woods. "No father of mine would ever do such a thing. That would be beneath him."

"I need to discuss several important issues with you, number one being Alessa."

"Aha—there it is." Damon shook his head in disbelief. "What about her? I notified you of her re-appearance. We tested her as you demanded, and she passed everything you threw at her, proving her loyalty to the Spartans. What else could you possibly want?"

"There is talk about Alessa's destructive abilities, that the gods have forsaken her."

"Seraphine established her microchip had glitched, enabling her to control technology. It's not that deep." Damon opened his front door and ushered his father in, holding his hand toward the older man.

Stepping over the threshold, his father continued. "Yes, but—"

"You have always had it out for Alessa. Since she was a child. But especially after I declared my love for her and told you my intentions—"

His father laughed under his breath. "As if you would have actually—"

Damon stepped forward and stood face-to-face with his father. "She has mother's band. I was going to ask her to be mine forever as soon as she returned from her mission, but as you know, that didn't happen. And Alessa is Spartan in every way that matters."

His father's eyes narrowed. "Then why aren't you with her right now? I can only assume you're with that Brielle woman for some reason."

Damon brushed his father's question off. "That's none of your concern; I'm not discussing my relationships with you."

"As long as you eventually end up with a strong Spartan woman, I don't care who your rebound relationships are with. But I certainly did not come to discuss who you are fucking."

"Then why are you here? Spit it out," Damon growled.

"Alessa's elder has been trying to convince both the Council of Elders and the Consilium of Lucas Greenfield's involvement regarding the next attack on humankind and his ties with Eric Lansing."

Damon stilled, listening intently to his father. "And?"

"And he is failing miserably. There is no hard evidence of him being Lucas Greenfield except for a few personality quirks and a 'feeling' he gets about the man. As far as him being behind a sinister plan against humanity, the facts point to him being a simple farmer and helping his father with his company his entire life. There is nothing to support Alessa's elder's claims, so we will announce the rejection of his proposal to continue monitoring Lucas and his request to take him out."

Damon froze. "I had meant to discuss this with you; had I realized you were still here and easily accessible, I wouldn't have waited. The final decision hasn't been made just yet?"

"No, but it might as well be. There's no reason to continue encouraging her delusions."

"Let me do some investigating. Give me, say, three weeks to find some plausible evidence."

His father tilted his head. "One week."

Damon reluctantly agreed. "One week, but do not make any decisions until I have presented my argument."

Damon's father laughed and turned toward the door. "I don't understand why you are doing this for her. It's not like you owe her anything."

"If Alessa is one thing, it's trustworthy. If she says he's got something up his sleeve, I believe her."

His father placed his finger upon his chin in feigned contemplation. "Didn't she claim you died a few months ago?"

Taken back, Damon blushed. "Well, yeah, but—"

"Yet, here you are alive and well and with another woman, I might add. You are putting your reputation on the line to help a woman whom you swear is trustworthy but refuse to demonstrate any semblance of believing what she says to be true."

Damon opened the door, his chest heaving up and down as he found it hard to maintain his composure. "I think it's time for you to leave."

His father stepped out of the front door into the woods. "Your facts don't add up, son. I know you think you know Alessa, but maybe you don't. Not truly."

After watching his father walk away, Damon slammed his front door shut. Pressing his back against the wood, he slid down the door to the ground. Placing his hands on either side of his face, his head fell forward as he let the gravity of his father's words hit.

If I can't believe Alessa, who will? And what if she is right about everything? What then?

CHAPTER THIRTY-FOUR

The next few days flew by as Camden and Alessa continued watching footage of Lucas Greenfield at his company events.

When Lexi and Quade found the time, they helped Alessa hone her newfound abilities and sparred with her. Lexi loved to teach her new moves from the motherland.

Quade bent over, hands on his knees, panting loudly as he and Camden finished a sparring session. "Damn, you are quick for a big guy."

Camden swallowed and wiped his sweat off on a nearby towel. "Growing up in a home where it was encouraged to kill the weakest definitely has its benefits."

Lexi's jaw dropped. "Like, actually kill?"

Camden wiped the back of his neck. "Yes. From the time I was five until ... I don't know, maybe ten, there had been, maybe, ten lives taken every year."

Quade squirted water into his mouth before shaking his head. "Spartan history is pretty twisted, but that's dark, man."

Camden shrugged nonchalantly. "I didn't know any better;

it was how I was raised. My strength and speed are what helped me become a..."

Camden eyed Alessa, who, after stepping back behind Lexi, shook her head back and forth.

Lexi's eyes narrowed. "Become what?"

Camden looked to Quade, panicked, and cleared his throat. "Um...a fighter."

Knowing Camden's secret, Quade interrupted and directed his attention at Alessa. "Today's lesson involves identifying where electronics are by their distinct sounds."

Alessa's forehead scrunched up. "As in that high-pitched whining noise they make?"

Quade walked them out back to the outdoor portion of the building. "Is that what electronics sound like to you?"

She shrugged and tilted her head in consideration. "I guess so. Each kind of buzzes, like I can feel its radio waves."

"Hmm, interesting." Gently grabbing her shoulders, Quade positioned her in the middle of the stone patio beneath the bright sun. "I want you to stand here and close your eyes."

Alessa's navy blue skirt blew around as she slowly exhaled beneath the warm Colorado sun. "Okay..."

"I want you to focus all your energy on finding all the hidden electronics. They go out quite a ways."

Alessa's eyes popped open. "Are you serious?"

"Quite."

"Sorry, I know you're just trying to help," Alessa apologized while closing her eyes again. Shaking out her arms, Alessa stood tall and inhaled deeply, feeling the familiar burn behind her eyelids as her microchip glitched. Using her abilities, Alessa reached out toward the distant humming until she could feel the marrow of her bones vibrate.

Finding the first of the hidden electronics, her breathing

sped up as she replayed the visions in her mind of her discovering Brielle was alive and with Damon. She relived Brielle touching Damon, and as her heart filled with hate, she could feel the tiny pinch of the electronic bursting into flames.

Camden clapped his hands together. "I knew you could do it!"

Quade nodded in approval. "Well done. Only a dozen or so more to find and destroy."

Already feeling stressed, Alessa sighed before returning to the task at hand.

An hour later, Alessa was emotionally exhausted after finding all the devices.

"Is that it?" she asked, slumped over on a nearby cement bench.

Quade tilted his head. "You tell me."

Closing her eyes, Alessa focused all her energy on sensing the surrounding area's electronics. After feeling the nearby Spartan's microchips, Alessa's eyes darted open as she realized she had somehow locked in on Damon and Brielle.

Brielle's microchip felt different for obvious reasons since she had a temporary one, but Damon's gave off a different vibe than the others she had felt. *I wonder what that means.*

"Yeah, I've got them all," she responded as Camden snuck up behind her and placed his large hands atop her shoulders. As he massaged the knots from her upper back, Alessa melted at his touch and smiled, grateful.

Announcing her departure, Lexi cleared her throat. "Thanks for letting me watch you in action, but I need to get back to researching Lucas Greenfield's whereabouts and personal estates so we know the easiest way to get to him."

Camden looked down at Alessa. "And we have our own festivities to attend."

Alessa's eyes narrowed suspiciously. "Do we?"

He grinned mischievously.

Sticking their arms out toward one another, the men grasped each other's forearms, and Quade pulled Camden in to whisper into his ear. "Treat her right. She's been through a lot."

Camden pulled back and responded in all seriousness, "That's the plan."

They let go of one another. "Good," Quade winked. "I'm going to head home to Soren and Sera."

Camden wrapped his arm around Alessa's waist, helping her stand up.

"What was that about?" she asked.

"You'll see," Camden reassured as they started toward home.

Alessa brushed her hair out of her face and sighed. "I'm not sure if I have much energy left to do whatever you had planned."

"Well, first, let's get some food in you. I was thinking Italian. Or at least as Italian as I can get in a city of Spartans."

Alessa laughed as she placed her hand on Camden's secured on her hip and tripped forward.

He caught her with ease. "You okay? Need me to carry you?"

Laughing at the ridiculous notion, Alessa shook her head back and forth. "No. I need a second to get my footing. I'm not sure if you can tell, but focusing all of my energy on the electronics is emotionally draining."

Trying to walk forward again, Camden firmly held Alessa, his arm hooked on her elbow. "Why is that? I haven't ever experienced what you're going through."

Trying to figure out how to explain it, she licked her lips, looking down at the ground. "You know when you play a video game and are super focused? Or, better yet, when you're in battle and putting all your energy into the physical moves you're performing? That's how it is for me, but mentally and emotionally, since I have to funnel all my rage every time I cause something to erupt."

"Interesting." Camden led them down the path away from the city's center.

Alessa looked back toward the mess hall she could no longer see. "I thought you said we were eating."

"We are. I just didn't say where." He walked with her off the path, and they arrived at the edge of the small lake, where a table had been set up, complete with candles and plates of pasta.

Alessa glanced up at Camden and grinned excitedly. "Are you serious?"

Proud of himself, Camden smiled and helped her to her chair. "You've been training so hard and haven't had any time to relax. You need one night to remember what it's like to feel human."

Picking up her fork, she looked at Camden with tears. "Thank you."

He nodded his head at her food. "Eat up."

"I am starving," she confessed, scooping the pasta into her mouth.

After finishing dinner, they both sat back and sighed in satisfaction.

"Wow, that was delicious," Camden smiled at Alessa.

Alessa sighed, slow and content. "Okay, time for some deep conversation."

He chuckled. "Okay?"

"You know pretty much everything about my life at this point: My birth parents' deaths, my sister's disappearance, my boyfriend"—she shook her head—"I mean, ex-boyfriend, my upbringing..."

He crossed his arms. "And?"

"It's your turn to open up. About your past, your home, anything. I mean, did you have any pets? Did you ever search for your biological family? Did you have a girlfriend?"

Camden groaned. "It's not that interesting."

She rolled her eyes. "As if."

His eyes narrowed, questioning her statement. "What does that mean?"

Alessa scoffed and shrugged. "It means, I very much doubt it. Okay, then. Tell me just one thing I don't know about you."

Camden leaned forward, resting his elbows on his knees, and rubbed his hands together. "I, uh—I can't have kids."

"Oh. Is there something—" She eyed his zipper.

He laughed, glancing at the ground. "Everything works just fine." His eyes met Alessa's. "Some might say, 'perfect.'"

Her cheeks blushed as she inhaled deeply and nervously looked to the side of the table.

"The Elite sterilize their boys at the age of fifteen, so we can't get sidetracked with families of our own."

Alessa's jaw dropped. "Oh, shit. I'm sorry the option of being a father was taken away from you."

Camden held his hands up. "There's no guarantee I would have been amazing at the gig, but I would have given it my all had I been given the chance. Guess we'll never know."

She absentmindedly played with Damon's ring on her finger. "Thank you. For telling me."

Camden cleared his throat and sat upright in his chair. "Yeah, well, you asked, and I aim to please."

Alessa sat back in her chair. "And on that note, what do we do now? It's still pretty early."

His teeth flashed pearly white as he grinned mischievously. "I thought you were too tired to do anything else."

"Cam, I know you; there's no way we're just eating. What else do you have up your sleeve?"

Seraphine squealed after stepping around the bushes. "Alessa!"

"What?" Alessa jumped up and hugged her friend. "What are you doing here?"

"She's not the only one," Quade joined in while carrying a chocolate dessert.

"It's a party, right?" Lexi asked from behind Quade, holding speakers.

"What is going on?" Alessa laughed.

"You needed a break, and in all honesty, we did as well. So, Camden invited us for a game of sand volleyball and a night swim."

Alessa looked back at Camden, who grinned and shrugged innocently.

"Volleyball? Oh man ... I hope I don't puke. I ate enough pasta for an army," she laughed nervously.

After setting down the speakers, Lexi hooked her arm through Camden's and pulled him toward the outdoor volleyball court. "You're on my team."

His right eyebrow arched, and he flashed a smile. "Only if you can guarantee we'll kick their asses."

Lexi grinned confidently. "Is failure ever an option?"

Alessa caught the volleyball Quade threw at her. "So, who's sitting out? Or is it going to be two versus three? I'm good with whatever."

Seraphine plopped down in an elevated chair on the sideline, directly beside the net. "I volunteer as the ref."

Alessa tossed the ball back and forth between her hands.

"Are you sure? You're not one to sit out on a game of volleyball."

Seraphine exhaled loudly. "Oh, I'm sure."

Alessa's eyes narrowed suspiciously while her friend sat down.

Seraphine dismissively flicked her wrist in Alessa's direction. "I'm fine. I'm just exhausted from training for a new procedure."

Camden smirked as he got into position on their side of the net. "If you say so."

With a shake of her head, Seraphine announced the beginning of the game. "Does anyone need the rules explained to them?"

Everyone shook their heads back and forth.

"Okay, then. The first team to 25 points wins. Alessa, you and Quade serve first."

After playing for nearly two hours, Camden and Lexi stood at the back of the court, talking closely.

Leaning down into her, Camden put his hand on her shoulder. "Lexi, this is *the* point. If we get this, we win. Don't fuck this up."

Rolling her eyes, Lexi huffed, brushing his hand off her shoulder. "As if."

Backing up to his spot on the sand, Camden bent down.

Awaiting her friend's serve, Alessa exhaled before she clenched her teeth in concentration. The scene before Alessa changed for the briefest of moments from the volleyball court to the darkened underworld. Hades' castle stood tall before her as birdlike creatures circled above in the artificial sky.

"Move!" Quade screamed, pulling Alessa back to reality just in time for the volleyball to smack her in the face.

Lexi covered her mouth. "Oh shit!"

Camden scrambled toward Alessa, ducking under the net and rushing to her as she knelt on the ground, holding her profusely bleeding nose. "What were you doing?"

Blinking through the pain, Alessa cleared her throat. "Uh, I'm not exactly sure. Hallucinating, maybe?"

Seraphine shoved Camden to the side. "Move! Let me see if it's broken."

The doctor held Alessa's face, and through the swelling and bleeding, she could tell it was indeed broken. Scrunching up her nose, Seraphine *tsked*. "It is broken, but it isn't that bad. I need to reset it real quick. Hold still."

She placed her thumbs on opposite sides of Alessa's nose and looked into her friend's eyes. "Breathe in."

While Alessa inhaled, Seraphine jammed her thumbs into either side of Alessa's nasal bone, which crunched with the force of being put back into place.

Alessa grunted. "Ugh."

"I'm so sorry," Lexi apologized, helping Alessa to her feet.

"If I got upset with everyone who accidentally hurt me, I'd have no friends. We're good." She touched the wet blood on her lips.

Camden tilted his head toward the lake. "Let's get you cleaned up. Good thing we have a large body of water just over there."

With a wide grin, Lexi stripped out of her emerald green dress and ran toward the shore, revealing a lavender bra and matching panties.

Camden laughed as they watched her jump into the water. "Is that girl intimidated by anything?"

Alessa's eyes narrowed as she unzipped her dress, exposing her magenta bra. "If you have feelings for Lexi, you have my permission." She allowed the fabric to pool around her ankles.

Camden glared down at Alessa. "Permission for what?"

She wiggled out of her athletic shorts. "You know…"

"Alessa, let's get something straight"—Camden placed two fingers beneath Alessa's chin and tilted her face to his—"if I wanted her, I'd have her. She's not the one I want."

Camden was so close his hot breath bounced off her lips. "Now, let's go get that blood washed off." He let go of her and strolled toward the shoreline, peeling his button-up shirt off his sweat-drenched torso.

Suddenly breathless, Alessa forced herself to inhale the cool night air. "Well, fuck me," she cursed.

CHAPTER THIRTY-FIVE

After what felt like being sucked through a wind tunnel, Alessa was suddenly standing before an extravagant castle.

She was dressed in a sapphire blue, traditional Spartan dress with a split extending up her skirt, exposing the entirety of her right thigh. Her arms were adorned with strands of gold and white jewels cascading down from her muscular biceps, and sitting atop Alessa's head was a leaf crown made of gold.

Looking up at the large black castle made out of sparkling gemstones, her eyes lifted to what should have been the sky. Instead of an indigo-blue hue, the atmosphere had been replaced with a white, whirling vapor beneath a layer of vibrant red-orange.

To the left of the castle was a luscious green field filled with brightly colored flowers swaying in the non-existent wind.

Alessa walked toward the ebony castle ahead of her as if her legs were being instructed to move forward without conscious thought. "Hades," she mumbled.

Crossing the bridge made of red brick, she looked over the

side and saw a river of wispy white figures swimming back and forth in an endless loop. "What in the world are those?"

She reached the castle doors, and the enormous double doors opened. Looking around hesitantly, she finally entered.

The vibrant colors and shiny surfaces were reflected throughout the elaborate entry. "Huh..."

"Didn't expect my realm to have so much ... color?" a male voice boomed.

Alessa whipped her head to the right, where Hades was sitting atop his throne, which was made of black onyx.

His handsome, dark features surprised Alessa. Even the scar above his left eye, going through his eyebrow, looked strategically placed to emphasize the danger he embodied.

Alessa's jaw dropped, and she slowly stepped toward him. "How is this—?"

"This is not your first time being here. Do you not recall our first encounter?" Hades arched an eyebrow as Alessa stood before him, confusion written across her face. "Let me remind you, I expect my payment in full, or I will bring you back—"

"Four souls in exchange for your one. Our deal is done," Alessa muttered, remembering the words.

Blue and white birds flew above them in a make-believe sky beneath the ceiling.

"You do remember," he grinned sadistically.

Nodding slowly, her eyes drifted toward the dark three-headed dog beside the underworld king.

"And yet, knowing full well the repercussions, you haven't followed through with your end of the bargain. That's a choice."

Alessa opened her mouth to speak but was silenced by Hades lifting a finger.

"And as we agreed, I need four souls for your deal to be upheld."

"But I did give you four. I gave you many more than what was agreed upon."

He smiled as if enjoying an inside joke. "No, no, my dear. You have not delivered your part of the bargain regarding the four specific souls we had agreed upon."

"What does that matter?" Alessa's arms flailed defiantly.

Hades' head whipped violently toward her, and he stood up. Marching down from his throne, Hades' black and gold embroidered tailcoat flailed behind him. "Every soul has a different point value tied directly to their death count. Their death count doesn't have to be taken by their hands per se; it could be indirectly related to them. So Eric's soul is—"

"Priceless," Alessa groaned.

Hades grinned and clapped his hands together. "Precisely."

The white, wispy clouds above them had begun darkening into shades of grey, and even the birds' colors had become mute.

She looked past Hades, her eyes unfocused. "So if Eric isn't here, my suspicions are—"

Hades placed his hands on Alessa's biceps. "Correct! Lucas has pulled a fast one." He wiggled a finger. "I am quite impressed; that bastard really wants to live."

"Okay..." Alessa backed away from Hades' cold touch. "Then I will still uphold my end of the bargain. I will get you Eric, I mean Lucas, for you to add to your collection."

"Yes, but when?" He turned and held out his arm, summoning a bird to land. "I have given you more than enough time, *Alessa*," Hades said her name as a man would to his lover.

Her eyes flared bright red, and she balled her hands into tight fists. "What do you want from me? I am trying my—"

The room darkened, and the birds transformed into crows. The cawing bird turned pitch black as it landed on Hades' extended arm. "Soon, there is to be a pivotal moment in which you will be forced to make a decision that will bear heavy consequences if you choose incorrectly."

Her face scrunched up in frustration. "What is that supposed to mean?"

Hades tilted his face down with a sadistic grin.

"Can we please not speak in riddles?" she begged.

He rubbed his hands together. "My dear, if I were to give you the answers to everything, what fun would that be?"

"I'm not sure if you've noticed, but life is hard enough without the king of the underworld fucking with you," she growled.

His jaw flexing, Hades stepped toward Alessa. Cerberus followed suit, walking up behind his master whilst baring his teeth. "No human has ever dared speak to me so. I shall remind you that I hold your life in my hands."

She froze, unable to pull back her emotions but unwilling to risk angering the king of the underworld any further.

"I'll be watching. Now go," Hades dismissed her with a flick of his wrist.

Cerberus lunged at Alessa as the birds bombarded her from the false clouds.

She sprinted through the corridors of the castle for the entrance doors. Tripping over the threshold, one of the dog's teeth tore the skirt of her dress, and as she fell forward, her head emerged from the lake's surface.

While coughing water from her lungs, Alessa treaded the lake, searching for the shoreline. After seeing her friends asleep on the sand, she swam for land.

Crawling onto the dirt, Alessa rolled onto her back. As her chest heaved up and down, she stared at the sun barely rising over the horizon.

"The fuck was that?" she cursed, trying to catch her breath.

CHAPTER THIRTY-SIX

Cain's fist was held high above Kai as her body slammed to the ground. As her ribs smacked the hotel's hard, patterned carpet, a groan escaped from between her lips.

Shaking his head back and forth, he rubbed his sore knuckles. "I told you what would happen if you failed again."

Her head bobbed back and forth as she fought the pain from where his fist had struck her cheek. "You—you did. I'm sorry."

"You're sorry?" Cain crouched down in front of Kai. "Sit up." He wrapped his fingers around her arm and yanked her upright.

A whimper escaped between her lips, but she quickly bit her lower lip to silence herself.

"I told you we need to know the list of questions before every interview, so there is no reason to question Lucas's motives. We need to make sure every move is premeditated and calculated. There's no room for error."

A tear fell from her eyelashes as Kai looked down at Cain's

shiny dress shoes. Without a word, she shook her head up and down.

Cocking his head to the side, Cain eyed the dark red spot that was already appearing on her cheekbone. Cain made a 'tsk' noise and caressed Kai's face. "I *did* warn you."

Her insides jumped at his touch, but she held fast. Faking a half-smile, Kai placed her hand on the back of his. "I should have done better. I will do better."

Cain leaned in and pressed his lips hard against Kai's. "You'll have to."

Opening her eyes, she found his stormy green-grey eyes staring intently into hers, and for the first time, she recognized the rage behind his beauty.

Even after the lashings she had received after the Spartans had stopped Eric's agenda a few months prior, Cain's eyes had never held an ounce of hate. It should have been a major red flag, but he had done an incredible job of making her feel like she had deserved the punishment. Then, he had shown such kindness when helping her wounds heal by applying ointments and salves to reduce the pain and scarring, all while he verbally manipulated her.

"My uncle will not tolerate another mistake like today, my pet," Cain cooed while helping Kai to her feet.

Placing his first two fingers beneath her chin, he lifted her face, examining her cheek. "I'll get you some ice for that; it's starting to swell."

He gently pressed his lips to her bruise before pulling away.

As he marched out the door, Kai stared into the mirror on the wall. Feeling numb, she walked toward the dresser, holding her clear makeup bag.

After digging out a bottle of coverup, she opened the lid

and poured some medium beige onto her stippling brush before pressing it against her darkening cheekbone.

A single tear fell from her eye as she suddenly wanted nothing more than to return to Sparta and her life with her sister, but that would never be possible after she erased Alessa's memories.

I never wanted any of this. I just wanted someone to love me, but he's not the man he made me believe he was. She exhaled shakily from between pursed lips.

I'll never see home again. I'll never see Lessie again. Even if I did, she wouldn't know who I was. I'm glad I saved her life, but I'm sad that I lost her. Oh gods, what have I done?

While staring into the mirror, Kai froze, reliving a specific memory in which she, as a teenager, sat side by side with a young Spartan man. While sitting outside in the grass, they talked and laughed about nothing in particular when his mother appeared out of nowhere and swooped in to ruin their fun. Yanking him up by the arm, his mother chastised him for wasting his time with Kai.

"How dare you ignore the other eligible women of Sparta for the likes of her? She's not a bloodborn Spartan! As far as the Wellborns are concerned, she will never have any prospects as high on the social ladder as us, so you'd better get that ridiculous notion out of your head right now."

Kai closed the book she was reading and watched the young man walk away with tears in her eyes. He glanced back at her one last time before never speaking to her again.

Returning to the present, Kai cried silently, painfully watching the tears stream down her cheeks in her reflection.

CHAPTER THIRTY-SEVEN

Camden and Alessa sat in the library's basement, staring at the three-dimensional visual representation of Lucas Greenfield's plantation hovering before them.

Alessa sighed and closed the image file with a swipe of her hand. "Okay. I feel like it's a solid plan."

Camden leaned back in his chair. "As solid a plan as one can get without the permission of your leaders." His eyebrows raised while quizzically glancing at Alessa. "You're sure about this?"

"Yes. It's happening soon."

He pressed the tips of his fingers together. "How could you possibly know—"

Not wanting to tell him about her meeting with Hades, she cleared her throat. "I should let Damon in on the plan."

Camden sat up straight in his chair. "Are you sure we need him?"

Alessa glared at Camden. "Yes, Cam. Having him and his men on our side will put the odds in our favor when we attack Lucas. You may hate him, but he is one hell of a warrior."

Camden cleared his throat and rose to his feet. "Maybe he had an off day when we sparred, but alright. I trust you. I'll go find Quade while you do that."

She wrapped her arms around Camden in a tight embrace. "Thank you for everything. It's almost over," she whispered into his ear, excitement in her voice.

Camden nodded in silent agreement as Alessa turned around and ran from the room.

Running his hand through his hair, he exhaled. "I hope you're right."

As Alessa approached Damon's cabin, alone in the woods, she passed by the lake they had made love in so many times. Her heart raced, and she closed her eyes against the painful memories.

Walking quietly through the darkened trees, every fiber of Alessa's body was set aflame with the knowledge she was about to be alone with Damon in their once-shared home.

With a deep breath, she stepped onto the small porch and lifted her hand to knock on the front door.

Alessa's hand froze in mid-air, just before the dark wood, and in a last-second decision, she gripped the black door handle and turned the knob.

Opening the door, Alessa's heart ached as she looked around at the familiar artwork and the table on the side of the room where they had made love just a year prior.

Hearing a noise, Alessa called out. "Damon?" After not getting a response, she stepped further into the cabin. "Damon, you here?"

Rounding the corner, Alessa froze at the sight of Damon atop Brielle in his bed.

Damon's olive skin glowed beneath the skylight above the bed, and with every thrust, Brielle let out a satisfied squeal.

Swallowing vomit, Alessa exhaled loudly and sprinted out the front of the cabin into the darkening night.

"Fuck, Alessa!" Damon yelled from the cabin, realizing what she had just walked in on.

"Oh, come on, she'll be fine," Brielle breathily encouraged Damon to continue. "Don't go!" she demanded while grabbing his forearm.

He withdrew himself in a panic and jumped out of bed. "No, no, I have to make sure—"

"What's the problem? She knows we're together. You think she didn't know we fucked?" Brielle demanded angrily.

He hurriedly pulled on cargo pants and ran out the front door. "Alessa!" he yelled, running after her through the trees. *Shit. Where would she go?*

Alessa ran up beside the pool's building and bent over. With her hands on her knees, she vomited into the grass. "Fuck," she cried while wiping her mouth.

"Alessa!" Damon's voice echoed through the trees.

Standing up, Alessa inhaled a shaky breath and opened the doors to the swimming pool. Tears fell as she exhaled. *Pull yourself together; you can't let him see that he broke you.*

Running into the pool house in only dark cargo pants, Damon's muscular chest was heaving. "Alessa, I'm—" He stopped himself and rubbed the backs of his eyelids with his fingertips. "What did you come to see me about?"

Unable to turn around and look him in the eyes, she snapped, "Shouldn't you be finishing about now?"

Running his hands through his hair, Damon sighed in frustration. "You're not being fair. You knew about—"

Failing to keep her emotions in check, Alessa marched toward the deep end. "No! You know what isn't fair? Me having to watch you, the only man I have ever loved, die in my arms only to come home and find out that you fell in love with the bitch that killed you."

He rolled his eyes. "Not this crazy talk again—"

She stood before the pool, staring down into the water. "I find myself holding my breath, hoping you'll change your mind and want me again, but that's never going to happen, is it?" She looked at him, and as he stayed silent, Alessa bit her lower lip and nodded.

"Maybe this is what I needed. Perhaps instead of being angry, I should be thankful. Now, I can finally put the ridiculous notion of us ever getting back together out of my head."

Damon stepped forward with his hand reaching out, wanting to comfort Alessa somehow. "Alessa, I—"

"Don't. Please don't. I can't take it anymore. It's just too much." Her voice broke as she looked him in the eyes. "I can't pretend anymore that I'm okay with just being friends."

"What are you—"

Unable to hold back her emotions anymore, she cried. "I need to let you go."

"Don't do this, Alessa. I still want you in my life," Damon begged as he rushed toward her. Taking her hand within his own, he held tight while placing his free hand on the side of her face.

She licked the tears from her lips and looked into his eyes, emotionless. "I don't want you in mine. You're no good for me,

Damon." She shrugged him away. "You used to be my rock; now you're my kryptonite."

Damon's heart was crushed beneath the weight of Alessa's confession. "I didn't mean—"

With tears streaming down her face, she removed his hand from her skin and took her hand from his before turning away. "Go home to Brielle."

"Alessa, no, I won't let you—"

Cutting him off midsentence, she dove into the pool.

As the warm liquid wrapped itself around Alessa, she closed her burning eyes and screamed from the bottom of her lungs, releasing an unhinged cry into the depths of the blue water.

Large bubbles floated up from the bottom of the pool as Alessa screamed beneath the water's surface, and her dress swirled around her, clinging to her curves.

The lights above flickered, and as the door behind him flew open, Damon slowly backed up.

"What did you do?" Camden screamed at Damon as he stripped his shirt from his torso and dove in after Alessa.

Embracing Alessa, Camden wrapped his arms around her shaking body and brought her to the pool's surface.

Swimming to the stairs, Camden carried a sobbing Alessa in his arms and sat down in a nearby lounge chair just as the lights exploded from up above.

Damon backed out of the door and stood outside the poolhouse.

"He's gone," she sobbed in Camden's tight embrace. "He's truly gone."

A searing pain shot through Damon's temple as he heard Alessa repeat the familiar words.

CHAPTER THIRTY-EIGHT

After being unable to sleep that night, Damon marched toward Alessa's cabin with the rising sun. He couldn't get over what had transpired between them last night.

Why can't I stop feeling as though I betrayed Alessa even though I'm with Brielle?

Coming over the hill, his eyes landed on the figure sitting on a wooden chair on the front porch. "Camden," Damon growled.

Looking up from Damon's laptop, Camden grumbled. "What do you think you're doing here?"

Damon rubbed his hands nervously against one another. "I need to see Alessa. I need to apologize—wait, is that my missing laptop?"

Camden smirked. "Why, yes. It was your laptop. But it's ours, now."

"How did you get that?" Damon demanded, his hands balling into fists.

Camden eyed Damon and scoffed. "If you don't believe anything Alessa has already told you, you certainly aren't going to believe me. And no." Camden slammed Damon's laptop closed.

"No, what?" Damon asked.

Camden glared up at him from his seat. "No, you don't need to see Alessa."

The man's protective demeanor took Damon back. "I'm sorry?"

"You've said enough. You've *done* enough. You are no longer welcome here." Camden stood tall.

Damon stepped angrily toward the blond Russian. "You have no idea what I've been going through, trying to maintain my honor while still loving Alessa."

Camden's eyes narrowed, and he leaned into the dark-haired Spartan. "And you came here to tell Alessa what? You never stopped loving her?"

Damon's lower jaw dropped as he struggled to find the words.

"You think that's what she needs to hear? That the man who broke her is still in love with her while fucking the enemy?"

Damon's face dropped as he realized Camden was right. Alessa didn't deserve to be strung along while he continued a relationship with Brielle.

"Why do you think you still have feelings for Alessa when you're with Brielle? Not that I want to help you get Alessa back, but have you ever heard of worms?"

Damon tilted his head in disbelief. "Yes ... are you suggesting Brielle—"

Camden shrugged his muscular shoulders. "I'm not suggesting anything. I'm telling you that after researching for too many hours about what could've happened to you, for Alessa's sake, that is the only explanation."

Damon stared off as he contemplated the possibility of Brielle mind-controlling him while she somehow simultaneously erased specific memories.

After clearing his throat, Camden bumped into Damon's shoulder as he passed. "If you ever loved Alessa, you'll let her go. Give her a chance to be happy."

Damon glared at him, narrowing his eyes. "With who, you?"

Camden tilted his head toward Damon. "I have never once faltered in having her back. The same can't be said for you."

Damon lunged for Camden, but expecting the move, the Russian whipped the laptop over to the side of the porch while blocking Damon's hit.

Moving as if in a choreographed dance, Damon swung and punched the air as Camden blocked every move before he landed a kick square in the center of the Spartan man's chest, sending him flying backward off the porch.

Damon landed on his back with a grunt on the grass in front of Alessa's cabin.

Picking up the computer, Camden shot daggers from his eyes. "If you come near her again, I'll kill you."

Staring at the Bodyguard from the ground, Damon's irises flashed silver as he breathed heavily.

After he turned around, Camden opened the cabin door before he let it slam closed between him and Alessa's ex.

CHAPTER THIRTY-NINE

A winded Quade ran down the path toward Alessa and Camden as they approached the training building. "Alessa! Alessa!"

She stopped Quade from ramming into the two of them and held him at arm's length. "What is it?"

Licking his lips in a frenzy, he breathed heavily in and out, catching his breath. "The Consilium has met and it's been decided..."

"Spit it out," Alessa urged.

Quade shook his head apologetically. "I'm so sorry. They decided Lucas Greenfield was not a threat. They will send orders to stop us from using our resources to investigate him further. There will be a cease order, and just under two days from now, everyone will have received official orders to stop enabling you."

"Hold on a minute. The almighty Consilium has decided it is in everyone's best interest to drop the highly suspicious actions of a highly influential person with unlimited resources?"

"Yeah, I know, it doesn't make any sense," Quade agreed.

Her skin tingled as rage boiled just beneath the surface. "And if I continue my investigation, I'm the enemy? What the fuck?" Alessa screamed in frustration. As the sound reverberated off the trees and bushes, there was a visible reaction of the limbs bending and the leaves scattering. "So they're making it official. Well, if I'm being made into the enemy, I might as well act the part."

"I hate to say it, but I agree. If you're going to make your move, it can't wait." Quade wiped the sweat from his brow.

Camden looked back and forth between Quade and Alessa. "What does this mean as far as our attack on Lucas?"

Alessa licked her lips, pacing back and forth with her hands on her hips. "We forgo the actual attack on Lucas and focus on the extraction of Kai." She turned to Quade. "You know that by helping me, you're associating with—"

Quade waved a hand in mid-air. "Yeah, yeah. I'm assisting a criminal in their eyes and will be punished. But technically, I can play the naive card and state I hadn't received any orders of that capacity. And even if they physically searched my memory, I could deny knowing anything. Wouldn't be the first time I've had Sera fudge my microchip's memory."

Alessa fell into her friend's chest and wrapped her arms around him. As she stayed in his warm embrace, he quietly said, "You are like my sister, Alessa. I would gladly lay down my life for you."

"Well, let's just hope it doesn't come to that today." She laughed to herself and wiped a tear away from her eye. "Do you think you'll have time to update those you trust about the plan to extract Kai?"

Quade stepped back, holding Alessa by the upper arms. "I have more than enough time to request troops. Believe it or not, there is a group of us who believe you are truly protecting humankind and not just fucking around with the Lucas Greenfield theory."

"Well, that's a relief," she sarcastically remarked before grabbing Cam's arm nervously. "We should get to the library's basement and reserve a conference room. But we must act casual, or else they'll know something's up. Got it?"

Quade excitedly rubbed his hands together. "You'll want to find out Lucas Greenfield's current location, pinpoint your sister's whereabouts, download the plantation's blueprints—"

"Yeah, yeah, I know what to do. This isn't my first rodeo, Quade. I need you to do your part, and we will do ours." She ushered Camden toward the library.

"I'll call you to find out which room you reserved. And Alessa?" Quade called out.

She turned back around. "Yeah?"

"Make sure it's one of the soundproof ones." He flashed a grin and winked. "I'll send Alex your way as soon as he can get free."

"Got it, thanks. Go gather your people." Alessa and Camden hurried toward the library, her arm tucked into his, nervous about the coming days.

A few hours later, Alessa looked up from the table they were using to draw the three-dimensional diagram of what would transpire that night. "And you're sure she'll be there?" she asked, worry dripping from her voice.

Alex nodded assuredly. "The woman we've planted on the inside has reassured us Kai is scheduled to be there."

Camden stood protectively over Alessa. "And Lucas?"

"He does have a break in his upcoming schedule, but he shouldn't be there until late morning."

Camden nodded. "Good. That's one less thing for us to have to worry about. We can snatch up Kai and get in and get out."

"Correct. With Lucas Greenfield away from home, it should greatly reduce the amount of security detail," Alex agreed.

Quade closed his hand into a fist, exiting the three-dimensional imagery. "As long as everything goes to plan, this should be a simple extraction. Once we're out of there and on the way home, we will debrief Kai. We have a secure location off base to take her to interrogate her."

Alarmed by his choice of words, Alessa's head darted in his direction.

Camden placed his hand on her shoulder. "It's only to keep her safe and get her side of the story before we bring her back. We know she's your sister, but we need to make sure she hasn't been compromised."

Alessa bit her lower lip to keep herself from talking.

Camden leaned into Alessa and whispered in her ear. "If we need to take your sister and run, are you good with never seeing this place again?"

Realizing this could be the last night she ever set foot in New Sparta, Alessa was hit in the pit of her stomach with feelings of nausea. As Damon's face flashed before her eyes, Alessa nodded up and down jerkily.

She anxiously twirled Damon's ring around her finger as the group dispersed, and as Camden and Quade stepped off to the side, she stared at the band. *It's time.*

"Hey, Cam, I need to do something. Don't wait up for me."

Camden held his hand up for Quade to wait before he hurried over to Alessa. "Do you want me to go with you?"

Alessa slid the ring from her finger. "I'm sure."

She got up on her tiptoes and wrapped her arms around the backside of Camden's thick neck. "I need to do this by myself. I'll meet you at one o'clock out front."

Camden squeezed his arms around Alessa's midsection before reluctantly letting her go. "Don't do anything stupid."

"When have I ever—"

He interrupted her question with a tilt of his head while arching an eyebrow as if to say, 'You're joking, right?'

"Okay, okay. I'll see you later," she laughed while rolling the ring between her fingers.

At some point along the way, the sun had set as Alessa hurried down the path toward Damon's cabin, leaving the way lit only by the bright stars above and a few torches. She kicked the bottom of her magenta skirt and focused on the ground before her.

How long have I been walking?

Alessa meandered close to the lake before she rounded the corner.

Lit torches illuminated Damon's cabin on either side of his doorway.

Her breathing hitched, and she closed her eyes, unintentionally reliving the memory of her standing before Damon and Brielle in bed with one another just a few nights prior.

Her irises flickered red, and the flames grew brighter as she opened her eyes. "Huh, that's new."

Mesmerized, Alessa looked up at the fire while she approached the front door.

"Alessa?" Damon said, clearly surprised. He stood in the open doorway in a black tank top and dark grey cargo pants.

"Oh—uh—yeah—uh," Alessa stammered, having forgotten the reason she had come in the first place.

For a moment, he stared at her in silence. Alessa's tight-fitting magenta dress wrapped around her breasts and back.

Stepping to the side, Damon cleared his throat while ushering her in. "Please come in."

"Oh—um," Alessa shook her head and stepped back, not wanting to see Brielle.

"She's not here. She left on business."

Alessa's jaw dropped, and her tongue pressed against the inside of her cheek as she stepped over the threshold while spinning the ring between her fingers.

Damon cleared his throat, anxiously rubbing his hands on his pants. "I wanted to—I'm just so sorry about the other night." He shut the front door.

She closed her eyes and shook her head back and forth. "That's not why I'm here."

Damon's eyes fell to his mother's ring in Alessa's grasp. "Alessa, you don't need to—"

She licked her lips before interrupting. "But I do. I—I do. You're not mine, and I shouldn't have this anymore." Alessa held out the small piece of jewelry.

"I gave that to you with every intention of—"

"I'm not here to start a fight." She stepped toward Damon and pressed the ring into his chest. "It doesn't belong to me. Maybe it never did." She shrugged with tears in her eyes.

Pressing his hand against hers, Damon's cheeks reddened, and his chest dropped as he exhaled loudly.

"No matter what I've said out of anger, I am happy you're

alive. I only want the best for you"—Alessa bit her lower lip—"even if it isn't with me," her voice cracked.

Damon narrowed his eyes and played with the ring between his fingers. "Why does it sound like you're saying goodbye?"

Alessa's hand dropped, and she wiped a tear away, thinking she might never see home or Damon again once she left the compound that night.

"You never know what tomorrow will bring," she lied through a sad smile.

His eyes scrunched up, etched with concern. "What are you hinting—"

"I can't do this—" Alessa turned and hurried toward the front door.

Turning the handle, she pulled open the door only to have it slammed shut in front of her.

After having rushed up behind Alessa, Damon's hand lay splayed upon the wooden door, his arm outstretched next to Alessa's head, holding the door closed.

Silence stretched between the two as no words were spoken; only their echoing breaths could be heard.

Stepping forward, Damon's chest radiated heat against Alessa's back.

Feeling his warmth, Alessa's breathing turned ragged, and she squeezed her eyes shut, tilting her head back toward the ceiling.

Leaning forward, Damon's forehead pressed into the back of Alessa's dark head of hair, and he smelled her. His cock twitched in primal response, and he growled. *No one but Alessa matters. No one.*

Damon wrapped his arm around her, throwing the ring

onto the entryway table, and while pressing his fingers against the side of her face, he spun her around.

Facing one another, he dove into Alessa's lips, pushing her back against the wooden door.

As their lips urgently moved against one another, she wrapped her arms around Damon's neck.

Picking Alessa up around the waist, he carried her toward his bed.

Breaking away from their passionate entanglement, she looked into his eyes. "Not the bed," Alessa pleaded.

Damon's eyelashes spasmed in understanding, and he grabbed the back of her neck, bringing her back into his lips. Changing direction, he headed for the chaise.

As Damon set her down, Alessa grabbed either side of his tank top's neckline and ripped it in two, exposing his strong chest.

Pressing her lips against the skin stretched tight over his muscles, Alessa kissed her way down to his belt.

Placing two fingers beneath her chin, Damon lifted her face and stood Alessa upright.

He growled hungrily, rubbing his thumb up and down Alessa's neck before reaching behind her. Damon kissed up and down her neck and the top of her chest while he untied the long, thick straps from behind her back. Lifting Alessa's arm, he placed her hand on the back of his neck before kissing the inside of her right bicep, intentionally running his lips over their matching tattoos.

Releasing Alessa's breasts, Damon pulled down the top of her magenta dress down to her belly button, exposing her abdominal scar.

Having forgotten about the injury, Damon's breathing faltered as his eyes fell upon the puffy, jagged skin. His knees buckled, and he held Alessa in place as she wriggled to escape his grasp.

"Baby—" He kissed up her mid-section, tracing the scar with his soft lips.

Closing her eyes, Alessa shook her head back and forth, trying to avoid reliving the trauma. "Damon, no, please, don't—"

"I am so sorry I wasn't there for you—"

His apology was cut short as Alessa fell into his arms and pressed her lips against his, kissing the salty tears from his lips.

Damon's erection lengthened as Alessa straddled him, her warmth pressing against him. With a guttural growl, he pulled her head to the side and sensually dug his teeth into the skin on her neck.

She moaned loudly, and her body shook as he marked her like he used to when they were together.

Damon pulled down what remained of the dress's skirt, and looking up into Alessa's eyes, he leaned forward and pressed his lips against her inner hip.

Damon stood up, and Alessa unzipped his pants as she licked his bottom lip.

Moving backward toward the chair, Alessa followed Damon as he stepped out of his pants, one leg at a time.

Alessa placed her hand on his naked chest before pushing him back onto the chaise.

He stripped out of his black boxer briefs as she wiggled out of her panties, and as he lay back, Alessa crawled on top of him, straddling his legs.

Damon gripped Alessa's hips as she lowered herself down onto his thick erection, and as his length slid deep inside Alessa, Damon's eyes rolled back.

A moan escaped from between his lips, and all coherent thoughts disappeared from his mind as she rose.

Alessa's breathing hitched as Damon's ridge gripped at the edge of her entrance, and grabbing her hips, Damon pulled her back down onto him and thrust.

Alessa moaned loudly as Damon hit her G-spot.

Sitting up, he wrapped his arms around Alessa and pulled her close. Pressing his mouth against her breast, Damon wrapped his lips around her erect pink nipple.

He flicked his tongue against Alessa's smooth skin, and she wriggled atop him as lightning bolts of ecstasy shot from his mouth into her.

As Damon moved from one breast to the other, Alessa rocked her hips back and forth, up and down.

Their moans echoed one another as he broke free from Alessa's breast and stood upright in one swift movement.

Holding Alessa up, Damon withdrew himself before setting her down on the chaise.

"Damon, wha—"

Spreading her legs, he stared at her swollen pink lips. "Gods..." His eyes raised to meet hers as he dove into her.

Alessa's lips separated in a gasp of pleasure, and her eyelids closed as her head flung back.

Damon lapped up her juices as his tongue moved rhythmically inside of her, and as Alessa's hips moved back and forth, her raspy breaths increased in both frequency and volume.

Damon licked up her center to the tip of her pleasure, and Alessa gripped a handful of his hair as her body jerked. He moaned low and deep, holding her in place.

Goosebumps popped up all over her skin as Damon sucked and licked her most sensitive part.

With the appearance of stars in her vision, Alessa found the strength to beg. "I want you. I need you to fill me."

Glancing up at her, Damon's eyes darkened in ecstasy. Pushing up off his stomach, he positioned himself directly over Alessa, placed one hand behind her arched back, and pushed off the chaise, thrusting inside of her.

Her full lips separated, and an erotic whimper escaped as he hit her spot over and over.

"Baby, look at me," Damon demanded, his hips thrusting.

Her eyelashes fluttered, and she looked up into his activated bright silver eyes. Feeling the familiar burning behind her eyes, Alessa squeezed her eyelids shut. *No, no, no.*

"Open your eyes."

She shook her head back and forth as he stopped moving altogether. "No."

"Sydämen liekki," he demanded.

A tear escaped from the corner of her eye, and Damon brushed it away with his thumb. "I accept you. As you are, now."

Opening her eyes, Alessa's irises were flickering between blood red and pale blue.

He looked back and forth between her eyes before leaning down and kissing her deeply.

After Damon bit and sucked her lower lip, he growled, "Let go," before thrusting Alessa so hard, he lifted her entire body entirely up off the chair.

Fireworks exploded in her vision, and Alessa's irises glowed red as the ecstasy she was feeling threatened to consume her.

Her breathing quickened as Damon's speed intensified, and their moans echoed one another as they felt themselves losing control.

The lit candles glowed brighter, and smoke rose from the electronics throughout the cabin.

Alessa shuddered hard as she came. "Damon!" she screamed.

"Oh gods, yes. Alessa," he bellowed out, joining Alessa in ecstasy.

Damon's cock filled Alessa, milked by her intense pelvic contractions, and he slowed the speed of his pumping, focusing more on deepening his reach.

Her hips rocked, allowing Damon in as far as he could go, and as she licked her lips, she moaned one final time. "Uh, yes!"

"Mmm," he groaned, leaning down into Alessa. He turned her head to the side before biting and sucking on her neck as he finished spilling into her.

She gasped, her hips jerking in response to the sharp pain mixed with pleasure.

The flames around the room flared a good foot into the air, and every electronic in the room exploded as she climaxed a second time.

The sudden stroke of his cock made Damon's eyes roll into the back of his head, and he released her skin, bringing her lips back to his.

Consuming her satisfied moans, Damon pressed his lips to hers and sucked her tongue inside of his mouth.

As Alessa's orgasm lessened, he slowly withdrew himself while continuing to worship her breasts.

Glancing up from her nipples, he looked around the room at the smoke and destroyed electronics and laughed. "Well, that was interesting." His eyebrows raised.

Her cheeks blushed red, and Alessa pressed her lips together as her eyes faded to blue.

Laying down beside Alessa, Damon covered their naked

bodies with a blanket he snatched up off the floor beside the chair. "Don't clean up. I want my warmth slowly coming from you as you lie beside me."

He lay his head down and faced Alessa while closing his eyes.

Tears welled up in her eyes as her fingers traced the outline of his jaw. *I wish I could tell you I'm leaving tonight, possibly forever. I wish I could tell you how much I still love you and how much walking away will tear me apart, but I can't. I can't tell you any of this. Because if I do, you'll risk it all to come with me, and I can't have you doing that. I won't let you risk your future as a Spartan and risk being tracked down for the rest of your life. Your blood will not be on my conscience. Never again.*

Damon's breathing slowed as he fell into a deep sleep.

"I will always love you," she whispered and kissed him, leaving the taste of her tears upon his lips.

Pulling away, Alessa covered Damon with the navy blue blanket and ran to the bathroom with her dress and panties in hand, where she quickly cleaned up and dressed.

Tip-toeing back into the room where Damon lay soundly asleep on the chaise, Alessa side-eyed a pen and paper on the table.

After writing a brief letter, she placed the paper beneath his mother's ring on the table next to the front door. Turning around one final time, she watched Damon's chest rise and fall before she inhaled a shaky breath.

Determined to save her sister, Alessa straightened her spine, opened the front door, and disappeared into the dark woods.

CHAPTER FORTY

Alessa stood beneath the shower head as the hot water washed away the memory of Damon's touch while she mentally prepared for her sister's extraction.

Turning off the shower, Alessa grabbed the towel and after wrapping the fabric around her torso, she hurried to her bedroom, where she haphazardly scooped up some clothes and shoved them in Damon's backpack.

As Alessa sat down on her bed, there was a knock on the cabin's front door. "Yes?"

Her friend's muffled voice shouted from behind the door. "It's me, Sera. I thought you might need some help getting ready."

"I do, actually. Come on in." Alessa wiggled into her panties as her friend made her way to the bedroom. She grabbed her Spartan uniform and held it up before her chest.

"Wow," Sera sighed. "I never thought I'd see you back in that again."

The thick ebony strip going down the center of the corset had criss-crossing straps meant to hold a decent number of weapons. A deep, vibrant crimson covered both sides, extending to the back, and the dark fireproof fabric was stretched thin across the top. A bit of fabric extended from the bottom of the corset down to the top of the wearer's thighs in the form of a short skirt.

The bulletproof shoulder strap attached to the black choker that Damon had given her as a present years ago lay on the bed. Its purpose was to cover Alessa's left shoulder as well as protect her heart.

Her black elastic pants were splayed out next to the protective device. They were decorated with tight straps to hold additional weapons, thus allowing the warrior to move unencumbered.

Alessa turned her back to Seraphine. "You and me both. Did you also bring your top so I can help you get into your uniform?"

Sera blushed as she started lacing Alessa's corset. "About that ... I won't be joining you tonight."

Alessa's peered over her shoulder. "Why not? Is everything okay?"

Continuing to lace Alessa's corset, Seraphine smiled. "Yes, everything is fine."

Alessa's eyes narrowed. "What then?"

"Nothing's wrong." Seraphine shook her head with a chuckle. "I'm pregnant."

Alessa's eyebrows rose in surprise. "Oh! H-How far along are you?"

"Eight weeks. We just found out it's a girl."

"Wow." Alessa swallowed the lump in her throat. "Uh, congratulations."

Seraphine turned Alessa around and pulled her into a tight

embrace. "Please try everything in your power to come home. I want my daughter to know her Aunt Alessa."

Pursing her lips together, Alessa stayed silent, knowing in her heart that she probably wouldn't be returning to New Sparta. "Mmhm." She nodded her head, pulling away. "I will try."

Turning back around, Alessa focused on breathing slowly in and out while Seraphine secured her corset.

Noticing the bite mark on Alessa's neck, Seraphine's fingertips caressed the bruise. "What's this?"

Brushing her hand away, Alessa cleared her throat. "Oh, it's —it's nothing."

Seraphine licked her lips and tilted her head. "If you don't want to talk about it, just say so."

Alessa was thankful her friend couldn't see her face as her cheeks burned red. "Okay, I don't want to talk about it."

Seraphine smiled wide. "I know you didn't ask my opinion, but I like Camden. I think he's good for you. *Clearly*, you don't disagree."

Alessa's eyes widened as her pulse quickened, and she stared straight ahead. *She thinks the mark is from Cam.*

"There. Perfect." Seraphine nodded her head in satisfaction.

Sitting down, Alessa pulled on black compression socks before she tugged her pants on, one leg at a time. Breaking the silence, she spoke. "I really am happy for you. For Quade and you both. You know, I completely understand if Quade didn't—"

Seraphine interrupted. "No way. Don't even suggest it. My husband would never let you do this alone. We are both good with him going to extract Kai. I mean, it's *Kai.* How could he not help?"

Alessa nodded as she stood up, tugging up her tight black pants. "Thank you." She shrugged the shoulder protector on, securing it with a buckle across her upper chest. As Alessa stood before the floor-length mirror, Seraphine clasped the choker behind her neck.

"Wow," Seraphine exhaled.

Alessa stared at her reflection silently.

Spinning around, Alessa pressed her hands on her friend's lower belly and spoke. "Little one, you hang tight while I rescue your Auntie Kai." She stood upright, placing her palm upon her friend's cheek. "And you are not to worry about us. We will be just fine. I've got Quade and Camden to watch my back as much as I vow to watch theirs."

Alessa plopped down on the bed and reached for her black combat boot.

"What about Damon? I thought he was to be included if anything were to be decided about extracting your sister. I know you and him aren't in the best of—"

"No. We *cannot* involve Damon. It has nothing to do with my personal feelings anymore. It's one thing for Quade to follow me into battle, but Damon could lose his place as a High-Borne Wellborn. I will not have that guilt on my conscience.

"Quade and I have spoken, and he doesn't have orders from the Ephor to avoid me yet, so we need to act before they can use that against him."

Seraphine sighed. "I understand, but I still don't like it. You would have a much better chance of getting in and out with Damon and his men."

Alessa zipped up her second boot. "We don't have that as an option. I'll take who I can get and who won't be severely punished for helping me." She stood upright. "It's time." Alessa scooped up her backpack and shield before walking out of her bedroom.

Seraphine followed close behind Alessa out into the darkness.

After their short jog through the woods, to avoid attracting unwanted attention, Alessa and Seraphine arrived at the entrance of New Sparta.

Under the cover of the trees, the group of warrior Spartans, along with their small arsenal, awaited Alessa's arrival.

While strapping an additional weapon to his back, Camden turned around to confront Alessa. "Where have you been?"

Seraphine eyed Alessa in confusion but answered for her friend as Alessa stood silently with her lower jaw slack. "Oh, uh, we were talking about stuff, and I was helping her dress."

Camden's eyes narrowed. "Mmm," he mumbled.

Seraphine glanced over at Alessa questioningly.

"Uh, would you please put my shield on?" Alessa handed Seraphine the smaller, condensed shield and stood with her back to her friend.

While squinting her eyes in confusion, Seraphine bit her lower lip to keep herself from asking questions while she secured Alessa's Spartan shield in the center of her corset's back.

Alessa nervously licked her lips and stepped forward to collect her weapons, nodding at her redheaded friend. "Thanks for joining us, Lexi."

"Are you kidding me? Going against what's expected of me is what gets me up in the morning." Lexi winked before shoving a small gun into the side of her pants.

The women Spartan warrior uniforms were similar in that the corset tops were made of bulletproof fabric, but each was customized to its wearer. The colors, shapes, and accessories were made to every warrior's preferences; however, each stuck to the traditional colors of red, black, grey, and gold.

All in all, about thirty Spartans had volunteered to help Alessa extract Kai, all fully knowing exactly what they were getting themselves into.

Sighing loudly, Alessa finished accessorizing every inch of her uniform with a different weapon before she turned to Quade and Camden.

Quade grinned. "Ready to go get your sister?"

Alessa exhaled a shaky breath. "Let's do this."

The Spartans split into two groups of fifteen and loaded into the vehicles.

Camden sat down beside Alessa, their legs resting against one another. "So, how exactly does this work?"

Quade closed the back door and secured it before he signaled for the transportation device to be used.

Alessa adjusted herself on the uncomfortable seat lining the side of the truck. "Anyone with a microchip manufactured by our people can transport to a location entered into the database."

Camden gripped his gun. "I have a temporary microchip. I assume it will work just as well as your more permanent implanted one?"

Alessa smirked and shrugged.

"Wait, what is that supposed to mean?" He panicked. "What happens if it doesn't work?"

Her eyebrows rose and her eyes widened in feigned alarm. "Your head might explode. Guess we'll find out."

Quade and Lexi snorted in laughter from across the back of the enclosed truck.

Camden's eyes widened. "The fuck you say?"

The vehicle disappeared mid-sentence, landing in

Louisiana on the border of Lucas Greenfield's sugarcane plantation.

Lunging forward, Camden fell out the back of the truck, vomiting in the grass.

Quade chuckled. "That happens to everyone the first time. Or ten." He jumped out of the back of the vehicle, weapons raised.

Alessa placed her hand upon Camden's lower back, but he swatted it away.

"Activate and raise your weapons," Quade ordered as they began making their way through the tall plants.

Standing tall, Camden's eyes glowed gold.

Alessa gasped. "Cam, you can't let them—"

He held up a hand to silence her. "I told them. They all know."

"All of them? And they're not fighting over who gets to kill you first?" Alessa asked, flabbergasted.

Camden side-eyed her as they walked carefully out into the open. "I guess my time in New Sparta has earned me a modicum of trust. Plus, I can only assume the majority of them don't really give a damn if I live or die, so to them, I'm just another body."

"Ugh!" a hidden Bodyguard grunted as he hit the ground after he was stabbed by a Spartan.

"What? Why?" Alessa stammered, returning her attention to Camden.

"I didn't have a choice. I needed them to trust me. Completely. It was the only way I wasn't going to get myself killed," he tilted his head and smirked.

"Ah!" another hidden Bodyguard hissed before hitting the ground, dead.

Quade interjected. "All my warriors know is he's got your

back, and so do I. That makes us all brothers. Ex-Bodyguard or not."

Everyone's activated irises glowed in the dark of the night, and as they closed in on the plantation, Camden interrupted the silence. "Aren't real sugarcane plants' leaves green?"

Alessa nodded her head toward the plants. "Yes. But since these are not true sugarcane, these leaves are light amethyst in color."

Camden's golden eyes glowed in the dark of night as he smacked his lips together. "Interesting. Who would've thought something so beautiful could have a sinister purpose?"

"Do we know what that purpose is yet?" Lexi asked, her violet eyes glowing from behind Alessa.

The sound of knives slicing through human flesh echoed through the plants as several Spartan warriors fought hidden Bodyguards in the shadows.

"Not yet." Camden shook his head.

"But since we have deduced Eric Lansing and Lucas Greenfield are undeniably the same person, we know for a fact that he doesn't exude puppies and sunshine."

Lexi snorted. "More like cockroaches and radiation."

Quade raised his finger to his lips. "Shh. We're here."

While standing amongst the amethyst-colored plants, Camden's golden eyes stared over at Alessa's crimson irises, reflecting the glow of the plantation's porch lights.

He eagerly licked his lips and raised one of his guns before his chest.

Alessa blew a steadying breath from between her lips. "Ready?" she mouthed.

With a nod, Camden positioned himself behind Alessa in order to defend her from any surprise attacks.

Alessa was looking in through one of the plantation's many windows when she gasped. "Lucas."

Her stomach dropped when she realized that since Lucas was unexpectedly home, they had grossly underestimated the amount of manpower the plantation would have.

As she sprinted toward the side door, the sounds of battle broke out.

CHAPTER FORTY-ONE

Stretching his arms above his head, Damon groaned with the popping of his joints and movement of his sore muscles. Slowly blinking his eyes open, he expected to see Alessa asleep beside him but was taken back when he found the spot beside him empty and cold.

Confused, he sat upright and threw the blanket off. "Alessa?" he called out. A terrible feeling hit the pit of his stomach. "Alessa, where are you?"

After pulling on his briefs, he ran to the front door and opened it. Looking out into the darkness, he bellowed from the doorway. "Alessa!"

His voice echoed through the trees, and after receiving no response, he slammed the door to his cabin. "Fuck."

His eyes darted to a piece of paper on the entryway table, with his mother's ring set atop.

Moving the ring, he snatched the paper off the table and read the note.

Damon,

Thank you for loving me, if only for a moment.

Goodbye.

"No, no, no, no." Damon balled the piece of paper up and chucked it onto the floor, sprinting for his closet.

Realizing the secret meaning behind her letter, he hurriedly got dressed in his warrior uniform. "What were you thinking doing this without me?" Damon cursed the air.

We swore we'd never say goodbye; it's too permanent a word. It meant we wouldn't be coming home, and we'd always refused to believe that. But if she purposefully put that in the letter, that means...

He pulled on his black cargo pants, wriggled into his compression shirt, and secured his black and red fitted iron chest plate. After clipping on his weapon straps, he tugged on his black combat boots and bolted out the front door.

Busting into the armory, Damon nearly ran into Thaddeus, Marcus, and Justice.

Thaddeus held up his hands. "Whoa, there."

Damon ran around his fellow warrior. "Perfect. I need you to discreetly gather a group of, say, thirty warriors to head out now."

Marcus's forehead scrunched up. "Damon, what are you talking about? We haven't received any orders—"

Damon huffed as he snatched weapons off the wall and shoved them into his straps and pockets. "This would be off the books. It's a personal favor. My father knows nothing of it, and we're going to keep it that way." He turned and stared directly at three Spartans. "Is that clear?"

The warriors' backs stiffened. "Yes," Marcus responded.

"You got it," Justice nodded their head.

"Crystal clear," Thaddeus said before speaking into his high-tech walkie-talkie. "The first thirty warriors to respond are to report to the armory, fully dressed in their gear. It is a 'Code Grey' and requires the utmost discretion. I repeat, discretion is required. If anyone does not feel up to the task, continue your posts and keep your damn mouths shut, or there will be consequences."

A cacophony of voices reporting their names responded, and within twenty minutes, Spartan warriors were geared up and ready to head out as Damon stood before them.

"I appreciate you all showing up knowing what 'Code Grey' means. You all trusting me with your lives is the highest honor anyone can bestow upon me. I will let you know; I know nothing about this mission."

The warriors looked at one another in confusion.

"I believe Alessa and a small group of our people may have gone against the Consilium's orders and transported to Lucas Greenfield's plantation to extract her sister from Lucas Greenfield's plantation."

He stared at the warriors standing before him.

"Wait, you mean Kai? You think Kai's alive?" Justice asked, stepping forward.

Damon silently nodded while repositioning his weapon. "I completely understand if anyone wants to step down from this mission. Your participation could end poorly for you, even though I hope my father takes it upon himself to grant us forgiveness. I will let them know you knew nothing about it until just before we left. But enough talking, we need to get moving. Is anyone uncomfortable with participating with the information I just gave?"

Every single person refused to move a muscle.

Exhaling a loud breath in relief, Damon held his gun in front of his chest. "Let's move out."

The Spartan soldiers ran toward three military trucks and piled into the back.

Justice closed the door behind the warriors, and as Damon sat down, he closed his eyes.

Marcus squeezed Damon's shoulder. "We'll get them out," Marcus said reassuringly.

Pressing his lips together in a forced smile, Damon nodded as Justice announced their teleportation. "Three ... two ... one..."

CHAPTER FORTY-TWO

"Quade!" Alessa screamed, bolting for the entrance. Barging in through the doorway with her weapon raised, she fell into pure chaos.

Her fellow Spartan warriors were spread thin, engaged in battle with silver-suited Bodyguards.

"Alessa!" Camden sprinted after her and impaled a Bodyguard who had been charging toward Alessa with a machete held high.

"What the fuck is he doing with a machete?" Camden demanded while extracting additional hand-to-hand combat weapons from his straps.

Glancing to the right, Alessa saw at least three Bodyguards abandon the fight and sprint out of the house's side door. Her head darted toward the bizarre behavior, and as she realized why Rogue Command Bodyguards were running away from a battle, she and Camden broke free from the fight and took chase.

Reaching back to pull an arrow from her quiver, Alessa entered the enclosed glass greenhouse behind the Rogue

Command Bodyguards who had surrounded Lucas Greenfield and were running for the exit.

Aiming at the group of men, Alessa screamed at the top of her lungs as he was about to hit the door. "Eric!"

He whipped around, and their eyes met.

Knowing in her heart she had been right all along, Alessa glared deep into Lucas's stormy grey eyes as she drew back the bowstring.

Kai's screams echoed off the glass walls at the same time she released the arrow, and as she turned her head toward the sound, instead of striking Lucas, the arrow hit a Bodyguard standing a few inches to the right of him, straight through the eye.

As the Rogue Command Bodyguards dove in front of Lucas, one of the men standing in front aimed a weapon at Alessa and Camden. Releasing the targeted sound wave in their direction, the glass walls vibrated and shattered.

"Shit!" Alessa grabbed Camden and they dove out of the way as glass shards flew around them.

Lifting her head, she glared at Lucas.

Staring back at Alessa, he sported a smug grin while pushing backward out of the greenhouse.

"Dammit!" she groaned in frustration. Shaking her head back and forth, Alessa jumped up and ran back into the house, away from the incoming Rogue Command Bodyguards. "Hurry! We've got to find Quade!" Alessa yelled to Camden over the sounds of death.

As one of the Spartan comrades fell, dead, in front of them, Camden raised his smaller gun and aimed it at the attacking Rogue Bodyguard. Shooting the charged barbed balls into the man's gut, Camden pressed his thumb into the button on the trigger. The Bodyguard's entire body vibrated as he was electrocuted and collapsed to the ground, smoke rising from his nostrils and mouth.

"Jade, no..." Alessa gently closed her fallen comrade's eyes before she jumped up, fueled by anger.

"Quade!" she screamed, moving down the hallway, scanning each room for her friend.

As they came to the end of the hallway, the house opened into a grand ballroom.

Spotting Lexi in the back of the large room, Camden yelled her name as he stood under the arches of the room's entrance. "Lexi!"

She had just taken a hard kick to the stomach and was falling backward as her attacker aimed his flame thrower at the wounded Spartan.

Panic gripped his heart, and Camden sprinted toward Lexi. He extracted his condensed shield from his back, and as he slid on his knees across the floor, his shield expanded to its full size. Camden dove in front of her at the last second, blocking the fire.

As the flames danced up the front of the shield, Lexi and Camden stared into one another's eyes, panting heavily.

The hot flames receded, and Camden plucked a dagger from his chest strap, stood upright, and rotated, sending the dagger straight into the attacking Bodyguard's right eye socket.

From across the room, Alessa sighed heavily upon finding Quade alive, surrounded by at least fifteen Bodyguards.

Grabbing a specialty grenade from her arsenal of weapons stashed in her belt, Alessa yelled for her fellow Spartan warriors to find cover. "Shields up!"

After she threw the weapon up, the device flashed red twice upon embedding itself in the high ceiling.

The Bodyguards looked around in confusion as every

Spartan stopped fighting and took a knee, covering themselves with their expanding shields.

As the machine beeped, acid rain poured down onto the unsuspecting Bodyguards, who had remained out in the open.

Their bony fingers clawed at the flesh melting from their faces.

From beneath the protection of her shield, Alessa scanned the room for her sister, knowing she would've sought shelter.

Finding Kai hiding beneath the grand piano, Alessa's breathing hitched. "Kai..."

Pulling the only Strongroom Bubble she had on her, Alessa stood upright with her shield still overhead.

Realizing what Alessa was doing, Quade yelled at her. "Alessa, I got you! Go!"

Holding the shield above her head, protecting her from the acid still trickling down, Alessa sprinted toward Kai.

Seeing Alessa run toward her, Kai's eyes squinted in disbelief. "Alessa?"

With her arms raised above, Alessa smacked her forearms together, triggering arm protectors to spread across her exposed skin.

At the same time the acid ceased falling from the ceiling, Alessa hit the ground. Gliding across the slick tile on the side of her thigh, Alessa slid beneath the grand piano and wrapped her arms around her sister.

Alessa grabbed Kai, and they slid together from underneath the piece of furniture. Her eyes unglitched back to blue as they knelt on the ground in one another's arms, and Alessa immediately slammed down the Strongroom Bubble upon the tiled floor.

As the protective shield expanded around the sisters, Cain threw himself against the translucent blue shimmer. "Kai!" he screamed just before the bubble blocked out sound from the outside.

Alessa held her sister as they stared up at the handsome man's distraught face before he was shot in the arm by a Spartan, forcing him to retreat.

Watching the man run away, Alessa's eyes narrowed. "Who the hell is that?"

Turning around to face her sister, Kai's eyes widened in disbelief. "Lessie? Wh-What are you doing here?"

Alessa held back tears as she ran her hands down Kai's face. "What am I doing here? What are you doing here, with Eric, no less? How did you get wrapped up in this mess? What were you thinking—"

"I'm so sorry," Kai cried, wrapping her arms around Alessa's neck. "I'm so sorry for everything."

"What happened?" Alessa shook her head back and forth as her sister struggled to explain herself.

"I fell in love with Cain, Eric's nephew." Kai looked out of the transparent bubble at Cain fighting the Spartans. "At least, I thought I did. Now, I realize he manipulated me and probably never loved me."

Kai pulled back from her sister and held her at arm's length. "Did you help create the serum that erased my memory?"

Kai wiped her nose with her hand and stared down at the ground. "I did. It was all me."

"Why? How could you do that to me?" Alessa asked, her face scrunched up in confusion.

A Bodyguard ran up to their bubble and smacked it with his machete. The women flinched as it bounced off the protective surface before they continued their conversation inside the protective bubble.

"When Cain told me their plan to kill you, I convinced

them to inject you with the serum I made. It contained medication to simulate death, so when they dumped you, they'd thought you'd be dead, but—"

"I wouldn't be. But how did you not know the hell they'd put me through? They tortured me ... for weeks."

Kai cried. "I am so sorry, Lessie. I was told they would give you the injection and dump your body as soon as they got ahold of you. After realizing how long you had suffered, I struggled to keep up the facade to help you escape." She grabbed her sister's hand. "Cain made me believe so much that I now know isn't true. But how are you here right now? Did my memory loss serum not work?"

"It did ... for a while. Then Bodyguards came after me, and Damon found me and helped me remember." Alessa's face scrunched up in confusion. "Why would you want to erase my memory? Faking my death, I understand."

Kai squeezed Alessa's hands. "My serum was supposed to be a gift to you."

"What? What do you mean—"

"I know how much the loss of our parents had taken from you and how you have always blamed yourself for making me a Spartan, knowing this wasn't the life I would've chosen for myself."

Alessa silently listened to her sister's explanation.

"I wanted to give you a new life, one without loss and guilt."

"But also one without Damon?" Alessa demanded.

Kai scoffed. "I know you love Damon, but I wanted you to be able to live a normal life, so, yes, I sacrificed him for your peace. I am so, so sorry it didn't work, though."

"I'm not," Alessa grabbed her sister's arms. "I knew from

the moment I awoke something was missing. I would've never stopped searching for you."

"I'm sorry, Lessie. I fucked everything up." Kai buried her face in her hands.

"Shh. Not now. We have our entire lives for you to make it up to me. We only have a minute or so left in this protection, and I still need to know how badly I need to fuck this Cain guy up."

Kai wiped her tears away. "He made me believe he loved me, but every day, I see more of how dark his soul truly is."

Alessa clenched her teeth as anger pulsed through her veins. "What has he done to you? Has he hurt you?" She tucked some strands of Kai's hair behind her ear. "How did the two of you even meet?"

"That's too long of a story for right now. All you need to know is they fed me their bullshit about making the world better and wanting to do what was best, and I stupidly fell for it." She shook her head back and forth. "I just want to get out of here and go home, to forget that this happened, like it was a bad dream."

Alessa's heart fluttered. "Oh, thank the gods. That's the only reason we're here right now. YOU are the mission. We may not be able to return to Sparta, but I don't care. Wherever you are is my home."

Tears welled up in Kai's eyes. "Oh, Lessie. I love you—"

CHAPTER FORTY-THREE

When they opened the truck's doors, bullets whizzed past the Spartan warriors. They hit the ground before answering the gunfire with their own.

"Was this expected?" Marcus shouted over the sounds of battle.

"No." Damon looked at the plantation, already littered with fallen bodies from both sides of the battle.

"Go get them. We'll get as many of our people out as possible while maintaining a clear path for you to return."

Damon nodded his head toward the others and waved his arm for them to follow him. "Keep your eyes open. Bodyguards will be positioned within the sugarcane fields."

He turned to face all of his Spartan family, raising his weapon in front of his chest. "To die in battle is the most courageous way to leave this world; we should all be so lucky, but let us strive to live to fight another day."

Damon bellowed a warrior's cry, sprinting through the lavender sugarcane plants. Bodyguards popped up left and right, aiming at the Spartans.

Approaching the large plantation, Damon burst in through the front door. "Alessa!" he hollered over the grunts and screams.

He dodged to the left as a silver suit dove at him with an electrified knife in hand.

"Alessa, answer me!" he yelled as he ran.

Pulling weapons from the straps wrapped around his torso, Damon fought back against the Bodyguards, one after another.

Moving from room to room, he looked into each doorway before moving on to the next. "Alessa, dammit!" he cursed before his eyes darted toward the end of the long hallway, and every hair on his arms stood up as he heard the disembodied voice say, "Go to her."

"Alessa," he said breathlessly, darting for the ballroom.

Turning the corner, he saw the remnants of several deceased Bodyguards lying on the floor whose skin had melted away. Peering up, he saw the weapon buried deep in the ceiling.

As he scanned the room, Damon's gaze landed upon Alessa and Kai. Their arms were wrapped tightly around one another in a desperate embrace.

He sighed in relief. *Alessa found her. Kai's alive, just like she said.*

Watching the Spartan enter the room, Cain took advantage of the man being distracted by Alessa and charged Damon, running a sharp knife across his bicep.

Failing to dodge the blade, Damon grunted as it sliced his skin. "Ugh!"

Cain grinned wickedly at the Spartan. "Give my regards to Hades."

Damon touched the blood coming from the wound. "'Tis' but a scratch," he laughed incredulously.

Cain confidently passed the deadly knife back and forth between his hands, taunting the Spartan warrior. "One laced with poison."

Glancing over at his arm, he recognized the faint tingle of numbness spreading from the wound. *Oh shit.*

Thinking Damon was an easy target, Cain lunged for him.

Moving quicker than Cain had expected, the Spartan dodged the man, spun him around, and kicked him in the middle of his chest.

As Cain flew back through the air, a look of surprise across his face, Damon pulled a dagger from his arsenal, and after raising it above his head, Damon brought his arm forward, letting go of the golden hilt.

The black leather-wrapped golden hilt and blade spun through the air toward Cain's chest.

—

Unbeknownst to those who fought in the ballroom, Hades hid amongst the shadows, leaning up against a tall white pillar in a corner of the room.

—

The shimmering blue protective bubble surrounding the sisters was evaporating in a jagged line from the bottom up.

—

Cain fell back as if in slow motion, and just before the sharp blade would have pierced the far left side of the man's chest, Hades extended his arm and flicked his first two fingers. The dagger slid to the side, missing its target altogether, and continued past Cain, rotating in the air.

———

The protective bubble had evaporated up to Alessa and Kai's chest, and by the time Alessa looked up and realized a blade was flying toward them, there was nothing she could do. "No!" she screamed while spinning her sister around, prepared to take the hit herself.

Kai cried out as Alessa whipped her body around, the weapon having already unknowingly buried itself between her shoulder blades.

———

With a satisfied sneer, Hades disappeared into the night.

———

Holding her sister tight, Alessa stared past Kai, surprised she couldn't yet feel the blade's sharp edge.

Kai stood still for a few moments before her eyes widened.

Alessa held her sister out at arm's length. "Kai?"

As the searing pain spread from her center, Kai lifted her hands, reaching up and over her shoulders, desperately seeking the source of the pain. With blood seeping out from the corner of her mouth, she fell forward into Alessa's arms.

"Lessie," she panicked.

Alessa screamed as her sister collapsed, revealing the deadly weapon sticking out of her back. Recognizing the decorative hilt of the blade, Alessa gasped. "Oh, gods! Is this—is this Damon's?"

Bright red blood quickly spread onto Kai's daffodil-yellow silk dress shirt, encircling the wound.

Alessa's eyes darted around the room, searching for Damon.

She wanted to do nothing more than pull the deadly object out from her sister's body, but with all her training, Alessa knew doing so would guarantee Kai's death.

"What do I do? The fuck do I do? Okay. You're okay. You'll be okay," Alessa repeated as she knelt on the floor, holding her sister.

Blood spilled from Kai's mouth, and she coughed, spraying red into the air.

"No. No. No, you can't do this to me. I just got you back," Alessa begged through heart-stricken tears.

Feeling a mysterious wave of guilt, Alessa locked eyes with Damon as he stood watching them, unmoving, near the room's entrance.

He stared at Alessa and Kai, utter devastation etched into the lines of his face as he fell to his knees.

"I'm ... so sorry ... for everything," Kai croaked as her body shook violently.

Alessa's voice trembled as she failed to hold back tears. "Shh. Save your strength. We're going to get you out of here."

"I'm cold, Lessie. I'm so ... cold."

"Oh, um, let me..." Alessa searched the room for a source of heat but came up empty-handed.

Kai inhaled a noisy breath before she spoke. "Thank you ... for ... being my ... big sister. I love ... you ... Lessie. I'll always love..."

Kai's body went limp as her eyes closed, and her head fell to the side.

Alessa's heart stilled, and her breathing hitched. "Kai?" Her eyes darted back and forth as she searched for signs of life. "Kai?"

Shaking her sister, all the blood drained from Alessa's face. "No, no, no. This isn't happening. This can't be happening."

Rage, as she had never felt before, burned within Alessa's heart as she screamed her sister's name. "Kai! No, Kai!"

Having been the cause of Kai's death, Damon dropped to his knees in despair. "No ... Kai. I didn't mean—"

Hearing Alessa's cries, Camden turned his attention from the Bodyguards to find her sitting on the floor, holding her sister's body. "Oh, no, Alessa."

Watching Alessa's frame tremble, Camden knew they didn't have much time before Alessa lost control.

Without a moment's hesitation, he pushed Lexi toward the exit and yelled for her to get out. "Run! Get out of the house, now!"

Confused, Lexi tilted her head and narrowed her eyes.

"I said go! Get as many Spartans out as you can!" Camden screamed as he ran across the room toward Damon. "Spartans, retreat!"

Not understanding the urgency of their situation, the majority of the Spartans continued to fight.

His voice echoed off the tile floors as he sprinted across the ballroom. "Get out now!"

Slamming into Damon, Camden cursed. "Get up, Damon. We've got to get out of here."

Damon tried to use his numb arm to push off the ground but fell back down. "But ... Kai. She's ... she's..."

"I know, but if you stay here, you will die as well. Alessa is about to lose control. You don't remember what happened the last time, but no one is safe near her. Now, get up!"

Snapping out of it, Damon got up and took off after Camden out of the closest exit.

Memories of Kai flashed before Alessa's eyes as she held her sister's limp body, finally stopping on a toddler version of Kai lying dead in Alessa's arms.

Her eyes, whites and all, were stained red as her glitch took over.

Tilting her head back, Alessa screamed at the top of her lungs as an electromagnetic pulse resonated from deep inside of her. The invisible wave shot across the house, engulfing every electronic in flames and causing every microchip inside her fellow Spartans and the Bodyguard's brains to explode instantaneously.

Every single person who remained in the house collapsed to the floor, dead, just before the glass windows and doors exploded.

Camden and Damon jumped out the back door, and shards of glass flew as loud explosions followed close behind.

Landing safely in the grass, they both looked back at the house engulfed in flames.

"Alessa!" Camden yelled as Damon sat in stunned silence, the tingling sensation spreading throughout his torso.

Jumping up, Camden ran back toward the house but was pushed back by the intensity of the fire. "Alessa, where are you?" he yelled through the doorway.

Camden was about to re-enter the plantation when he spotted Quade coughing with his back against a nearby tree.

"Where's Alessa? Have you seen her?" Camden demanded.

"I don't know." Quade coughed, his warrior's uniform singed at the edges.

Holding his arm above his head, Camden ran back into the house, searching for Alessa. "Alessa!"

He found her sitting in the middle of the ballroom floor with Kai's body in her arms, rocking back and forth.

"This can't be happening again; not again," she was crying.

Gripping the ornate hilt, Alessa yanked the dagger from her sister's back before tossing it to the side of the tiled floor. "No. No. No. This isn't real. This can't be real."

Cautiously approaching Alessa, Camden extended his hands out in front of him in a gesture of peace. "Alessa..."

At the sound of his voice, she jumped like a frightened cat, her red irises flickering red as she held her sister closer.

"It's Cam. I'm here. Alessa, I'm here."

"Why does this keep happening? Kai was innocent. She was only here—in this life because—because of me," she sobbed.

Camden reached out and touched Alessa's upper back.

"Don't touch me!" She shrugged him away and pressed her sister's empty vessel against her chest. "Everything I touch burns and turns to ash. Everyone I love dies."

The dark smoke swirled, threatening to overtake the room's remaining oxygen.

Camden's lungs burned as he fought off the urge to cough. "That's not true. I'm here, Alessa. I'm still here. I've got you." He cleared his throat and wiped away the tears in his eyes caused by the intense heat. "I've got you." Camden crouched down. "Let me help you; let me help Kai."

Staring up into Camden's golden irises, Alessa released her tight grip on her sister, allowing Camden to scoop Kai up in his arms.

The room was falling around them as they sprinted for the only remaining exit not blocked by fire: a picture window.

Alessa reached into her strap and pulled out a small bomb. Throwing it at the glass, she hit its detonator, and the glass shattered.

CHAPTER FORTY-FOUR

On their way back to the transportation trucks, the Spartans passed by several of their fallen warriors.

Amidst the field of amethyst sugarcane, Damon bent down unsteadily and closed his fallen friend's eyes. "Marcus. Thank you for your sacrifice. You will be buried with those worthy of the highest honor."

Another of the Spartans picked Marcus up from underneath his arms and lifted him onto his back before carrying him back to the trucks.

While standing beside the vehicles, Damon watched someone familiar emerge from the smoke. "Alessa?" he tripped forward, hope gripping his heart.

Watching the two figures step forward, he saw a lifeless Kai being cradled against Camden's chest.

Swallowing back tears, Damon stammered. "Fuck. I can't believe I—Alessa, I—"

"YOU!" Her rage emanated from every pore as she struggled to keep her glitch in check upon seeing the man who murdered her baby sister.

Recognizing the hate written clearly across her face, Damon froze.

Charging toward Damon, Alessa punched him in the jaw. "YOU! How could you?"

With the force of her hit, Damon was forced to his knees. He adjusted his jaw with the hand he could still feel as he looked up at her apologetically. "I don't know how it—I'm so sorry—"

"She loved you! How could you do this to her? To me?" Alessa screamed over his apology.

Damon's gaze dropped. "I came to help you, to save Kai. This was not supposed to happen. The dagger shifted mid-air! It shouldn't have—"

"Stop!" Glaring at him, Alessa's eyes flickered red as she dropped every one of the remaining Spartans with the sensation of a spike being driven through their skulls. "Just stop. Hades warned me this would happen. It should have been you." She turned away and walked toward the first truck. "It should have been you..."

Following Alessa, Camden climbed into the back with Kai still in his arms. "Take us back, please," Camden instructed the driver.

Feeling Alessa's release, Damon heard the back doors close, and guilt poured from every ounce of his being as he watched the vehicle disappear into the night.

CHAPTER FORTY-FIVE

As they returned to New Sparta, they were greeted with absolute chaos.

The back of the truck opened, and the sounds of the wounded intermingled with the orders being barked by the medical staff. Medics scrambled about, tending to the gravely injured, while off to the side lay a row of Spartans who had departed from this world.

Numb to the scene unfolding before them, Alessa stepped down from the vehicle.

Spouses and children were running down the main road frantically, trying to find out whether their loved ones were amongst the deceased.

Alessa walked forward as if in a daze as Seraphine shouted orders to her fellow medics. "No, not like that! If you ever want him to walk again, you can't tie the tourniquet that tight." She loosened the tie and re-wrapped it. "There, that's better."

Seraphine wiped the back of her hand across her forehead, leaving a bloodied smear. "Give me the suturing gun. Where is the soldering iron? I'm going to need you to—" Seeing Alessa, she froze.

"Alessa! Alessa, where is Quade? Have you seen him?" Seraphine demanded.

Alessa stilled and looked absentmindedly around into the crowd. "Quade?"

"Yes, Quade. My husband! What's the matter with you?" Seraphine's eyes darted behind Alessa, and she gasped as she saw Kai's limp body in Camden's arms.

"Oh, shit!" Sprinting forward, the doctor pressed her fingers into the side of Kai's neck. "Kai? Gods, no, no," Seraphine pleaded. "How long has she been down? Maybe we can still—"

Shaking his head, Camden tilted her body so the fatal injury was exposed.

"I can fix it," Alessa mumbled, emotionless.

"Oh, gods," Seraphine covered her mouth with a shaking hand. "I—Alessa." She extended a hand toward her friend but was interrupted by the wail of someone in agony. "I'm sorry, but I have to go. There are so many to tend to."

Seraphine turned toward Camden. "Please send word if you see Quade."

He nodded his head in silent agreement before readjusting Kai's limp body closer to his chest. "Where are we taking her?"

Damon's father marched up to Camden and Alessa, pointing his long, bony finger. "You will NOT be bringing that abomination into our home."

A large group of older men from the Council of Elders rushed toward Alessa as they stood before the fountains. "How dare you go behind our backs after we explicitly instructed you not to seek out your sister. Wh—What were you thinking?" he yelled.

Alessa's head tilted slightly to the side as she absorbed everything they said about her flesh and blood. "You did no such thing."

He swallowed, surprised by her defiant response. "Well, we were about to, and somehow you knew about that. That had to be why you chose to act tonight."

Alessa glared at him, feeling the burning sensation build up behind her eyes.

"All these lives lost, all the blood spilled tonight, is on you!" He pointed at Alessa's chest. "You will be put on trial for your actions. Your sister was—"

Alessa's eyes flared bright red, and she stepped forward, pressing her chest against the man's pointed finger. "My sister was what? What more could you complain about? My sister is DEAD. Because of you! Because of the Council of Elders and the Consilium's inability to protect our people and all of humanity. Your refusal to take action against Lucas Greenfield is what caused this. Just wait, I guarantee as time goes on, the truth about the imitation sugar will come out, and people will die. They always do when Eric, I mean Lucas, is involved. And if I am to be held accountable for tonight's loss of life, then you should all be held accountable for every single death, both Spartan and general population, that is associated with Ambrosia."

Alessa's jaw clenched as she struggled to maintain her composure. "My sister was my world, my everything. She just needed a place to live because of me! And all she ever wanted was control of her own life and in order to do that she had to run away from this fucking place."

The electronics within eyeshot were visibly vibrating in response to Alessa's building rage.

Tears swam in her red irises and Alessa's body shook as she

stepped toward Damon's father, menacingly. "You can put me on trial and find me guilty of trying to save my flesh and blood from the enemy while you failed her. You can do whatever you want to me, *after* I take care of my sister."

The men audibly gasped at Alessa's disrespectful tone. "I—If you think your traitor will be allowed to lie with our warriors—"

Alessa's head whipped back around to face the elders. "I would never trap my sister here. If I can't save her soul from the underworld, I will at least set her physical form free."

Camden stayed close to Alessa in case the group of Spartans decided to attack.

Done with their discussion, Alessa turned her back and walked away. "I am not to be bothered until the sunrise after next."

Damon's father's voice shook as he tried to regain dominance. "If you think—"

She whipped around, stopping the group of men with the deadly glare of her red irises. Focusing on the microchips within the Council of Elders' heads, she brought them to their knees. Her left eyebrow raised as she peered down at them and addressed them. "I will meet you at the cliff the morning after next for my trial. Until then, I will be preparing my sister for her final rest."

Releasing the hold on their microchips, the men exhaled simultaneously and fell forward. Staring up at her in shock, they remained on their knees, watching Alessa march away while Camden held Kai in his arms.

One of the council member's jaw dropped. "Did she just—"

Damon's father clenched his teeth together before responding. "Yes. She is out of control and a danger to us all. I must call the Consilium to discuss matters further."

CHAPTER FORTY-SIX

After walking down the path for a half hour, Camden grunted while re-adjusting Kai in his arms. "Alessa, where are we taking Kai?"

"Our elder's cabin."

"Okay. Then what?"

"We're going to get some sleep. The next few days are going to be rough."

Camden's eyebrows scrunched up in disbelief. "Sleep? You think I can go to sleep after such an intense battle?"

"Okay," she huffed. "Shower then, I don't really care." She veered off the main path toward their small wooden cabin. Opening the door, she stood to the side so Camden could squeeze in with her sister.

He stood motionless in the main entry, awaiting instructions.

"Oh, right. You can lay Kai down on her bed for now."

Camden followed Alessa toward the bedroom on the left side of the hallway, across from the bathroom. As she opened the light brown wooden door, he followed her in.

Laying Kai down on the bed, Camden stretched her limbs out on the bed.

Alessa grabbed the fresh flowers from the vase on the bedside table. "Purple flowers are her favorite." Alessa smiled.

Camden side-eyed Alessa while standing up. "Are you doing okay?" he asked hesitantly.

"Yeah, why?" she responded calmly.

Anxious, Camden rubbed his hands up and down his thighs. "You seem far too calm after everything you experienced tonight."

"You mean to say me nearly ripping the heads off my elders was calm?" She laughed, devoid of humor, with a shrug of her shoulders and placed her hand upon the muscular bulge in his shoulder. "Don't worry about me. Go take a hot shower."

Reaching up, he gently squeezed her hand. "Are you sure I should leave you alone right now?"

"I'm just going to sit here with my sister. Take one of your epically long showers. You've earned it."

Camden hesitated. "Want to join me? I mean, it'd be just to clean off, nothing sexual."

Alessa smiled, thankful for his thoughtfulness. "Not right now. I'm going to spend some time with Kai."

He bent forward, resting his forehead against hers. "You stay right here. Don't do anything stupid."

Dropping her hand, she smiled and dragged the chair next to her sister's bed. "Go." She sat down and peered over her shoulder at her friend. "Thank you. For everything."

His back straightened as he started taking off the layers of warrior gear. "If you need me, just holler."

After watching him leave the bedroom, Alessa waited until she heard the shower turn on before speaking to her sister.

"I am so, so sorry." She squeezed her sister's cold hand. "I will do everything in my power to bring you back. This is not our final goodbye. I swear it."

Letting go of her sister, Alessa stood up and entered the hallway. Quietly peering in the cracked bathroom door, she saw Camden's large shadow behind the shower curtain. Eyeing his cell phone, she grabbed it off the counter.

She set a forty-minute timer titled 'Save Alessa from the lake. Bring a knife & look for the boat' before returning his phone beside the sink.

Retracting her arm from between the door and doorframe, Alessa tip-toed toward the front door.

Bolting out the front door, she sprinted toward the lake. While formulating a plan, Alessa's chest was heaving up and down as she reached the shoreline. "Where's the boat?" she asked breathily while looking around, bent over with her hands on her knees.

Locating it behind a nearby bush, Alessa pushed back its leaves, exposing the small wooden boat amongst the shadows in the night.

She sighed in relief upon seeing the anchor at the bottom of the boat. "Good, now all I need is—" Alessa looked nearby for a heavy rock to weigh her down.

After finding a small boulder, she pushed the boat toward the water and hauled the small boulder into the boat. Careful not to drop it too hard, she grunted loudly as she placed the deep grey stone in the boat.

Breathing heavily, she walked over to the small shed and grabbed a long rope from a hook hanging on the wall.

After throwing the coarse rope into the bottom of the boat, Alessa pushed it out onto the dark still water. When she had rowed far enough into the water to ensure her body would be fully submerged but close enough to the edge for Camden to hopefully find her, Alessa stopped and dropped the anchor over the boat's edge.

With her shaking, bloodied hands, she tied the frayed rope around her corseted midsection, and after letting out a maniacal laugh, Alessa scooted to the edge of the wooden bench. "Am I crazy for thinking this could work?"

Gripping the boat's edge, her knuckles turned white as she rocked the boat back and forth. "Here goes nothing."

She exhaled noisily as the boat rocked faster until the closest side foundered and the boat flipped.

After a sharp intake of breath, Alessa was pulled down into the lake's depths by the weight of the boulder tied around her midsection. Sinking deeper, bubbles escaped her lungs, drifting to the water's surface as Alessa lost consciousness.

CHAPTER FORTY-SEVEN

Damon's truck rocked back and forth as he and the other Spartan warriors were transported back to New Sparta.

After the back doors opened, he and Quade entered the bloody scene unfolding before him.

Seraphine screamed over the groans of wounded men and women. "Quade!"

Her husband ran into Seraphine's open arms and lifted her off the ground in a tight embrace. Their lips crushed desperately up against one another's. "I was afraid you had fallen."

Quade placed his hand on the side of her face and grinned. "Don't be so eager to replace your husband just yet."

She stretched her neck and kissed him again before realizing Damon was standing directly beside them. "Damon! Thank the gods you're alive."

Damon fell to his knees before them. Leaning forward, he showed her the discolored gash across his upper arm. "Guy's dagger was soaked in poison," he said through chattering teeth.

Quade squatted beside his friend and held him upright.

Seraphine's eyes widened in concern. "Let me see what I have here to treat that." She ran to an open brown bag and dug to the bottom. Extracting a small ampule, she held it up. "Got it!"

She broke the glass with a gauze pad and drew the clear liquid into a syringe. "It'll make you tired, but it should be just for the day. The injection may burn a little."

As she jabbed the needle into his injured bicep, Seraphine pushed the plunger, injecting the light green liquid into his arm.

As the hot liquid started into his tingling extremity, Damon clenched his teeth together.

Seraphine extracted the needle before she turned around to gather additional supplies. "I need to clean this wound..."

Damon shook his head while struggling to stand up. "I'll clean it later."

With Quade helping him stand upright, Damon turned. "Thanks," he bellowed over his shoulder as he limped away.

Quade glanced over at his wife. "I should—"

Seraphine nodded, giving him a quick hug. "Agreed. Go on; I have plenty to keep me busy. I'm just glad to know you are okay."

Darting after his friend, Quade licked his lips before yelling out. "Damon! Hey, Damon, wait up!"

Chasing Damon back to his secluded cabin in the woods, Quade placed his hands on his knees and bent over. "What ... was ... that ... about?" he gasped between breaths.

Exhausted, Damon burst through his front door and grabbed a backpack from under his bed. Ripping open his dresser drawers, he haphazardly threw in articles of clothing with his working hand.

Quade followed him into his house and stood before Damon's bed. "What are you doing? I don't think you're in the right frame of mind to be leaving to go anywhere."

Shaking his head back and forth, Damon threw one last article of clothing into the bag before shuffling toward the bathroom.

When Quade hurried over to help his friend, Damon's head whipped toward him. "Leave me be," he snapped, pushing him away.

Quade stood outside the bathroom as Damon slammed the door in his face.

Turning on the shower, Damon painfully stripped out of his bloodied and dirty uniform before stepping into the hot water streaming down from the shower head.

"Damon, talk to me, man. What's going on? Is this about Kai?"

Placing his hands on the stones on the side of the shower, Damon growled and punched the wall, bloodying his knuckles.

Unable to find the words, Damon silently showered the blood, sweat, and tears from his skin.

As the tingling sensation was replaced by pain in his upper arm, Damon emerged from the steaming bathroom with a towel wrapped around his waist. "I need your help."

Quade was sitting on the ground with his back against the wall as he looked up at Damon. "All you have to do is ask. What do you need?"

Damon held his towel together with one hand as he headed for his closet. "I need information on a doctor in Philadelphia who has the capability of implanting worms."

Quade stood up, confusion written on his face. "Worms? As in—"

Damon strolled toward his closet. "The technology that targets specific moments within one's memories."

Quade's eyes narrowed curiously. "I can do that for you, brother, but why?"

Damon inhaled deeply while reaching for a navy black fitted T-shirt. "I shouldn't feel this way about Alessa if I truly loved Brielle. Alessa may have been right all along: Brielle may be controlling me. Like, right now, I don't give a fuck about Brielle, but I can't stop thinking about Alessa, and how I—I …. and the fact that both Camden and Alessa swear certain events happened that I have no memory of—something isn't right, and I need answers. If I find the only person capable of assisting Brielle with this twisted request, as close to where she lives as possible, I might get some answers."

Damon walked over to his dresser and dropped his towel. Grabbing a pair of boxer briefs and black combat pants, Damon finished getting dressed.

"I need some time to get the information you're requesting. And Kai's being laid to rest tonight. Are you sure you don't want to be here for that?" Quade asked.

Damon clenched his fists before extending his fingers. "You're right. I should stay for her final rest, but I will leave immediately afterward. Can you get the information before this evening?"

"Maybe. Let me get to it." Quade turned around to leave but froze in place. "Damon, I'm sorry about Kai, but she knew you loved her. That you didn't mean to—"

Facing away from Quade, Damon held his hand up. "Stop. I know you mean well, but just stop."

"Okay, brother. If you need me, I'll be in the comms room gathering your intel."

Damon nodded as Quade left through the open front door.

Staring absentmindedly at his bedside lamp, Damon screamed at the top of his lungs. Lunging toward it, he swept his arm forward, and as his hand struck the porcelain, the lamp shattered against the cabin's wall.

Continuing the destruction of his house, Damon ripped frames from walls, tore bedsheets from his bed, and after picking up one of his sharpened daggers, he stabbed the chaise. Dragging the blade down the length of the chair, he exposed the stuffing.

With his chest heaving, he looked across the room at his anguished reflection in the full-length mirror. He charged toward it, punching his reflection.

Most of the shards of glass fell to the ground while the others protruded from the back of his hand.

Sliding down the cabin's wall to the wooden floor, Damon's head fell into his hands as he bellowed out in agony. "I'm sorry. Kai, I'm so sorry."

CHAPTER FORTY-EIGHT

Gulping the underworld's stale air, Alessa pressed her hand against her heaving chest.

Alessa had been stripped of her dirty warrior uniform and was wearing an elaborate gown.

Bejeweled golden bangles adorned both arms, and as she stood, the deep red skirt transitioned into black, billowing out from her bare feet. Looking up at the large castle before her, Alessa pressed her hands against her corseted stomach. "I did it. I did it!" she exclaimed.

Running toward the open castle doors, she burst into the underworld's castle. "Hello? Hades? I must speak with you!"

She found him standing at the edge of his koi pond, feeding the brightly colored fish. "I am always here, Spartan. What do you wish to speak to me about?"

Approaching him slowly, Alessa held her hands up apologetically. "I'm sorry. I am so sorry I didn't—"

Hades raised an eyebrow and side-eyed Alessa. "Did you not take Eric, I mean Lucas, out when you had the chance?"

She gulped nervously. "I tried, but—"

He held up a single hand. "Silence. I warned you what would happen. *You* chose the outcome."

She stilled, and the billowy fabric of her gown took a second to catch up. "*I* chose for the love of my life to kill my sister?" She felt the heat behind her irises.

Camden had just gotten out of the shower and gone to his bedroom to pull on a pair of underwear and mud-brown cargo pants when he heard his alarm going off.

He picked up his phone, confused. "That's strange. I don't remember setting an alarm."

His heart sank as he read the alarm's title.

"Fuck! Alessa, what did you do?" he gasped, running to the kitchen counter, to the butcher's block. After grabbing a blade from the block and a small flashlight hanging on the kitchen wall, Camden bolted out the cabin door.

Hades chuckled as he threw the last bit of food to the fish below. "You hold no earthly powers here, human." Exhaling loudly, he shook his head. "Why do you seek my audience? You must have come here knowing the outcome would not be in your favor."

Standing before the god, Alessa's hands balled into fists as she struggled to keep her anger in check. "I am fully prepared to offer my soul in exchange for my sister's."

His face scrunched up in disbelief. "What makes you think I'd ever agree to that when keeping you in the mortal plane benefits me so much more? I've already made a deal with you once, but you couldn't keep it. I no longer am interested in what you offer."

Alessa lunged for Hades and grabbed ahold of his arm. "I'll give you anything—anything you want to save my sister."

———

Rounding the corner, Camden ran up to the shoreline and frantically looked out into the darkness while flashing the narrow beam of light across the water's surface. After a few deep breaths, Camden screamed. "Alessa!"

By the light of the full moon, he saw the outline of a small boat that had capsized but had stayed in place. "Alessa, no!"

Diving headfirst into the water, Camden swam out to the boat as fast as he could. Bobbing up and down in the water, he inhaled deeply before biting down on the flashlight and swimming his hardest to the bottom of the lake.

After locating Alessa's floating body attached to the rope and rock, he vigilantly dragged the blade back and forth across the old rope. Finally, feeling the rope give, he grabbed Alessa around the waist and kicked as hard as he could toward the surface.

———

Hades' smile turned into something wicked as he grabbed Alessa's hand and peeled it away. "You think rather highly of yourself. Only a handful of humans have asked me a favor, yet you have asked several. What makes you so special?"

As the god strolled away from the large pond, Alessa watched the fish follow his movement. As they swam in the dark blue water, the fish transformed into human beings, their bodies wriggling toward the god for attention.

Alessa's hands flew to cover her mouth as their arms and legs flailed, reaching for Hades to pull them from the depths of their despair.

"Spartan, you intrigue me, but I'd be labeled weak if I gave one human a second chance. My final answer is no. Your sister shall remain with me in the underworld."

Looking into the faces in the water, she saw Kai's face amongst the strangers. Feeling a painful punch to the chest, Alessa gasped. "Kai! No, Hades, please—"

He whipped around, enraged. "I said NO!"

Irate, Alessa clenched her teeth together as her irises burned red. "You'll regret this," she growled.

Feeling another powerful punch to the chest, she fell to her knees.

Tilting his head to the side, Hades' lips raised in surprise. "Is that a threat, lowly Spartan?"

Water poured out of Alessa's mouth, and as her chest felt as though it were splitting in two, she grunted. "It's a promise."

Opening her mouth wide, lake water poured out. The flames within the lit torches throughout the underworld's castle blazed high as she screamed.

Disappearing from the underworld, Alessa slammed back into her body, earthside.

Hades' head whipped back and forth as he searched the room for the source of the intensifying flames.

Nyx, the primordial goddess of the night, emerged from a dark corner, wearing a dress as dark as the night sky, set with shining gold stars scattered throughout its corseted bodice. "What was that?" she asked, her voice dripping with intrigue as her silky alabaster legs emerged from between the slit on the long, tight-fitting silk skirt.

Rubbing his hands together, Hades scoffed as if disinterested. "Nothing, I'm sure."

Her eyes narrowed. "Has that ever happened before? A human use their powers like that in another realm, such as ours?"

Hades stood tall in defiance, answering with his voice cloaked in indifference. "Not that I can recall."

Nyx smiled, staring at the wet spot left on the floor by the Spartan. "And are you sure of your answer to this human?"

Annoyed, the god of the underworld's face scrunched up as he strolled to his throne. "Of course I am. I am a god. I will not be intimidated by a mere human."

Nyx bent down and dipped her fingers in the water pooled on the floor. "What if she is the one the prophecy speaks of?"

"Hold your tongue," Hades snapped.

Standing upright in her seductive gown, Nyx smiled wickedly. "If indeed this human is the one, she is destined to be the first of her kind. How does this prospect not intrigue you?"

He stared at his nails absentmindedly. "Why would you want to tip the scales in this woman's favor? We rule this realm together, equally. Is that not enough for you?"

Nyx glared at the young god. "We barely tolerate one another, you and I. And if you just made an enemy of the woman destined to become the most powerful of all humankind, all the better for me to be on her good side."

Spotting Kai in the mass of swimming bodies, Nyx sauntered over to Kai. Reaching her hand into the warm water, she grasped hands with the soul of Alessa's sister and plucked her from the others.

The naked woman stood before her, dripping water, and as Nyx snapped her fingers, a warm towel appeared in her hand. Draping it across the shoulders of the naked woman, she smiled sweetly. "I think I shall keep an eye on this particular Spartan."

Hades rolled his eyes. "You can't be serious."

"I most definitely am. If I am to believe the Oracle and my children, the Fates, the human foretold is prophesied to have the ability to allow me the ability to walk in the light of day, no longer being tied to purely shadows." She ran her fingers through the woman's blonde hair. "You and I have a lot to discuss."

Hades stepped forward. "You can't have her. The souls are mine to do with as I please."

Nyx turned her head, her eyes boring into the king of the underworld. "You forget your place, young god. I am your elder and will do as I please."

With a deep growl, he disappeared from his seat on the throne.

The primordial goddess Nyx stepped back and waved her arms, instantly dressing Kai in an indigo form-fitting dress. Grinning, she stepped forward, taking Kai's arm within her own, and walked the Spartan toward the castle's front doors. "Now, darling, tell me your and your sister's origin story. I want to know everything."

Laying on her side, Alessa vomited all the contents from her stomach while clearing her lungs of lake water.

Camden vigorously rubbed Alessa's back. "That's it, keep it coming."

When she finally calmed down, Alessa's breaths were loud and exaggerated as she started to hyperventilate.

Camden dug his fingers into her shoulders and shook her angrily. "Why did you do it? How could you even think to—"

"I had to try. I had to—" Crying, she collapsed into Camden's arms.

Gripping his muscular neck and back, Alessa shook in his arms. "He won't give her back. He won't give ... her ... she's-she's gone. Kai's gone," Alessa sobbed uncontrollably.

Awaiting the rising sun, Camden ran his fingers through Alessa's wet hair as they held one another in the dark of night.

CHAPTER FORTY-NINE

After trudging slowly back to her elder's cabin, Alessa and Camden found Seraphine and Lexi standing before her home.

Lifting her head to look at her friends, Alessa stilled. "What are you doing here?"

Seraphine stepped forward. "We're here to help you prepare Kai for her transition. Why are you all wet?"

Alessa stuttered, unable to form the words. "I—uh—we—"

"She took a swim," Camden interjected.

Alessa blinked away the confusion. "I guess I didn't think—"

Lexi pressed her hands together. "We're not going to let you do this alone."

Exhausted and emotional, Seraphine wrapped her arms around Alessa and burst into tears. "I'm so sorry, my friend. This was not the outcome any of us were hoping for."

Burying her face in Seraphine's shoulder, Alessa squeezed her eyes shut as Lexi turned toward Camden. "We've got it from here."

Camden stepped forward, his brown cargo pants soaking wet. "I don't think I should—"

Lexi held up a hand to stop him from continuing. "No men are allowed at the preparation of a woman's body."

He stepped back. "I see." He peered over at Alessa and then back at Lexi. "Keep an eye on her. She's not dealing well."

Lexi nodded in understanding. "We need to get started."

Camden walked up behind Alessa. "If you need me, just call. Do not hesitate. Got it?"

Alessa flashed a sad smile. "Got it."

With a deep exhale, both women stood on either side of Alessa and took her by the hand. Walking forward toward the back of the treeline, Seraphine squeezed Alessa's hand. "If you went swimming, why is Camden wet?"

Alessa shook her head. "It doesn't matter. Did you already—"

"Move her to the board? Yes," Lexi answered.

"We knocked on the door, and there was no answer. We moved her with the utmost respect," Seraphine explained.

Alessa closed her eyes as they walked up to her sister's lifeless body lying on the thin, dark brown wooden boards. After inhaling a steadying breath, Alessa stopped short of touching the wooden slats and squeezed her eyes shut.

With a shaky breath, she opened her eyes and looked down at her baby sister's pale face. Feeling her heart shatter, Alessa grabbed the side of the wooden table and hit her knees, and she screamed out loud.

Lexi's heart broke for her friend. "Let us help you."

Seraphine held Alessa by the arm and rubbed her back. "You're not alone."

Wiping her tears away with the back of her hand, Alessa's legs shook as she stood up. "Can I have a pair of scissors?"

Lexi silently walked to their makeshift table and plucked the red scissors off the top before handing them over.

Standing before her sister, Alessa moved to the foot of the wooden table and gripped the bottom of one of her sister's black pant legs. She cut the entire length to her waist one at a time before splaying the fabric open.

After slipping the black pants off, Lexi covered her bottom half with a weighted white blanket. Alessa continued cutting her yellow shirt, bra, and underwear off until she lay naked beneath the blanket.

Seraphine said a lengthy prayer to the gods as Lexi prepared the water to bathe Kai.

Pushing the purple flowers to the side in the bowl, Alessa dipped a small cloth into the fragrant water.

Starting with Kai's forehead, Alessa gently pressed the cool cloth to her sister's worry lines, which remained etched into her skin. Washing the dirt and soot from her sister's skin, Alessa pushed her sadness down deep so she could complete the task without breaking down.

Kai's once full, bright pink lips were now pale and cracked. Cleaning further down her body, Alessa washed away the dried blood from the mortal wound caused by Damon's dagger, and her breathing hitched as she struggled to hold it together.

Moving away from her shoulder, Alessa cleansed down her arm, and the water ran down her wrist, dripping from her fingertips.

After she dipped the cloth into the clean water again, Alessa moved the sheet to clean her sister's abdomen, thighs, and calves before she finally moved to the foot of the table.

Lexi said another prayer aloud as Alessa finished cleansing her sister's feet. With the final touch of the cloth, the three Spartans stood silent before the young woman's body.

Seraphine touched Alessa's shoulder. "Would you like us to leave while you anoint her?"

Alessa swallowed back tears and nodded. "If you wouldn't mind. I think I'd like to say my goodbyes the same way we arrived here, just her and I."

Lexi placed the dirty cloth in the bowl before picking it up. "You don't need to explain anything. Take your time."

Painfully biting her lower lip to keep from breaking down, Alessa watched her friends leave before she turned back alone to face the heartbreaking truth: she was standing alone in front of her dead sister's body.

"I know you're not in there anymore, but I need you to know how sorry I am." Her voice cracked. "I tried but couldn't save you in life or death. You'd probably kill me if you knew I tried to exchange my soul for yours." Wiping away her tears, she laughed, devoid of humor. "I drowned myself to grant an audience with the king of the underworld, himself." She glanced down at the grass. "I can hear your voice telling me how dumb that was, but I had to do something. I couldn't just let you die for my mistake."

Alessa took a steadying breath and blinked back tears as she looked up into the bright sun. "How am I supposed to live without you?" she choked. "I don't think—I don't think I can continue without you. You've always been here with me; I don't know that I have anything else to live for."

Alessa collapsed on top of her sister's chest, wrapping her arms around her cold body. After a few minutes of crying hysterically, Alessa wiped the snot from her nose and tears from her face.

"I guess I don't have a choice if I'm going to make killing Eric my new goal in life," she cried. Hovering over Kai's face, Alessa bent down and gently kissed her sister's lips.

"My soul has been crushed, and my heart shattered more than I would've ever thought was possible. Sera had said it's debatable whether or not I'm still human, and I'm starting to think she might be right."

Exhaling loudly, Alessa stood up and moved over to the table. Dipping her fingers into the oily concoction, Alessa pressed her fingertips against Kai's forehead, then down her cheeks.

Smoothing the blessed ointment onto Kai's collarbone, Alessa massaged the lilac oil onto her sister's waxy skin.

The only noises were those from nature: birds chirping, the wind blowing through the leaves upon the trees, and squirrels chittering as they chased one another.

Picking up the thin, soft white cloth Seraphine had left on the table, Alessa draped it over her sister's frame, covering her naked, shiny body.

When she had finished, Alessa sat in the tall grass, facing away from her sister, and stared into the distance, her heart numb.

The sound of Lexi's voice made Alessa jump. "We brought you food."

"Oh!" Alessa pressed a hand to her heart. "Um, I'm not hungry."

Seraphine sat beside Alessa and took the plate from Lexi. Handing it to Alessa, she instructed, "You will eat. It's only half a sandwich and some grapes."

Alessa forced a grateful smile and took the sandwich from the plate.

"How are you doing?" Lexi asked as Alessa took a bite.

Alessa nodded her head with a mouthful of deli meat. "I'm hangin' on." *By a thread.*

"Would you like help dressing Kai?" Seraphine asked.

"Yes." Alessa took another bite of her sandwich. "I still need to go back to the house and grab some clothes for both of us."

"Why don't you do that while Sera and I keep Kai company?" Lexi asked.

Alessa absentmindedly nodded in agreement. "Okay." She stood up, turned toward Kai, and, without thinking, said, "I'll be right back."

Her breath hitched upon catching herself saying something so ridiculous to a corpse. "I meant to say that to you," she explained to Seraphine.

Seraphine accepted her actions without question. "Don't take too long; her muscles won't be easy to move for much longer."

Shaking her head clear of the disturbing images that came to mind, Alessa jogged back to her cabin.

Hitting the front steps, Alessa exhaled as she entered the entryway. Eyeing the bathroom, she stripped off her warrior's uniform on the way to the shower. Turning the knob, she stood below the streaming water, allowing the liquid to wash away the unseen scars that remained.

After quickly scrubbing the blood and dirt from beneath her fingernails, Alessa dried off before she stood naked in front of her closet. *What would Kai want me to wear?*

Plucking a dress from a hanger, Alessa wriggled into it before her full-length mirror. After putting on the floor-length traditional Spartan gown, she pressed the black overlay against her stomach, forcing the deep red fabric underneath to show through. *Yeah, I think you would've liked this. Now, it's your turn.*

Alessa walked into her sister's bedroom and looked through

the dresses in her closet. Eyeing a burnt orange ombre sweetheart dress, she reached forward.

Unclipping it from the hanger, Alessa smiled. "This is perfect."

After Alessa returned, they dressed Kai altogether.

Seraphine sighed as she readjusted the bottom of Kai's skirt. "She loved this dress."

Exhausted, Alessa lay in the grass beside her sister's elevated wooden table and closed her eyes.

"We'll be back after sunset. Try to get some rest," Seraphine said to Alessa.

Taking Lexi by the arm, Seraphine led her away, leaving Alessa alone with her sister.

CHAPTER FIFTY

"Lessie? Lessie, wake up," Kai whispered.

Slowly blinking her eyes open, Alessa's eyebrows scrunched up in confusion. Her sister was looking down at Alessa from the wooden tabletop.

"Kai? Kai!" She jumped up and wrapped her arms around her sister, nearly knocking her off the wooden slats.

Kai hugged Alessa back. "I don't have long. I need you to listen to me—"

Alessa pressed her hand to the side of Kai's cheek. "How are you—are you really here?"

Kai flashed a sad smile. "In a manner of speaking. The primordial goddess Nyx gifted me a moment in your dreams, but I don't have long. I need to ask you to do something for me."

"Anything. I would do anything for you," Alessa grabbed her sister's hand and sat beside her.

Kai squeezed Alessa's hand. "I need you to forgive Damon. This isn't his fault. Hades—"

Alessa jumped up in anger and faced her sister. "You haven't even been dead twenty-four hours, and you're asking me to forgive the man who killed you? No. No, I will not. I cannot."

Kai gently stroked Alessa's arm. "I'm gone, Lessie; he's all you've got now. You need to know that Hades—"

Alessa shook her head back and forth, ignoring Kai's words. "Damon is not all I have. I've got Sera, Lexi, Quade ... Camden. Damon is not the end all be all, and I can't just forget what he—"

Kai placed her hands on Alessa's upper biceps. "I'm sorry, but I'm out of time. I need you to know that I am being taken care of. Please don't blame yourself for my passing. Hades was the one behind—"

Alessa grabbed her sister's hand as she started to vanish. "I love you, Kai. Please don't leave me."

"You're waking up now. I love you, Lessie. Never forget—"

Alessa sat upright and looked up at the darkened sky.

Hoping her sister was alive and well, Alessa stood up eagerly. "Kai?"

Finding her sister's corpse lying still and cold, Alessa choked back tears. "Kai?"

"Are you ready?" Seraphine asked from behind her.

Jumping at the sound of her friend's voice, Alessa spun around.

Seraphine, Quade, Soren, Lexi, and Camden were standing nearby. Each of them was holding a lit torch while additional Spartans showed their respect further away atop the hill.

Nodding toward the figures on the hill, Alessa swallowed nervously. "I didn't think anyone else would care."

Quade stepped forward, the flickering light from his flame

illuminating his face. "Not everyone agrees with the council. Especially those who fought last night and realized you were right about Eric—I mean, Lucas. We are ready to go against the Consilium to do what is right for humankind. It is our sworn duty to the gods."

Alessa's jaw dropped in surprise, and she lunged at Quade. Wrapping her arms around him, she buried her face in his neck. "Thank you."

Seraphine moved close and touched Alessa's hand. "It's time."

Opening her eyes, Alessa looked at the large pile of timber. Inhaling deeply, she released Quade and nodded at Seraphine.

Camden handed Lexi his torch before standing at the head of Kai's wooden plank tabletop. Quade handed his torch to Seraphine before approaching Kai's feet, and Seraphine said a prayer in Greek as Alessa stared at her sister in shock.

Seraphine ended her beautiful words with, "Kai, you were loved as much in life as you will continue to be in death."

Alessa nervously cleared her throat as Camden and Quade grabbed the wood and lifted Kai into the air between them.

After carrying her across the wild grass, they gently set Kai down on the wood pile before returning to Alessa's side.

Lexi handed Camden's torch back to him as he stood as close to Alessa as humanly possible.

Wanting to protect her from what was about to happen but knowing there was nothing he could do, Camden tried his best to be strong for her.

Soren stepped forward and gave Alessa his lit torch, and with a single tear falling down his face, he nodded in encouragement.

Forcing herself to flash a grateful, sad smile, Alessa's

knuckles blanched white as she gripped the wood beneath the flame.

Alessa slowly stepped across the small field toward Kai, watching the light dance upon her sister's face. *Keep it together. Don't fall apart. Keep your shit together.* Exhaling loudly, Alessa licked the tears from her lips and bent down next to her sister's ear. "I love you so much. I'll carry you in my heart until the joyous day I finally join you in the underworld."

Standing upright, her arm dropped, and she threw the flaming torch into the wood pile.

Never losing sight of her sister, Alessa took slow steps backward as if in a trance until she bumped into Camden's muscular chest.

As she startled, he cooed in her ear. "I'm here."

Hearing his words, Alessa somehow found the strength to stand tall, and she watched her sister's physical body become stardust once more.

From off in the distance, Damon stood amongst the trees, offering his private condolences as Kai's pyre burned high.

Watching Alessa struggle was by far the hardest thing he had ever had to endure, and not being able to comfort her in any way was genuinely agonizing.

Gripping the rough bark of the tree, tears streaked down his face. As the onlookers on the hill started to fall out, Damon growled and punched the thick trunk, bloodying and bruising his knuckles, before turning to leave.

"I know I can't bring you back, but I promise on my life to seek justice in your honor. I love you, Kai," Damon promised into the night air before he grabbed his backpack off the forest floor.

Swinging it over his shoulder, Damon headed for the teleportation area at the city's entrance.

As the last of the onlookers on the hill left, Lexi walked away in silence before she was followed closely behind by Quade, Seraphine, and Soren, thus allowing Alessa and Camden time to honor her sister in private.

Alessa broke the silence first. "Cam?"

"Yes?" he asked, moving closer to her protectively.

"I don't know how I'm going to survive this," she said through tears.

Camden looked at the side of her face. "You're going to take one day at a time."

Looking up at the heavens, she blinked away the tears. "What if I don't want to survive without my sister?"

Camden grabbed Alessa's arm and spun her toward him. His eyes, forest green with flakes of yellow and brown scattered throughout, stared deep into her soul. "Don't say that. I couldn't imagine a world where you're not in it. Not now. Not ever."

Her skin burned where he was gripping her hard, and all she wanted was for him to grip tighter and touch more of her. Alessa needed to feel again. Something, anything besides the overwhelming sadness that was threatening to consume her.

Alessa's heart beat fast as an intensity burned within her core, spreading like wildfire throughout her entire body. The light from Camden's torch danced upon his face, outlining his perfect lips, and before she could talk herself out of it, Alessa pressed her body against his.

As their lips crashed into one another, Camden felt the heat radiating off Alessa and pulled away, his eyebrows furrowed in concern. Placing his free hand upon Alessa's cheek, he bent down. "Are you sure?"

Nodding fervently, Alessa pulled him down as she stood on her toes. "Yes, yes."

As their lips touched again, Camden no longer held himself back and dropped the torch into a patch of dirt.

Looping her arms around his thick neck, Alessa jumped into his outstretched arms. As she wrapped her legs around Camden's midsection, he placed his hands underneath her backside, holding her against his chest.

With Alessa in his arms, Camden walked toward the treeline as they desperately kissed one another.

Pressing her back up against a tall tree, Alessa moaned into Camden's open mouth.

Opening his eyes, Camden's irises flashed golden as adrenaline coursed through his veins, and as he held Alessa in place, he kissed down the side of her neck onto her collarbone.

Pulling Alessa's dress off her shoulder, Camden exposed her right breast. He pressed his lips against her hot skin, leaving a trail of kisses in his wake, and upon reaching her erect pink nipple, Camden exhaled a breath of hot air.

Goosebumps popped up all over the surface of Alessa's pale skin, bathed in the light of the full moon. Writhing in anticipation, she ran her fingers through his sandy blond hair, and as Camden's tongue played with her, Alessa grabbed hold of his soft locks and moaned loudly.

Camden wrapped one arm around Alessa's lower back

while his other firmly grasped her breast, holding her in place as she writhed against him.

The space between her legs grew slick, and she gasped. "Uh! Cam."

Without missing a beat, he pulled down the opposite sleeve, exposing her left breast, and his hand continued ripening her nipple after his mouth left to harden her other nipple.

Gently pinching her left nipple between his fingers as he flicked his tongue around her other nipple, Camden groaned as his bulge begged to be set free.

Panting, Alessa lifted his mouth from her chest back to her lips.

Camden leaned into Alessa and placed one hand on the tree trunk above her head. While grasping her behind the lower back, he lifted her to him, and as she grabbed the sides of the collar on his black silk button-up, Alessa bit down on Camden's lower lip while ripping his shirt open.

Buttons flew off the front of his shirt as he sucked in a sharp breath before he released an excited groan. "Fuck."

Exposing the six-foot-three Russian man's toned chest and abs, Alessa licked her lips in anticipation.

Lunging forward, Camden pressed Alessa back against the rough tree bark, and while kissing her breasts once more, he inched up the long skirt of her dress.

Slipping his fingers beneath her panties, he felt how wet she had gotten for him.

Camden watched her face melt as he slid his first two fingers in until the last knuckle. "Mmm..."

Slowly pulling his fingers back out, Alessa's breathing hitched before he thrust them back inside, forcing a loud moan from between her lips. "Oh, gods!"

Moving the tips of his fingers up and down in a rhythmic pattern, Camden lifted Alessa's chin to see her expression.

Her cheeks were flush, her words incomprehensible as her panting picked up pace with the gyrating of her hips.

"Cam ... Cam," she breathed as he brought her to the brink of arousal.

"Let go," Camden encouraged before his lips crashed into hers.

High-pitched squeals came from Alessa as her entire body shuddered upon his hand.

"That's it, let it all go." Camden held her upright as her orgasm finished coursing through her, and her body threatened to go limp.

Opening her eyes, blood-red irises looked hungrily up at Camden as he removed his fingers and sucked her juices from each finger.

Her eyelids fluttered as she watched him, and before she knew it, Alessa was undoing his belt. Pulling it free from his loops, Alessa whipped the black belt off to the side, dropping it carelessly on the ground.

Unbuttoning his pants, she unzipped him and pulled them down to where he could kick his slacks off easily.

Standing before her, Camden grasped the skirt of her dress and yanked the fabric down in one fell swoop. The dress pooled at her bare feet, and she stepped toward Camden.

Gripping the top of his boxer briefs, Alessa stood up on her tip-toes to lick and suck on his lower lip before she slipped the elastic band over his engorged cock.

He sprang out from the confinements of his briefs, and Alessa licked her hand from wrist to the tip of her fingers before she wrapped her hand around his tip.

He twitched in the palm of her hand as she stroked back

and forth, faster and faster, and as his lips hungrily consumed hers, he removed her back from the tree, and they moved together further into the tall grass.

With one hand behind Alessa's back and one behind her neck, Camden laid the Spartan down on the ground before positioning himself between her legs. As Alessa lay naked in the field, the full moon's pale light reflecting off her skin, Camden knelt and kissed down her neck, in between her breasts, and down her scarred stomach. Pressing himself against her warm entrance, he could feel how wet she was.

Spasming in anticipation, Alessa moaned aloud.

He paused, looking down at Alessa. "You're sure this is what you want?"

Her eyelashes fluttered. "This is what I need."

Thrusting his hips, Camden dove inside Alessa, and her back arched as she took him deep.

"Uh! Cam!" she moaned aloud. Her entire body moved up and down as he thrust his hips forward and back, and as the intensity built, Alessa arched her back.

"I want—I want..." she breathed.

"Yes? Tell me what you want. Show me," Camden urged.

Opening her red irises, she wrapped her legs around Camden's back and, using all of her strength, pushed him up and over.

Straddling Camden, Alessa hovered atop him before sinking down.

Partially sitting up, Camden's mouth opened in pure ecstasy, and his head tilted back.

Alessa rotated her hips as Camden pulled her chest to his mouth. Sucking her nipple in between his lips, Camden's tongue licked around her areola before flicking her hardened nipple.

Unable to hold back any longer, Camden moaned her name. "Alessa—uh!"

She responded by riding harder and faster, and as he thrust up into her as far as he could, an explosion went off inside Alessa. Feeling him pulse inside her, Alessa's breathing faltered as her mouth opened wide and her head tilted back toward the stars.

The torches surrounding them intensified as their bodies shuddered against one another, the flames reaching for the sky.

Their muscles tensed as they came, hard, and while they focused on catching their breath, they smiled at one another.

With a laugh, they kissed one another before Camden fell back against the grass and Alessa collapsed to the side of him.

"Had I known it was going to be like that, I would've been more persistent," he said breathily.

Lying naked on her back, intertwining her legs with his, Alessa smiled and released a content sigh as tears stung her eyes. "That was exactly what I needed."

CHAPTER FIFTY-ONE

Appearing in a side alley in downtown Philadelphia, Damon held his backpack's strap tight as he jogged away from his drop-off point.

The brisk wind bit his nose and stung his cheeks as he crossed the street. *Good thing I decided to get the leather jacket lined with self-heating fleece because, damn, it's cold out here.*

Damon pulled the dark blue ballcap further over his face, not wanting to draw any unwanted attention. Keeping his head tilted toward the sidewalk, Damon walked the two miles to the doctor's last known location per Quade's intel.

Turning a corner, Damon squinted at an abandoned, broken-down building. "This can't be right."

A pair of holographic glasses popped out from his gadget with a flick of his wrist. After putting them on, Damon saw what had been masked: a set of stairs going underground to the side of the building, which the naked eye would not have been able to see.

"Smart," Damon grumbled, tucking the holographic glasses back into his wristband.

Approaching the building, he stepped behind some bushes and pulled out a few smaller weapons. Looking down the steps, Damon took a deep breath and said a few words of encouragement before descending. "You've got this."

When he reached the door, he looked around to ensure no one was there. Damon shoved a wedged device between the door handle and the jamb, walked halfway up the stairs, and then pressed a button.

The metal door heated up, causing the structure to creak. As it hit a weakened point, the device shot a sharpened tool between the jamb and door, separating the door from its lock.

Damon ran for the entrance, extending his arms, weapons in hand, and walked stealthily in through the compromised door.

Making his way down the dark hallway, Damon peeked around the corners, moving toward the only illuminated room.

Stepping to the side of the hall, Damon peeked into the glass at the top of the wooden door.

A teenage boy was strapped down to the tilted chair, his eyes open wide in terror as an older man wearing a white lab coat and eye magnifiers approached him with a spinning blade in hand. His two assistants were standing off to the side, a mix of horror and intrigue written across their faces.

"Please don't!" the kid wailed.

Pressing his back against the wall, Damon held his hands up, a gun in each, before kicking the door in.

Busting in through the doorway, he aimed and shot each of the assistants between their eyes. As they dropped dead to the floor, Damon aimed his weapon at the doctor.

With a frustrated groan, the doctor stopped his tool from spinning. "Excuse me! I am trying to"—he whipped around to confront the assailant—"you. It's you."

Damon grimaced. "So you remember me?"

"Why, yes. It's been some time, though. A young woman brought you—"

"Brielle?" Damon asked through clenched teeth.

The man wiggled a finger. "Brielle. That was her name. Yes. Brielle." He turned back around, and his tool made a *whirring* sound as it turned back on.

Damon stepped toward the doctor. "Stop!"

The doctor grumbled under his breath. "You're interrupting me, young man. I was in the middle of—ugh—you'd never understand. What I do is too complex for someone of your low intelligence."

Damon's eyebrows raised. "Are you calling me dumb as I hold a weapon to your head?"

The doctor groaned in frustration. "Why did you come here?"

"I need to know what you did to me. So it can be undone."

The doctor grinned maniacally.

"Did you insert worms into my brain?" Damon demanded.

The doctor nodded slowly, up and down. "Yes, we did."

Tilting his head to the side, Damon exhaled. "How many?"

"Eight wigglies burrow themselves into your brain, eating the events Brielle had me target." He eyed the large screen hanging from the ceiling.

Damon's eyes grew wide as he realized what they had done. "You watched my memories, and then she chose which ones to erase?"

The doctor flashed his teeth. "Precisely."

Pissed off, Damon cocked his gun. "How do I remove them?"

"You can't. What's done is done," the doctor replied nonchalantly.

Damon's free hand balled into a fist. "Fuck you! You had no right to take my free will, to steal my life."

The doctor shrugged nonchalantly. "It was nothing personal. She paid me handsomely, so I did as she asked."

Damon lunged at the doctor, and the man screamed, slicing through the air with his spinning blade. Dodging the weapon, Damon slammed the doctor backward, pinning him against the wall with his forearm.

"Ah!" the old man exclaimed as he dropped his tool. "Don't hurt me."

Damon growled. "Give me one good reason I shouldn't kill you right here, right now."

The doctor side-eyed Damon from his chokehold. "Have you been feeling rather off lately? Found yourself doing things you don't recall wanting to do?"

Damon's face dropped in alarm. "How did you know—"

"That pendant she wears around her neck."

Damon pictured the amber, teardrop-shaped gem Brielle always had around her neck. "What of it?"

The older man licked his lips. "It gives her control. Destroy the pendant as well as the implant within your front cortex, and you will destroy her ability to control you."

"The fuck you say, old man? You not only took away my memories, but you also gave that psychotic bitch the ability to control me?" Damon turned on the spinning blade.

The doctor put his hands up in front of him and cowered before Damon. "No! Please don't," he begged.

Damon sliced through the straps holding the kid to the table. As the kid jumped up from the steel table with tears in his eyes, he thanked Damon before running out of the hidden lab. "Thanks, man."

Damon stomped back to the doctor and grabbed his arm.

Dragging the man to the table, Damon pushed the doctor onto his back and slapped handcuffs around the man's wrist and secured them to the bed before walking to the other side. Picking up duct tape, Damon pressed the rotating blade within the doctor's palm before securing the device by wrapping the silver tape around his wrist.

"What are you doing? I—I told you everything you wanted to know," the doctor panicked.

Damon plucked his backpack from the floor with a loud exhale. "Relax, I'm not going to kill you."

"But you are going to leave me here ... like this?"

"I'm leaving you with two options. Option one, you stay bound to that table, hoping someone comes along to save you before you starve to death. Or option two, you cut through your wrist to free yourself."

Damon turned his back on the doctor and headed for the door.

The doctor spit onto the floor. "You might as well kill me! It would be quicker."

Damon pulled the strap tight on his shoulder. "That's the point. If I outright took your life, you wouldn't receive the punishment you deserve. If you did this to me, how many others have you hurt?"

As soon as the Spartan was out of earshot, the doctor confessed to nobody in particular, with drool dripping from his lips, "I've heard the woman's pendant isn't the only trigger, and those worms have adapted to their environment. Good luck regaining control."

CHAPTER FIFTY-TWO

Arriving back at New Sparta in the midday sun, Damon marched through the center of town, heading straight for the medical ward.

Damon passed by a group of women and paused after hearing Brielle's voice.

"Damon!" She excused herself from the small group and ran toward him. "Where have you been? I've been looking all—"

Violently slamming his backpack down to the ground, he screamed, "Stop! Just stop!"

Taken back by his aggression, Brielle froze. "Sugar bear, what's the matter? What happened to—"

Trying his best not to throttle her, Damon stepped forward, his hands balled into tight fists. "What happened to me?" He laughed without humor in his voice. "YOU are what happened to me. I should have never gone to your apartment that night. I should've never trusted you would help—"

Brielle glanced nervously at the growing crowd. "What are

you talking about? You're not making any sense." She reached for his hand. "Just come back to the house, and we'll talk—"

"No!" he pulled his hand out of her grasp and backed away. "I will never go anywhere with you, ever again. I trusted you to help me, and you have done nothing but lie and deceive your way into my heart and my bed. Gods, Brielle, what the fuck is wrong with you?"

Brielle's jaw dropped, and her eyes filled with tears as she tried to justify her behavior. "I never meant to hurt you. I only wanted you to love me."

Damon's eyebrows furrowed in confusion and anger. "By getting rid of the competition? By erasing memories of the only woman I've ever loved? By implanting electronic bugs in my brain?"

Realizing he knew everything and that she had lost control, Brielle's lower lip trembled as she slowly backed away from Damon.

"You don't actually love me, and I most definitely don't love you. You hired a doctor to implant devices in my brain to trick me into loving you. If I didn't have a moral code when it comes to women, I would beat the living shit out of you." Looking down at the ground, he licked his lips. "Brielle, I hereby banish you from New Sparta. Forever."

Snapping out of her stupor, Brielle lunged forward and desperately clung to his arm. "You can't possibly mean that. Damon, you wouldn't—"

"Oh, I very much mean it. From henceforth, you are never to step foot in this city or any of our sister cities."

Her face dropped as she grabbed her pendant and pressed it furiously. "But I love you, and you love me. I know you do! Damon, don't do this."

Eyeing her pendant, Damon snatched the gem and broke

the chain from around Brielle's neck. Lifting it high, he smashed it down onto the ground before pulverizing it beneath the heel of his black combat boot.

Leaning forward into Brielle, he growled, "You will never again have power over me."

She laced her hands together and fell before Damon. "Please, just come with me. I promise I will never, ever—"

Grabbing Brielle, Damon picked her up and carried her over his shoulder, kicking and screaming, to the city's barrier at the city's entrance.

"You can't save Alessa! The elders are convening as we speak and plan to hold her accountable for her crimes in the morning," Brielle taunted. "Put me down! Damon!"

Placing her back on her feet, he reached behind her ear and painfully snatched the temporary chip from the back of her ear.

Collapsing to the ground, Brielle spasmed in pain and screamed as her body rejected being on the inside of the forcefield without a Spartan microchip.

As the Spartan guards appeared behind Damon, he instructed them, "Escort this woman through the barrier and take her far enough away that she won't find her way back."

Damon glared down at the woman he had just spent the better half of a year loving and felt relief as he said his goodbyes. "I hope you find peace, but it won't be with me."

As the Spartan warriors picked Brielle up off the ground and carried her away, she screamed for Damon. "Don't do this! Ah! Damon!" Her voice trailed off as they crossed the barrier.

Ignoring her cries, Damon walked back toward the medical ward. Picking his backpack off the ground, he passed by the audience who had gathered to watch the spectacle.

Entering Seraphine's office, Damon tossed his backpack onto a medical bed on the side of the room.

The backpack slamming against the tiled wall made Seraphine jump. "Jeez! Damon. Where have you been?"

"Brielle hired a psychotic doctor to implant worms in my brain, which erased the memories I had of Alessa from the night I found her, as well as every memory I had with her since then, up until she arrived back in New Sparta."

Seraphine dropped her pencil and stared at Damon. "So that's how she did it."

"They also implanted a device to control me," he swallowed. "To make me love her instead of Alessa. I need you to take it out."

"Do you know where the device is—"

Damon ran his fingers through his hair. "My brain."

Seraphine scoffed. "You want me to perform brain surgery on you? You know I can't do anything about the worms. There are too many variables, and they move as if they're living creatures because, well, they partially are. The worms will probably be in there indefinitely."

Damon balled his hands into fists and inhaled deeply. "I am aware. But the chip that's controlling me, you can get it out, right?"

"I won't know anything until I scan your head and get the results back. Even then, nothing is guaranteed until I'm in there and get a visual."

"That'll have to do," he nodded, staring into the distance.

Seraphine stepped forward, her hands pressed together. "You do realize there's no hope of you recovering the memories the worms deleted, right?"

Licking his lips, Damon nodded. "Yes, I'm aware. I'm sure you'll want to do a few scans, but then I need it out. Immediately."

Seraphine raised her eyebrows. "So, you want the surgery, like, now?"

Damon laid down on the table beneath the scanning equipment. "I need Brielle out of my head as quickly as possible. Besides, I don't have time to be down and out. I've got things to do and people to save."

CHAPTER FIFTY-THREE

It was mid-afternoon, and the sun was masked in the overcast sky.

Alessa sat alone near the final resting place of her sister's body. She was both amazed and happy the wind had already distributed Kai's ashes over the side of the cliff.

"Good," she sighed aloud. "You deserve to be free after a lifetime of being contained."

Staring off over the cliff's edge, Alessa spoke out loud. "I know this is going to sound strange, but New Sparta has always felt like home to me. I mean, it wasn't at the beginning of our lives, but from the first day our elder brought us back, I felt at home." Alessa choked back tears. "The physical trials never bothered me. I didn't have an issue with proving myself to the others in the community, and even though we were outcasts, I had all the love I ever needed. From you, our elder, from Quade, Seraphine"—she laughed, thinking of the goofy young boy—"Soren, and especially"—she paused—"Damon."

Clearing her throat, she bit her lower lip, holding back tears. "But lately, I don't feel the peace anymore. And now that you're gone and Damon is"—she wiped tears away with the back of her hand—"I don't think I can continue living here. There are too many memories, too many ghosts."

While playing with a blade of grass, she sighed. "And I know you asked me to forgive Damon, but I can't. Not yet. Maybe someday..." She looked at the snow-capped mountain peaks, her heart heavy with grief.

"I want you to know that no matter where I am, you will always be with me in my heart. Or, you never know, the Consilium and the Council of Elders may decide to kill me in the morning, so maybe I will be seeing you much sooner." She laughed without an ounce of humor.

"However, if the gods allow me to live just a little while longer, I promise to avenge your death and make Lucas and Cain pay with their lives. And you better believe if I am the one to end their time on earth, it will not be peaceful nor painless."

"Alessa, it's time to go!" Camden bellowed across the field.

Whipping around, Alessa yelled back. "Okay! Be right there!"

Standing up, she smoothed out the long skirt on her dark teal dress. "Guess this is goodbye for now. I love you, Kai."

"Coming!" she shouted at Camden, running toward his outstretched arms.

"You're sure about this?" Camden asked, nervously pacing back and forth behind the table.

Alessa, Quade, and Lexi stood at the table, their hands firmly planted on the cool metallic surface. Memorizing the three-dimensional holographic image before them, they studied the floorplan for Lucas Greenfield's secondary residence, a large pueblo in New Mexico.

"Yes, this is our only shot," Quade responded with a stern nod.

Camden exhaled loudly. "The Council of Elders has already convened with the Consilium, and they plan to announce Alessa's execution in the morning?"

Quade's lips pressed into a hard line. "That is what was reported to me."

Lexi shook her head back and forth. "No, absolutely not. We will not allow it. It's not Alessa's fault the Council didn't listen to her about Lucas being a douchebag reincarnate."

Alessa placed her hand upon Camden's upper shoulder, and he stilled. "It's now or never. The Consilium clearly has some vendetta against me and can't see Lucas Greenfield for who he truly is."

Camden joined the others at the table. "We're still unsure what his plan is with the bioengineered sugar. So far, not a lot has come about it, but the long-term side effects are still unknown."

Alessa grimaced. "That's what I'm most afraid of. I'm just glad I accidentally took out the rest of the sugarcane he was growing when I blew up, quite literally, but there's no telling what it's done to those who have already consumed it."

Lexi plopped down in a rolling chair. "Only time will tell."

Camden turned his head toward Quade. "How many are prepared to head out?"

"Well, we lost 12 warriors last night, and that's not including the wounded who cannot help us," Quade responded.

Feeling the heavy burden of guilt, Alessa bowed her head.

Quade grinned. "But, by word of mouth from those at the

battle, we've gained support. Your fellow Spartans believe in you, Alessa."

Her head whipped upright. "What? Seriously?"

"Yes. You've gained quite a following. You might turn out to be one hell of a leader."

"How many are we talking?" Camden asked.

Quade shrugged. "One hundred or so."

Alessa's jaw dropped in surprise. "Wow."

Camden's eyebrows raised. "With those numbers, we might have a fighting chance of taking Lucas down. For good."

Alessa nervously bit her lower lip. "And everyone has been made aware of the potential punishments for helping me?"

Quade nodded. "They have, yet they choose to stand by your side and fight."

She sighed. "So, it's decided then? Tonight at eleven o'clock, we'll head out."

Camden scooted protectively closer to Alessa's back. "Spread the word. And make sure everyone gets a copy of this map so they have it memorized inside and out."

Quade reached out and grasped Camden's forearm tight. "I know if we had met in this lifetime at any other point, we would've killed one another, but, brother, am I glad to be on the same side as you."

The side of Camden's lips turned upward in a friendly smirk. "Likewise."

"I need to update Sera and report back to the others." Quade released Camden and walked out of the room.

Lexi remained seated and kicked her feet up on the table. "If you two don't mind, I want to stay here and talk strategy."

Alessa sat down beside her friend. "I wouldn't have it any other way."

Camden stood upright. "And while you two discuss the

mission, I will grab us some food. It's going to be a long day and night."

Alessa pointed up at a section of the pueblo while standing next to Lexi. "Sounds great, Cam. Um, will you grab me something caffeinated as well?"

"Oh, I'd like a black coffee, please," Lexi piped up.

"Your wish is my command, ladies." Camden grinned over his shoulder as he left the room.

While standing up and walking around the table, Alessa sighed.

"What is it?" Lexi asked.

"After the way things turned out a couple of nights ago, the last thing I had on my mind was going back to war so soon, and this will truly be a bloody battle, not a recon mission gone badly."

Lexi placed her hands on the table and looked at Alessa's blue eyes through the hologram of Lucas's pueblo. "Let's get something straight. What happened was not your fault, and honestly, I'm not sold on it being Damon's fault either with what Cam said Hades hinted at."

Alessa startled. "Wait, what do you mean by it not being Damon's fault? He threw the weapon that killed Kai."

Lexi rocked her head from side to side. "Yes, but didn't Hades tell you he'd take what was dearest to you?"

Alessa stared off into the distance, her brain misfiring. "Is that what Kai was trying to tell me?" she mumbled. "Hold on, Cam told you about my meeting with Hades?"

Lexi tilted her head. "Yeah. Was he not supposed to? I think he just needed someone to vent to; he wasn't saying anything bad about you."

"Oh, yeah, no, I trust you." Alessa huffed, and her cheeks

reddened. "I'm just surprised he said anything to anyone. He doesn't trust easily."

Lexi shrugged and glanced nervously to the side. "Uh, I guess so. But back to your concerns about tonight. What are they?"

Alessa sighed and dropped her head. "Of failing my sister, our people, and all of humanity."

Lexi grinned. "Oh, is that all?"

Alessa scoffed. "And I know this is dumb, but I didn't clean my uniform after coming home the other night, so I have no idea what I'm going to wear tonight."

Lexi walked to the closet and slid open the door. Grabbing the hanger, she held up Alessa's clean uniform. "You mean this uniform?"

Alessa's eyes squinted in astonishment, rushing forward. "How did you—"

Lexi shrugged nonchalantly. "I had a feeling. I may not have grown up at this location, but I am a Spartan. I know how the Council of Elders and the Consilium think, and you and I both know they would not sit by while you took charge. Not only are you a woman, but you are also not of pure Spartan blood. That matters to them. Me? Not so much."

Alessa fingered the corseted top of her cleaned uniform. "Thank you for everything. You've really shown up for me. Whenever I've needed a friend these past few months, you've been there."

"It's almost like the gods sent me or something." Lexi winked before handing Alessa's uniform over.

Alessa tilted her head in consideration. "That is an interesting way to look at it." She cleared her mind by shaking her head back and forth. "Now, back to studying this map. We only have a few hours before we get this show on the road."

CHAPTER FIFTY-FOUR

Dressed in borrowed Spartan warrior gear, Camden returned to Alessa's side, standing protectively beside her. "You ready?"

She pumped her weapon. "Always. You?"

"You betcha. I just caught everyone up on the objective."

Alessa's right eyebrow raised. "You mean, kill Lucas Greenfield?"

Camden pressed another weapon into his belt. "You got it. I don't want any fuck ups. This could very well be our last attempt."

"I couldn't agree with you more."

Camden turned Alessa toward him, placed his fingers beneath her chin, and lifted her face to his. "Stay safe, my flame."

Alessa smiled, placing her hand atop his. "You too."

"Okay, you two, break it up." Quade pushed his way between them. "We've got a psycho to kill."

Stepping back, Alessa rolled her eyes with a smirk. "Understood, Spartan."

Quade pointed toward a hologram map projected into the

air. "We are strategically placing ourselves a good half mile away from any streetlights, cameras, anything that'll give away our arrival. We will establish a forcefield as soon as we land so the general population can't see or hear what we will do. To them, it will look like any other night at Lucas's quiet abode."

Camden licked his lips in excitement. "Okay. So what's the plan for getting into his house?"

Quade flashed a sideways grin. "Carefully."

Camden's eyebrows furrowed together with his lack of response.

"Time to load up," Quade announced, and the Spartan warriors piled into the backs of the trucks.

Camden sat beside Alessa, his weapon at the ready. "You ready for this?"

Alessa's eyes flashed red as she encouraged her despair and anger to consume her. "I'm getting there."

As they were transported, the feeling of being disoriented ended just as fast as it began.

Quade nodded toward Alessa and placed his hand on the door. "We're here."

The Spartans piled out, scattering throughout Lucas Greenfield's private property. Several held forcefields as they surrounded his property in a large semi-circle. Slamming the sharp bottoms into the dirt, they pressed the illuminated button atop each device, and it shot up a false wall up to the heavens, masking their activity to the outside world.

Camden jogged behind Alessa. "How is this not on their radar, the movement caused by our initial arrival?"

"We program our arrival to register on their devices as a flock of birds landing. We show up as a blip, so we go unnoticed if they don't pay close enough attention, which no one ever does. As far as why they don't see us individually, that would be thanks to our specialized microchips."

Camden touched the device attached behind his ear. "Interesting."

Alessa stopped running and froze, her senses on high alert. "Do you hear that?"

Camden nearly smacked into her back. He shuffled his weapon back and forth between his hands. "No, what?"

"It's like a high-pitched whistle." She looked up to see the outline of a bomb against the starry night sky. "Take cover!" she screamed. Grabbing Camden by the arm, she pulled him off to the side.

They dove onto the ground as the bomb struck.

The specialized bomb sent a shockwave that pulsated and pulled everyone back into it, snapping a few of the warriors' necks.

Alessa glared up ahead and growled. "They know we're coming."

Camden stood up and held his hand out for Alessa. "What should we do?"

She grabbed his arm, and he hoisted her back onto her feet. "I suggest we run faster. We can't let this opportunity slip by," Alessa answered.

Camden nodded in agreement. "Let's go."

Quade bellowed out over the surprised groans. "Looks like we're in for one hell of a battle. Remember, come back with your shield or on it! To die in battle is the greatest honor. Up and out, soldiers! And move quickly. The falsity of surprise has been made evident."

As they ran beside the other Spartan warriors, Alessa repeated the mission's objective in her mind: *Kill Lucas. Kill Lucas. Kill Lucas.*

As the Spartans approached Lucas Greenfield's four-story modern pueblo, the Bodyguards hid in plain sight, using technology to mask themselves high above on elevated platforms.

The Bodyguards gave away each of their positions with every shot, and a Spartan warrior chucked an electronic disruptor up in one of the shooter's directions. As the disruptor struck the attacker's platform, it sent an electric current through the air, revealing their hiding spots.

"Two o'clock!"

"Four!"

"Nine o'clock!" Spartan warriors cried out as the Bodyguard's snipers were shooting them.

A handful of Spartans stayed to take out the snipers while the rest continued.

"This is already turning out to be an exciting night," Camden said.

Alessa shouted back over her shoulder, "It was either this or sit on my ass at home and wait to be executed. I would much rather see Hades again on my terms than be killed by Damon's father."

Camden followed Alessa, weapon at the ready. "Let's try to avoid you meeting anyone in the afterlife."

She laughed dryly. "I've made peace with my death, just as long as I arrange the appointment for Lucas to meet with Hades before I arrive."

Camden's lips pressed together, stern, and his muscles stiffened.

"Hey, if I die taking out the man who was ultimately responsible for my sister's death while saving humanity at the same time, I'll consider that a glorious death."

Camden caught sight of a Bodyguard hiding behind

shrubbery, aiming at Alessa. As the man's finger touched the trigger, Camden shot two back-to-back bullets through the Bodyguard's forehead.

Camden breathed deeply before continuing forward. "You are not dying tonight. Not if I have anything to say about it." His eyes darted back and forth. "You know, you should be behind me."

A bullet ricocheted off Alessa's shoulder blade armor, and with a loud grunt, she aimed in the direction the shot came from. Tossing a ball of electricity toward the camouflaged attacker, she yelled for her team to stay out of range.

As the ball hit the three-second mark, it exploded ten feet in all directions, and a Bodyguard appeared before them, shaking back and forth on his knees before falling flat on his face onto the dirt ground.

Alessa scoffed. "Thanks, but no thanks. Maybe if I were an innocent princess who needed a man to protect her, but that's not my M.O."

Camden flashed an impressed grin. "Understood, Spartan."

CHAPTER FIFTY-FIVE

"Awaken, warrior. Your goddess Nyx demands it," the primordial goddess whispered in Damon's ear.

His head flopped to the side as he struggled to wake up.

"You need to save Alessa," Nyx urged. "I understand you feel guilty for Kai's death, but you need to know the truth. Hades moved your blade's trajectory and caused Kai's mortal wound. You are not at fault."

Hearing her confession, Damon's heart rate monitor beeped faster with the nauseating sensation that his stomach had flipped.

"Now, get up and save the woman you love," she demanded.

The sound of a woman's crying reverberated off the walls as Damon lay in the medical bed, slowly opening his eyes. Feeling his pulse inside of his head, Damon groaned with his first failed attempt at sitting up. His hand pressed against the bridge of his nose as he moaned, "Ugh."

"Oh, shit. Damon, is that you?" Seraphine closed the holographic image she had been looking at, wiped the tears from her eyes, and rushed to his bedside. "With the amount of anesthesia they gave you, you shouldn't be awake for at least one more hour."

"Where's Alessa?" Damon mumbled.

Not entirely understanding, Seraphine leaned into him. "I'm sorry, say that again."

He cleared his throat before speaking again. "Where is Alessa?"

With worry lines crossing her forehead, Seraphine patted the back of Damon's hand. "You shouldn't be worrying about anything other than your recovery. You just got out of brain surgery less than two hours ago. You shouldn't even be able to speak yet, let alone be worried about—"

Damon stared up at her, his eyes activating silver, and covered her hand with his hot palm. "Sera, what aren't you telling me?"

Licking her lips nervously, she wiped away a tear that streaked down her cheek.

Damon swallowed painfully. "What is it?"

"They've gone," Seraphine sighed.

"Gone. Who's gone? Gone where?" he demanded, struggling to sit up.

Damon's pain broke through the anesthesia, and he held his head in his hands.

"A group of our people left to fight Greenfield Farms, to try to take out Lucas Greenfield before he could do any more harm."

Damon's eyes squinted against the pain while he tried to justify her motives. "But her trial wasn't until the morning. She could've had a chance to—"

Seraphine scoffed. "You're not an idiot, Damon. Alessa

never had a fighting chance. Everyone knows the Consilium was going to put Alessa to death in the morning."

He shook his head back and forth in denial. "It hadn't been decided yet."

Seraphine's eyes narrowed. "Maybe I give you more credit than you deserve."

Damon nearly leapt out of bed. "My father would have never—"

Seraphine balled her hands into fists. "Who do you think your father requested to have the medication on hand to disable Alessa's microchip? Who do you think made the heartbreaking decision to tell her husband to go to war, to go against our leaders, to save her best friend's life?"

Damon's jaw dropped as he sat back against his pillow in stunned silence.

"That's right. Because of your bloodthirsty father, I had to choose between my best friend and my husband."

Damon shook his head back and forth. "I'm so sorry."

Seraphine walked over to the counter, mindlessly arranging the instruments on the countertop. "You're not the only one whose life has been dragged through shit lately."

Ripping the IV from the back of his hand, Damon stood up, swaying back and forth unsteadily.

"Shit, Damon, you need to lie back down. You're not ready."

He brushed the doctor away and hobbled toward the exit doors. "The hell I'm not. Get me a shot of dopamine."

Seraphine's eyes widened as she shook her head. "I can't do that. I won't do that."

Damon turned his head to look at Seraphine from the corner of his eyes. "Don't make me repeat myself. It wasn't a request. It was an order, Spartan."

With a loud sigh, Seraphine's heels clicked as she opened the walk-in cooler.

Damon leaned onto her desk, breathing slow and deep through the sharp pain at the bridge of his nose.

As she approached from behind, Seraphine demanded Damon expose his left upper arm. "I'm going to need your left bicep."

Tearing the hospital gown from his body, the fabric fell to the floor, pooling around his feet. Damon stood before Seraphine in his black boxer briefs, extending his arm for the doctor.

She held the needle in front of his bicep. "Are you sure about this?"

With Damon's jaw clenched, he reached his arm around and put his hand upon hers, helping Seraphine jab the long needle into his muscle.

After withdrawing the needle, she nodded in understanding. "Can you do just one thing for me?"

Damon shrugged into his shirt before pulling on his pants. "Anything."

"Bring Quade home to me. Please? We need him." She rubbed the tiniest bulge on her lower abdomen.

"I will do everything in my power to bring your husband home. I swear it."

Seraphine inhaled deeply and stared off into the distance. "With his shield or on it."

After one last glance at his friend, Damon ran from the room to get dressed for battle.

A moving image of his father appeared on the holographic screen before Damon. "I was told you just got out of surgery. What are you doing?"

"Did you order Alessa's execution?" Damon interrupted. His jaw muscles tensed as he struggled to contain his rage.

His father pointed at the screen. "I told you. I told you not to get involved with that girl, but do you ever listen? If I let her live, she would undoubtedly be your downfall."

Damon ran his hands through his hair, disgruntled. "What are you talking about? She has never done a thing against us."

His father's eyebrow arched. "Except go after you. The natural born grandson of the king of the East."

"That doesn't matter to her. Besides, she doesn't even know the full extent—"

His father scoffed. "How could she not know your family history?"

"Oh, she does know. About the people who truly matter, like Mom and Cassius."

His father turned away from the camera. "I don't have time for your foolishness."

"The possibility of me becoming the future king of the East is so slim, it's laughable to consider. I'm not even the first to inherit the title. There's you."

Damon's father laughed. "I am too old."

"And then there's your eldest son, my older brother, Cassius. He would never abdicate the position. He was born to be the next king of the East; I would abhor all it entails."

His father cleared his throat. "Yes, well, you never know what the gods have in store for you."

Damon scowled. "The fuck does that mean? By that justification, what if the gods favored Alessa, and by declaring

347

her the enemy, you have just made yourself an enemy of the most powerful beings?"

His father's face scrunched up in disbelief. "She is just a lowly human being. That girl has no Spartan blood running through her veins and should stop acting like it. It's insulting."

Damon pushed his chest out and stood tall in front of the camera. "And yet the gods have blessed her with life, time and time again, and she has recently gained favor with the primordial goddess Nyx."

"You lie," Damon's father scoffed.

"I would never lie about something as serious as the gods. You should know that. Also, for your information, this call was more than an interrogation. I am notifying you, the Council, and the Consilium that I am gathering a small group of Spartans, and we are attacking Lucas Greenfield."

"You will do no such thing!" Damon's father's voice bellowed through the speakers.

Damon didn't flinch as the man's voice boomed. "That may have worked when I was a young child, but I am now a thirty-year-old man. The time for intimidation is over, Father. I am following orders given directly from the goddess of night. Any of my fellow Spartans will be coming with me because they also believe in this mission." He glared defiantly at his father. "If you want to piss off the goddess Nyx, that's on you.

His father's jaw dropped as he stared at the camera.

"So, the leaders of our civilization have a decision to make: will they maintain their prideful front and supersede doing what is right, or will they admit their fault in this and help take down the biggest threat to humankind?"

His father stood before the camera, dumbfounded. His mouth opened and closed, but no words came out until he finally cleared his throat.

Damon rubbed his hands together anxiously. "I see. Well, you know where my heart lies, and I have declared my intentions. I guess the only thing for you to decide is whether or not I go to the afterlife with Alessa tomorrow. Goodbye."

Damon's father held out his hand toward the screen as it blackened. "Damon, wait—"

Turning around, Damon readjusted the strap across his chest and inhaled deeply before jogging to the front of the city, where his companions were awaiting his arrival.

Thaddeus held Damon's primary weapon out for him. "All clear?"

Grasping the handle, Damon nodded toward the empty vehicles. "We need to move quickly. They've been gone for a while, so who knows what we'll be greeted with."

After crowding into the back of three vehicles, the warriors shut the doors and pressed the transport device.

With the sound of screams and loud explosions, Damon blinked his silver eyes open, and he burst out of the vehicle's back doors to a scene straight out of an action movie.

Every one of the yard's bushes and trees were lit on fire. The windows to the house had been blown out, shards of glass littered the front yard, and Spartans had placed a forcefield around the place of residence to hinder outsiders' view and prevent them from hearing the fight.

It was just another night to the rest of humanity, and Lucas Greenfield's pueblo remained the same as before the Spartans arrived.

"Damon, down!" Thaddeus yelled just seconds before a screaming missile narrowly missed Damon's head.

Nodding toward his friend in thanks, Damon raised his weapon and shot toward the launched missile. Hearing a loud shriek, Damon felt the adrenaline surge hit, and excitement vibrated throughout his veins.

CHAPTER FIFTY-SIX

Alessa held up her wrist and spoke into the band around it. "Quade, I have this feeling in my gut that Lucas isn't going to be inside the house, but as you can probably guess, I have no basis for these feelings, so you still need to take your group in."

"As much as I trust you, I have to agree with taking my group inside," Quade responded. "There are four levels to the pueblo. I'll need most of the warriors to explore each one thoroughly. Fifteen soldiers will scope out the west side of the house, and you can take the east with ten additional. When we reach the front steps, I'll notify Gage to send the thermal drone to hover overhead."

Alessa spoke into her wrist. "Understood. May the gods be with you."

"You and Camden as well," Quade said.

The radio went silent as they approached Lucas Greenfield's home. Other than the bushes and trees placed for aesthetics directly in front of Lucas's home, the incoming Spartans were out in the open.

Camden swallowed before peering over at Alessa from the side of his eyes. "Ready?"

Hearing the drone fly high above, Alessa tilted her head back. "Never have I been more ready for anything in my life."

The drone quietly positioned itself above the roof before shooting its thermal radar in every direction. As the beams of light reached out, touching the edge of the barrier, the Spartan warriors flicked their wrists, projecting a single see-through eye covering in front of each of their faces. The Bodyguards that had been invisible were illuminated bright red.

Not realizing their positions had been given away, the Bodyguards sat unmoving, awaiting orders.

Every single Spartan took a knee and aimed at a different Bodyguard.

"Now!" Quade bellowed from the depths of his soul. The ear-shattering sound of hundreds of bullets exploding from their chambers simultaneously echoed throughout the grounds as they shot at the Bodyguards hovering above them.

With the realization of their discovery, the Bodyguards tried to fight back from their elevated positions.

Unable to wait out their invasion any longer, Quade burst through the front doors before he called out to his fellow Spartans. "Twenty on each floor! Clear your entire floor before returning to the main! Go! Go! Go!"

With weapons raised, Camden, Alessa, and their team ran to the east side of the pueblo. Encountering at least thirty Bodyguards on their side of the house, they lost several Spartans while searching for Lucas.

Alessa clenched her teeth together in frustration. "Where is that bastard?"

Reaching the far end of the house, her fellow Spartan warriors halted. "All clear!"

"Fuck!" Alessa groaned, disappointed and upset. "I really wanted to be the one to take him out."

Looking off into the distance, Camden squinted. "Do you see that?"

CHAPTER FIFTY-SEVEN

Damon burst through the front door, fighting to get into Lucas's pueblo. "Alessa!" he bellowed out. "This is way too familiar," he mumbled to himself.

The Spartan warrior fighting next to Damon made a gurgling noise before they fell to the ground, choking on their blood.

Extracting two shortened swords from his straps, Damon pressed their hilts into his hips, fully extending their blades, as a Bodyguard charged him while they spun their double-edged sword artistically in the air.

Damon charged the Bodyguard with a maniacal grin, and as their blades crashed against one another, they clanged loudly.

Bringing one of his blades over his head, the Bodyguard expertly blocked Damon's advance with a flick of his wrist.

Damon lunged forward with the sword in his left hand and was blocked again.

Spinning in a circle, Damon brought both blades together and struck the man's double-edged sword in the middle, pushing the Bodyguard off balance. As he backed up unsteadily, Damon turned his back to the Bodyguard and stabbed backward toward their stomach.

Sucking his abdomen in, the Bodyguard narrowly escaped being impaled.

While still facing away from his attacker, Damon knew he had missed by the feeling of his empty blade. Flicking his wrist, Damon spun his second sword up in the air as the Bodyguard brought his sword down hard, slicing across Damon's protective chest armor.

Doing a front flip out of the Bodyguard's reach, Damon caught his sword and landed on the floor. Feeling the heat from the surface of his armor melting, Damon growled.

The Bodyguard sported a sideways grin as he stared Damon down.

Bringing the heat, Damon bellowed a warrior's cry as he rushed forward. "Ahhhh!" Spinning his dual swords in a figure-eight pattern, he whipped around, striking the Bodyguard in his discreetly protected ribs.

Damon's eyebrow raised in surprise. "You're wearing armor this time."

The attacking man tore the buttons from his dress shirt, exposing the thin armor beneath his clothes. "Had a feeling you'd show up. We weren't taking any chances."

Damon smiled flirtatiously. "Any chance you'll continue undressing so I can see how far your armor extends?"

The Bodyguard wielded his double-edged sword. "You'd like that, wouldn't you?"

Damon bobbed his head about. "That's kind of why I asked." Coinciding with a loud burst of firearms, he lunged forward.

While being struck in the leg, Damon grunted, but as the

bullet went out the back of his thigh, he never wavered from his attack.

The blades sparked, striking against one another.

The Bodyguard backed up while spinning his sword to protect himself.

Eyeing the doors to the garden area, Damon pressed harder, advancing on the Bodyguard. Intentionally not aiming to kill but only to press his opponent further back, Damon sliced through the air.

Their blades danced with one another until Damon gave one last powerful hit.

As the Bodyguard's back pressed against a tiny sharp edge from the door's medieval decorations, the Bodyguard gasped and turned their head for the briefest moment.

Taking advantage of the Bodyguard's surprise, Damon threw one of his blades toward the Bodyguard's head, and as they became distracted by blocking the flying blade, Damon bent forward with his left knee extended.

Slicing his top sword clean through the Bodyguard's neck, Damon stood above his dead opponent, with blood dripping from his sharp blade.

CHAPTER FIFTY-EIGHT

Alessa turned her head to see where Camden was looking. "See what? What am I looking for?"

She stared into the darkness, unable to see what he was referring to. Alessa saw nothing besides the random trees outlined throughout the backyard and scattered bushes.

"How are they—" Camden mumbled, walking toward a shimmering outline as if in a trance.

"Cam, Cam! What are you doing? The battle is back there." Alessa hurried after him. "There's no way they'd hide Lucas out in the open. Especially after the thermal rays. He would be glowing like every other person."

The rest of their group followed them, weapons at the ready.

Camden tilted his head in curiosity. "We've never fought like this before; never had this technology. It's almost like they are using technology similar to the Spartan's ability to shield your cities, but how would they have gotten that information?" Camden hesitantly approached the wall of shimmering light.

"Do you see that? It's reflecting the light off itself, so we see our surroundings, just like your city's defenses."

Finally seeing the shimmering outline Camden was referring to, Alessa's eyes widened in shock. "Does that mean—"

Each of the Spartans standing beside them grunted as a small blade impaled them through the chest. As they fell to the ground, dead, both Camden and Alessa were grabbed and pulled through the shimmering wall.

After passing through a bright light, their weapons were snatched from their hands, and they were aggressively shoved down to their knees.

Glowing collars were secured around their necks as they knelt on the white concrete ground before Lucas Greenfield, Cain, and their men.

Twenty-five elite Rogue Command Bodyguards surrounded them. The Bodyguard's eyes glowed gold in the light cast from the few lights surrounding the elaborate swimming pool.

Camden's eyebrows furrowed together as he peered over at Alessa apologetically. "I'm sorry, I should've known—"

Camden was struck in the middle of the back by a Bodyguard's gun.

"Shut up, traitor!" Lucas Greenfield growled.

Alessa glared at the man she hated most in the world. "How the fuck did you survive?"

Lucas looked down at her, restrained on either side by a Rogue Command Bodyguard. "Oh, silly Spartan. It had been our backup plan for quite some time."

Alessa glared up at Lucas. "But how do you have the same scar? Are you in someone else's body, or—"

His eyes narrowed, and he smirked. "Observant, aren't we?

I had the surgeon add the scar to this body so that way I would never forget what happened to me in my childhood. Why I continue working so vigilantly to create a better world."

Alessa scoffed before her eyes darted toward the young man beside Lucas. "You're Cain, aren't you?"

He flashed his pearly whites while being handed a thin black steel rod. "So, you've heard of me."

Alessa smiled with murderous intention. "My sister told me everything. I cannot wait to get my hands on you."

He made a pouty face. "With the limited amount of time you two had before your Spartan friend killed her, I highly doubt she told you *everything*."

Alessa's breathing stilled, and her stomach flipped as he struck a nerve.

Cain struck a black metal baton up against the palm of his empty hand. "One thing I do know about my pet's untimely death is I will avenge those who took part in it."

Alessa tilted her head. "So you're going to kill yourself? And your uncle? That's great news! Why don't you go ahead and get on with it? That saves me time."

Enraged, Cain charged Alessa. "I LOVED her. I would have never—"

"Cain, enough," his uncle chastised. "You know she can't be touched." Lucas pointed at Camden. "Him, on the other hand—"

"Where did you get the technology to mask yourselves?" Camden asked after regaining his ability to breathe.

Lucas whipped around to face Camden. His eyes were large and wild. "We had a little help."

Cain marched toward Camden, glaring at him while Lucas touched Alessa's shoulder. "I'd love to continue this discussion, but we've got a helicopter to catch."

The Rogue Command Bodyguards behind Alessa forced her up onto her feet.

She dug her heels into the ground, trying to activate as she was dragged across the grounds toward the grounded helicopter. "What do you mean by 'we'? The fuck? I'm not going anywhere with you!"

Camden's veins bulged out of his neck as he failed to active while struggling against the men of the Rogue Command. "Alessa!"

Holding the baton above Camden, Cain flashed an evil grin. Bringing the weapon down hard, he smacked the side of his face.

Alessa screamed as Camden's head slammed against the cold ground. "Cam! Gods, no! Stop!"

Cain struck Camden again and again. Even after he fell over onto his side, Cain continued smacking him; all the while, his bones were audibly cracking, and bright red blood sprayed across the light grey concrete.

Walking purposefully toward the helicopter, Lucas didn't even look back at the sounds of his nephew torturing Camden.

Alessa's blood boiled as she was dragged behind the men, kicking and screaming. Fighting back against the mechanism around her neck, she focused all of her rage and hate on the glowing device.

Light grey smoke rose imperceptibly from the device around her neck as her irises flickered red and blue.

CHAPTER FIFTY-NINE

Damon's chest was heaving, and his sword was drenched in blood as he stood before the headless man.

Wiping the sweat from his brow, Damon nodded in satisfaction before he spun the sword in his hand.

Screaming, Damon fought his way to the back of the pueblo. "Alessa! Camden!"

Bursting through the double back doors, Damon scanned the yard. "Gods help me. Where are you?"

Closing his eyes in the middle of the chaos, Damon focused all his energy on finding Alessa.

Suddenly, Nyx's crystal clear voice broke through all the noise and guided Damon toward the far side of the yard. "Look beyond the horizon and see what lies beneath the moonlight."

Gripping a sword tightly in each hand, the Spartan warrior sprinted toward the yard's edge, where a patch of grass was bathed in moonlight.

Unable to make out any discernable enemy, Damon charged in the general direction until he heard Alessa screaming. Choosing to trust Nyx and his instincts rather than his eyes, he crossed his arms in front of his chest and jumped through an invisible forcefield.

After crossing the barrier, Damon landed on his feet, struggling to comprehend the chaotic scene before him.

CHAPTER SIXTY

Camden lay unconscious in a pool of blood with the glowing device wrapped tightly around his neck.

The Bodyguard closest to Alessa shot her in the upper arm with a tranquilizer, and she cursed at him while struggling to escape.

"Camden!" Alessa cried out in desperation.

The world began to tilt as the panic and rage built inside of her, and just as she blinked her eyes wide to keep herself awake, the device around Alessa's neck cracked just the tiniest bit.

Cain rushed Alessa, but as he lunged for her, she extracted a hidden double-sided dagger that was laced with venom, and she cut up the left side of Cain's face, slicing him from his jaw to eyebrow.

With a feral yell, Cain raised the metal rod and struck the side of Alessa's leg, breaking her femur with a sickening crunch.

Watching Alessa's leg crush beneath the steel rod, Damon snapped. Dropping the swords, he extracted six discs from his arsenal of weapons and threw them on the ground in various directions as Alessa screamed in agony.

A few seconds after their release, the ground beneath each of the discs exploded, taking any Rogue Command within their vicinity down into the earth.

Damon sprinted toward Alessa as her unconscious body fell in slow motion.

Withdrawing his firearms, he killed the three Bodyguards surrounding Alessa, one of which unfortunately blocked his shot at Lucas.

Catching Alessa just before the back of her head hit the concrete, Damon exhaled loudly.

Shooting a death glare at the man who broke her leg, Damon realized it was the same individual who had wounded him with the poisoned blade in the previous night's battle. *I will hunt you down, and I will kill you.*

Focusing on getting Alessa out of danger, Damon reluctantly allowed Cain to scramble toward the helicopter.

Cain held his face in his hands as his skin sizzled from the poison Alessa had coated on the blade.

With Alessa in his arms, pressed against his chest, Damon ran back to Camden. Squatting down beside the gravely injured man, Damon smashed his Strongroom Bubble on the ground, and a blue shimmering shield surrounded the three Spartans.

Damon lifted his wristband to his mouth and watched the helicopter rise into the sky. "Spartans abort. I repeat, get out and get home. The objective is unobtainable."

As the Rogue Command Bodyguards shot at Damon, he pressed his specialized transport button and vanished.

CHAPTER SIXTY-ONE

Materializing back into existence, Damon appeared at the city's entrance with Alessa in his arms and Camden lying broken at his feet.

Running up to Damon, Lexi gasped. The color drained from her face after seeing the extent of Camden's injuries. "Oh, gods."

Damon swallowed hard. "Get Sera. Now."

Snapping back to reality, Lexi's eyelashes blinked back tears as she searched for the doctor. "Sera! Sera, we need you over here! Now!"

Using the transportation devices, the trucks carrying the warriors reappeared one after the other. Most Spartans were injured to some extent; however, some were too far gone to be saved.

Damon peered down at Alessa's unconscious form before grabbing the broken device from around her neck and throwing it off to the side.

"I'm sorry, babe." He held her up against his face and rocked back and forth with his eyes closed. "Sydämen liekki—"

Running toward them, Seraphine pointed at Camden and directed her medical staff. "Carefully get him on a stretcher. His nose, jaw, collar bone, shit ... everything's broken, and that hip looks popped out of place—careful! His injuries need to be addressed immediately. Get him prepped for surgery immediately!"

Seraphine touched Damon's shoulder. "Damon, Damon, let me see her."

He looked up at Seraphine with tears streaking down his face. "I failed her, Sera. I couldn't stop her from getting hurt, but I'm going to do everything in my power to protect her from my father and the Consilium. I swear it."

Seraphine nodded, and her eyes fell from Damon's. "Okay, Damon. But we need to take her and evaluate the extent of her injuries right now. Are you doing okay?" She pressed two fingers against a cut on his cheek.

Damon pushed her hand away. "Nothing that won't heal itself in a few hours. Just take care of Alessa." He watched the medical staff wheel her away, knowing there was no way in Hades that Seraphine would let him go with her.

The doctor stood up and turned away when Damon called out to her. "Hey, make sure that asshole lives or Alessa will never forgive me."

Inhaling deeply, she flashed a nervous grin before hurrying after Camden and Alessa. "That's the goal. Just make sure someone looks at that cut!"

Inhaling deeply, Alessa slowly blinked. The sounds of disjointed beeping assaulted her senses, and as she tried to lift her hand to block the harsh lights, she was surprised by the weight of a hand wrapped around her own.

Damon was asleep on her small bed, with one arm outstretched, holding onto her for dear life.

Feeling her move, Damon's head raised unsteadily, and he stared at her. "Oh, Alessa, thank the gods you're awake," he sighed. The recently stitched laceration on his cheek was in the final stage of healing.

Alessa's voice cracked as she spoke. "Did Lucas—"

Damon confirmed her suspicions. "Bastard got away. Again. Oh, Alessa, I'm so sorry for everything. For not believing you when you said my memories had been tampered with, for not believing you about Brielle." He looked down at her hand and shook his head. "I never truly loved Brielle. She wasn't my home. It was you; it was always you."

Alessa felt her stomach flip as she struggled to understand what he was saying. "So, what, you remember now?"

He licked his lips nervously. "I don't remember the lost time, and I most likely never will, with what they did to me. Brielle's been controlling me the entire time. We'll talk about it later; it's not important right now.

Pulling her hand out from under his, Alessa's eyes darted around the small makeshift room made by closed curtains surrounding her in the crowded post-op ward. "Where's Cam?"

Damon cleared his throat. "Um, Camden, right. His injuries were a bit more extensive than yours. He just got out of an eight-hour surgery."

Alessa's breathing hitched as she bolted upright in bed. "Damon, where is he?"

Hissing with the stabbing pain radiating from her upper thigh, she grabbed her right leg.

"I told them you hate the way pain meds make you feel, so

they gave you a minimal amount. Would you like me to call them to give you another dose?"

Exhaling slowly, Alessa grimaced. "Thank you for telling them that. I don't want any more right now. But about Cam—"

"He's alive. For now." Damon tilted his head to the side in contemplation.

She threw the covers off her legs and winced when she tried moving her broken femur. "I need to see him."

Damon scoffed while holding his hands directly in front of Alessa, stopping her from attempting to get up. "You can't get out of bed, let alone walk."

Alessa glared up at Damon. "If you don't take me to him, I will crawl."

Rolling his eyes at her stubbornness, Damon huffed and peeked around her pulled curtain. Pointing at Alessa, he ordered her, "You, stay," before he disappeared behind the curtain.

Biting her lower lip anxiously, Alessa pulled out the IV and held her blankets on the site to stop the bleeding while she waited impatiently for Damon to return.

Tugging back the curtain, Damon emerged with a specialized wheelchair. "If I can't stop you, let me enable you in the safest way possible."

He lifted the half of the chair that held her injured leg in place before approaching her bedside.

Alessa stuttered uncomfortably as they awkwardly danced back and forth with their arms. "How are we—"

"Just stop—" Damon interrupted. "Let me just—put your arm around my neck."

Alessa wrapped her arm around the back of Damon's muscular neck, and as their skin touched, a familiar shock of electricity passed between them.

Pushing the feeling deep down, Damon gently picked Alessa up and set her in the wheelchair.

Grunting with the painful movement, Alessa clenched her teeth as Damon secured her leg in the chair.

"Ready?" he asked as she adjusted her position.

Alessa nodded excitedly. "Yes."

Walking down the hallway together, they received looks of respect and gratitude as fellow Spartans bowed their heads in Alessa's direction.

She narrowed her eyes in confusion. "What is that about? Nothing I have done is worthy—"

"You have a following," Damon interrupted.

Alessa rotated painfully, looking back at Damon. "Who, me?"

He nodded and chuckled. "Yes, you. You may very well be the first Spartan citizen in our history to have enough support from the people to prevent the Consilium from ending your life."

Alessa inhaled shakily before swallowing. "I had forgotten all about that."

"I wouldn't worry about it too much. They'll have to get past a lot of your supporters to take your and Camden's lives. Me included."

Alessa's breathing faltered with the weight of what Damon had just admitted.

He sighed and pushed Alessa in front of the clear glass doors of the ICU. "Here we are."

The doors opened automatically, and Alessa brushed his hands away. "I've got it from here. Thank you, Damon."

"Alessa, I hope you can forgive me. I mean, not yet, but maybe someday," he said quietly behind her. "I promise to spend every minute of every day for the rest of our lives trying to make it up to you."

Tears rolled down her cheeks as she stared straight ahead in silence.

Licking the salty tears from her lips, Alessa exhaled a shaky breath as she pushed her wheelchair forward.

Watching Alessa roll away from him toward another man, Damon's heart shattered as he stood in the doorway.

Reaching Camden's bedside, Alessa's eyes widened as she took his hand. "Hey, Cam. It's me. I'm here." She squeezed his hand reassuringly.

Glancing up at the beeping monitors and the liquid-filled tubes leading up to the hanging bags of fluids, Alessa's eyes overflowed with tears. "Don't you go dying on me. You are not allowed to leave me, not after everything we've been through together."

She licked her lips. "You fight Hades with every ounce of energy you can muster. Don't let him take you. You can't let him win."

Alessa brushed back Camden's blond hair out of his face as several nurses entered his room in the ICU.

"No one but medical staff is allowed in here," the nurse chastised. "You know that, Spartan."

Alessa squeezed Camden's hand tighter. "Yes, but—"

"No buts. You need to leave. Looks like you have healing to do of your own."

Knowing her arguing with the nurses wouldn't win her any brownie points, Alessa pursed her lips together and nodded jerkily. She leaned into Camden's ear. "I'll be back, and make sure they give you the good stuff."

The first nurse grabbed Alessa's wheelchair handles and

rolled her toward the clear glass doors. "Let's get you back to the post-op ward, Alessa."

Alessa's head whipped around, and she looked up at the nurse. "Do I know you?"

"No, but I know of you. You're the Spartan true at heart who communes directly with the gods."

Alessa shook her head back and forth. "You've got me confused with someone else. I was not born a Spartan."

"You misheard me. I said Spartan true at heart."

Alessa's eyebrows furrowed in confusion. "Spartan true at heart? What is that supposed to mean?"

They turned the corner to the general post-op ward. "It means you follow what you believe to be right whether or not our leaders agree, which is unheard of. Lucas Greenfield would have been taken care of if they had heeded your concern. Now we have to wait for him to resurface once again."

Alessa exhaled as they parked before her partition. "Because, inevitably, he will."

"Precisely," the nurse agreed. "I highly advise you get your rest so you heal properly. You will need to begin training sooner or later."

Alessa grunted as the nurse helped her into bed. "Thank you..."

"Tessa."

Alessa hissed in pain as she repositioned herself in the bed. "Do you know if Quade and Lexi are doing okay?"

Tessa nodded. "Yes. They have both already inquired as to your condition and were updated. They have clearance to visit tomorrow. Today, you must rest."

As Tessa turned to leave, Alessa reached out and grabbed her wrist. "And our losses?"

"So far, we've lost thirty-six, but eight are still in surgery, and others are in the ICU."

Recognizing the distress on Alessa's face, the nurse placed her hand upon Alessa's before leaning in toward her. "Do not blame yourself for our elders' mistakes. This should've never been put on you. It is their fault we've lost warriors. Not yours."

Trying to hold it together, Alessa closed her eyes while laying her head back on her pillow.

"I'm going to head out. Peace be with you, Alessa."

Feeling the aftereffects from the breathing tube used in her throat during surgery, Alessa turned toward her bedside table for her water.

With her arm outstretched toward the half-filled glass, she saw the familiar outline of a small piece of jewelry sitting atop a white folded piece of paper.

Picking up Damon's ring, Alessa opened the paper and read, "Come back to me, Alessa. Please come back."

CHAPTER SIXTY-TWO

Lying beneath the darkened night sky, Damon stared up at the constellations and free-floating stars when, unbeknownst to him, his eyes flickered silver as his activation was triggered. He pressed his fingers into his eye sockets to numb the dull ache.

Releasing the button on the keyboard, Cain sat back with a wicked grin spread across his bandaged face. "And that is how it's done."

Lucas Greenfield stared into the monitor. "Just like that, and we've got the Spartan under our control?"

Cain pressed a button and spoke into the microphone. "Lift your hand and hold it in front of your face."

Damon's eyes turned silver as he unknowingly looked at his hand floating in front of his face.

Cain's eyebrows raised as he tilted his head toward his uncle.

Lucas Greenfield flashed a sideways smile. "Brilliant."

Brielle scoffed from a nearby chair. "I told you it would work."

As animalistic shrieks and growls were heard from the next room, she scrunched her face in concern. "What is that god-awful noise?"

Cain's eyes widened in sadistic excitement. "May I show her, Uncle?"

Lucas nodded and flicked his wrist toward the door to the next room. "Of course, you may. By this point, she's proven herself trustworthy."

After Cain jumped up from his chair, Brielle followed him through double doors that led into the next room.

A large glass cube was being used as a cage in the center of the room. Alone inside stood a hyperventilating, filthy man in dirtied, torn clothing. His long, greasy hair stuck to the sides of his face, his wide-open eyes never blinked, and his bloodied mouth gaped open.

Cain walked closer to the subject in the cage. "It appears our genetically modified sugar has some unfortunate side effects such as aggression, loss of inhibition, and"—he swallowed—"cannibalism. It only seems to occur when an individual consumes alcohol, and their blood alcohol reaches a level of at least .10%."

Brielle pointed at the growling, drooling man. "Are you telling me every single person who consumed Ambrosia and then drinks a bit of alcohol can become *this*?"

Cain shrugged nonchalantly. "When we did the study over three years, we kept the study alcohol-free while they lived in our facilities, not realizing they could have adverse reactions." Cain craned his neck to the side, instructing Brielle to follow him through the next set of doors. "No experiment is without risks."

Brielle's high heels clicked against the floor as she followed him to the next room, where no less than ten people stood before a large water tank on an elevated surface. Each person had on a long white medical jacket, their mouths were gagged beneath their wide, red eyes, and their hands tied behind their backs.

"We at Greenfield Farms understand that mistakes happen, but someone needs to be held responsible, and the initial scientists seem the most logical."

Making eye contact with a Rogue Command Bodyguard beside the first scientist, Cain bowed slightly. With the pull of a lever, the scientists were dropped into the water simultaneously.

The muffled screams and sounds of the drowning people echoed throughout the room as water splashed out of the container.

***

Hades, the king of the underworld, and Nyx, the primordial goddess of the night, watched the violent scene play out before them from the comforts of their underworld's castle.

Hades' head tilted in intrigue. "What is happening to humanity?"

Shaking her head, Nyx inched toward the scene, hovering before them. "I'm not sure. I will go consult my daughters, the Fates."

His lips separated in a sadistic grin as the new souls appeared beneath him in his pool. "Whatever that is, I'm here for it."

Nyx side-eyed Hades in disgust before vanishing from the palace.

As the splashing noises ceased, Cain and Brielle strolled back into the room, where the deranged man was locked inside the glass cage.

Brielle's heels clacked against the tile floor as she slowly walked toward him.

The man's veins bulged from his massive muscles, and there was so much blood on him that she couldn't tell whether it was his or someone else.

As Brielle got closer, she noticed the whites of his eyes had blackened.

After sniffing the air between them, he lunged at the transparent wall with a nauseating screech. Attempting to claw his way out, his nails broke off, leaving streaks of blood on the glass.

Brielle stood so close to the glass that she could feel the vibrations every time the man struck the wall.

Leaning in, Brielle stared at the deranged man, who was going mad with the overwhelming urge to kill her, and as she watched the crimson blood drip down the glass before her, Brielle grinned wide. "What are we going to do with you?"

READY FOR MORE?

Keep a look out for book three in the Glitched Series.

ABOUT THE AUTHOR

Eisley Rose is the author of *Glitched* and *Shattered*. She is also a registered nurse, a stay-at-home mom, and an entrepreneur who lives in the greater Kansas City area. She loves reading, writing, painting, attending concerts, playing tennis, watching movies, and playing board games with her family. Her love for science formed the backbone of this story, but she also adores anything creative and openly embraces the unique.

"If you choose to be one thing in this world, choose to be unequivocally, unapologetically, you."

— Eisley Rose

facebook.com/eisleyrosebooks

instagram.com/eisleyrosebooks

goodreads.com/eisleyrosebooks

youtube.com/@eisleyrosebooks

amazon.com/Eisley-Rose/e/B0CSMD89HQ

tiktok.com/@eisleyrosebooks

threads.com/@eisleyrosebooks

bsky.app/profile/eisleyrosebooks.bsky.social

REVIEWS APPRECIATED

Please feel free to leave a review online.